Troop of Shadows

Book One in the Troop of Shadows Chronicles

Nicki Huntsman Smith

NHS Marketing, LLC

Copyright Notice

Copyright © 2022 by Nicki Huntsman Smith

All rights reserved. No part of this publication may be reproduced, distributed, or transmitted in any form or by any means, including photocopying, recording, or other electronic or mechanical methods, without the prior written permission of the publisher, except in the case of brief quotations embodied in critical reviews and certain other noncommercial uses permitted by copyright law.

Terms and Conditions
The purchaser of this book is subject to the condition that he/she shall in no way resell it, nor any part of it, nor make copies of it to distribute freely.

All Persons Fictitious Disclaimer
This book is a work of fiction. Any similarity between the characters and situations within its pages and places or persons, living or dead, is unintentional and co-incidental.

Credits
Credit to Henry Wadsworth Longfellow for the poem "A Shadow".

Acknowledgements

I would like to thank the following:

Lori, my editor, proofreader, and grammar consultant extraordinaire. Thankfully, comma placement doesn't vex her as profoundly as it does me.

My test readers, Lisa and Al, who provided advice, suggestions, and top-notch cheerleading.

My British friend, Tony, who made sure Dr. Harold Clarke sounded like the real deal.

My mom, whose belief that I hung the moon is so unwavering, I sometimes believe it too.

My friends and family, who have always accepted my eccentric interests and overt nerdiness with minimal eye-rolling...as far as I know.

Lastly and most importantly, my husband Ray, without whose constant encouragement, gentle nudging, infinite patience, and support on a million different levels, this book would never have been written. I owe him everything.

Preface

During the initial chapters of this book, I introduce four groups of survivors. I've given a handful of these characters their own third-person point of view. As a reader, I enjoy experiencing the action and storytelling from more than one perspective, especially when recounted by colorful, diverse, complex, and frequently flawed personalities. I decided this technique would work well to more vividly tell the story I wanted to tell. Happy reading!

Prologue

Colleyville, Texas - October

Dani cursed the weight of her backpack. The final two items from the ransacked Walgreens, crammed in as an afterthought ten minutes ago, might cost her everything. After surviving the last twelve months of hell only to be thwarted now by a can of Similac and a twelve-pack of Zest soap, would be sadly anticlimactic. Despite running at a full sprint down a dark suburban street, dodging overflowing garbage cans while eluding three men who would steal her hard-won tubes of Neosporin and likely rape and kill her in the process, she snorted at the thought of a fictional headline: *Young Woman's Life Ends Tragically but Zestfully Clean.*

Damn it, she would ditch the backpack. She could come back tomorrow night for it, but right now staying alive outweighed any future benefit its contents might provide. As her pursuers rounded the corner behind her, she darted across the front lawn of a house and leaped over a cluster of dead juniper shrubs. A year ago, those shrubs had been green, manicured, and providing curb appeal to the upscale neighborhood; they functioned now as a hurdle component in the obstacle course Dani navigated on most nights.

She angled toward the side of the house and around the corner, only to come to an abrupt stop next to a six-foot barricade. Residents of these sprawling bedroom communities situated between Dallas and Fort Worth clung to their privacy fences as fiercely as their rural counterparts did to their firearms. Why all those day-trading dads and cheerleader moms required such secrecy was beyond Dani. She didn't care. All that mattered was how difficult they made her nightly forages. Only idiots or people with a death wish traveled alone on the streets anymore. The clever ones navigated through backyards and drainage ditches, shadowed easements and alleyways, avoiding open spaces and other humans.

Especially humans traveling in groups.

Stealth and caution were second nature to her now, and she was pissed at herself for loading up the backpack with more weight than she could easily carry at a full run.

Rookie mistake.

She flung the pack into the undergrowth of a once meticulous garden, making a mental note of the enormous red tip photinia which camouflaged the bundle in a leafy shroud. She hoped to be alive the next day to retrieve it.

She clambered up the fence, finding a toehold on a warped plank, and squirmed over the top. A silver fingernail of a moon did little to illuminate the backyard. Weak starlight reflected off the inky surface of a half-empty, kidney-shaped swimming pool. Her Nikes gripped the concrete deck as she skirted the murky water and made a beeline for the back of the yard that was, of course, separated from its neighbor by a privacy fence. It was a tall one too — a full ten feet. There were no bushes or trees to use for leverage either. She scanned the area for anything that might serve as a step ladder.

Of all the yards she could have chosen for her escape, she'd picked one with a damn ten-foot fence.

Her heart raced from the sprint, but not from panic. Gone was the young woman from a year ago, the full-time floundering college dropout and part-time surly Starbucks barista who spent too much time reading books and not enough time looking for a job that would allow her to move out of her parents' house. She was too smart for her own good, everyone had told her. She should have taken that secretarial position in North Dallas, but she would have lost her sanity in that environment. The tedious filing, the ringing phones, the office politics — in other words, hell on earth for a girl with an IQ over a hundred and fifty.

Despite the recent horrors, she'd come into her own at last, after twenty-one years of meandering through life unfocused and unchallenged. The extra twenty pounds she'd been carrying courtesy of Freddy's cheeseburgers and Taco Bell burritos were gone, thanks to her newfound self-discipline and endless hours of Krav Maga training with Sam. Not only had she transformed her body, she'd elevated and strengthened her mind as well. Before the power had gone out, she'd watched countless tutorials on T'ai Chi, Qigong, and Buddhist meditation. During that same window — when people were beginning to get sick, but before most of them had died — she'd combed book stores and libraries within a fifteen-mile radius. When the country went dark and people realized that life-saving information was no longer available with a few keystrokes, Dani had amassed reference material on subjects as diverse as hydroponics and combat first aid, ancient meat drying techniques and bomb making. Between martial arts lessons with Sam, she spent every spare minute absorbing the printed esoteric knowledge like a greedy lizard on a sun-drenched rock.

Knowledge was survival.

When the first of the men slithered over the fence into the backyard, she hadn't found anything to use as a foothold. Another figure followed behind him. She closed her eyes, took a deep breath and released it from her lungs, slow and measured, then took off at a full run toward them. While she ran, fingers slid down to a leather sheath secured to her belt. Two seconds before she reached the first of her would-be assailants, a Ka-Bar — the grandaddy of tactical knives — was in her hand.

Dani used momentum and every ounce of her one-hundred-twenty pound frame to slam the first man into the second, knocking both assailants off-balance and unprepared for her next move: a vicious stab to the groin of the first. He collapsed to his knees. She followed with a backhand movement, opening up the throat of his companion. A similar gesture to the man with the injured groin silenced his moaning.

June (Sixteen months earlier)
Archaeological site, Ancient Sumerian city of Uruk 30 km east of As-Samawah, Iraq

"This is big, Harry." The American anthropologist spoke to Dr. Harold Clarke, key council member of the British Institute for the Study of Iraq, whose connections were responsible for funding the current multi-national excavation project.

"Indeed, it would seem so, Thomas."

The clay tablet was still embedded in the rock that lined the floor of the ancient Sumerian cave. The previous artefacts found in the area in recent months dated from 3200-3000 BCE, but this new find appeared to be much older. The scratches were difficult to decipher in situ, but were certainly cuneiform. Still, these were somehow different. Harold and the American, who was also an expert in ancient logophonetic languages as was Harold himself, knew it instantly. After delicate brushes had whisked away the last grains of sand and the first photographs taken, a hasty charcoal rubbing revealed something that startled both men and left Harold with an uneasy feeling in his stomach. Although crude in its rendering, next to the wedge-shaped Sumerian symbol for 'god being,' was a detailed representation of the double helix.

***

Liberty, Kansas
September,(Thirteen months earlier)

"Steven, will you please drag yourself away from the kitchen and mow the front yard? The neighbors are beginning to grumble. I saw them gathering up torches and pitchforks this morning. Better hurry."

The man sighed, irritated but amused. He glanced up at the woman carrying an overflowing basket of clothes to the laundry room. Even after fifteen years of marriage, she still took his breath away. How had a socially awkward nerd straddled with debt courtesy of dual master's degrees in mechanical and electrical engineering, gotten so lucky?

"Clever girl. Your nag-to-funny ratio is flawless, as usual."

She blew him a kiss and began stuffing clothes into the ancient Kenmore. Steven lifted the last of the mason jars from the pressure canner using rubberized tongs designed for the task, then placed the hot jars on the kitchen table. The contents, cubed chicken and broth, still boiled inside the glass. Seconds later the lids began to pop, indicating a vacuum seal. He knew it was silly, but the sound always made him smile. It said, *"You did it right, Stevie Boy! Good job! Now your family won't starve during the zombie apocalypse!"*

Except for his wife Laura, he kept those thoughts to himself. As far as his son knew, the whole 'prepping' thing was just his dad's quirky hobby. But Steven knew better than most how vulnerable the country's power grid actually was. Detonating a nuke twenty-five miles above the earth would spawn an electromagnetic pulse and devastate the grid, setting the country's technology back more than a hundred years. What terrorist group or enemy rogue nation doesn't have wet dreams about crippling the United States? An EMP would be an effective, relatively easy way to do it. All electrical devices stop working and everything goes dark. Supply chains are broken, food becomes scarce, and the fabric of society unravels quickly and violently. Steven could picture the bastards salivating at the thought as they crouched in some Afghani cave.

Those who prepared now might survive if they were sensible, cautious, and discreet. He'd never shared his obsession with his friends nor his co-workers at Kansas Electric — not that he had many friends, and his co-workers tended to avoid his eccentric behavior — so discretion came easily.

He'd filled up the root cellar with first dozens and then hundreds of canned vegetables and concentrated soups, tuna fish, and Spam. The canned items segued to rice, sugar, salt, pasta, and a large variety of beans stored in Mylar bags and food-grade buckets. He'd discovered the shelf life of peanut butter was surprisingly short, so he purchased a powdered version in bulk. High-acid foods like tomatoes and fruit degraded their metal containers, so he learned to can them himself in mason jars. Commercially canned meat was cost prohibitive, which led to buying a pressure canner at the Goodwill store in Salina and educating himself on methods for preserving poultry, pork, and beef. When done correctly and stored under optimal conditions, his food would last for years — decades even, despite the assertions of the FDA and the *Ball Blue Book Guide to Preserving*.

He'd built the cellar himself with the help of his oldest son, Jeffrey, whose stringy thirteen-year-old muscles and quiet tenacity had proven invaluable. They'd completed the job over a weekend six months before, and it was almost filled to capacity. He eyeballed the pint jars still bubbling on the kitchen table, considered Laura's reaction to the idea of a second cellar, and decided that battle would be more easily won with the leverage of a tidy yard. She didn't embrace this business of planning for the end of the world, but she did tolerate it. Barely. And for that, he loved her even more.

He kissed her cheek, squeezed her backside, and headed out the door to the shed where the lawn tools were stored. On the way, he noted the newly installed wind turbine fifty yards from the house near the back fence line. The three propeller-like blades spun with an eerie robotic grace, conjuring electricity from the movement of air with silent efficiency. When he received his annual bonus, he intended to add solar as a back-up for those times when Mother Nature's bluster didn't cooperate. For now, the turbine powered only the well pump; they still relied on Kansas Electric for everything else and would continue doing so until Steven could work out the glitches with his off-grid system. He experienced moments of anxiety when he thought of all that still needed to be done. If his family were to remain safe in a world suddenly turned upside down, he better get cracking.

Starting with mowing the lawn.

It was an important chore only in terms of his marriage — and therefore immensely important — but his mind had already leapt ahead to the next project. He estimated the yard work would take him until lunchtime, which meant a good five hours of daylight left to start on the new root cellar. He could put a big dent in it if Laura didn't have other chores lined up for him, assuming she green-lighted the plan in the first place.

As he pondered the best angle from which to approach that marital-landmine-riddled task, his cell phone vibrated in his jeans pocket.

The display showed an image of a smiling woman with dark hair and more than a passing resemblance to Steven.

"Hey, sis. Long time no hear. What's new in the sexy world of molecular genetics? Have you discovered the gene responsible for penis length yet? I'm asking for a friend."

"Hey, little brother. What's happening in the steamy world of mechanical engineering? Did you finish the schematics for that female sex bot? You're destined to be rich, you know."

He could hear the smile in her voice but also something else. Fatigue? Worry?

"Not as rich as you if you get that penis thing nailed down. What's up, Julia Petulia? How's Stan?" He knew she despised the pet name, especially now that she was a big-shot scientist with diplomas covering the walls of her office and the letters 'Ph.D.' printed on her business cards.

"Stan's fine. Still no sign of the cancer, thank god. He's dealing with the normal bullshit at the firm."

"You doing okay? You sound tired."

"I'm exhausted. Work has been kicking my ass. Which is why I'm worried that I may be overreacting..."

Steven didn't know much about her current project, just that she'd been studying the phenotype of a particular gene in order to determine its mutation characteristics...the usual stuff. He was a smart guy, but the human genome didn't hold any great interest for him, so he usually zoned out when Julia rambled on about her work. She probably did the same during their conversations about his work, although recently she'd asked about disaster preparedness, which had struck him as odd.

"Overreacting how?"

"The behavior of the molecule I've been working with is like nothing we've ever seen before. And not in a good way."

She had his full attention now. "What do you mean? Not good how?"

"The way in which it's expressing is unprecedented. It's been dormant until now. We knew its nature was developmental, meaning it would become active at a certain stage of its lifespan, versus how a 'tissue specific' DNA molecule can make hair fall out because it's located in the scalp."

His attention began to wane. Julia sensed it and hurried on.

"This gene has suddenly self-actuated in most of the samples we've collected. This is crazy behavior — DNA is highly individual — but this gene is acting identically in almost all of the samples, at nearly the same time...like a collective consciousness thing."

"I'm with you so far I think, but where's the bad news in this? What's it doing that has you guys at Stanford so nervous?"

Silence on the other end while she formulated a response. Seconds ticked by. Steven was beginning to wonder if the connection had been dropped when she finally spoke.

"In layman's terms, it seems to be telling all the cells in the body to self-destruct, which should be impossible, yet it's happening before our eyes. If we're right about this..."

"What? What does it mean?"

"Steven, if we're right about this, it would mean the end of humanity as we know it."

He suddenly found himself sitting on the overgrown lawn.

Press conference given by the Centers for Disease Control
Atlanta Georgia
November,(Eleven months earlier)

"It's not airborne. We know that for sure. But it's not clear how the disease is spreading." The man behind the makeshift podium spoke into more than a dozen microphones representing a huge variety of national and world news affiliates. His face was pale and haggard, suggesting days of sleep deprivation, but his carefully prepared speech and quiet, self-assured demeanor conveyed confidence. The scientific community would prevail over this dire threat — that was the message he intended to project.

"It's neither bacterial nor viral. Its characteristics are similar to autoimmune diseases such as rheumatoid arthritis or lupus in that certain cells of the body attack other cells. Specifically, it works in the vascular system and is analogous to SNV — systemic necrotizing vasculitis — but the onset occurs over hours rather than months or years.

"We are working around the clock to get a handle on this. We understand that people are afraid, but panic only makes the situation worse."

He pointed to a female reporter from Reuters.

"Will the PSI be raised?" she asked.

"That's up to Health and Human Services. Since this isn't influenza, the protocol is different. However, I expect the Pandemic Severity Index to be upgraded to level 4 within the day so that additional federal and state resources may be utilized."

He nodded to a dark-skinned man from Al Jazeera News.

"Is it spreading as rapidly in other countries as it is in the United States? Is there a demographic it favors?"

"We believe the event is happening worldwide at the same frequency and diffusion as it is here. There is no evidence to indicate that any segment of the populace is at higher risk than any other. It appears to be an equal opportunity illness and is presenting in all ages, all ethnicities, and both sexes without bias."

"Director Frieden!" A young man from CNN didn't wait to be called upon. "What is the mortality rate?"

He'd been dreading this question. Facts and candor would adversely affect a society already exhibiting hysteria, and the White House had issued a mandate two hours ago that panic must be contained even at the price of the truth. He'd withheld most of what they knew about the disease to everyone except his fellow scientists at the CDC, and of course the group from Stanford who had initially tipped them off about the gene mutation.

"It's still relatively low," he lied. "But we haven't been able to determine accurate numbers at this point."

If people knew the mortality rate, it would spark the immediate breakdown of social order and more people would die as a result of the pandemonium. This was the balm with which he soothed his conscience. Withholding the truth now would be saving lives.

At least for a while longer.

Even though every person on the planet possessed the DNA molecule responsible for the widespread deaths, not everyone's were self-actuating...yet. Those in whom it had, were dead within a day or two.

When it happened, it was quick and catastrophic. The vascular system became inflamed and blood flow to vital organs grew restricted. Death from suffocation or kidney failure occurred mere hours after the first sign of chills and fatigue. The speed with which the body responded to the directive given by the gene was unprecedented, and any therapies they might develop to battle it would take months or years. Director Frieden knew from his research that at the rate the illness was occurring in the population, they would never beat it in time. Fate had placed him at the helm of the Centers for Disease Control during the most significant event in human history.

Its demise.

Chapter 1

Colleyville, Texas - October (Now)

The third pursuer straddled the fence now, his mouth open in surprise at the sight of his accomplices on the ground and a woman in shadows standing beside them. Moonlight glinted off the blade she held in her hand. When he began to scramble back over, frantic and panicked, Dani thrust the Ka-Bar at the dangling denim-covered calf.

The man screamed as he slid the rest of the way down the other side.

She scrambled over after him.

He huddled at her feet, clutching a serrated steak knife in one hand, and his wounded leg in the other.

"You bitch!"

Tattered clothes hung on his skinny body like a neglected scarecrow. Most people were skinny and tattered these days.

"Who started this, asshole?" she replied in a reasonable tone.

"We're hungry! I got a little sister at home too. We're all starving. It looked like you had stuff."

"And you thought it would be cool to take my stuff because there were three of you and one of me?"

"Yeah, that's right. I don't know you. Why should I care?"

"Because we're not animals. Well, technically we are in a biological sense, but in terms of cultural anthropology, we're not. Not yet, at least." Even in the gloom she could see the man's quizzical expression.

She sighed. "Where do you and your sister live?"

"You think I'm gonna tell you? So you can come kill the rest of us?"

She knelt beside him, pressing the blood-darkened blade against the scrawny neck.

"I'm not killing anyone else tonight if I don't have to. Give me your pig sticker, handle first. Don't make any fast moves or I'll open up an artery," she said, with the quiet confidence of someone who has done so before.

The man obliged, grudging and slow, then lay back on the ground, pulling his injured leg up to his chest.

"It hurts!" he hissed through teeth that hadn't seen a good brushing in months.

Dani shook her head in silent disapproval. Oral hygiene was more important now than ever before. No longer were there dentists to tend to one's abscesses and root canals.

"Here's how this is going down. I'll play doctor on your leg, you'll say thank-you to the nice lady, and then you're going to hightail it back to your little nesty nest. *Capisce*, amigo?"

She fetched her backpack from under the shrub, then squatted next to her attacker as she unzipped it. She withdrew a small red case stamped with an iconic white symbol. These days, she never left home without basic first aid supplies.

He nodded. "Hey, I'm sorry about that bitch thing."

"No sweat, bro. I shanked you, and I wasted your buddies. It's understandable."

"Maybe we can help each other out. You seem like you got your act together. Maybe you could join up with us? My sister is kinda worthless, but she's real pretty and she sings like an angel. It's nice to listen to her...makes you forget all this shit for a few minutes, know what I mean?"

Dani ignored him. She tended to the leg wound with the efficiency of an emergency room nurse.

"I got some skills too, ya know," he said, petulant now.

"Really, Einstein? What might they be?"

"I'm real good at math!" he blurted.

She laughed. "If I ever need to know the sum of the square roots of any two sides of an isosceles triangle, I'll look you up. I appreciate the offer, sport, but I'll take a pass. I've been doing just fine without the benefit of singers and math wizards."

Dani had the wound cleaned and bandaged in less than three minutes.

"Now count to a hundred, slowly, then you can leave. Don't come looking for me. Don't come back to this area at all — I have dibs on this particular piece of real estate. Understand?"

"Fine."

She was already two houses away when she heard, "One one thousand, two one thousand, three one thousand..." She smiled as she sprinted down the darkened street toward home, her footfalls soundless in the night.

Chapter 2

Stanford University in California

Julia sat in the deserted lab. The woman who had called her brother about a rogue DNA molecule was gone. Strands of gray streaked her dark hair — vanity had taken a back seat to the most important research she'd ever done — and her shoulders were perpetually slumped from hundreds of hours bending over her microscope.

After she lost Stan, she'd moved into her lab. She slept on a small sofa in her office, used the shower in the attached bathroom, and ordered in her meals until the restaurants closed. When the staff and other scientists died or disappeared, she'd returned home, loaded the bulk of her shelf stable food and cases of bottled water into her new Land Rover, and brought it all to her office. She'd purchased the vehicle and supplies soon after her conversation with Steven — the day she'd told him about Lixi. The power had gone out, but the building was equipped with a backup generator. Sufficient diesel fuel remained in the maintenance shed to keep the lights on, the air conditioner cooling, and the electron microscopes, thermal cyclers, and centrifuges functioning for longer than she planned to stay.

It would soon be time to leave what had become her sanctuary, but also her prison. Until then, she was consumed with unlocking the secrets of the molecule which had annihilated most of the population and which she'd coined Lixi, the Greek word for 'termination.'

No longer must she endure the sideways glances from co-workers when she talked to herself. She was all alone now except for the orange tabby that had followed her back from the fuel shed a few days ago. The sound of her own voice kept the mocking silence at bay while she worked. But at night, when she lay in bed, the insidious feelings of solitude and isolation squirmed into her realm of consciousness, dreaded and unwelcome. She missed her husband, she missed people in general, and she missed the weekly, static-filled conversations with her brother. Those had ended two months ago when a hailstorm damaged the campus radio tower. The crushing aloneness sometimes felt unbearable, but she was close to deciphering the genetic code that had led to the fall of humanity. Could there be any more daunting yet meaningful task left in the world?

The clock was counting down though. She and Steven had agreed on a date. In the meantime, she would continue her research, but when that day arrived, she would leave. Must leave. And it was almost here.

The thought terrified her.

The last time she'd been 'out there' on her food and water run, she'd witnessed the ugly and violent collapse of society. Starving people behaved no differently than starving animals. Probably worse. On the drive from her home in Palo Alto back to Stanford, her Land Rover was attacked twice. Those horrific memories never left her.

For years she'd complained about the inconvenient location of her lab which was situated in a remote, older section of the campus, but now she realized the inaccessibility had kept her safe. No one had bothered her because no one had found her.

But there were people alive out there; she knew that better than anyone. What had happened to that tiny fraction of humanity that hadn't succumbed to the disease? Were they banding together in civilized groups or had they formed marauding packs willing to commit unspeakable atrocities?

Soon she would find out firsthand.

***

Logan sat on the pier, gazing out at the choppy gray water. It was chilly, so he zipped up the black windbreaker. Alcatraz loomed in the distance, craggy and formidable. Not for the first time he considered loading up a boat with supplies and making the rocky island his home. Its remoteness made it appealing in some ways, but the isolation also intimidated him. And the place was creepy. The tour he'd taken as a kid with his mom left him feeling unsettled and anxious for days. At the time he'd thought some of those angry men who had lived and died there might still be around, their spirits clinging to the last place they'd lived. He had nightmares about it for a long time afterward. But that was years ago. What he'd experienced these past months put those childhood nightmares to shame.

When the pretty news lady on Channel 6 reported death tolls in the thousands, he'd emptied out his savings account and spent every dime on firearms and ammunition. He'd ruled out using any of his money on food — he figured he'd be able to scrounge for it — and he prepared for the coming apocalypse, which would be bloody and violent. He quit his job at Dave's Doughnut Shop and worked on becoming skilled with his new weaponry. By the time the truth came out about the plague — something called the 'mortality rate' — he could hit a four-inch target at a hundred yards. A one-inch target at fifty yards. That in itself was nothing to write home about. Heck, with his Sig Sauer tactical rifle and Konus scope, a child could do that. He was especially proud of his accuracy with the subcompact handguns. Considering the truncated barrel and reduced grip area, it was a minor miracle for an amateur to hit an adversary at ten feet. Logan could leave a tight, six-hole grouping on the paper targets at Harvey's Gun Range from fifty feet away. His new buddies at the range seemed to think this was pretty cool. One of them said he was an 'idiot savant.' He didn't much care for being called an idiot, but later, after he checked his mom's old Webster's dictionary, he decided he liked the savant part.

His stomach growled, which startled him out of one of his Quiet Spells. His mom had named them that. She was dead now, as were most people he'd known in the Before Time. He reckoned he should go scrounging for some food. It had always been difficult for him to focus for very long — except when it came to guns — but over the last few days he'd put some serious thought into leaving the Bay Area and heading south. A gang of thugs had taken over the Fisherman's Wharf territory, so it wasn't fun to visit the place that had been a childhood favorite. He'd killed a few of them, but they kept coming. Some of them were even girls, which mystified him since they sure didn't act like the girls that came into the doughnut shop, or the ones in his Sunday school class. These girls acted as mean as the men, and they wore leather boots and carried knives.

He supposed that meant it was okay to kill them too, but so far he hadn't. His mom told him it was important to be nice to females because they were fragile and weren't as strong as he was. After the incident with the girl in middle school, they'd moved to a new neighborhood. They had the birds-and-bees talk and spent a lot of time going over 'acceptable and unacceptable behavior.' She fretted that there'd never been a positive male influence in his life, since his father skipped out long before he was even born, and none of the guys his mother dated seemed to stick around for long.

He missed his mom. She always made him feel better when the Bad Thoughts came. Now that he was by himself, he'd begun to listen to them. What did it matter now? She'd said he might go to jail if he let the Bad Thoughts control him, but he was pretty sure there was nobody left to put him in jail. He hadn't seen a police officer in months. He decided he no longer needed to follow all his mom's rules from the Before Time. The notion that he could now make up his own rules was...what was that word?

Thrilling, said the Bad Thoughts.

Chapter 3

Twickenham, United Kingdom—11 miles South of London

Harold bumped his toe against the ball and claw foot of his antique desk, spilling his tea, and eliciting a rare expletive from the anthropologist. Under different circumstances, the candlelight and gas fireplace would have provided a cozy ambience to his study. Now they signified a monumental reversal of technology and modern life. Candles were necessary to light his home after the power had gone out, and the fireplace was the only form of heat available to him now, short of burning furniture and books. He supposed when the gas stopped working, he'd be forced to consider such a solution. But for the moment, the fireplace still heated the study where he slept, and the cooker in the kitchen continued to boil water for his Earl Grey, and to warm the tins of stockpiled soup. The mountain of food he'd acquired before the end was down to a meager mole hill.

Something would need to be done about that soon, but not yet. Not just yet.

A year ago, when he and his colleague from the States found the first of the strange tablets, they'd known it was different from any other previously discovered Sumerian artefact. For one thing, it was much older, possibly dating from 8,000-10,000 BCE. That flew in the face of the scientific community's generally accepted date of 3200 BCE for the first appearance of language-driven writing. It was cuneiform, the earliest form of linguistic written expression. Its predecessor, known as proto-writing, utilized ideographic and mnemonic symbols to convey basic information such as quantities and animals, but was not an actual representation of a spoken language. Cuneiform was true writing. By definition, that meant the content of an utterance was encoded, so what was written by one individual could be reconstructed and understood by someone else with a fair degree of accuracy.

In evolutionary terms, cuneiform represented a prodigious leap for humankind. But the cuneiform chiseled onto the tablet they'd unearthed in Uruk was even more complex and advanced than anything seen before. It took him months to decipher the additional characters which, up to that point, had not appeared in any other Sumerian artefact. And while he'd been working on this project — certainly the most significant archaeological find in the history of humanity — humanity perished.

The irony was not lost on him.

During his career, there'd never been time to get serious about a woman, so he had no spouse or children to mourn when the end came, and his parents had been gone for years. His work was his life, so the people he missed the most weren't family or friends but colleagues, who would have relished the tantalizing mystery spread out on his cluttered desk: photographs of the Urak tablets. They'd found seven in all, each more mysterious than the last. He had made enormous progress in deciphering the new characters, but the resolution on some of the photos vexed him. He was close to completing the task but several elements stubbornly refused to give up their secrets.

Harold sighed. He knew what must be done next, but the thought of leaving the relative safety of his flat made his stomach churn. Twickenham and Richmond had been a war zone in the final days. Many people died and the ones who remained were desperate and hungry. He'd had the foresight to barricade himself in his third-floor flat for what would be the violent and ugly collapse of civilisation.

He knew there were still a few people about because he sometimes spotted them through his shuttered window. However, based on what the news reports said before the power went out, most of the global population would have succumbed to the disease the media had termed 'Chicxulub,' so named for the dinosaur-killing asteroid. When he first heard it, Harold couldn't deny the cleverness of the term. At least he'd thought it was clever until people started dying by the millions. Now, it filled him with bitterness, but also determination to see if his hunch was right about the tablets. He would need to study them in person, which meant a dangerous eleven-mile journey on foot to London. As people tried to flee the cities, the roads had become clogged with the sheer volume of vehicles they were never intended to accommodate; and they remained so to this day. He learned this a few weeks ago when his curiosity overcame his fear and he ventured out to reconnoitre.

A block from home, two men dressed in shabby clothes and one skeletal woman cornered him in an alleyway, brandishing knives and demanding food. He'd given them the contents of his pockets: an energy bar and a bottle of water. They'd been about to press him for more when something startled them and they ran off. He took off in the opposite direction, making it back to the safety of his flat with a racing heart and a sprained ankle.

The experience left him anxious about venturing out again, but he knew he must at some point. The necessity had now become more pressing. He needed answers which could only be found by studying the Urak tablets firsthand. What he'd garnered thus far from their ancient author defied belief and challenged everything he knew about the origins of modern man. Even more compelling were the titillating hints about the end of humanity. They pinpointed a date, one that coincided precisely with the past year, when earth would be cleansed of the destructive genus known as *Homo sapiens*.

How was it possible that a text, written more than ten thousand years ago, had predicted the exact year in which humankind would essentially be wiped off the planet?

CHAPTER 4

LIBERTY, KANSAS

"Jeff, quiet as a mouse, okay?" Steven whispered to his son, who had grown in body, mind, and spirit this past year.

The death of his mother had devastated the boy. For weeks after, he barely spoke. Then a month after her death, Steven suspected his son had experienced some kind of epiphany, which transformed him almost overnight into the young man standing before him now in the bunker. The fourteen-year-old was determined to succeed in every project he undertook, whether at his nightly school lessons with his father, the self-defense techniques they learned together from the DVDs Steven bought before the end, or the daily drudgery of chores. He never complained and he never gave up. Steven sometimes worried about the man his son would become in these unprecedented times, but he refused to obsess about it. How did that Nina Simone song go? *It's a new dawn, it's a new day. It's a new life for me.* Never had those words been more relevant or poignant...for him, his son and the few remaining humans who had survived Chicxulub.

After the phone conversation with his sister a year ago, he'd nixed the plans to build a second root cellar and constructed an underground bunker instead, despite Laura's objections and the debt they acquired as a result.

It was the smartest decision he had ever made.

Debt had no meaning now, and he had provided a safe haven for his family, which now included only himself, Jeffrey, and their eight-year old Labrador retriever, Molly. As horrendous as the death of his mother had been to Jeffrey, losing Laura almost killed Steven. The agonizing grief felt too huge to be contained, much less endured. With claws and fangs, it threatened to tear its way out of his chest, seeking sanctuary in a vessel which could accommodate its immensity. For months after, the only salve for his pain, the only spark of hope in a bleak wasteland of misery, was his son. He must live for Jeffrey. Otherwise, he would have used his recently purchased Glock 17 to blow out his own brains.

Of course now, months later, he was glad he hadn't, even though he missed his wife every minute of every day. He and Jeffrey had accomplished amazing things together. Some days he felt content. Satisfied, if not happy. But there were also days like today, when the threat of losing everything clarified how tenuous was their continued existence.

"Dad," Jeffrey whispered, pointing toward the 30.06 Springfield he had just finished cleaning but hadn't yet returned to the weapons locker.

Steven gave him a terse nod, placing a finger against his lips. *No more talking.* The blast resistant door was soundproof but the ventilation duct wasn't. Noises from inside could be heard above and the last thing they needed was for the intruders to discover the concealed vent, which he'd covered with a pile of dead tree limbs thirty feet away.

Jeffrey nodded, lifting the loaded rifle, and gripping it with the confidence of a young man who knew how to handle firearms. Steven felt a frisson of pride. He'd done a good job with his son this past year, teaching him skills and knowledge he would need to know if he ever had to survive on his own. And he would not let those Neanderthals trampling about above them take that away.

Steven hadn't camouflaged the bunker; there'd been too many pressing tasks to do first. The bottom half of the rebar-reinforced concrete structure was buried six feet deep in the sandy Kansas soil, and the top which rose six feet above ground, would ultimately be covered with dirt and fescue sod, leaving only the blast-resistant door visible. Since the opening faced away from the house and toward a barren cornfield, trespassers would likely never see it since there was nothing in that direction to draw their curiosity. He also intended to plant trees and shrubs to disguise the mound, but it was too late for any of that now.

The intruders were kicking on the two-inch steel door. He couldn't hear them, but he could see them. Two men had appeared on the seven-inch monitor of his closed circuit camera system, run by a solar power generator built from scratch. Three wireless cameras with motion sensors were placed discreetly throughout his property: one near the steel door, a second located at the front door to the house, and the third was positioned at his driveway entrance where it connected to the semi-rural residential street. When the electric current wasn't running through it, he knew the metal fence wouldn't keep out someone who was hell-bent to gain access, despite the razor wire. Their best defense would be a forewarning and the precious moments it would give them to hide. The signaling mechanism Steven jerry-rigged into the cameras was triggered by movement — the old Motorola pager he carried had vibrated ten minutes ago.

The late afternoon sunlight had taken on a golden cast which intimated the arrival of sunset. It was Steven's favorite time of day, and they'd been in the bunker with the door open, finishing up their weekly firearms maintenance. He had been teasing Jeffrey about the Evans girl, who was expected for dinner along with her mother in an hour. He knew of twenty or so people still alive in Liberty. There may be more out in the neighboring farms, but if so, they kept to themselves. It was Jeffrey's good fortune that one of the survivors had been the prettiest girl in Janie Stark Middle School's eighth grade class.

Now, all thoughts of the pleasant evening they had planned vanished. Father and son scrutinized the small black-and-white screen. The men didn't appear to be starving, as other drifters had been. They seemed well-fed, and they moved with the fluid efficiency of trained military personnel. Their mismatched clothing belied the possibility they were there on government-sanctioned business. And since Steven had seen zero evidence that the United States government still existed, he knew this meant big trouble.

The man on the left withdrew a pen and notepad from a shirtfront pocket, scribbled something with lazy indifference, and held it up to a camera which Steven had believed to be well-hidden in the low branches of a giant cottonwood tree.

COME OUT SLOWLY, HANDS UP, NO QUICK MOVEMENTS. YOU HAVE TWO MINUTES BEFORE WE START LOOKING FOR YOUR VENT AND DROP AN M26 DOWN THE PIPE.

Steven wasn't familiar with military vernacular, but he did know what an M26 was. He knew the kind of devastation the fragmentation grenade would cause. The thirty-foot underground air duct ran mostly horizontal, so unless it could make 90 degree turns and still keep going, it would never reach them. But the explosion would create enough rubble to plug the shaft and cut off their air supply. They had sufficient oxygen to last a few hours...maybe a day. Then they would suffocate.

Steven analyzed the situation and devised a resolution in less than ten seconds. He would never allow these men or anyone else to take what he and his son had worked so hard for. He had anticipated this exact scenario and taken counter measures in advance of its happening.

After two minutes that felt like two hours, the men moved away from the steel door. Steven wished there had been time to place a fourth camera near the air vent, but it had been a matter of limited resources and more pressing priorities.

So they wouldn't be able to witness the springing of the trap Steven had set for anyone venturing into its vicinity, which was just as well. He didn't want Jeffrey to see the resulting carnage if it worked, and he had no reason to assume it wouldn't.

The mechanics were crude but effective. He had patterned them after the basic Punji trap used by the Vietcong in the '60s. When someone stepped on the wooden treadle — concealed by twigs, rocks, and other debris — the spiked end would spring up and strike the person in the face and chest. Six-inch box nails extended sufficiently through the half-inch plywood as to elicit devastating results. Though the injuries sustained might not be fatal, the victim would be in agony, and blinded if his height fell in the average range. Then Steven could finish him off.

Whatever that might entail.

He suffered a moment of doubt when he considered the confident demeanor of the intruders. He hoped whatever their military experience, it hadn't included training on the type of trap awaiting them.

They would know soon enough.

Chapter 5

Near Prescott, Arizona

Pablo's Journal, Entry #382

I admit the solitude is beginning to wear on me; a soft but insistent pressure on my chest and head...insidious in its methods since it was initially a boon of sorts. A gift of freedom from oppression and prejudice, presented as a magnanimous yet bloody favor by the Grand Liberator, which the pundits called Chicxulub. Now there are moments when my loneliness reaches such depths that I would relish the companionship of the very ones who sought to limit and subjugate me. Anyone. Anyone who is human. And by human, I don't mean those devils cloaked in filthy rags that strut about the courthouse square, brandishing their weapons and screaming of their prowess to the wind and those who might be listening. I will not call them animals, because most animals have honor and decency, as Bruno can attest. But I would happily share my fire with someone who might have hated me before — hated me because my skin is brown and my kind were willing to perform tasks which they considered beneath them. During our evening, we might achieve an accord. He (or she) might be surprised by how well I speak English better than most Whites. They would not be threatened by this because color no longer matters, but also — perhaps — because at that moment, in the warm glow of the fire and with the glittering stars above, they would realize their former bigotry was misguided.

And since I'm fantasizing, I think I'll make this person Scarlett Johansson. A man can dream can't he?

Pablo chuckled to himself, prompting the German shepherd at his feet to lift his head and gaze up at his human. He tucked the Bic into a jacket pocket, rubbed the furry head and looked up at the night sky. He missed television, along with the thousands of other modern conveniences lost when civilization imploded. Good food was also at the top of the list, not this canned offal he'd been eating for months. His mother's perfectly seasoned chiles rellenos...oh my...he might trade his left *huevo* for one bite. Okay, two bites. Two bites would be worth sacrificing a testicle, for sure.

He sat outside the abandoned cabin he'd stumbled upon in the foothills of the Bradshaw Mountains after fleeing the madness and anarchy of the Quad City area. The sun-bleached boards were barely held in place by nails coated in rust. The place might have been used for hunting, or perhaps gold-panning, situated as it was next to a tributary of the Agua Fria River. Thirty feet away stood an outhouse, still intact, and complete with the traditional crescent moon opening carved into the door. The nearby stream provided clean water and an occasional bluegill or mullet, treasures more valuable than any nuggets of gold. Within minutes of pulling them from the water, Pablo roasted them in the fire pit next to the cabin. Fresh food was a special treat these days and he knew he would soon need to find additional sources, or be forced to venture back into Prescott.

Under these strange circumstances, he had discovered a level of inner peace unknown to him during his life as the son of illegal immigrants. He no longer had to endure the snubs, nor the feeling of being socially inferior to those who benefited from the labor of his people. For his family and friends, these realities were normal and did not warrant discussion. To Pablo, they had made life almost unbearable. The disparity was infuriating. Why couldn't they see this? Why did they just accept their fate, their lowly position in society, as if they'd been born peasants in Medieval England?

It had been gnawing away at him for years, like a miserable crow plucking at some ancient road kill. Nobody else saw it and nobody else cared. Things were what they were and probably always would be so.

Then Chicxulub cleansed the planet of almost all people, indiscriminately, like a tsunami scouring the shoreline and destroying five star hotels and poor hovels without bias.

Pablo's unusual, light gold eyes — eyes his father jokingly said must have come from the mailman — filled with tears. He missed his family so much, but he couldn't say he was unhappy now. He sometimes just felt nostalgic for all that had been, and lonely for the sound of a human voice or the touch of fingers on his face.

His focus shifted from the night sky to the large spiral notebook on his lap. Elegant handwriting covered almost all of the pages; he'd need to find a new one soon or risk losing his mind. The daily journaling had become more than a way to pass the time and document the end of the old world. His literary ramblings were a coping mechanism, offering escapism as well as moments of catharsis.

He hesitated a moment, then flipped back to the first entry from more than a year ago...

Pablo's Journal, Entry #1

Papa died today. The pain is intense, as I knew it would be, but there is also some joy because he is now with Mama. I have always struggled with religious faith, much to my parents' dismay, but as it turns out, I DO believe. I NEED to — because to NOT believe in an afterlife, a continuation of our spirit, is abhorrent. Their souls are together now as they were in life...billions or even trillions of energy molecules soaring through stardust and frolicking in the heavens. Perhaps they are corporeal again, reincarnated into the bodies of newborn babes, destined to find one another on this earth as they have done many times before. They would scold me for such thoughts, of course. Good Catholics don't believe in that nonsense, but the truth is we don't know. Nobody does — not the priests, nor the televangelists, the Buddhist monks, nor the ayatollahs. So for me, I believe in whatever brings me comfort to contemplate. I don't know of any other way that makes sense.

I will bury Papa in the vacant lot across the street so as not to contaminate the soil of our vegetable garden in the backyard. It may be risky because people are becoming panicked. Like corralled horses catching the scent of wolves on the breeze, they seem to be dancing on a razor's edge and capable of sudden, explosive violence. Several of them pounded on our door yesterday while Papa was slipping away. The locks held and the plywood on the windows were secured with molly screws — Papa had been wise about that — and finally they went away.

I know they are hungry. I am also hungry. I hope I never become like them though. I hope I never get desperate enough to steal food belonging to another person in order to fill my own belly. When we lose honor, we lose everything. In the aftermath of this pandemic, when there are so few humans left in this world, I can't imagine anything more important than honor. Except love, perhaps. And I think these two things cannot be separated.

Maybe I'm deluding myself. Maybe I too will get hungry enough to snatch the last crust of bread from the mouth of another man, but I hope not. Oh, I hope not.

When the disease began taking people a month ago, it was thought to be some kind of influenza. Every evening we would watch the news for the latest information. "Fifteen deaths in the Midwest, twenty-seven in New England, and thirty-eight on the Pacific coast have been reported today. The medical community is recommending that everyone who has not already done so to get a flu shot immediately. Even though the efficacy of the current vaccine is unknown, doctors believe it might at least help with the severity of this new strain, if not prevent it."

Mama and Papa would exchange worried glances and say nothing. Our survival in this country had been achieved by staying under the radar, which meant no medical treatments requiring proof of citizenship or documented worker status. And they refused to take charity from the free health clinic, where such paperwork was not required. From the beginning, I knew a flu shot wouldn't make a difference. I think others suspected as much too, but it didn't keep the mobs from storming their local Walgreens, the grocery store pharmacies, and the government-run clinics. Soon, the stock of vaccines was exhausted.

But people kept dying...by the thousands.

When a young female reporter from NBC announced a week later there had been ten thousand deaths in Seattle, her voice trembled. The news anchors no longer clung to their façade of composure — their faces reflected the fear everyone felt.

That's when the supply chains began to break down. The long-haul truckers stopped making their runs because they were either dying or afraid to leave their families. Union Pacific, BNSF, and other railway companies that transported food from the Midwest ceased operations because their employees were dying or not showing up for work. The independent farmers and the workers at the agricultural conglomerates which grew and harvested the food, and the tens of thousands of others who supplied the necessary labor in between all these links in the chain, were dying just like everybody else.

The grocery stores emptied for good.

I marvel when I think how precariously balanced was the system that put food on the table of most Americans. Such a tiny percentage of our society was self-reliant, which left the remaining vast majority not only utterly dependent on their local Safeway or Trader Joe's, but also blissfully unaware of how tenuous was their lifestyle. When the store shelves became as vacuous as the minds of the citizenry that embraced television shows such as The Bachelor and Keeping up with the Kardashians, *it seemed a reckoning, of sorts...as if people had gotten what they deserved by virtue of their stubborn ignorance. I realize this sounds harsh, but it seems a true statement to me.*

I don't know why I was spared, but I am happy to be alive and I will make the most of the time I have left in this world.

So today, while there is still daylight, along the top of our fence I will install the barbed wire Papa and I bought last week. I will bring the chickens inside before dark so they will be safe from those desperate enough to risk injury either from the wire or Bruno, who insists on staying outside to keep watch over what remains of his family. And tonight, I shall bury Papa under both cover of darkness and three feet of American soil, which was always his wish.

POEM — Blue Marble

The blue marble spins and twirls
Never mind my pain, it has orbiting to do

Another day, another cosmic revolution
The blue seems glacial now, chill and wintry
Before, a cerulean embrace
Now, a hollow place
Of ice and freezing climes
Its vocation, not maternal but infernal
And I, in its frigid gyrating grasp
A solitary mourner

The fire had burned down to luminous embers and the waning moon crested the stunted mountain peaks twenty miles to the north of Pablo's cabin. He sighed and closed the worn, yellow cover of his journal. This had been the first time he'd allowed himself to experience that day again through his own words. He had never gone back and read anything he'd written, and despite the sadness it stirred in his soul, it also felt curative...cleansing. Perhaps he would read more tomorrow night, but for now it was time to sleep.

"Ready for bed, Bruno?" he said, rubbing the soft head again.

Instantly, he knew something was wrong. Bruno's body was tense and rigid. The huge German shepherd ears seemed to hone in on a sound, like a radio dish picking up a weak signal. The low, rumbling growl confirmed it. Somebody or something was out there in the desert. Pablo stood, reaching for the ancient shotgun always kept within reach, and racked the slide. Bruno's growls intensified as Pablo scanned the terrain, a thousand textures of gray in the moonlight.

Then he heard a scream.

Chapter 6

Colleyville, Texas

Dani was still smiling when she arrived home. The dentally-challenged, would-be thief had been typical of the type of people she encountered after Chicxulub, with a few exceptions, of course. Sam was one of them. She shook her head, mystified by the capricious nature of fate and the irony that a person such as herself would be cast adrift in a sea of morons.

Well, at least they were fun to play with.

She flicked her Zippo and lit several candles in the kitchen of her parents' home. She had nailed plywood to the windows months ago — it wouldn't do to allow candlelight to announce her presence to roving marauders. The kitchen door was her only means of ingress and egress at the sprawling, two-story suburban house, and it boasted three sets of Schlage deadbolts, which she locked behind her. She had converted the place into Fort Knox — a long and arduous process but worth the effort. When she was at home, with the boarded up doors and windows, the bolts and the booby traps, she felt safe. It was the only time she let her guard down. Her continued mental health depended on regular reprieves from the 'high alert' mode in which she spent most of her time.

She shrugged out of the backpack and set it on the dining table. When she turned around, a muscular man of medium height stood three feet away between her and the door. His lips curled back in a grin of anticipation. Without hesitation, she shifted her stance into something one might see in a boxing ring — arms bent at the elbows, chin down, shoulders forward. With her left arm, she threw a perfect cross body punch. It caught the man on the jaw and wiped the smile off his face.

"That hurt, Dani!"

"I thought this was another one of your sneak attack lessons, Sam. I'm sorry. How bad is it?" She reached for his face, turning it roughly toward the candle.

"It doesn't feel like a walk in the tulips, I can tell you that."

Dani laughed. Sam's mixed metaphors always cracked her up. She had never been able to determine if the scrambled clichés were intentional or not. Finally she decided she didn't care. It was best not to look a gift laugh in the mouth.

"Suck it up, sissy boy. You've given me much worse." She smiled at her friend. "What's for dinner?"

Sam rubbed his cheek, gazing at her with the joy of a golden retriever welcoming his master home after the work day.

"I was thinking tomato soup and grilled cheese with some of the peasant bread I made last week. We still have plenty of propane for the Coleman. My mom used to make us tomato soup and grilled cheese every Friday night." The family memory evoked a beautiful smile.

"We've talked about this," Dani said, her voice gentle. "We have to be careful about using up too many of our resources before winter. I know it doesn't get that cold here, but it gets cold enough. Don't you think we should save as much of the propane as we can? It's only October, and it's seventy-five degrees out. What about regular cheese sandwiches for tonight? We'll open that last bottle of cabernet...how does that sound?"

"It's just that the dehydrated cheese doesn't taste too good unless it's warm and melty. But I understand. I get two glasses of wine though. It's only fair."

Dani nodded with a smile. She had no idea what Sam meant by 'fair' in this context, but she'd realized a long time ago that his thought process was fundamentally different from hers. Sometimes she wondered if he'd been in remedial classes growing up, and then out of the blue, he'd spout off with some complex philosophical statement. He was a mystery, for sure. She respected him and his opinions, especially when it came to self-defense. The man was a genius at martial arts. He wasn't too hard on the eyes either, but she didn't return Sam's feelings, which she suspected went well beyond friendship. She couldn't explain it. She liked boys, and the pickings were mighty slim now, but despite his many fine qualities — a big heart being one of them — she didn't feel anything of a romantic nature for him.

Like her father used to say, it is what it is.

As they puttered about the kitchen preparing their meal, she relayed the events of her evening.

"That could have been bad," he said, his brow creased with worry. "What if you hadn't been able to take those guys? You should've let me come with you."

"We've been over this. I have to learn how to protect myself. If I needed you to take care of me every minute, how would I fare in this world if something happened to you? You know it's important for me to be self-sufficient."

His nod was slow and noncommittal.

Dani punched him in the arm and said, "Hey, let's go sit outside to eat. It's a gorgeous night."

"You sure? You think it's safe enough?"

"Yeah, for a little while."

They carried their dinner and wine back through the kitchen door and into the backyard, which at just shy of an acre, was large even by the standards of the upscale neighborhood. Murky water filled only the bottom half of the swimming pool. It had been used to flush toilets and wash clothes for months now. Her parents only lived eight years in their dream house before the plague took them, along with almost everyone else.

As they ate their dinner, she indulged in a rare moment of nostalgia, remembering the people who adopted her as a three-week old infant, and never, not for one second, treated her as anything other than their own offspring. Dani missed them so much sometimes it felt like burning icicles formed in her chest every time she thought about them. Living through their deaths and acquiring the critical knowledge necessary for survival in this new world had been a trial of monstrous proportions. But she'd done it.

She just wasn't sure *why* she'd done it.

When Chicxulub raged through the global population like a biological wildfire, a survival instinct surfaced that she never knew she possessed. She had been watching the latest death tolls on the news one evening with her parents, when something shifted inside her. A tiny but insistent seedling grew overnight as she lay in bed devising a strategy. By morning, the seedling had burgeoned to an intense desire to live, even when others were dying en masse. She created a methodology for living under the adverse conditions she knew were imminent for anyone who survived.

And some did survive, like her. But most of them now subsisted on whatever scraps they could scavenge from the looted stores or the homes of dead neighbors. Dani did more than scrape by. She thrived. Before the end, she had used her father's credit card to order as much shelf-stable food from companies like Mountain Home and Lindon Farms as they would ship at that time. She wasn't the only person who'd had the same thought, and inventories depleted rapidly. She made trips to Costco for bottled water, over the counter medicines, batteries, camp gear, and a lengthy list of other items.

She had met Sam on one of those shopping forays while standing in the vitamin aisle at a Wal-Mart. She soon discovered the hunky Krav Maga instructor had much to teach her, lessons even more important than the information she had garnered from all the books she'd collected. In the following months, he had taught her the art of self-defense. That training had saved her life tonight, and not for the first time.

She studied Sam's profile in the starlight. His sculpted jaw was covered in reddish gold stubble, and his straight-edged nose and full mouth would be at home on a Greek statue, perfect in their symmetry. A guy like him wouldn't have looked twice at a chubby nerd like her under normal circumstances.

But he had. Thank god.

She was still a nerd months later, but the chubby girl was long gone, and happily so. Sometimes she felt guilty that in between the moments of grief — the loss of her parents, the loss of humanity — she was kind of digging this Brave New World thing. If that was immoral or evil, she didn't care, and she couldn't deny her feelings.

After all, it is what it is.

She still asked herself ten times a day, why her? Why Sam? Why the skinny dude with the bad teeth? Why had they survived and not the seven billion or so others?

Sam startled her out of her reverie with a sudden, firm grip on her knee and a finger held to his lips.

Someone is out there. He mouthed the words and pointed to the darkened area beyond the pool.

Five figures detached themselves from the shadows with inky fluidity and walked toward them with measured, confident movements.

"We are so screwed," Dani breathed.

***

Stanford University in California

"One more time. I have to do it one more time," Julia mumbled.

She had done the test twice now with the exact same results, results that were so incredible, she struggled to believe them herself. Yet the evidence was there. The tests had been flawlessly executed, and her findings would be validated after the third run. The most colossal breakthrough in genetics and nobody was here to share it with her. Except for the stupid cat.

Well, he was better than nothing.

"I know this sounds unbelievable and yeah, yeah, I know looking for specific personality and talent dimensions in genetic polymorphisms is a bit farfetched, but there was a compelling twin study done with mind-blowing results before mine, so shut your trap, Brains."

The cat, whose name had recently been shortened from Shit-For-Brains, merely gazed at Julia with an inscrutable expression from the comfort of a blanket-lined cardboard lid. She had always thought cats were creepy, but the little dipshit was a warm body, at least. Despite their brief time together, she realized she'd grown attached to him. And when she talked to him rather than just out loud to herself, she felt less crazy.

Somewhat.

"Yes, I know they weren't able to replicate their results, but I did. And I'm about to do it for a third time, so put that in your pipe and smoke it."

The feline began to clean his orange fur with vigor, giving no indication that a pipe quest was imminent.

"There's still so much to do, but the dopamine D4 receptor in almost all my viable samples indicate marked intelligence. That's freaking huge, Brains. Do you know what that means?"

He stopped grooming and studied her with mild interest, as if anticipating the weather forecast.

"The samples — the ones where the Lixi molecule in the DNA never flipped on, meaning the human donors would have survived — the weird thing is, in about half of those which presented with this trait, the serotonin transporters also indicated an increased spike in anxiety levels, neuroticism, and psychosis."

Brains went back to his toilette, underwhelmed by the news.

"Stupid cat. You don't get it do you? This could mean Chicxulub targeted certain types of people. Or more accurately, skipped over a tiny percentage of humans who carried these genetic markers. And what that indicates is a distinct and sudden macroevolution.

"What it *means*," Julia continued, her voice filled with awe, "Is that most people were meant to die out quite suddenly, and the few who didn't are special. Very special indeed."

Chapter 7

Liberty, Kansas

Steven and Jeffrey watched the tiny camera monitor inside the bunker. If Steven's trap had worked, only one of the two intruders would reappear. The minutes ticked by at what felt like half-speed. What the hell were those guys doing out there?

Finally, one of the men emerged on the left side of the screen. The clarity of the high resolution Sony captured fresh stains on the man's clothes, but his movements were fluid, confident. It must be his companion's blood.

This wasn't a worst-case scenario. If he and his son only had to deal with one assailant instead of two, their odds of success were vastly increased. Steven could see in Jeff's eyes that he had reached the same conclusion. He nodded at his father with a somber, adult expression.

They both knew what they would have to do next. Then something neither of them anticipated appeared on the monitor.

Molly, the yellow Labrador retriever — a family member for seven years — came into view. She sat happily by the man in blood stained clothes, who now held a gun to her head as he posed with a mocking grin.

The message was clear.

"Okay, son, here's what we're going to do."

A minute later, Steven opened the steel door and stepped outside with his arms held high.

"Here I am. Look, nobody has to get hurt here. I have plenty of food and I'll give it to you. Just don't harm the dog."

"Nobody has to get hurt? Tell that to Rodrigo, asshole. Your little trap put a nail in his brain."

"I'm sorry. I had to take measures to protect myself. You can't blame me for that, can you?" Steven ambled to the right, away from the open doorway, arms still held up in a gesture of submission.

"Who else you protecting? You got a pretty little wife down there? A daughter I can have a little fun with before I blow her brains out?" The man was agitated. Steven got the impression losing his partner had unhinged him — or maybe he'd been unhinged to begin with. There was something odd about his eyes.

"No, no one else, I swear," he said with a calmness he didn't feel. "Look, let's be cool. If you go ape shit postal on me, I won't be able to tell you where my stockpile is. The stuff in the bunker is just the tip of the iceberg."

The man's eyes gleamed as he smiled broadly. Maybe he was going for charming, but the combination of the bared teeth and the disturbing eyes produced a ghoulish effect on what should have been a handsome face. Steven felt the hair on the back of his neck stiffen, like Molly's hackles did now that she realized the man smelled like bad doggy-mojo.

"Is that so?"

Steven could see the poorly veiled interest and knew the hook was set. Now all he had to do was reel in the fish before the fish killed him.

"Follow me up to the house and I'll rock your world."

He continued to walk, arms still raised, hoping his body language exuded a defeated air.

Twenty more feet...come on you creepy bastard...

"Whoa, hold on. You think I'm stupid?" the man said, stopping in mid stride. He grabbed Molly by the collar and thrust the gun's barrel against her head again.

"What do you mean?"

"You got another booby trap in there, don't you?"

"No, of course not. Why would I booby trap my own house?" he replied and began walking again. *Ten more feet...*

"No. Stop right there. What are you up to, asshole? You better tell me right fucking now or I will put a hole in this furry skull."

"I don't know what your problem is. All the best stuff is in the house. Just follow me and I'll prove it to you."

Steven took another step toward the house. Wedged in a front pocket of his baggy jeans was a Taurus 380 compact, but his aim wasn't precise with the small handgun and he didn't know if he was fast enough to retrieve it and shoot it before the creep shot Molly.

"Why would you have all the *best stuff* in the house and not the bunker? Makes no sense now, does it?" The man smirked, pleased with his logic.

"Because the bunker is where you're supposed to assume the best stuff is. See? I figured that's what people like you would think, which is why I didn't bother to hide it. Of course the good stuff isn't just lying around the house, either. See those bushes over there on the left side of the house? There's a door to a storm cellar under there that isn't accessible from inside the house. It's padlocked and the keys are here in my pocket."

"I knew it! I knew something wasn't right. Guys like you think you're pretty smart. Guess you're not so fucking smart now, are you?"

Steven continued to walk toward the house as he'd been talking. The man's attention, if not his feet, followed.

"You got me. What can I say? I thought I was pretty smart but you outsmarted me, for sure."

"Damn straight! Now, what the hell do I need you or this stupid dog for anymore?" The man glanced down at Molly, still held by the collar.

Now, Jeff!

Steven pulled the handgun from his pocket at the same moment Jeffrey sprung through the bunker door, drew a bead and fired. The intruder's revolver and Steven's pistol discharged a half second later. Molly yelped, a heart-rending sound in the stillness. Their assailant collapsed to the ground.

"You okay, Dad?" Jeffrey called while keeping his eyes, and the Springfield, fixed on the man who lay unmoving.

Steven rushed to the bleeding heaps — one flesh and one fur — the Taurus leveled at the man's head. A three-quarter inch hole above the right eyebrow confirmed what he suspected. Steven's shot went wide — he knew it the second the bullet left the chamber. Jeffrey's was the kill shot. What would that knowledge do to the delicate psyche of a fourteen-year-old boy?

He shifted his focus to Molly. The dog lay on her side holding up a front paw. Blood was everywhere.

"You're okay, girl. Where did the bastard hit you?"

She whimpered as Steven examined the yellow fur of her head and body. He breathed a sigh of relief. Jeffrey stood behind his father, his cool blue eyes scanned the perimeter, alert and prepared to protect his family.

"How bad is she, Dad?"

"I think she'll be okay. It looks like the bullet grazed her skull, took off a chunk of her ear, and went through her paw. She's in pain, but she'll survive."

"You think I need to go check on the other guy?"

Steven had all but forgotten the second intruder. He pondered the situation for a moment before nodding.

"Good idea. Be careful. I'm going to take Molly in the house and dress her wounds."

Even if the other man weren't dead, he had to trust that his son could take care of himself. He wouldn't be around forever, and Jeffrey had just proven his competence.

Steven watched his son walk to the back of the property. The fluidity of his movements and the confident manner with which he carried the rifle evoked conflicting emotions. Pride mingled with apprehension, a cocktail that set Steven's stomach churning.

Chapter 8

Twickenham, United Kingdom

Harold was almost ready. He had donned his waterproof Barbour coat, the pockets bulging with supplies. Next, he wriggled into his backpack, heavy with reference books and notes from the anthropologist's research this past year. Worst case, if he got stranded at the headquarters of the British Institute for the Study of Iraq in London, he would still be able to work. As good as his personal library was, the BISI's was superior. He had delayed as long as he could. He needed to examine those seven tablets in person, touch them with his fingertips, and scrutinize magnified details which the pixelated photographs couldn't provide.

It was risky, of course. Just two nights ago he had been startled out of a troubled sleep by a scream which sounded less than a block away. The following day, he readied himself for the journey on foot to London and also managed to sneak in a two-hour nap. He would travel at night, and even though the thought of skulking about the streets of Twickenham, Richmond, and the rest of the boroughs terrified him, he knew it would be the safest way. If everything went smoothly, he should arrive before dawn at the BISI located in the St. James district, about a mile from Westminster Abbey.

Thank goodness he still had his keys. Gaining access to the wealth of knowledge found in the four story facility, which housed the British Academy as well, would be difficult otherwise. The electronic alarm systems would no longer be functioning, so getting into the building shouldn't be a problem. The problem was getting to the building.

Harold took a deep breath, moved the armchair from under the doorknob of the front door, unlocked the two deadbolts, and stepped into the darkened hallway. He flipped on the HexBright, switching the output to the lowest setting. It was bright enough to illuminate the detritus left by the apartment building's former occupants who were now most likely all dead. The last vestiges of humanity took the form of empty Highland water bottles, plastic rubbish bins, and so many newspapers that he was reminded of a parakeet he had once owned whose cage was regularly lined with them, a task performed by a housekeeper who was probably no longer alive.

The flashlight illuminated a Daily Telegraph headline: *"Another 10,000 Die in Dublin"* and one from The Daily Mail: *"Chicxulub Leaves Swath of Carnage in Africa — More Than a Million Dead!"* The narrow beam came to rest on a third one from The Mirror: *"Why Is God Punishing Us?"*

If his theory proved correct, as incredible as it seemed even to him, Harold knew this cataclysmic event had absolutely nothing to do with God.

CHAPTER 9

NEAR PRESCOTT, ARIZONA

The scream's echo resonated for a few seconds in the chilly desert air. Sound carried so well here, it was difficult for Pablo to determine how close the person was. And he was certain it had been a person, not a coyote or a mountain lion, prevalent here, as were wolves and the occasional black bear. Nor was it the cry of the red fox, which could sound eerily similar to a woman wailing. He had seen and heard them all during the months since the aftermath of Chicxulub drove him from his home and into the questionable safety of the desert and surrounding foothills.

He didn't fear those predators. At least not in the way he did their human counterparts. You could predict the actions of such creatures, and he respected them, as they in turn respected Pablo and his shotgun. But his experience with the humans who had survived the plague changed his fundamental belief system of what it meant to be human. In almost every instance of interaction after the plague, people had proven either unpleasant or downright violent.

It was a mystery and an irony that he would survive the global scourge, only to find himself in such poor company. With the exception of Maddie, of course. And he couldn't bear to think about her. Not yet.

Pablo waited another twenty minutes, shotgun ready. No further screams followed and he noticed the normal wildlife sounds were returning now: the scurrying of kangaroo rats and black-tailed jackrabbits, the *hoo-hoo* of a great horned owl answered by another farther away, and the haunting *whip-poor-will* of the nightjar.

He felt unsettled. He replayed the scream in his mind, questioning whether it had been a fox after all, and decided his initial assessment was correct. No, it was a cry only a human could produce. He hadn't seen another living person in two months, so the idea both titillated and terrified him. Titillated because he was lonely, and terrified because of his experiences with the remnants of humanity before fleeing Prescott. He entertained a brief thought of venturing out into the desert, but he knew how dangerous it would be to do so at night. He promised himself instead to head out at first light, which seemed a reasonable compromise.

"There will be no rest for me tonight, Bruno."

He saw the dog had curled up again at his feet, a good sign. He opened his journal and flipped back through hundreds of pages.

Pablo's Journal, Entry #12

While I watched the news this evening to see the latest death tolls, the power quit working soon after the broadcast began. I knew it was inevitable but when it happened, so sudden and conclusive, I felt it was a harbinger of more terrible things to come and perhaps the final blow to our species. The mindless yet magical act of banishing darkness by the mere flip of a switch was something we all took for granted. It is a simple task to light a candle in the dark, but only if one has the foresight to place the candle and match at the ready. Otherwise, we end up stumbling about, blind and unsure of where we're going. I know this will be the fate of most. They will stumble and fall, and others will come up behind them in the night and pick their carcasses.

Perhaps in less advanced countries it won't be as severe because they do not rely on modern conveniences. But our lazy, dependent culture has been an insidious cancer in the corpulent body of our nation. And now, what Chicxulub doesn't take, the malignant tumor of passivity and slothfulness will.

Before the electricity went out, CNN reported astounding numbers of deaths all over the world. How accurate the reporting was at that point, I have no idea. In his press conference, the President tried to exude confidence, but it seemed clear to me he was in shock. How awful to be the most powerful man in the world yet impotent to stop the end of life as we know it. Everything is crumbling, unraveling, dissolving. Humanity is an elaborate and ungainly sandcastle built much too close to the tide.

Pablo looked up from the notebook, not seeing the cold, glittering stars, but rather images conjured by the writings from a year ago. He remembered that day as a portent, and also a turning point. He had known it at the time, but in the days to follow he would experience the aftershocks first hand.

Pablo's Journal, Entry #28

It's been a month since Papa passed. It seems that almost everyone in Prescott is now dead except for a small percentage of people. What that number is, I cannot guess. One percent? Five percent? Who knows? The smell of human decomposition wafts through my bedroom window at night, a discordant mingling with the lovely scents of acacia and desert lavender. My water supply is dwindling more rapidly than I had planned. It's been a dry year, which diminished what would have otherwise been a bountiful harvest from my garden. Still, I probably have more than most, and if someone came to me now and ASKED for food rather than demanding it at knife point, I would happily oblige. That has yet to happen. If not for Bruno and Papa's shotgun, I would be starving just like the rest of those poor, lost souls. What am I to do? Put myself in danger by seeking out those I might help only to become a victim too? I admit my sense of self-preservation has triumphed over any altruistic thoughts I entertained. Maybe in my own way, I am just as lost as those who beg their god for salvation or an end to their misery.

At least I am not hungry. Last night's expedition to the Safeway in the valley on Highway 69 proved successful. I had a feeling it might not have been looted as thoroughly as the ones in town because of its size and location, and I was correct. But it wasn't unguarded. Two men were holed up there, keeping watch in shifts while the other slept. It took me hours of surveillance and eavesdropping to establish their routine, but once I had it figured out, I made my move. I slipped through a jagged opening in one of the glass panes on the left side of the store, slicing my shoulder in the process. My jacket caught the worst of it. It's a small wound but I must not let it fester. To survive Chicxulub only to die of infection from a scratch is not the ending I see for my life. I gained entry, searching in the gloom for the man who would be sleeping. Thank goodness for obesity (words I never imagined saying before), because I found him easily, summoned by cartoonish snores while he lay on a filthy pallet in a back room. Before he could come fully awake, I gagged him with the bandana I brought for the task. Then I bound his hands and feet with nylon rope, using a quick release knot so he could escape after I was gone.

Then I targeted the second man...the problematic part. I am confident of my physical abilities, but because he was armed with a rifle and appeared alert while making his rounds of the store's perimeter, I knew he could be dangerous. My goal was to take only what I needed, leave the rest for them, and not hurt anyone in doing so. They appeared well-fed, and I didn't feel any guilt over this minor plundering of an embarrassment of riches. When he woke up, I am sure he had a considerable headache, but I'm certain the blow from the wooden stock of my shotgun didn't inflict any permanent damage. Well, mostly sure. What does this say about me, the man who was so certain of his honor only a month ago?

It became apparent why they had been so vigilant in their guard duties: squirreled away was enough food to feed dozens of people for months. I located their hoard in a stockroom near the sleeping man. They had removed everything from the shelves that was salvageable and stashed it out of sight. I loaded up the Jeep with cans of salmon and chicken, powdered milk, and enough Bush's *beans to create a mushroom cloud of methane gas. I left them with much more than I took.*

The mission was worth the risk and I arrived home safely, but with the tank depleted. Tomorrow, I will need to locate a new source for gasoline as well as more water.

Always more water.

Pablo remembered that day as clearly as the day the power went out because it had been a turning point as well, but on a personal, existential level. He had taken from others, something he thought he would never do. Yet he knew there had been justification. The men in the Safeway had more than they could eat in a year, and he had been down to a few potatoes and carrots from the garden. He hadn't killed them, nor left them with nothing. It chafed his conscience at the time, but in the following months, he had incorporated a healthy dose of pragmatism into his belief system. Honor and integrity still mattered, as they always had, but as one of the few remaining survivors, he felt it equally important to stay alive.

"It's a bit of a balancing act, isn't it Bruno?"

He scratched the pointed ears again with affection, barely rousing the German shepherd from slumber. Bruno huffed a deep sigh and went back to sleep. Within seconds, his back legs began to twitch. Pablo smiled, trying to imagine the dreams his furry companion might be having. Was he chasing jack rabbits, darting between the sagebrush and cactus? Was he dreaming of the cute little Chihuahua that had lived down the street back home?

Another scream pierced the night. This time, he got a better sense of the direction from which it had emanated. It sounded two hundred yards to the south, this side of the stream.

"Damn it! That was not a fox."

Bruno growled, fully awake now.

The next moment he stepped into the dilapidated cabin, grabbed two bottles of water, a granola bar, and a handful of shotgun shells, stuffing everything into the pockets of his jacket. He hesitated for a second, then reached for the Maglight which held the last of his D cells. Replacements must be obtained in town, and he had been putting the trip off. Starlight sufficed to illuminate his way, but he might have need of the flashlight later.

"Let's do it."

The German shepherd stayed close as they trudged over the rocky terrain, skirting mounds of cacti and trampling scrub brush, on as direct a path toward the source of the scream as Pablo could estimate. An unnatural hush blanketed the night, unnerving him and ratcheting his anxiety to a degree not felt since leaving Prescott. Nature seemed to be pausing, holding its breath for an event it knew was about to unfold.

He stopped, signaling for Bruno to stop as well. No longer violated by the muffled noises of dog and human, the eerie desert silence was complete. He waited.

A stifled whimper floated out of the gloom fifty yards ahead.

Pablo ran now. Something about the voice was familiar. His mind raced as he sprinted through the night, heedless of ankle-twisting rocks and spiny needles that could draw blood.

Could it be? How was it even possible?

"Hold it right there." A man's voice stopped him in his tracks. "Not another step or I'll slit this gal's throat."

Pablo flipped on the Maglite. In the sudden brightness stood a bearded man and a woman who crouched at his feet. The man clutched her long, rust-colored hair in one hand and pressed a hunting knife against her slender neck.

No, no, no. It can't be.

The man jerked the woman by her hair, forcing her to lift her face into the light.

Although it was swollen, dirty, and smeared with blood, he still recognized Maddie's lovely face.

He had seen her die months ago...

Chapter 10

Colleyville, Texas

Dani slipped the Ka-bar out of its sheath at the same moment Sam flicked open his switchblade. In the clear night air the unmistakable metallic sound of a bullet being chambered came from the vicinity of the dark figures walking toward them.

"Never bring a knife to a showdown," Sam whispered.

"Good evening!" The man's voice was deep and rich, but his face, along with the other four, remained shadowed.

"Stop right there," Dani said. "We'd prefer not to Ginsu anybody tonight."

Laughter resonated in the darkness, all honey and baritone. The five figures came to a halt.

"Duly noted. Andrew, please stow your weapon. The rest of you as well. We don't want to offend our new friends."

"But they have knives!" Andrew's stutter was the cracking voice of a post-pubescent boy.

"Clearly they would, but if we mind our manners, we need not worry. Am I correct in my assessment, young lady?"

Even after such a brief exchange, Dani recognized an intellectual kindred spirit. She hoped she wouldn't have to kill the owner of the melodious voice.

"I don't make promises I can't keep."

"I see. Might we have a chat with you and your partner? The five of us and the two of you? No tricks. You have my word as a man of honor."

Dani understood the underlying message. Yes, she and Sam were outnumbered and outgunned. Should they take their chances and see what these people wanted, or assume the worst and attack now?

She knew it was illogical, but something told her the man would keep his word. She and Sam were a formidable team, but you can't outrun a bullet. She made the decision.

"Fine. You have five minutes. Come closer where I can see you, but not so close that I can smell what you ate for dinner."

The rich laughter continued as the shadowy group stopped ten feet from the patio table. Sam flipped on a lantern, flooding the strangers in unnatural light and illuminating their faces.

Four of them were in their teens, she guessed, but tall and muscular for their ages as their black, sleeveless shirts revealed. The muscles, no doubt, were the result of being conditioned to survive days such as these. Two girls and two boys of various ethnicities, all wearing the grim expressions of adulthood thrust upon them too soon. Dani's eyes were drawn to the man with the resonant voice. His smile was warm and seemingly genuine in a face of polished ebony. The eyes exuded a keen intelligence as she expected they would, and his close-cropped hair was dusted with white. Forties perhaps? Certainly no more than fifty. His arms were more heavily muscled than the youths', revealing a level of physical fitness to match that of his intellect.

"Close enough," she said, not bothering to sheath her knife. "Now, what brings you to our humble abode? Don't lie because Sam here can sniff out bullshit from a mile away. It's a knack he has. Comes in pretty handy too."

"How delightful. And such a useful talent. Perhaps some introductions first though? I find it preferable to converse when I know with whom I'm speaking. I'll go first. My name is Isaiah. Last names no longer seem relevant, so just Isaiah. As you heard, this young man to my right is Andrew." An elegant gesture indicated the boy with the creaky voice. "To my left here are Malik, Amy, and Daniel. All well-behaved young people, I assure you. And who might I have the pleasure of addressing?"

Dani felt the heat of Isaiah's focus, as defined and intense as a laser sighted on her forehead. She gazed into the obsidian eyes, two glowing hellish pools. She knew with instant clarity that the man in front of her, despite his impeccable manners and flowery words, was the most lethal human being she had ever encountered. If she didn't handle the situation flawlessly, she and Sam were dead.

"I'm Dani. What can we do for you, Isaiah? Are you here to see a man about a horse? If so, you've come to the wrong place. We're on hoof these days just like everybody else, but not the four legged kind."

She smiled, mustering all the charm a nerdy girl could manage. She sensed Sam next to her on heightened alert.

"Dani, I have a proposition for you, one that will be beneficial to all involved parties. Shall I proceed?"

"I have the feeling that if I said no, you would proceed anyway."

"Perhaps, but let's assume for both our sakes that you said yes." He flashed another smile which might have lost a measure of its previous warmth.

Dani decided to dial down the smart ass. She offered a polite, differential nod. "Please continue."

Her sudden courtesy seemed to mollify him, which told her much about the personality behind the dazzling smile and honeyed voice.

"Very well." He swiveled a wrought-iron chair away from the table and sat down, a relaxed general surrounded by trusted soldiers.

"It occurred to me some time ago that civilization will need to be rebuilt from the ground up. The old ways of doing business are over. Democracies never last. History has shown us this over and over. Now give me an empire and I'll show you a system of government with some longevity! The Byzantine Empire, the Empire of Japan, the Ottoman Empire, and of course, the Romans. The Romans were brilliant people. Clever, industrious, and wonderfully effective in maintaining order. Wouldn't you agree?"

"The Carthaginians, Parthians, and Gauls might take issue with you on that." She regretted the words the second they flew from her mouth.

He frowned, studying her with more intensity than before. The next moment the smile was back, like the sun erupting through a cloud.

"What would you expect from a bunch of conquered Frenchmen?" The laughter was genuine. He was pleased with his cleverness.

Lovely. A classic narcissistic sociopath with delusions of grandeur. We are surely in some deep shit.

She risked a covert glance at Sam, who studied Isaiah like a ferret contemplating a cobra.

"Point taken." Her smile was friendly and benign.

"Excellent! Let me continue. As I said, civilization is over, and that tiny fraction of mankind that still remains is a seething, chaotic miasma of violence and villainy, frenzy and fury, turbulence and tumult."

Knavery and knivery!

She almost said the words out loud, but caught herself in time. This guy was the worst kind of insufferable douche bag — the kind who thinks he's smarter than everyone else in the room.

"You see my point, yes? We need organization. We need rules. We need consequences. Anarchy has prevailed for months now and it's time to rein it all in. Someone needs to take charge and corral all that energy into productive, constructive behavior."

"Someone like yourself?" She struck the tone of a polite student with a raised hand and the correct answer on her lips.

"I can think of no one better." Isaiah's smile was exuberant, charismatic, and utterly insane.

Chapter 11

San Francisco

Logan had been heading south for two days now with only eight miles to show for his efforts. Traveling at night was safer but it also took him longer to navigate the roads and highways in the dark, which were clogged with the abandoned cars of people trying to run away from the collapse of their world. Where were they all going in such a hurry? Maybe they thought they could outrun the sickness or that it hadn't spread to the country.

Logan had known better. He'd watched the CBS Evening News every night for as long as he could remember, and Scott Pelley told him the disease was in all four corners of the world. Even little black children in African villages were dying, so why would the residents of San Francisco think they'd be better off in Mexico or Arizona? He had yet to figure this out, and the cars blocking the roads were a big nuisance.

He stopped at daybreak in Little Hollywood Park about a half mile from the 101. He had good memories of the times his mother brought him here when he was little. They had lived on the next block over for a while, before the neighbors began complaining about him, forcing them to move somewhere else. There was more rust than paint on the merry-go-round, and the slide would take a chunk out of the backside of any child reckless enough to brave its serpentine length of uneven steel plates. But Logan felt good here, so he planned to spend the daylight hours dozing and resting under the bleachers next to the basketball court.

He had scavenged a package of Twinkies, some pretzels, and a bottle of Sprite from a looted convenience store. Everything was picked over now, and he thought he might soon have to start eating the things that he killed. The idea wasn't appealing. He didn't kill to survive, after all. He killed because it felt good and also because the Bad Thoughts told him it was part of the Grand Design. He wasn't sure what that meant but the 'whys' of things didn't bother him too much. He loved this new freedom where he could just be himself and do all the things his mother had always called 'unacceptable behavior.'

He removed the cellophane and took a huge bite, sitting cross-legged on the asphalt as the early morning sun filtered through the aluminum benches in glowing strips, warming his skin and illuminating the filthiness of his jeans. He hadn't thought about new clothes until now, as he gazed at the stains and accumulated grime from many days of wear. He sniffed under his arms and realized he smelled terrible. His mother would never have allowed him to go so long without a bath, but he didn't mind the smell. The Levi's may need to be replaced though. They were getting stiff and uncomfortable from all the dirt and dried blood. Maybe he would go shopping tonight.

He marveled at the spongy lightness of the cake and then the burst of creamy sweetness. His mother had never let him have Twinkies because she said that sugar always got him 'wound up.' He was a little angry at her now for denying him this delicious pleasure for so long. He would put Twinkies on his list along with the new pants. And more bullets. Definitely more bullets. He was down to three boxes.

Movement on the playground caught his attention. A fluffy cat emerged from some shrubs, its grayish fur matted and as dirty as his jeans. Logan smiled as he put the remainder of the Twinkie back in its wrapper and reached for his 9mm, which was lined up on the blacktop next to his other firearms. It had been a tough decision selecting which of his weapons to bring on the journey. If he had brought them all, he wouldn't be able to carry his backpack and the other supplies he needed. But because the Ruger had proven to be reliable, had yet to jam, and felt good in his hand, it made the cut. He remembered the clerk trying to push him into buying a Glock, but the other gun sang to him, even before he'd fired it at the range that first time. The Sig Sauer tactical rifle and the Colt revolver could wait for now — something in his head told him the animal preferred the Ruger. If he could honor the desires of his victims, which he received telepathically, he would do so. It just seemed right.

He released the safety and targeted the feline fifty yards away. He exhaled half the air in his lungs and clutched the pistol in a classic two-fisted grip. Ever so slowly he had begun to squeeze the trigger, when a small girl sprang from the bushes. He lowered the gun and watched her. He thought she looked about the same age as one from his third grade class.

She was after the cat.

"Linus, come back here!" Her voice was musical, like the delicate notes of the wind chimes his mother always hung on the back porch of whatever house they moved to.

"Linus, now! I mean it!"

Her dress was yellow, her sneakers were bright blue, and her hair was carrot orange; she belonged in a cartoon, so vibrant were her colors. He was transfixed. His mouth went slack with concentration as he watched her graceful, pixie-like movements. The cat ignored her and continued ambling toward the other side of the playground. The girl's eyes darted about, as if she sensed someone watching her, but he knew she wouldn't spot him in the shadows of the bleachers. Her gaze slid over him without registering his presence. It was always strange when this happened. He had begun to suspect he might have acquired invisibility during these last few months.

"Linus, it's not safe!" She was getting exasperated now, reluctant to go much farther from the concealing shrubs.

The cat stopped and swiveled its whiskered face directly toward Logan. The scruffy ears pressed against its head and a low, threatening sound came from its throat.

He had already figured out that his invisibility didn't work on cats, so he wasn't surprised by the sudden hissing when it came. Cats really liked to hiss.

The Ruger pivoted from the furry head to the head with the carrot-colored hair. He pulled the trigger and watched in fascination as a hole appeared above the right eye and below the orange fringe. The pixie girl folded to the ground as her legs turned to rubber, just like the Coyote did when the Road Runner knocked him over the head with a giant Acme hammer. Two seconds later, the next bullet blew off the top of the cat's head.

Logan beamed. Those guys at the shooting range were right. He was very good at this.

He jogged over to the bodies and gaped at the cartoon girl's wide open eyes, which perfectly matched the blue of her sneakers. He wondered if she planned that or if it was just one of those 'happy accidents' his mom had always talked about. He glanced over at the dead cat, forgetting the blue eyes and matching shoes.

He had a new project this morning: he was going to skin that cat and see if there really was more than one way to get it done.

Chapter 12

Liberty, Kansas

Steven and Jeffrey had dug a rectangular hole in the ground on the other side of their back fence line. The sun hung close to the flat Midwest horizon, creating a spectacular light show as its rays navigated the cumulus clouds. Sunsets didn't get much better than this, Steven thought, marveling at the infinite shades of pink, lavender, and orange water-coloring the western sky.

He watched his son, who was sweating almost as much as he was from the exertion of carrying the dead men and digging their shallow grave. They laid the bodies face down in the three-foot deep hole and began shoveling the soil on top of them.

"You did well. I'm sorry you had to take a life, but I'm proud that you did it. It was him or us. You know that, right?"

"Of course." Jeffrey seemed surprised that such an obvious fact would require voicing.

"How do you feel about it?"

"I feel fine, Dad. Look, let's not make a big deal out of this. They were bad guys. They wanted to take our stuff and kill us in the process. End of story."

Steven paused with his foot propped on the shovel blade, studying his son for any signs of emotional trauma. He saw nothing other than acceptance.

He sighed. "Okay, I won't harp on it, but it was a big deal even though it was justified. I don't ever want you to forget that. Taking a human life is about as big a deal as it gets. You did the right thing...*we* did the right thing, but it should never be taken lightly just because it was necessary for our survival. Do you understand what I'm saying?"

"Yeah, I do. I don't take it lightly. Those guys are dead and we made them that way. We're responsible for that. Where are they now? Did their souls fly out of their bodies and go down to hell or up to heaven? Do places like that even exist? When we killed them, was that it for them? Lights out forever? Or will they be born again in another place and time? We don't know and we can't know until it happens to us. And we made those guys find that out today, whatever *that* is. All we can do in the meantime is just keep on living in the present. Do the best we can do and treat people as kindly as they deserve to be treated.

"That's the way I see it." He began tossing shovelfuls of dirt into the grave, finished with the subject.

Steven hid his smile. He had made a few mistakes in his lifetime, but he'd also done a lot of things right. He had been a good husband to Laura, a good son to his parents, even a good employee at Kansas Electric. He could be proud of most of his life's work, but raising Jeffrey to be the young man standing before him today was by far his finest accomplishment.

***

Freshly bathed an hour later, Steven and Jeffrey sat at their kitchen table. The candlelight created a warm coziness and Steven noticed the way it illuminated the pleasing contours of Natalie Evans' lovely face. Jeffrey's puppy-dog eyes indicated similar thoughts about Brittany, who was a carbon copy of her mom. A steaming bowl of new potatoes, green beans, and smoked pork sat in the middle of the farmhouse style table. Steven had covered it with Laura's best lace tablecloth, a wedding gift from her mother. It was used for special occasions and he knew that Laura would approve of its use now; she'd always been pragmatic. The thought of his wife evoked a momentary stab of pain, but he banished it. As Jeffrey said, we have to live in the present.

"Steven, I'm so impressed. You're saying all this wonderful food was home canned? Even the ham? I didn't know canning meat at home was even safe. I think I read something about botulism being an issue." Natalie's voice had a delightful raspy quality that suited her smoky gray eyes and long, dark hair.

"That's a common misconception which stems from the practice of using the water bath method for preserving all types of food. Water bath canning only raises the internal temperature of the food to 212 degrees — the temperature of boiling water — which is not hot enough to kill clostridium botulinum spores. It's fine to can foods this way if they are high in acid, like fruit, because the acidity is naturally anti-bacterial. Low acid foods, such as meat and most vegetables, including green beans and potatoes," he indicated the ceramic bowl in the center of the table, "Need some help. Botulism spores are in the dirt and in our food, but they're harmless when dormant. The problem occurs in the anaerobic environment of a vacuum-sealed can. That means airless. Under these conditions, the spores grow, and in the process they produce a deadly toxin. By heating the food to a temperature of 240 degrees when it's put in the jar, the spores are destroyed and can never germinate. That temperature can only be achieved by using super-heated steam. Boiling water doesn't cut it. Thus, the pressure canning."

Steven felt a pang of embarrassment as he realized his enthusiasm about long-term food storage might not be shared by Natalie.

"I'm sorry for the over explanation. You must think I'm a real dork."

"Not at all. I find it all quite interesting. You must have gotten a lot of experience with this canning business when people started panicking over empty grocery store shelves."

"Actually, my interest in disaster preparedness began before the pandemic, but I was mostly just a dabbler back then. I did tons of research while the internet was still working."

She seemed interested in the subject — one of Steven's favorites — but he knew he shouldn't get carried away. Natalie and her daughter didn't pose a threat, but it wasn't wise to reveal all the measures he and Jeffrey had taken to assure their safety and survival. Operational Security rules still applied and were more critical now than ever. The location of the root cellar, camouflaged from prying eyes, was the number one reason for OPSEC. People would kill them for a fraction of what was contained there, as illustrated earlier today.

The thousand-gallon underground propane tank that fueled the gas stove was perhaps their second most important secret, since consistent heat for his pressure canner was crucial. For items requiring less critical temperature control, the fireplace with its adjustable cooking grate worked fine, and as far as anyone knew, was their only heat source. Adding to those treasures was a lengthy list of other assets Steven had procured before the end came, thanks to the heads-up phone call from his sister. He had bought medicines, firing and non-firing weapons, ammunition, books, a huge variety of vegetable, grain, and fruit seeds, an Aquasana Whole House water purification system in case the well went dry.

And nearly a ton of shelf-stable food.

On top of all the canned goods, he had amassed hundreds of pounds of rice, legumes, quinoa, pasta, spices, salt, sugar, oats, and winter wheat — all placed in Mylar metal bags with oxygen absorbing packets, heat sealed, and stored under perfect conditions in the cool, sunless, dry cellar. It could last for decades.

"I do know what anaerobic means, by the way," Natalie said with a wink. "I have my masters in English Lit, a subject which is not appreciated nor embraced by my offspring." She gestured to her daughter who was busy exchanging smitten glances with Jeffrey across the dinner table.

"I'm sure she has other interests, right Brittany? What did you like to do in your old life?"

Natalie laughed. "Brittany's previous life included lots of shopping at the mall, drooling over celebrities, and texting all her girlfriends about said mall and said celebrities."

Steven raised an eyebrow, curious now about the dynamic between mother and daughter.

Brittany gave her mother an exaggerated eye roll and smiled at Jeffrey's father.

"I love taking walks at sunset. Now that there's no television and my iPhone doesn't work, it's my favorite thing to do. Sometimes my mom won't let me go because she worries about 'marauding gangs of rapists,' but I'm fourteen now, and I know how to be careful."

Brittany shifted her dazzling smile from Steven to Jeffrey, who almost spilled his water glass. She was a pretty girl, and Steven marveled again at the stroke of luck that females such as these were among the survivors.

"Oh and I play the piano when I'm totally bored. Mom wishes I'd play more often but I have to be in the right mood, you know?"

Her mother assumed a world-weary expression and gave a dramatic sigh.

"Yes, the girl is practically a musical prodigy but unfortunately for me, while she has talent to spare, her ambition and desire are sadly lacking. Ironic, huh, Steven? I guess it doesn't matter now, anyway. Flawlessly playing Rachmaninoff's Concerto Number 3 in D minor is not a talent that will serve either of us well in this new world."

Steven noticed both females had helped themselves to seconds of the green beans. Their manners were impeccable, but they'd been discreetly shoveling in the meal as fast as possible. He wondered about their provisions. He couldn't imagine anyone having the foresight to fill an entire cellar with shelf stable food as he had done. If they had started a vegetable garden after Chicxulub, it may not be producing food yet.

Steven had just harvested his first crop of fall produce: cauliflower, kale, carrots, and cabbage. The pumpkins and butternut squash would be ready soon, perhaps before the end of the month. He hadn't anticipated feeding anyone other than his family, but could he let other folks starve when they had so much? People like Natalie and Brittany? Doubling the number of mouths to feed would put a huge dent in his plans for canning much of his harvest and refilling those jars that he and Jeff had emptied during the past year. It was October in Kansas, which meant the first snow could arrive within weeks. They would need plenty of food to get through the winter, when temperatures dipped below zero and blizzards could be expected at least once or twice before April. He had been focused on the future needs of just the two of them, planning expansions to their garden, perhaps adding livestock in the spring. Other than Julia, he had never considered feeding other people. Was that about to change? Would providing for these two be taking food out of the mouth of his son? His logical brain said yes, but his conscience told it to shut the hell up. He would never knowingly let decent people go hungry.

A wave of relief washed over him, having reached a decision on an ethical issue which may not even come to pass. But as he watched Brittany reach for another helping of potatoes, he realized it very well might.

"That reminds me, I must thank you again for the use of your well. I don't know what we would have done without fresh water all these months. Our bottled water ran out a long time ago, even though I thought I did a good job of stockpiling back then."

It was Steven's turn to narrowly avoid a water glass incident when Brittany's mother turned the full force of her smile on him. She was a beautiful woman, no doubt about it. Steven could tell she had taken extra care with her appearance. Her cotton dress was clean and she'd even applied some lipstick. Who wore makeup these days? Did it mean something or was she just happy to have company other than her daughter?

"It's my pleasure. I only wish my system could do more than run the well pump and the refrigerator, but I bet we're the only house in Kansas with ice tonight."

"I think a toast is in order," she said, raising her glass of pinot noir, her contribution to the dinner. "May your plate be filled, your heart light, your laughter genuine, and your ice cubes frozen!"

The crystal glasses made a delicate clink when they came together. Steven took a healthy swallow and noticed her eyes stayed on him seconds longer than a polite toast required. Warmth flooded his cheeks, and judging by her feline smile, Natalie had seen his blush.

Chapter 13

Near Prescott, Arizona

"Maddie, is that really you?"

Pablo struggled to accept the reality before him, despite his brain's assertion that it couldn't be true. Maddie had died seven months ago in the parking lot of a Walgreens on Highway 6. Now, she was on her knees twenty feet in front of him, the flashlight's beam illuminating her thin face and the filthy hand clutching her hair. The man's other hand held a hunting knife at her throat; the point had pierced the delicate skin enough to draw blood.

Pablo's gaze fixed on the blood, mesmerized by what it conveyed. Maddie was alive. She was here, right before him. How was that possible? His eyes traveled up to the brute that held her captive. How she had risen from the dead was a matter that would have to wait. He dropped the shotgun and raised both arms.

"Okay, okay. Let's just stay calm."

"Damn straight, we're gonna stay calm. Right, girlie?" He emphasized the words with a rough pull of Maddie's tangled hair.

She groaned.

The man could have been an outlaw extra in a cheesy western. Every inch of him was covered in grime and what teeth remained in the grotesque smile were brown and jagged. A mere twelve months of hardship wouldn't have created this nightmare. He was the most revolting person Pablo had ever seen.

And he had captured and enslaved the woman he loved.

Pablo felt the familiar outrage wash over him. Before fleeing Prescott, miscreants, organized into gangs, paraded their captives and their weapons almost every evening in the square as a way of advertising their prowess to any would-be usurpers. They owned the town — that was their message. Pablo was only one man and he had recognized the futility of fighting their numbers and their depravity. Something in him, a fragment of his soul perhaps, had been lost when he turned his back on their helpless victims and headed for the relative safety of the desert.

Now, finally, here was a fair fight and perhaps a chance to redeem himself in a small way. Even if the man's victim had been a stranger, he knew he would still feel the same way.

"Please, let her go. I have food. I'll give it to you, if you'll just let her go."

"I want a lot more than that. I want everything you got...that little cabin, all your supplies, and that Jeep you got parked next to the road. It's all mine."

"Whatever you want. Just let her go. Please." He continued to take small, slow steps.

"Well, ya see, that ain't part of my plan, amigo. I get to keep her too. She's a sweet little piece, I'll tell ya that. Oh man, I ain't never had sweeter."

Maddie's dilated eyes locked onto Pablo's and he could see the truth of the words on her face.

Oh dear god. That thing has violated her.

A red haze clouded his vision. Still, he managed to keep his movements measured, even when rage demanded a rash and violent response.

"That scream of hers was part of the plan. I lured you out here so I could get you away from whatever stash of weapons you got in that shack. Improvin' my odds, get it? You fell for it too, ya jackass."

"So what now? Clearly, you don't intend to kill her. What's to keep me from rushing you?"

Keeping the knife pressed against Maddie's neck, the man let go of her hair and withdrew an ancient revolver from the pocket of his ragged jacket.

"I reckon this will."

A grimy thumb pulled back the revolver's hammer at the same moment Pablo whistled: two sharp notes echoed in the desert air.

There was a flash of fur from the right. The next moment gleaming fangs ripped into the man's forearm and powerful jaws locked onto the arm which held the gun. Pablo sprang toward them.

The man had released Maddie in his need to fend off the dog, but he managed to hold on to both the knife and the pistol in the process. The German shepherd jerked and tugged, neutralizing any threat of a well-aimed shot.

The man fired anyway. The bullet slammed into a cactus ten feet away. He raised the hunting knife, the blade began a downward arc toward Bruno's vulnerable chest.

Suddenly the rheumy eyes opened wide. The knife fell, dropping harmlessly to the ground. The man crumpled to his knees. Canine fangs still gripped his arm, but went unnoticed now.

Behind him stood Maddie, holding a six-inch glass shard in a bleeding hand. Her second thrust went into the base of his neck. The man toppled the rest of the way to the ground.

Pablo came to a halt five feet away, stunned. The gentlest, kindest human being he had ever known, rolled her captor onto his back and was plunging the shard into the still-moving chest. After a half dozen stabs, the glass blade shifted to the genitals.

Finally she stopped. A sob escaped her and she collapsed next to the body of a dead man.

Pablo watched Maddie sleep. After the longest night of his life, the sun had risen, blanketing the desert and her delicate features in golden warmth. When they arrived at the cabin, she had allowed him to wash and bandage the deep gash in her hand, but nothing else. She flinched when he wrapped his mother's colorful sarape around her shoulders, which told him he must respect her need for physical space. God only knew what she had been through these past months, and he might not know for a while. She hadn't uttered a single word so far.

He tried to get her to lie down on his pallet, but she shook her head. Instead, she sat on the ground by the fire and stared into the flames. Within minutes, her eyelids began to droop and she slid down onto her side, the tangled mess of hair coming to rest in the crook of a bony elbow.

Bruno left his spot at Pablo's feet and trotted over to Maddie's sleeping form. He sniffed her hair and her bandaged hand then curled up next to her. He didn't lower his head to doze; the alert brown eyes gazed into the desert while the canine brain analyzed all the information transmitted to it by the sensitive black nose.

Maddie was back with her two protectors again. Judging by her condition — half-starved, bruised and battered — she needed all the protection she could get. He couldn't imagine what she had been through. Even more curious was how she could be alive at all. He reached for his notebook and flipped back through many ink-filled pages.

Pablo's Journal, Entry #76

Tomorrow, we have decided to make a run south down Highway 89 toward the national forest. We've tried going north, but there's little in that direction other than death and empty food shelves. Even though it's winter, a warm front has swept through, ushering in temperatures in the seventies. Still, we must keep the windows of the Jeep rolled up as we drive through areas where people once lived. Otherwise, the smell of human decay wafts in like an invisible, viscous fog of finality. It is unnatural and unprecedented, this abrupt demise of humankind. I often contemplate explanations for this atrocity, but I suspect I shall never have the answer. The plague raged through my city, my country, my planet, with the wrath of an Old Testament god. For some reason I was spared, but why? Maybe it is not for me to know, and perhaps that is the price I must pay for my life: to never know the answers.

At least there is Maddie. It is wonderful to have the companionship of another person. How fortuitous that she is as sweet and kind as she is lovely. I wonder if our friendship will blossom into something more. I admit to having entertained more than a few romantic thoughts, but I won't press the issue. If she finds me as pleasing as I find her, then it will happen when she's ready. In the meantime, I will enjoy her company and the sudden flash of her playful smile which warms my heart more fully than a perfect summer day.

I love to watch her work out the logistics of our continued survival and comfort. She scans our provisions and in seconds she knows how many days it will last, down to the final calorie of food and ounce of water. It seems she has a calculator in that enchanting head. I think we are well-suited for each other in times such as these. Our strengths and weaknesses are balanced and in accord. When Bruno found her hiding in the closet of her parents' house three weeks ago, it was an auspicious day for both of us. She was relieved and thankful that I was not a member of the gangs that have been vexing the city of late. And I was delighted to assume the role of protector. My best friend took to her immediately, which is not his normal nature. In a short time, we have become quite the happy little family unit.

Maddie says we need more protein despite the abundance of beans in our pantry, the side effects of which we have both grown weary. So tomorrow we will forage to the south in search of a less gaseous protein source, and along the way, if we encounter a jewelry store, I will make a quick trip inside...alone.

Pablo's Journal, Entry #77

It has been a week since the ill-fated journey south, and I can only now bring myself to write about it. I don't know how this human body can contain so much pain. Perhaps if I document the events I will garner some small relief.

Perhaps.

Maddie and I had decided to travel during the day because the roads are even more treacherous to navigate at night, and the few people we'd been encountering when away from the city always avoided us, which was fine with me. About thirty minutes outside of Prescott, we reached the outskirts of the National Forest. I remembered there was a Walgreens store in the area, and we pulled into the parking lot. Of course I had my shotgun, and Maddie had slipped a knife into the satchel she always carried on our outings.

The lot was empty when we arrived. Maddie stayed in the Jeep while I conducted a quick reconnoiter. The glass door panels were broken, so access wouldn't be a problem. I gestured for her and Bruno to join me. I turned on my flashlight and the three of us stepped into the store. Staying together and alert, we determined the place had been ransacked, but because of my experiences in the past, we did a final check of the back stock room. An industrial metal dustpan and a few packages of Benadryl were scattered about the floor, nothing else. While Maddie collected the items and stuffed them in her bag, Bruno's ears pricked up and he emitted a low growl.

The next moment, our human ears were able to detect the sound of a car engine coming from the front. Maddie suggested we hide somewhere in the store, but with Bruno, that didn't seem like a good solution. Besides, I had the shotgun. I elected to investigate.

We headed to the front of the store. A Toyota Tundra was now parked near the shattered doors, and three men emerged as we watched from the shadows. All carried guns. I ushered Maddie and Bruno back to the stock room as one of the men began yelling.

"You folks better come on out of there! Keep your hands up and nobody will get hurt!"

We ignored the directive and kept running for the back, where I knew an exit would be found. I struck the release bar of the door and poked my head out. All clear. I motioned for her to follow; Bruno was right on her heels. I knew that if we timed it right, we could make a run for the Jeep when the men went inside looking for us. We edged up to the corner and I sneaked a glance around the brick wall. They were gone. I could hear them bellowing again from inside now.

We ran. We had almost made it to the Jeep when the men emerged from the store front. At that moment, Bruno changed course and headed toward them, barking more ferociously than I have ever heard before.

I yelled for him to come as I flung myself behind the steering wheel. Maddie leaped into the passenger seat, but after seeing Bruno running toward our assailants, she went after him.

Bruno stopped ten yards from the men and continued to bark furiously. One of them lifted his rifle and aimed it at him. As the shot was fired, Maddie darted in front. The bullet struck her in the shoulder, making her right side snap backward. Even though she wasn't facing me, I could tell the second round hit her in the chest. A third appeared to strike her abdomen as she fell.

I stood by the Jeep unable to move. Bruno stopped barking and ran back to me. I have a vague memory of screaming something, but the voice didn't sound like my own. All three men raised their guns and pointed them at me.

I can't recall what happened next, and I now realize I was in shock. I must have climbed into the driver's seat and somehow escaped with only a few bullet holes in the plastic windshield.

Bruno and I arrived home an hour later, unscathed but in utter despair.

A week has passed, but the loss is as fresh as it was the day I saw Maddie perish. It is agony so intense as to make eating impossible. I'm barely able to get Bruno fed and watered every day. The exertion is almost more than I can bear. I wonder if it is possible to die from a broken heart.

Poem — Fireworks

I said it couldn't be, wasn't written in the stars
Or chiseled in some divine daybook
She replied, in that sleepy smiling way that slays, slices right to my soul:
Dear boy, of course it wasn't written or chiseled
We are too prodigious for plans, our love too colossal
For orchestration from the meager heavens
It cannot be predetermined, corralled, nor sustained
An errant Roman candle on the fourth of July
She proved me right and was gone in a flash of barium and copper
Leaving the scent of black powder in her wake

Pablo closed the notebook, remembering the despair of that day as if it were yesterday. A fresh wave of shame washed over him as it had done for weeks after what he believed to be Maddie's death. Eventually he had managed to stuff it down into the depths of his subconscious mind. Regret was pointless, he'd told himself. But at random moments during these past months, it would surface: gut-wrenching remorse for his cowardly behavior. At the time there had been no doubt that her injuries were fatal, but he should have at least avenged her death, even if it had cost him his life.

As he studied her face, which seemed troubled even in sleep, he was overcome with anguish. What had he subjected her to by driving away that day? She had somehow survived the gunshot wounds, only to be victimized further. He cradled his head in his arms and let the sorrow and guilt build to a crescendo. How could he live with himself now, knowing what his cowardice had done to Maddie?

He felt a gentle pressure on his shoulder and raised his face to hers. She sat down beside him, wrapping an arm around his shoulders. Silent, glistening rivulets slid down her cheeks as she brushed away his tears.

"I'm so sorry, Maddie. I thought you were dead." He hated the tremulous way his voice sounded. It was the voice of a weak man, not a man who deserved to be her protector.

For the first time she spoke.

"I know, Pablo. Of course, I know that." She took a deep breath. "This is the only time we'll speak of it. Agreed?"

He nodded.

"It was the metal dustpan that protected me from serious injury. It was in my knapsack and two of the bullets hit it before they entered me. It must have deflected the energy just enough to keep them from going in very far. The shoulder wound was actually worse and took longer to heal."

"What about those men?"

Maddie laughed, a bright tinkling sound tinged with sorrow.

"As it turned out, those men saved me. The one who shot me said he'd been aiming at Bruno and hadn't meant to hurt me. They took me to their compound and some of the women there nursed me back to health. Later, our small group was ambushed and I was the only survivor. As it turns out, I'm an excellent hider. The parts that came after that, I don't want to talk about. The man who held me captive for a period of time was the one you met last night. We fled to the desert, as you must have done, to escape the barbarians in town. We watched you outside of your cabin for a day while he devised a strategy. The rest you know.

"Now do we have a deal? The past will forever remain in the past. No more guilt, no more regret, no more sadness. We are alive and safe for the moment, and I am happier than I have been in a very long time."

She sighed. It was the type of sigh that unburdens the soul. Shackled to that breath were whatever nightmares Maddie had endured these past months, plucked from their dark hiding place, and exhaled into the crisp air.

Pablo replied, "We have a deal. I will never leave you. Never."

"Good. Now what's for breakfast?"

The playful grin was back and Pablo didn't think the sun could ever make him feel warmer than that smile.

Chapter 14

Colleyville, Texas

"Isaiah, you've made a compelling argument. I'll cut to the chase and assume you're recruiting Sam and me for your cause. I must say that I'm intrigued. I can't deny there's safety in numbers, and even though we've been doing pretty well on our own, the idea of belonging to a well-ordered community is appealing."

Dani struggled to maintain a respectful tone, and keeping the sarcasm from her voice required intense concentration. They had one chance to get out of this alive, and it relied on this crazy bastard buying her load of crap.

"Most excellent!" The full force of Isaiah's smile was undeniably compelling. Dani suspected people like Saddam Hussein, Attila the Hun, and Joseph Stalin had similar smiles.

"So we are in agreement?" he continued. "You two will join our illustrious ranks, and together we will build a society of productive, law-abiding citizens, yes?"

She paused before she answered, appearing to think over the proposal. Finally she said, "We're in!" Her exuberance would only have appeared fake to anyone who knew her. She extended her hand, ready to seal the deal.

Isaiah's laughter washed over her like a warm summer rain. "I'm afraid we'll need something more permanent than a handshake. Not that I'm questioning your sense of honor, but in times such as these, an old school handshake is woefully inadequate to express true commitment. Andrew, please illuminate."

The young man stepped closer to the patio table, displaying his left arm, palm up. In the glow of the LED lantern, she could see a raised red scar which resembled the wheel of a boat — a circle with eight spokes fanning out from the center. It was large and well-healed, probably carved into the flesh at least six months ago. She got a sickening feeling in her stomach.

"A handshake or a signed legal contract would have sufficed in the old world, but no longer. I admit the process is a bit barbaric, but I think the result is the perfect representation of our new society. It's a Dharmacakra, the Buddhist symbol for order. The fact that it's incised onto the body without benefit of numbing agents or pain killers makes it the ideal method for proving one's sincerity."

The man was insane but certainly no idiot. Of course he wouldn't have accepted a mere verbal agreement. They would have to allow the tattoo torture or take on all five at once.

Before she could make the decision, Sam pushed up his shirt sleeve and extended his arm to Isaiah.

"Let's get this over with. The speedier the better."

Dani cringed. This time Sam's cliché mangling wasn't amusing. Not even a little.

***

"*Shit!*" Dani hissed as Sam held her arm over the kitchen sink. The thin stream of hydrogen peroxide converted to bubbling foam as it cleansed her wound. He dabbed at it with a paper towel, applied a heavy coating of Neosporin, then covered it with a large waterproof Band-aid from their medicine kit, as she had done for him minutes earlier.

"What the hell were you thinking? We'll have these sonofabitches for the rest of our lives. Now I know how all those farm animals feel when they get branded."

"There was no way we could have beat them.... not all at the same time. They had guns and knives. They were young, but I could tell they had some skills by the way they moved. And that crazy guy scares the heck out of me. I think he has more teeth than humans are supposed to."

Dani barked a laugh through the pain.

"You may be right about that. He sure is one scary dude."

"Yep, he sure is."

She had never seen Sam fearful until now. He must have picked up on Isaiah's sociopathic vibe.

"So what do we do now? I don't think we can stay here much longer." The wistfulness in his voice was unmistakable. They had created a surprisingly comfortable life together in just a few short months, and now they would have to leave it.

"You're right. We can't stay even one more night. These bloody boat wheels bought us a few hours — enough time to get the hell out of Dodge. They saved our asses, thanks to you. That was quick thinking."

"Where will we go?"

"I've been pondering that. Logic would dictate we go south to warmer climates, but something tells me the place to be when all the groceries run out is in one of those bread basket states."

Sam's quizzical expression prompted another pained laugh.

"The bread basket states are in the Midwest. They're where most of the country's food is grown. Nebraska, Iowa, Illinois, Colorado, Kansas, and Oklahoma. Also Minnesota and North and South Dakota, but it's way too effing cold there. What do you say? What state strikes your fancy?"

"I remember watching The Wizard of Oz with my mom and brothers when we were little. I think Kansas is where I'd like to go. There might be a yellow brick road we can follow once we cross the border." He grinned at his own joke.

Dani smiled fondly at her friend, wondering if he held out a smidgen of hope for just such a road. "You got it. Kansas it is. Let's get geared up. I want to leave Colleyville in a dust cloud within two hours."

"Okay. Maybe we can find some mountain bikes along the way."

He trotted out of the kitchen. She could hear him rattling around in the living room where they kept most of their supplies.

Bikes were a brilliant idea.

She liked Kansas as their destination for one specific reason, plus a lot of other reasons she couldn't articulate. Something about relocating there felt right. When there was time, she'd contemplate why that was. But for now, they needed to put as much real estate as possible between themselves and the psychopath with the beautiful voice and too many teeth.

Chapter 15

Stanford University

Julia knew it was time to leave the sanctuary of her lab.

Her supplies had almost run out. She'd been subsisting on a diet of slightly rancid peanut butter and stale crackers for several days now, and the bottled water was gone. She'd been raiding from the toilet tanks in the building's bathrooms for a week, and now they were almost empty. She hadn't allowed herself the luxury of using any of the water for clothes or hair washing for two weeks, and the Wet Wipes she'd been bathing with were almost gone. She sniffed an armpit and winced.

Her attention shifted to the tabby who didn't appear to be missing any meals. He refused to even consider the Skippy, so she'd been letting him out at night to hunt for his own food. Every morning he would be waiting outside the door for her to let him back in, and since he seemed to be putting on weight, she assumed his predatory skills were adequate. Too bad she couldn't teach him to share his spoils.

"Brains, I think it's time for us to leave. I know, it's a pretty sweet gig you've got here, what with the snuggly bed to sleep in and the crazy lady to pet you, but I'm hungry. It's time to head to Steven's."

After that phone call a year ago when she told her brother about the Lixi molecule, they had devised a 'just in case' plan. When Chicxulub began to emerge, they'd refined it. When Steven's wife died, followed by Julia's husband shortly thereafter, they had solidified it. While they were still able to communicate via the campus ham radio, Steven outlined the specifics of how she would travel from Palo Alto to his house. Next, they agreed on her departure date and then calculated, almost to the hour, precisely when she would arrive in Liberty.

Now it was time to implement the plan. Because Julia knew her brother better than anyone, she knew he and her nephew were alive, despite not having heard his voice in more than two months. Compared to most of the other survivors, herself included, they were probably thriving, because Steven would have planned for every possible contingency.

She spread a spoonful of peanut butter on a saltine and studied it with disdain. "Should have left a bit sooner while I still had decent food." She took a bite and grimaced. "Hopefully, the stuff at my house is still there, right, Brains? I see canned salmon in your future if you play your cards right."

The cat was curled up on the floor in a rectangular patch of a sunlight.

"Sleeping off a squirrel binge, huh, big guy?"

She squatted down to stroke the orange fur. He opened his eyes and blinked up at her through the dust-moted sunshine streaming through her office window.

"I wonder how well you'll travel. Do I need to put you in a crate, or will you behave yourself and sit politely in the passenger seat?"

The feline purred and closed his eyes, too sleepy to make such important decisions at the moment.

"We'll try the seat first, but we'll take the crate just in case. I can always store stuff inside it if I need the space. The first order of business is to haul some of the diesel from the shed."

It would be a journey of more than sixteen hundred miles, which would begin first with a quick side trip to her house in Palo Alto. She would need more than fifty gallons of gas. Steven had instructed her on the finer points of gasoline siphoning, which she would be forced to do after she used up all three of the five-gallon plastic cans she would take with her.

Apprehension blossomed in her belly. She would worry about the siphoning business later. Besides, if she even managed to survive long enough to use the fifteen gallons she planned to start with, it would be a minor miracle. She had no delusions about that. After all, she knew what type of people were out there, and she figured her odds of surviving the journey to Kansas were about the same as teaching Brains to share his squirrels.

The next two hours were spent filling gas cans and loading up her car. Every week for the past year, she had fired up the Land Rover's engine to keep the battery charged and to confirm that the gasoline was still viable. It would be a snug fit with the cans, some of her equipment, and the dozen or so binders containing her research from the past year. Steven would surely see those binders as an indulgent waste of cargo space, but she couldn't bear to leave all that hard work behind.

Yep, the binders were coming with her.

She emptied the last of the water from the bathroom toilet tanks and put it in the used water bottles saved for the task. There would be more cases at her house if it hadn't been looted. She shouldn't count on the remainder of her supplies still being there, but it sure would save a lot of time and stress if she didn't have to stop for food and water along the way.

The trip should take less than a week. Steven had worked out all the logistics for her, of course. Not that she couldn't have done it herself, but she knew he would worry less if she agreed to follow his plan. Her goal was to make two hundred miles per day, which might be optimistic considering how clogged some of the roads were likely to be. Once out of the cities, she would be able to make up for the time spent detouring around traffic jams of dead cars and dead people.

That was the part she dreaded most: all those inevitable bodies. The physical effects of Chicxulub came on suddenly and people had been in panic overdrive at the end. A mass exodus had occurred in the larger metropolitan areas. She planned to drive on the wrong side of the freeway when she left Palo Alto. With luck, the stench of human decomposition would have diminished by now. She was no biology major, but she understood the cycle of death. Seventy-two hours post mortem, rigor mortis subsides and bacteria within the body starts to consume the dying cells. Next, enzymes in the pancreas cause the organ to begin digesting itself. That's when the smell kicks in. As tissue decomposes, it emits a greenish substance along with methane and hydrogen sulfide gasses. Then the lungs expel fluid through the nose and mouth. It's about this time when beetles get interested — the blow flies had arrived at the party long before now, sometimes just minutes after death. A deceased body is a smorgasbord for the insect world, and nature utilizes these multi-legged critters to cleanse the planet of rotting dead things. If there are carrion eaters in the vicinity, such as crows or buzzards, the process goes even faster. Everything up to this point happens rather quickly, within a couple of weeks in most cases. After that, it's a matter of waiting out the drying phase. Approximately twelve months later, all that should remain of Uncle Bob is dried skin and bones. Of course all corpses, and the conditions under which they became such, are different.

Your results may vary!

Almost a year after most people who were going to die had done so, the worst of the stench should be gone.

It was her fervent hope.

By late afternoon the vehicle was gassed up and ready. She put a clean towel in the bottom of the stainless steel rabbit cage from the biology lab next door. It would be converted to a kitty prison if Brains got cantankerous on the long drive. He would not take well to being confined after his near-feral lifestyle, but she had no intention of leaving him behind. His company was better than being alone, and she had grown accustomed to his silly cat behavior. It was funny to think there'd been a time when she didn't even like cats.

An apocalypse makes strange bed partners.

The Land Rover was loaded. She headed back inside the building for a final night of comfort and relative safety before venturing into 'Here There Be Dragons' territory in the morning. She stopped suddenly, then turned back to the Rover, having just decided the Macallan 25 wedged into the glove box would not arrive at Steven's house with its seal intact.

Chapter 16

San Mateo, California

Logan figured he had walked about fifteen miles overnight, and as the sky in the east began to lighten, he knew he should set up camp for the day. He'd been traveling south on Highway 82 since the 101 was just too treacherous for easy walking at night. All the dead bodies didn't bother him, but the traffic jam went on forever, and the debris from the wrecks was begging to be stumbled over. He wondered if the people had placed all that metal junk in his way before they died just to be mean. He wouldn't put it past them.

He hadn't seen any living people since the little girl with carrot-colored hair. The thought of her made him smile. He'd gotten so wrapped up in skinning the cat that he had forgotten about her until now. It might have been fun to see what she looked like under her skin.

There was a sign on Highway 82 that said 'Peninsula Golf Course and Country Club, next exit.' On a whim, having never been to an actual golf course before, Logan decided to explore it. He trudged down the J. Arthur Younger Freeway for a mile or so before another sign indicated he should turn right on Alameda.

His first glimpse of it was not promising. He imagined it would be green and lush like the ones he'd seen on television, but this one was all brown and dead-looking. Still, the landscaping was neater here than most other places. He suspected he would find squirrels and perhaps other wildlife near all those trees. He had shot lots of squirrels these past months, and it always delighted him how they flew right off their little feet and up into the air from the force of the .22 bullets. Cats were heavier, so they weren't quite as funny, and dogs just fell over, so they were his least favorite.

He never ate any of the things killed. The cat-skinning was more about curiosity (*what's under the fur?*) than about preparing it for cooking. But his backpack was light at the moment, and the stores he'd passed during the night had been cleaned out. He might have to eat squirrel or cat if he didn't find regular food soon.

A two story building with a tall metal pole out front lay ahead. The ragged American flag blew in the warm October breeze, making him feel a little anxious. It made him think about laws and policemen and such, and Logan liked how in this new world he only had to worry about his own rules. He would never want to go back to the way things used to be.

He continued walking toward the building, averting his eyes from the flag. The extra-large wooden doors were locked tight, so he skirted around the corner. There was almost always a window he could break into in the back or on the side.

After about ten yards he found one, with the panes broken out. He slid his Ruger out of its holster and kept it in his hand as he climbed over the sill, which was free of glass shards. Somebody was a tidy burglar, he thought. Was he still inside? He thought about how good he was with the pistol and decided not to worry. His sneakers made no sound on the room's plush carpet.

It must have been quite a fancy place once. The medium-sized room looked like a *parlor* — a word his mom used — because several sofas had been placed here and there. The fireplace at the far end contained remnants of charred logs. He could start a fire there later and cook whatever he was able to kill that day. Maybe he could rig up some kind of spit, like cannibals did when they were roasting people in those old movies. The idea appealed to him and he decided he'd like to try it, even if he did find some packaged food somewhere in the building.

It would be fun.

He stepped into the next room, which was large and open. He saw the big doors off to the right, so he knew this was the *grand entryway,* another term his mom liked to use when she talked about rich folks and their houses. It truly was grand because there was even a dusty piano sitting under one of those rich-people chandeliers.

Logan wondered about the people who had come to this place in the Before Times. They must have had tons of money and probably drove Cadillacs. His mom always wanted a Cadillac, but never got one. They were too *pricey*. He felt sad then, thinking about her. She would have liked this place, even though it smelled like rat piss.

He was lost in thought and had let his guard down a bit when he heard the unmistakable sound of a bullet being chambered. It sounded like a Glock and when he spun around, he saw he was right.

Standing there with the gun pointed at his chest was a beautiful woman. His mouth dropped in surprise. She looked like one of those actresses on TV...the Rachel person on that funny show his mom liked.

She loved that program so much that she watched all the reruns long after they stopped making new episodes.

The woman was dirtier than Rachel but she sure was pretty, and the way she held the Glock, he knew she must be good with guns too.

Not as good as he was though. The thought made him smile.

The woman kept her weapon trained on the young man's chest. His sandy blond hair was shoulder length and filthy, probably not washed since the apocalypse. His shirt was caked with dirt and what looked like blood. In contrast, his jeans appeared brand new. Despite the twenty feet of distance between them, she could smell his body odor.

She sniffed in distaste. There was something off about the golden eyes and the creepy smile within the otherwise handsome face. She was getting a very bad feeling about the dude, which was saying a lot since she'd dealt with a lot of bad dudes the past year.

"Don't make even one tiny move or I will plant two bullets center mass before you know what hit you," she said.

The man's smile broadened.

Holy crap. That smile is freaky.

She toyed with the idea of killing him right then, but her sense of honor wouldn't allow it. He would have to make an aggressive move before she would shoot him. Her moral code required it.

"You look like Rachel," Logan said. "From that *Friends* show. You know the one?"

"Yeah, I get that a lot."

Her voice was low and sweet-sounding. He decided he would like to see her voice box from the inside. He knew it was located somewhere in the throat. He imagined a tiny music box with a twirling ballerina on top. He'd seen one in a toy store once.

"Obviously, you're here looking for food, but everything in this place belongs to me."

He noticed she spoke slowly now, like she was talking to a child. The thought irritated him, but he wasn't sure why.

"This is my home. You aren't welcome here. If you want to live, you'll turn around and go right back out the window you came in. Then you'll keep walking back down the driveway and on up the road. I want to see your backside on Alameda in five minutes. Do you understand?"

Logan nodded, but even as he did, his hand holding the pistol swiveled up with lightning speed.

He was fast, but she was faster.

Pain exploded in his shoulder.

"Why did you do that?" he screamed. He was so angry. His shoulder was killing him, but all he could think about was that somebody — a girl even — was better with a gun than him.

"I warned you. Plus you were about to shoot me, asshole. You're lucky I didn't aim for your heart. Now get the hell out of here before I kill you. Leave the Ruger on the floor."

"No, please don't take it. I need it to protect myself and to hunt for food."

"What about that Sig strapped to your back?"

"It's a .22 and I'm out of bullets for it," he lied.

The woman sighed. "Back up against that wall and keep both hands where I can see them."

He did as she instructed. She crossed the twenty feet to where the Ruger was lying. She released the clip, letting it fall to the floor, then tossed the empty gun to him. He caught it in his left hand.

"Now get the hell out."

Logan was seething, but he knew he'd been bested. The woman kept her Glock leveled at him as he clambered back through the window casing. The back of his neck tingled as he walked away. He could feel her eyes on him the entire way to the street.

Once he reached Highway 82 again, he stopped. He slid out of the backpack, unstrapped the rifle, and unbuttoned his shirt to study the wound. He could see the small hole in the front and could feel one also in the back. The bullet had gone straight through.

That was good. It really hurt, but he could lift his arm a little, so the muscles must not have been injured. He would be able to shoot with that hand, and even though he was almost as good with his left hand, he preferred to use the right. He would need to get something to clean it or it would get infected. His mother had been clear on the subject of infection — it was bad and could kill him. He'd have to find some medicine soon, and that meant traveling in the daytime.

He headed south on 82. Chaotic thoughts swirled in his mind. How had that Rachel girl been faster than him? Nobody was faster than him. All the guys at the shooting range had told him so. It didn't make sense.

Maybe she had magic.

He knew his invisibility didn't work on all creatures, but it seemed to on most humans. Maybe her magic kept it from working on her. That could explain it. He had a sudden thought that clarified everything: people who couldn't see him must not have magic of their own, but those who could see him, did have magic.

If they did have magic, he would need to be very, very careful with them.

The concept made perfect sense and he felt better, despite his shoulder, which hurt with every step. A sign said *Redwood City, 8 miles*. Soon after, another sign said *Palo Alto, 15 miles.* He sure hoped he could find a CVS or Walgreens sooner than Palo Alto.

Chapter 17

Liberty, Kansas

"Dad, I think Brittany's mom liked you."

Jeffrey's back was toward his father as they weeded the garden. Steven didn't have to see his son's face to know there was a shit-eating grin spread all over it.

"You may be right. Not sure how I feel about it. What are your thoughts? Do you like the Evans girls?"

Jeffrey straightened, contemplating the question.

"Brittany is pretty and sweet. I like Mrs. Evans too, but I don't think I like the way she treats her daughter. She seems sort of rude to her."

"I noticed that too. I'm not sure what kind of relationship they have."

The day was cool and overcast. After a hot summer and balmy September, their first hint of winter had arrived today in the form of a mild cold front. It made him feel anxious, despite knowing they were probably better prepared than anyone else in the area. Maybe even the entire state. He didn't indulge in this line of thought often; his focus needed to remain on the welfare of his son and himself, not strangers. He knew there were fellow doomsday preppers long before Chicxulub, but what were the odds any of them were still alive? He'd been avoiding all other survivors except Natalie and her daughter. He and Jeffrey had been sharing their water with them for months. Steven wondered if that might be expanding soon to include food, and at some point, their house. Between the semi-rural location, the electrified fence which ran on windmill-generated power, the garden, the near-full root cellar, and the buried propane tank, he knew they were safer, more comfortable, and certainly better prepared for the winter than the Evans girls.

Natalie hadn't said how they had fared last winter. The pandemic had just happened, people were still dying off, and the world was in chaos. Somehow though, they had managed to survive those harsh months. He knew she was intelligent, and he did remember that she'd mentioned some stockpiling. Was he underestimating her?

After seeing how much food had eaten last night and noticing they were both on the thin side, he had a feeling their situation might be tenuous. Should he suggest some kind of joint venture, or wait and let her approach him first? Any new people they took on must carry their own weight.

What skills could the females bring to the table? A literature major and a musical prodigy probably didn't have much survival expertise, unless they had seen the end coming and quickly self-educated. He decided he would just ask the next time they came to dinner. Before leaving last night, Natalie had been hinting around about a 'next time,' but Steven didn't take the bait. He needed some time to process everything, not only in terms of taking on the responsibility of more mouths to feed, but also the personal implications.

Then there was Julia.

If his sister were still alive, she would finally be heading this way from California. She had insisted on continuing her work until now, ignoring Steven's pleas to get the hell to his house where she would be safe. She'd flat-out refused. The disease had all but ended humanity and she would discover why, even at the expense of her own life.

Her supplies would be running low by now, and they had agreed that by the first of October, she would leave Stanford no matter where she was with her research. One year — that's what they both had agreed to.

It had been a couple of months since he'd last heard her voice. He assumed the tower at the campus had been damaged in the storm that had been raging during their last static-filled conversation. Their nightly attempts to communicate via low-frequency radio had been rewarded only sporadically, when the weather was perfect and the ionosphere cooperated. Sixteen hundred miles was a long way for the signal to travel, plus his amateur Kenwood system wasn't the best nor the most powerful. At the end, there'd been too many other critical items on which to spend the last of his credit.

Sixteen hundred miles was also a long way for a person to travel under adverse conditions. But if anyone could do it, Julia could. She was a brainiac with street smarts and more tenacity than anyone he'd ever known. If she did make it, how would she feel about bringing Natalie and Brittany into their fold? Steven was good at many things, but a keen understanding of social dynamics was not on that list.

He sighed.

In that uncanny way he had of sensing his father's thoughts, Jeffrey asked, "Are you thinking we should let them live here?"

"I think it's a bit premature to journey down that path at this point, don't you?"

Jeffrey nodded. "Dad, if you and Mrs. Evans got married, that would make Brittany my step sister, which would be weird since I think I like her. I mean not like a sister 'like' but like a girlfriend 'like.'"

"You've put some thought into this. And I see your point. I think times have changed though, and there aren't many people left to sit in judgment of anybody else. I think it would be okay to 'like' Brittany, and we could agree not to talk about the step-sister-brother thing. Anyway, I think we're getting ahead of ourselves. They might not even like us back."

"No, I think both of them like both of us. I'm sure of it."

Jeffrey's clear blue eyes gazed beyond their fence line, not seeing the dismal landscape of the depleted corn field, but something else. When he spoke again, Steven wondered at what point his son had become so damn grown up.

"The thing is, we need to be sure they like us for the right reasons. Not just because we have all the good stuff."

Chapter 18

Near Prescott, Arizona

"You know you're down to three cans of dog food? And the powdered milk is almost gone."

Pablo smiled as he watched Maddie inspect his supplies. Earlier, she had taken a bath in the chilly stream, squealing with delight when he handed her a bottle of jasmine-scented shampoo before trudging down to the water. Her long, strawberry blond hair was almost dry now and even though his clothes were absurdly large on her — the jeans had to be held up with a length of rope tied through the belt loops — she looked as lovely as ever.

Bone-thin of course, but beautiful.

He saw her tackling the math in her head and anticipated her words, if not the exact numbers, before she spoke them. He couldn't remember a moment in his life when he'd been happier.

"We have enough food for thirteen days and that's on a 1200-calorie-per-day diet. I hate to sound like a glutton, but if I'm going to put on some weight this winter, I'll need more than that. I'm afraid we're going to have to make a supply run."

Exposing her to the inherent danger in town was not an option. He'd lost her once. He wouldn't let it happen again.

"No, *we* don't need to make a supply run. *I* need to make a supply run."

"Not to undermine your authority here, Deputy Dawg, but we are a team. If you think I'm going to allow you or anyone else to treat me like a helpless female, or worse, a *victim*," she spat the word, "You've got another think coming."

Pablo was stunned by her vehemence, but his intense desire to protect her could not be so easily overridden by her need to feel independent.

"Maddie, be reasonable. You're not strong yet, plus you have a deep cut in your palm. Can you even use that hand?"

They had retrieved the ancient revolver and oversized hunting knife from her captor, the only items of value in his possession. She had refused to touch the gun, but she'd found some leather squirreled away in the cabin and fashioned a sheath for the knife, which she kept tied to her thigh.

"I have two hands. And who killed that creep? You? No. I did that. I'm perfectly capable of taking care of myself. I just didn't know it until now."

He sensed that pressing the issue further would only result in angering her, which was the last thing he wanted. Things had just begun to feel almost normal between them again, and he didn't want to jeopardize that delicate balance. An idea struck him.

Maybe there was a third option.

"I understand. But the last time I was in Prescott, things were dreadful."

"Yes, I know that. I've been there more recently than you."

"So perhaps we should rethink going there. Maybe we should try a different place. A different region."

"Like where? There aren't too many options around here."

"That's the point. Maybe we should think bigger...farther out. What about finding a farm somewhere in the Midwest? Plant some crops, round up some cows and pigs that are running amok. Even as we speak, I bet there's a gang of porcine thugs in Iowa spray-painting bridges and egging houses."

She burst out laughing. God, he loved that sound.

"Yeah, cows can be real jerks too," she said. "Once I saw a Holstein kill a man just to watch him die."

It was Pablo's turn to laugh.

"Don't even get me started on Holsteins. They lure you in with those cute little black and white spots, then they try to sell you life insurance. Once, two of them came to my door and asked if they could talk to me about Jesus. They're such assholes!"

As their laughter faded, he said, "So, where will we go, young lady? Got a hankering to see the big sky in Montana?"

Maddie gave a dramatic shudder. "Oh, no. It's way too cold there. Let's see...there's Indiana and Illinois, Missouri. What about Nebraska? It sounds safe, don't you think?"

"What about Oklahoma? It's closer and warmer than those other states, and I've always wondered how it would feel when the wind comes sweeping down the plains."

"Oklahoma is perfect. When do we leave?"

Pablo frowned, feeling suddenly anxious at the thought of leaving his refuge, despite its sad condition. He wasn't second guessing their decision, but when he imagined what might be out there beyond the relative safety of his small piece of Arizona desert, his stomach did a somersault.

Best to power through the angst.

"Let's leave in the morning. That will give us the rest of the day to load everything in the Jeep and strategize on the logistics. How does that sound?"

"It sounds wonderful. But first, there's something I want to do."

She took Pablo's face between gentle hands and kissed him. It wasn't the tentative kiss of fondness or friendship. It was the thorough, full-contact, knee-buckling kiss of passion, and it was the first of many.

Chapter 19

London

The sun had just begun to rise over the Thames, its weak rays struggling to pierce the oppressive leaden clouds. Harold suspected the cloud cover had likely saved his life during the harrowing twenty-kilometer trek from his home in Twickenham to St. James Park in London. In his old life as an anthropologist, he had managed to keep in excellent shape for a man in his fifties. The archaeological dig sites were rarely conveniently located and almost always required plenty of hiking and climbing. However, for the past year, he had been sequestered in his third-floor flat, doing nothing more strenuous than pulling an occasional book from the top shelf of his study, or opening tins of tuna fish with the labor-intensive manual device.

The overnight journey had almost done him in. The physical exertion was bad enough, but two encounters with groups prowling the streets of Richmond and then again in Kensington had almost proved deadly. Darkness and more than a little luck had kept him from being seen both times. He was surprised that his labored breathing hadn't given him away when the Kensington group meandered right past the Mini Cooper under which he'd been hiding. He vowed that if he survived the trip home, he would find a way to get regular exercise. If he intended to live, truly live, in this post-apocalyptic world — not just stay holed up in his flat — he didn't have a choice. Survival of the fittest, as they say. Perhaps he should relocate to the country? Eventually, he would have to grow his own food, a thought to which he'd only given fleeting consideration this past year.

His mind had been consumed with deciphering the seven Urak tablets.

He was close, but the digital photographs weren't sharp enough. He needed to get his hands on the tablets themselves to confirm his outrageous theory, touch the carved symbols with his fingertips, feel the subtle variances which conveyed a level of sophistication previously undiscovered in any ancient cuneiform writings. It didn't matter that there were so few people left with whom he might share his discovery. What mattered was discovering the truth. If his suspicions proved correct, it would mean the end of humanity had been no accident, and in fact, had been engineered and orchestrated from as long ago as twelve thousand years.

Perhaps even longer.

His keys to the front door of the five-story building opened the door without a hitch. No alarm sounded, of course, and it appeared that the place had escaped looting. Which made sense, when he thought about it. What sensible person would break into the BISI or the British Academy looking for food? All the Tesco and Sainsbury stores passed along the way appeared thoroughly pillaged. He thought about his meager provisions at home and added another item to his 'to do if I survive' list: go grocery shopping.

A quick reconnoitre of the building revealed it was empty and unscathed. He set up camp near the fireplace at the end of the Academy's main library. Most of his work would be done next door in the BISI archives, but the flooring there was cold tile. The plush carpeting in the library would do nicely for sleeping if he could round up some blankets and pillows. The Academy offered overnight accommodations, but he hadn't explored those yet, and he doubted the rooms would provide a way to keep warm without central heat. As much as he hated the thought of sacrificing any of the mahogany furniture, he would have to do so. Vapor, like tiny jet contrails, appeared when he exhaled; the temperature in the place hovered around 0°C according to the antique wall thermometer near the front door.

The first order of business would be to get some wood burning in the magnificent nineteenth-century fireplace. Now that he was here, the seven Urak tablets almost seemed to call to him, a siren song of possible answers to the questions that had vexed him for months. Still, a frozen anthropologist was not an effective one. He would get warm, sleep, eat, and then tackle the project.

Within a week, Harold expected to have the mystery solved and a clearer understanding of the most significant event that had ever occurred in the history of the human race.

Chapter 20

Denton, Texas

Dani and Sam made good time on Interstate 35 north, after slipping away into the night and leaving Isaiah and his Nazi youth army behind. The freeway was a parking lot of abandoned pickup trucks and SUVs; Texans adored their gas guzzlers as much as their privacy fences and firearms. The smell wasn't too bad, even though bodies could be seen through most of the windows. She figured enough time had elapsed to allow the smelliest part of the decomposition process to pass. Still, there was no way in hell she intended to open any of those car doors.

They hadn't found bicycles so far, and commandeering one of the corpse-free vehicles would have been pointless, unless it could sprout a rotor blade and hover above the gridlock. Once they were through Denton, the highway should open up a bit and perhaps they could find a car with gas and a functional battery. In the meantime, she told Sam they would grab a few hours of sleep before searching for bikes. She ignored his disappointment.

The sun was low in the sky when they woke. The warm October rays were like golden streamers, creeping under the concrete overpass where they had made camp.

"Now I know how homeless people feel," she muttered. In fact, there were remnants of past occupants near the spot they now occupied: a pile of ratty clothing, a half-empty bottle of something yellow that probably wasn't Mountain Dew, and a well-worn copy of Kerouac's *On the Road.*

"Our hobo had excellent taste in literature."

Sam followed her gaze, a troubled expression marring his sleepy face.

"I'm not much of a reader, myself. I never understood people who'd rather read a book than be outside doing stuff."

Dani studied him for a moment, before experiencing a flash of insight. She had wondered before if perhaps Sam had been in remedial classes growing up, but she'd never asked about it.

"Do you have trouble reading? Do the words get mixed up and you can't understand what they mean?"

"Yes! That's it exactly! I know what the letters are, of course, and I know the meaning of the words, but when I try to read a sentence, it just doesn't make any sense."

She looked at her friend with affection, thinking about the struggle his childhood must have been with a learning disability.

"You know what? I don't think everyone is supposed to be a good reader. Some people are meant to kick ass in other areas, like you with your martial arts. Seriously, dude, you're like a blond Bruce Lee."

"Aw, thanks," he said, crimson flooding his cheeks above the sparse beard. "Can we look for bikes now? We would make much better time riding than walking. I think it would be fun too."

This, of course, was the real reason Sam wanted to get to Kansas via bicycle. The little boy inside had never grown up. He was typical in that respect; she saw most men as taller, burlier, hairier versions of their little boy former selves. It was a complete mystery why men were the dominant sex in the world.

Perhaps that would change now that society had been reset, courtesy of Chicxulub.

"That's a great idea. Maybe once we're through the worst of the traffic, we can find a truck that still runs and we can carry the bicycles in the back of the bed. Then we'd make even better time."

Sam's face clouded, but he nodded.

They helped each other shrug into the heavy backpacks, keeping the straps from touching the still-painful arm wounds, and stepped out into golden sunshine. Gargantuan sheep-like clouds lazed across a backdrop of blue topaz. Dani had never lived anywhere else, but she couldn't imagine there was a place with a prettier sky than this one. She knew she'd made the right decision to leave their fortified home in the 'burbs, despite how exposed and vulnerable she felt now.

Juxtaposed with the unease was a sense of lightness and freedom that she had never experienced. At first, she felt sickened by walking away from the bulk of her stockpiled goods — all that food bought before the end or pilfered afterward and all the books from which she had acquired so much information. But perhaps it was time to put that knowledge to the test and do it somewhere they could make a new life. She assumed Sam would pick Kansas because he'd mentioned the Wizard of Oz on more than one occasion. It also happened to be her preferred destination as well. What she hadn't shared with him was her reason for wanting to go there. She didn't know much about her birth mother, but her parents told her that the woman had lived in Lawrence and that she'd been a young college student who, thankfully for them, had chosen adoption over abortion. Of course she didn't expect to run across her (she imagined fighting over the last jar of pickles in a looted Kroger with an older version of herself), but Kansas had just felt right.

She hoped it would be far enough away from Isaiah.

They hiked along the service road of I35 just south of the college town of Denton. The outskirts of the city were a retail Mecca of strip shopping and fast food dining. They had yet to see another living person since their adventure in Colleyville the night before, and she was still adjusting to the reality of so much death. Most people had stayed home to die, but a good percentage had tried to escape the disease by fleeing the city.

Which of course made no sense to anyone who had paid attention to what the CDC had said — and not said — in their press conferences. Chicxulub wasn't viral nor bacterial. It wasn't the Bubonic Plague, and it wasn't the H1N1 bird flu. It wasn't contagious, so why try to flee populated areas when you couldn't get the disease from another person anyway? After her parents had succumbed, Dani had known her best bet was to stay put in the relative safety of her home and wait out the inevitable unraveling of society.

She was probably alive today as a result of that decision.

They passed a Pet Smart, a Dollar General, a Subway, and a dozen other stores before they came to Sprockets Bicycle Shop.

Sam's smile was glorious.

Like most of the other businesses, the glass storefront had been busted out. In silent unison, they retrieved their knives and held them at the ready. Not for the first time, she contemplated trying to track down some weapons that carried a bigger punch. In close proximity she and Sam were deadly, but you couldn't roundhouse kick a person who was standing twenty feet away firing bullets at you.

She flipped on her mini flashlight, illuminating the interior as they stepped through the broken glass. Several racks of bicycles and a floor littered with boxes, air pumps, and some alien looking helmets, was all she could see. No humans, living or dead, were visible.

Sam was already gazing at one of the mountain bikes with the expression of a nerdy boy on a date with the head cheerleader.

"I'll give you two some privacy while I check out the rest of the store," she said with a smirk.

He gave her a distracted nod.

She made her way to the back, past circular racks of bike clothes and stacks of shoeboxes.

Good grief...you have to wear special shoes for these things? The idea annoyed her. She wasn't about to give up her lug-soled boots just to make a friend happy.

She aimed the beam behind the cash register. Nothing but more debris there and a few twenty dollar bills scattered about. Funny how what had previously been such an important thing in the world for most people now had no more value than kindling.

There was a door at the back of the store which probably led to a stockroom. It was unlikely anyone would be back there, but if she and Sam were going to be here for a while selecting and outfitting themselves for their cycling adventure, she needed to make sure. Better to be safe than dead, she thought. Sam's mixed metaphors might be rubbing off.

As she reached for the door knob, a foul odor assaulted her nostrils. The hours of grueling Krav Maga training kicked in and almost before she knew what she was doing it, she spun her body around, leading with the Ka-Bar.

Facing her in the circle of light was a leprechaun.

Or perhaps a human troll doll.

His bushy red hair stood straight up from his head like hairy flames. His beard was an exact version of the hair flames, but extended in the opposite direction, sprouting from every inch of his face from the nose down. Dani was so stunned by the sight, her mouth dropped open and her guard slipped.

That's when the troll sprang. Before she had time to react, his right hand pinned her knife-wielding wrist against the stockroom door. In his left was the biggest blade she had ever seen. He didn't point it at her, just displayed it, like a homely model on *The Price is Right.* His compact body was turned sideways, protecting the genitals from the knee-to-groin move she would have otherwise attempted.

"I could have killed you before you even knew I was there."

His voice was the deep rumble of a Colorado rock slide. Words like boulders crashed into each other, then tumbled to the ground with an abrupt heavy thud. It was both mesmerizing and scary, and without a doubt the strangest voice she had ever heard. Which was only fitting since it belonged to the strangest person she had ever seen.

"Duly noted," she said. Her internal danger-sensing radar was all over the board, refusing to reveal whether this creature meant her harm. An image of the overpass where they had been earlier flashed through her mind. Was this the Kerouac-reading hobo from under the bridge?

"Let's get down to business, girlie. I agree not to kill you and your comrade up there who's having the love affair with the Pivot Mach 429, and you won't attempt to kill me. Deal?"

She nodded. The troll released her wrist, sore from the strength of his grip. The little bastard was strong, and the keen intelligence in those blue eyes, dilated in the gloom of the bike store, told her not to try anything stupid. He would see it coming a mile away.

"I'm Fergus. Who the hell are you?" The deep gravelly voice was completely at odds with the man's stature. He couldn't be much more than five feet tall. She placed his age at somewhere between thirty and fifty — there was no telling whether he was a youngish troll or a middle-aged troll.

"I'm Dani. So what do we do now?"

With an elegant motion, the man slid his gargantuan blade into a shoulder sheath which extended down his back, then offered a grubby hand.

"We decide if we're to be friends or enemies," he replied. "Or perhaps something in between."

"Look, Fergus," she said shaking the hand while trying not to touch too much of its grimy surface, "We just want to get a couple of bikes and some gear and we'll be on our way. No trouble, okay?"

"What way would that be exactly?"

She could not get a read on this character. Why did he care where the hell they were going?

"North. We're going north. Now if you'll just let me by, we'll be out of your, um, hair before you know it."

She glanced at the bushy flames and wondered how a person could make their hair do that without benefit of gel or hairspray. Judging by the smell, his toiletries might include swamp mud and sewer water.

Fergus nodded as if 'north' explained everything. "I'd like to come with you."

He watched her reaction with visible interest. Blue lasers burned into her skull, seeking truth or perhaps just entertainment. She wondered if he was serious or just fucking with her.

"No can do, Fergus. Sam and I are a duo. We're not interested in adding a bass act to our world tour."

"Maybe Sam should have a say in this, or are you running a benevolent dictatorship?"

Dani's mouth opened but nothing came out. She had always been the one to call the shots. Sometimes Sam disagreed with her decisions, but she was usually able to mollify him, or even manipulate him so he would think his vote carried as much weight as hers. She felt some minor shame when she resorted to this, but she was nothing if not pragmatic. As the brains in the partnership, she knew her way was the smart way. The best way.

If not always, almost always.

Then she remembered that Sam had decided for both of them to endure Isaiah's painful loyalty test. That wouldn't have been her choice, yet it might have saved their lives. He had understood the danger and their odds of prevailing, while she would have let her arrogance get in the way. If they had fought Isaiah and his lethal band of Mini Mes, they might well be dead now.

"Fine. We'll ask him."

"Lead on, sister!" The troll stepped aside with a dramatic flourish of a grubby hand.

She gave him her best dirty look as she walked by, holding her breath as the troll-proximity became more than she could take. This little bastard had one-upped her twice now, but she knew what Sam's reaction would be: he'd never allow this little shit to come with them.

***

"What the hell, Sam! Why should Ronald McDonald get to tag along with us? He could be a serial killer, for all we know."

The afternoon sunlight streamed through the open storefront, highlighting the gold in Sam's hair and showcasing the strangeness of their new acquaintance. In broad daylight, Fergus was almost as odd-looking as she had first thought, and the now visible crinkles around his eyes confirmed that he was a troll of middle age.

Sam's hand stroked the seat of the mountain bike, letting his fingertips admire its contours, as he formulated his response. Dani crossed her arms and tapped her foot as she waited for an answer. His careful thought process always pushed the limits of her patience.

Finally he spoke. "You're right. He could be a serial killer, but he's probably not. If he wanted to kill us, he would have tried to already."

"Correction," Fergus said. "Would have *done so* already."

Dani rolled her eyes.

"If you say so," Sam continued, unperturbed by the man's confidence. "And the thing is, if we decide we trust him, why wouldn't we want to bring him with us? The more, the happier, right? But mostly, I think we'd be safer with a third person to back us up. Do you think Isaiah is the only bad guy we're going to run across? I doubt it. I like the idea of having another set of eyes to watch our backs and another set of hands fighting beside us."

"We don't know if we can trust him. We just met him!"

"Right, but he didn't hurt you."

"Maybe he wants to take our stuff."

"Would have *already taken* your stuff, if that's what I'd wanted." The flaming beard twitched.

Was the little fucker amused? The thought incensed her further. "This is insane. How many months has it just been you and me? Did we ever get into anything the two of us couldn't handle?"

"Almost. We almost didn't get out of Colleyville last night. That's what I'm still remembering right now. Think about it — if we'd had Fergus with us then, we could have kicked serious ass with those guys and we wouldn't have these things carved into our arms."

Two bushy red caterpillar eyebrows rose in sudden interest.

"Oh, what is this? Who is this Isaiah person? I'm intrigued. Please share."

Dani gave him a venomous look which evoked more beard twitching.

"Damn it, Sam. I'm not happy about this. I'm not happy at all." She resorted to a classic maneuver which had worked well in the past. He hated to see her upset. It damn near killed him, actually.

Sam frowned, moved his hand from the bike, and reached for Dani's. He squeezed it tenderly in both of his, and gave her one of his slow, beautiful smiles.

"I know you're not happy about it, but I think it's the right decision. I think you'll get over being unhappy sooner than you think. You usually get to make the decisions, right? Maybe you could let me make one this time."

Damn. The little red-haired sonofabitch would be coming with them.

"Fine," she said, feeling like a petulant five-year old in time-out. "But first he's going to *take a goddamn bath*."

She stormed out of the store, having no clue where she was headed, but determined to at least have the last word.

"Ouch," Fergus said, as both men watched her stomp down the sidewalk.

"You'll get used to that," Sam replied. His adoration for the young woman was as obvious as an 'I HEART DANI' tattoo on his bicep would have been. "She's a great girl, but she really likes to have her own way."

"I get that, Sam. I get that." Fergus smiled for the first time as he studied the young man's face, reading all the gentleness and decency that could be seen there.

CHAPTER 21

PALO ALTO, CALIFORNIA

Julia stood in the kitchen of her ransacked house. If she were the weepy type, she would resort to an extended, self-indulgent snotty cry at the sight of her once-beautiful home. The walls in most of the house were covered with spray painted messages from a long dead would-be philosopher: WE DESERVE WHAT WE GOT! PEOPLE SUCK! GOD IS CLEANSING THE WORLD OF THE EVIL MEN DO! And her favorite, prominently displayed above her lovely marble fireplace: CHICXU-LUBED HUMANITY RIGHT UP THE ASS!

She appreciated a well-executed off-color pun, but less so when rendered in red spray paint on the walls of her home. It was surprising that her reaction wasn't more visceral. She had lived here with Stan for more than a decade, and while as with any marriage, there had been plenty of hard times, it had mostly been a wonderful life in this house shared with a remarkable man.

Perhaps the twelve months spent sequestered in her lab had taken the edge off her grief. A house was just a house, and she still had all those wonderful memories locked away. Nobody, not even the spray paint-wielding philosopher who had desecrated her home, could ever take them away from her.

Although the human feces in the corner of the entryway did piss her off. Why crap on a floor? If the toilets weren't working, take it outside, for god's sake. She shook her head. Hell, maybe the painter was right. Maybe humanity did have it coming.

She navigated through the debris scattered on the kitchen floor; all those electric gadgets were useless now. The DeLonghi espresso maker lay in a dozen pieces against a wall, perhaps thrown there by a frustrated caffeine addict. God, she would gladly trade sexual favors for a double shot latte right now. She'd been drinking instant swill for months.

She stepped through the laundry room off the kitchen and out into the attached garage. She was surprised to see that Stan's black Mercedes was still there on his side of the garage, covered in a fine layer of dust but otherwise untouched. Food was a more pressing priority than luxury cars, it would seem. She gazed up at the ceiling and breathed a sigh of relief. It was intact. The aluminum ladder was still in place hanging on a hook next to where the rest of Stan's tools used to be. Most of them were gone now, but she didn't care. All she needed was the ladder and the drywall saw she'd bought a year ago for just this purpose. One of the last chores before her self-banishment to the lab had been to stash her remaining provisions in the attic above her garage. The idea to have a local handyman drywall over the opening had been Steven's, of course. At the time she'd thought it was overkill, but now she realized it had probably saved her life. Sure, there would be food out there, but how dangerous would it be to leave the relative safety of her vehicle to find it?

There would be more than enough freeze-dried meal packets, canned tuna for Brains, and bottled water to get them to Kansas, with plenty to spare.

It took her a good hour to finish the task. Sawing through all that drywall had been harder than expected. She finally made it through and pulled down the attic door, exposing the attached fold-out stairs. She clicked on the flashlight and climbed up. The beam illuminated plastic storage containers in a circle of light, dusty but otherwise untouched. If an angelic choir had spontaneously accompanied the sight of those bins, she wouldn't have been surprised. It was better than finding the Holy goddamn Grail.

Her stomach rumbled at the thought of food that wasn't stale saltines and near-rancid peanut butter, but there was no time for eating now. She needed to get back to the grouchy feline in the car. There had been so much bumpy off-roading getting around all the dead cars (filled with dead people) on the way from the university, that she'd had to lock Brains in his cage. He had tolerated it...barely. The expression of intense kitty loathing made her laugh out loud.

Twenty minutes later, two large bins of food, a first aid kit, and three cases of bottled water were stacked in the back seat of the Land Rover. It was a tight fit squeezed next to the lab equipment and research notebooks; the gas cans took up the cargo space in the back. They were loaded down, but they were in good shape. Better than she had dared hope.

She buckled her seatbelt, smiled at the caged Brains next to her who responded with a menacing growl, and turned the key in the ignition.

Nothing happened.

"Oh, you have got to be kidding me."

She banged her head on the steering wheel in frustration, took a deep breath and tried again.

Still nothing.

Had she left the headlights on while she'd been in the house? She checked the setting which was indeed set to ON rather than AUTO, and pressed her head against the wheel again. In the late morning sun, she hadn't noticed their beams reflecting on the garage door when she'd pulled up in her driveway.

All that preparation and planning to have it foiled before covering even one of the sixteen hundred miles to Steven's house. She thought of her little brother and how disappointed he would be by this rookie mistake.

She took another deep breath. *What would Steven do?* An image of colorful rubber bracelets flitted through her mind. Julia didn't believe in deities or put stock in religious dogma, but she had faith in her brother.

"Okay, Brains, we have to think like Steven. There should be jumper cables in Stan's trunk, but unless the battery still works after a year, they're useless. Gotta give it a shot though."

She fished her car keys out of her bag, which also contained a set for the Mercedes. Back in the garage, she pulled the release cord for the overhead door and lifted it manually. It screeched like a room full of howler monkeys. She winced, feeling an urge to hurry as she considered the ears that might have heard the noise.

After locating the cables, she slid into the Mercedes' driver's seat. Suddenly tears were streaming down her face, catching her by surprise. The leather upholstery still smelled of Stan's cologne.

She brushed the tears away with an impatient swipe of her hand and forced herself to focus, taking deep, shaky breaths. After a full two minutes of working through the sudden onset of grief, she pressed a damp index finger against the start button.

Not even a hiccup from the engine.

She slammed a frustrated fist against the steering wheel. At that moment, a scuffling sound came from the street. She scrambled out of the car then stopped short at the garage opening, not knowing what to do next.

In the road just past her driveway stood a young man. His blond, shoulder-length hair was filthy. Blood stains were splattered across the front of his denim jacket, and his right arm was in a makeshift bandana sling. When he spoke, his voice sounded almost childlike.

"Is your car dead?"

Julia had no idea what to do. He was the first living human she had seen in months. Something, some instinct told her to remain calm and to keep her gestures slow and casual.

Don't spook this guy.

"Yes, unfortunately. Not sure what I'm going to do now. I was an idiot and left the headlights on without the car running."

"Yeah, my mom did that once when I was little. Is it an automatic or standard?"

It was the voice of a grown man but with the inflection and cadence of a child. Her research gave her an insight into what she might be dealing with. She imagined herself as a trainer working with a skittish mare.

"It's a standard. Is that a good thing?"

"Yes. You can do the rolling start with a standard. It doesn't work on automatics though. At least, that's what our neighbor Mr. Cheney told us."

She felt a spark of excitement.

"How does the rolling start work? Can you tell me?"

The young man tilted his head back, studying the overcast sky. Julia glanced upward too, seeing only clouds. Acid churned with stale saltines in her stomach.

He was still gazing skyward when he spoke again. "You can see me, right?"

She was at a loss. "Of course, I can see you. You're right there in the street."

The man nodded. "Okay, then I can tell you how to get your car started. I like to be helpful when I can. My mom always told me I should help others as long as it's not against the law."

"Your mother sounds like a wonderful woman."

"Yes, she was. She's gone now, like everyone else. Well, almost everyone else. Rachel is living at the golf course, so at least she's not dead."

Julia had no idea who Rachel was, but she played along.

"I'm glad to hear that Rachel is alive. That's good, right?"

The man's face clouded as he shifted his gaze from the sky back to her. "At first I thought it was, but she wasn't very nice to me. She did this."

He lifted his wounded arm, wincing at the effort.

"Oh, my. What happened?"

"She shot me! I couldn't believe it. I was just there looking for food and she shot me in the shoulder. I couldn't find a Walgreens or CVS on the highway. I'm worried about *infection*." He whispered the word as if saying it too loudly might conjure an infection demon out of thin air.

"You should be concerned. It's a bad thing. The good news is that I have medicine in my car. Why don't I help you with your shoulder and then you can help get my car started. What do you think?"

The young man thought about it for moment, then nodded.

"Yes, I think that's a good deal."

He walked toward the Land Rover while shrugging out of his backpack. She noticed the rifle then. The pain from his injured shoulder made his movements awkward as he tried to wriggle off the strap.

"Can I help you with that?"

The sight of the gun made her nervous, but as long as she was kind to the man, something told her she would be okay.

"Yes, please. It's a Sig Sauer Tactical 2 with a Konus scope," he said with sudden enthusiasm.

She thought of the little kid with the round glasses from that Christmas movie, the one who was destined to 'shoot his eye out.' The image evoked a smile, which the young man mistook for pleasure at seeing his rifle.

He smiled too. "I'm very good with it. All the guys at the gun range said so."

"I'm sure you're excellent. What is your name, by the way? I'm Julia."

"I'm Logan. It's-a-pleasure-to-meet-you-Julia." It was a well-rehearsed speech, no doubt taught to him by his mother.

"It's a pleasure to meet you too, Logan. Let's have a look at that shoulder."

The bullet hole appeared to be straight through, which was fortunate for the young man, and her too — she didn't relish the thought of digging out a slug with nothing in her first aid kit to numb the pain. She soon had it cleaned, slathered with antibiotic ointment, and bandaged. Her only concern was whether any of the cloth from his clothing remained in the wound. It might fester, and without oral antibiotics, he could succumb to infection within a few days. Steven had told her about fish antibiotics, but there had been so many items on her To Do list that she'd never placed the online order. She had one round of Amoxicillin, wrangled from her pharmacist during Chicxulub.

And she didn't intend to share it with a stranger.

Julia felt his eyes on her as she finished up the bandaging and helped him slip his jacket back on, which smelled as if it had been pilfered from a landfill.

"Are you a doctor?"

"Yes and no. I have a doctorate degree, so technically I'm a doctor, but my specialty is in molecular genetics, not medicine like a medical doctor."

His expression was skeptical.

"You're a doctor but not a doctor?"

"I know it's confusing, but yes. I have a PhD in philosophy specializing in molecular genetics, which means that I can use the title of 'doctor' before my name. A person who has a PhD in medicine is a medical doctor. Does that make sense to you?"

He wore an expression of intense concentration as he studied her face, looking for traces of deception.

Finally, he smiled. "It sounds to me like you have a lot of tricks-up-your-sleeves."

There was the childlike cadence again. Julia wondered about his IQ, and then considered how a mentally challenged person like Logan had managed to survive so well after the pandemic. He seemed well-fed, and despite the gunshot wound and the disregard for personal hygiene, he looked healthy. Maybe that tactical rifle was the key. She supposed it evened up the odds. If he were as good with it as he said, maybe it compensated for the intelligence deficit. And considering what she had discovered in her research, he probably was as good with his rifle as he claimed.

"Are we ready to see about getting my car going? I sure hope you can help me."

"Yes. First we need to roll it out to the street. Then you'll have to steer and keep your foot on the clutch and I'll push you down the hill. That's what Mr. Cheney told my mom do. Then when you're going pretty fast, you'll need to pop-the-clutch and the engine should start. Does that make sense to you?"

Was he mocking her? She had just asked him the same question a few seconds before. She studied the strange golden eyes and decided he lacked the mental capacity for sarcasm.

"Yes, it makes perfect sense. You know, it seems like I've heard of this technique before but I've never had to use it. I'm not that smart about car stuff. Shall we?" She gestured to the Land Rover.

Logan's eyes opened wide as he looked through the passenger side window. A huge smile spread across his grime-smeared face.

"You have a cat?"

Chapter 22

Liberty, Kansas

"So, we don't have to use the pressure canner for the carrots and cauliflower, but we do for the kale?"

Jeffrey's interest in home canning was tepid at best, much to Steven's dismay. What could be more gratifying than preserving the food you've grown yourself and seeing those rows of colorful jars stacking up in the cellar? It was no longer a quirky hobby at this point, but a matter of survival. It was just a bonus that Steven enjoyed it so much.

He noticed his son's bored expression, then realized exactly what was happening. His fourteen-going-on-forty son was not giddy at the prospect of home canning the fall produce from their vegetable garden.

Imagine that.

At what point in Steven's life had his nerd scale crept into the red zone? He'd been a fourteen-year-old boy at one point too, and he remembered being interested in bikes, baseball, and fourteen-year-old girls. He should cut Jeffrey some slack. Still, the boy must learn the process at some point. He had absorbed everything Steven taught him about guns and booby traps and chopping wood. He would have to learn the boring stuff too. After all, his father wouldn't be around forever.

"Remember what I told you about acidity? High-acid foods like tomatoes and fruit don't need to be pressure canned. The acidity makes them naturally antibacterial. Cauliflower and carrots are low acid, but because we're going to pickle them with vinegar — very high acid — we can use the water bath method. The kale is also low acid and I don't want to add vinegar, so that has to go in the pressure canner."

Jeffrey gazed out the kitchen window at the mid-morning sun, his mind on something other than the plastic tubs full of washed vegetables and the stacks of sanitized mason jars.

Steven sighed. He glanced down at Molly sleeping in her dog bed. The sunlight filtering in revealed dirt on her bandaged paw and some red spots where the blood had soaked through.

"Would you rather change Molly's dressing than do this?"

"Yes! I'll get the medicine kit." He dashed out of the kitchen.

"You can chop up some more firewood when you're finished with that! We can't have too much going into the winter!"

"Okay, Dad!"

Steven smiled. He would make him learn on the next batch, maybe when the pumpkins and squash were ready to harvest.

His amusement changed to alarm when he heard shouts from the street near the end of his long gravel driveway. He touched the leather shoulder holster, confirming the Glock 9mm was in place, and he felt the weight of the small Taurus pistol in his jeans pocket. After the incident with the intruders two days ago, they went with him everywhere. His son was also armed with a Kel-Tec handgun, and his Springfield rifle was always within reach. The boy was far more accurate with firearms than his father.

"Jeffrey, get down here!"

He heard rapid footsteps on the stairs as he positioned himself by the front door. Through the oval leaded glass, he could see people on the other side of his gate. The street was fifty yards from the house, but he spotted firearms.

Townspeople. Steven recognized many of them, even though he hadn't seen them in a year or more.

"The fence isn't turned on, is it?" Jeffrey asked, peering around his father.

"No, we don't have enough power to keep it on for more than eight or nine hours a day. That's why I only turn it on at night."

"Could you flip it on now?"

Startled, Steven looked at his son.

"Those are people we know, Jeff. You want to fry Mr. Bollinger from the supermarket or Ms. Shuster, the librarian?

Jeffrey's face flushed bright red.

"No, but what the heck are they doing out there? They have guns."

"I see that. But we're going to remain calm and see if we can handle this situation peacefully and without anyone getting shot or fried."

Jeffrey nodded.

Steven opened the front door, allowing a few moments to make sure they didn't plan on opening fire. He counted about a dozen people he knew, and at least another dozen that he didn't. That didn't bode well. In most small towns, especially those of a rural nature, there is an unspoken camaraderie, a bond that exists due to proximity. But it also exists because of a commonality which connects them, whether it's shopping at the same grocery story or watching their kids play baseball in the same Little League games.

The unfamiliar faces in the group frightened him more than the firearms they brandished. There was no neighborly bond to exploit with strangers.

His mind raced as he considered his options. He could only assume they were here because they were hungry or angry or both. Would he give up his hard-earned food to strangers, especially when it might mean taking it from the mouth of his own son over the long winter? He thought of the months of hard labor, tilling the soil, weeding the garden, hand carrying buckets of water from the well when the rains held off in the spring. Of course, if he hadn't had the foresight to acquire the seeds and the knowledge to grow and store the food in the first place, he would be in the same predicament as the people in the street. Should he be penalized for his wisdom? Did honor demand he share the fruits of his and Jeffrey's labor with these short-sighted people who hadn't prepared?

The thought infuriated him. He was an honorable man. He didn't relish the idea of allowing people to starve when he and Jeffrey were well-fed, but these were dire times. He would never let Natalie and Brittany go hungry, but damn it, he didn't intend to feed the whole town.

"Jeff, go turn the fence on."

"But you just said..."

"I know what I said. Go turn it on. Now. And stay inside."

His son darted off as Steven stepped out onto the wraparound porch. He made a show of pulling his Glock out of the shoulder holster as he descended the wooden steps. He felt the warmth of the sun on his face as he walked toward the street. A measured gait would exude confidence and also allow time for Jeffrey to get the electricity running.

The crowd was silent as they watched him approach. Now was the time to speak. He hoped he chose the right words.

"What's going on here, Marilyn? Is that you, Ed? Gosh, I haven't seen you since the Wildcats series with the Blue Angels. When was that, two years ago? What a great season that was."

He addressed a tall scarecrow of a man with thinning hair and a shotgun clenched in his hand. The man had the decency to at least appear uncomfortable by being caught at his neighbor's house holding a menacing firearm. He shifted his feet and looked down, unable to return Steven's level stare.

"Chuck, how's your family? Did Carla and Bradley make it through?"

Gone was the slightly overweight, sanguine supermarket manager. In his place was this thin, baleful doppelganger, whose eyes had a haunted cast and whose hands held a Winchester bolt-action.

"My son made it, but Carla is dead." The words were clipped and hostile, and the troubled eyes never left Steven's face.

"I'm sorry to hear that. I lost Laura too. I almost didn't make it back from that, so I know how agonizing it was for you."

"Well, you seem to be doing all right. Actually, you look pretty damn robust compared to the rest of us." He waved his rifle over the heads of the people standing near him. People that Steven didn't recognize.

"If my son and I are in good shape, it's because we've been working our asses off."

"We've been working our asses off too." Marilyn, the former book Nazi at the town's library, was also a skinnier version of her already skinny self. Steven had never liked her, but his wife had become friends with the woman due to their mutual love of books. He struggled to recall details about her life.

She continued, "We've scavenged every bit of food there is to be found in a fifteen mile radius, fighting off all the others who had the same idea. Not all returned from those outings."

He knew she'd never married, and couldn't remember if Laura had ever mentioned family members. He realized he wouldn't have paid attention if she had. How many of Marilyn's loved ones had perished? He needed to choose his next words carefully or the situation could deteriorate fast. Hungry people were desperate people. Angry, hungry people were more so.

"I'm sorry to hear that, Marilyn. I know how difficult it must have been for all of you." He raised his voice so everyone could hear, making eye contact with as many people as possible. "But if you think it's been easy for me and my son, you're wrong. We've worked until our backs felt like they would break, until our fingers were covered in blisters. Then when the blisters began to bleed, we kept working. When my fourteen-year-old boy had leg cramps so painful he couldn't sleep at night because of all the hard work, I held him in my arms until exhaustion won out over agony. When you people were out scavenging, we were hoeing and planting and chopping wood and hauling water and devising strategies for our future in this world where food no longer magically appears in grocery stores.

"It's been hard for everyone who survived the devastation of Chicxulub. If my son and I are doing better than some, it's because we didn't just work hard, we worked smart." The last word echoed in the still morning air.

"Right, Steven, everybody knows how smart you are. You never let anyone forget it." Chuck's vehemence turned the adjective into something ugly.

He was baffled by the statement. Had he been a dick before? One of those pedantic jerks that enjoyed lording his intelligence over others less clever? He'd never thought so, but he knew he tended to be impatient, sometimes to the point of exasperation when people didn't grasp things as quickly as they should. But hadn't he been careful not to let that impatience show?

Perhaps he'd overestimated his poker face.

Suddenly, he heard the low hum of electricity running through the wires of his fence. Good. Very good. But an electrified fence wouldn't stop a bullet.

"Whoa there, Chuck. This isn't about anyone being smarter than anyone else. It's simply a matter of good planning. That's it. Nothing more."

"Wrong, Steven. It's about a lot more. It's about neighbors helping out other neighbors when times are hard. It's about being a decent human being and not letting people starve when you have tons of hoarded food."

What the hell? How did Chuck know about their food? Had Jeffrey broken protocol and told kids at school about his dad's weird little hobby?

Then Steven had an insight. As the supermarket manager, of course he had run into him on a couple of shopping trips. One time his cart had been full of ten pound bags of beans, and another time, he was buying a dozen cases of Spam when it had been on sale. It was just his bad luck that the man must have remembered those incidents after all this time.

"All those beans and Spam you saw are long gone. Much of what we're living on now was grown this past summer."

He saw confusion on the man's face, but it was soon replaced with open hostility, the same expression worn by most of the faces in the crowd.

"Bullshit. We know you have a lot more in there than green beans and potatoes. We've taken a vote and decided it's time for you to share. And we've got the firepower to make that happen." The man flipped off the Winchester's safety with a deft movement, never taking his eyes off Steven.

"So that's the way this is going down, huh, Chuck? You'll just take what you want from whomever has more than you? Is this what society has been reduced to? The law of the jungle?"

"When the natives on this side of the fence are half-starved and the natives on your side of the fence have more than they need? Yep, I guess you could say law of the jungle would apply here. This doesn't have to get ugly. Just open up your gate and let us take what we need."

The simmering rage Steven had held in check threatened to boil over. How dare these freeloaders think they could storm into his home and take what belonged to him and his son?

He sighted Chuck's surly face in mental cross hairs.

"Over my dead body." He slid the Glock out of his shoulder holster as others chambered rounds in their firearms.

"What a minute, folks!"

It was a familiar voice.

"Let's not get carried away. Nobody is going to shoot anyone...at least not today."

Natalie's voice exuded authority. The crowd parted, allowing her to pass through their ranks like an elegant, graceful knife slicing through warm butter. Had she been there all along? He hadn't noticed her until now. Was she part of this lynch mob? The thought infuriated him. She had just been a guest in his home two days ago.

She stopped five feet away from the fence, looking intently into Steven's eyes. Was she trying to send him a silent message? What the hell was going on here?

"Steven, try not to look like somebody just insulted your mother. Nobody is going to take what doesn't belong to them, right people? That's not who we are. Civilization may have ended but that doesn't mean we, the survivors, are no longer civilized."

"My kid is hungry!" Chuck yelled.

"So is my daughter. That doesn't make it acceptable to take what rightfully belongs to another person. Are we criminals now? Have we stooped to the same heinous behavior of the very people we loathed in our previous world? Thieving barbarians? That's not us. Right, Marilyn? We're better than that, aren't we, Ed?"

The scarecrow nodded. The librarian's eyes narrowed further, but she said nothing.

"I have an idea. One that I think is a fair and equitable compromise. Let's talk about it under friendlier conditions than this." She indicated the shotguns and rifles with a dismissive gesture. "I think a round table is in order. Perhaps you would open up your house for a few of the townspeople — representatives, so to speak — and we can discuss our options, in a calm, nonviolent manner."

"And in the meantime my kid starves?" A new speaker...one Steven didn't recognize.

"I'm sorry sir, but I don't know you. Are you new to our town?" Natalie's cool tone did everything but say the word 'outsider.'

Clever girl. Divide and conquer.

"I'm here now. That's all that matters." The man couldn't weigh more than 130 pounds; tattered clothes hung on him like laundry pinned to a clothesline. He was in worse shape than most of the locals. Where had he come from? Where had all these strangers come from?

"Clearly you are. Perhaps I'm overreaching, but I think Liberty residents...the people who lived here before the pandemic...get first dibs on legislating town business."

That's smart.

"But never fear, sir, we are kind people, and we will not let anyone go hungry if we can help it. Am I right, Steven?"

Again, she seemed to be communicating something with her eyes. He felt his anger draining away, and the effect of her words on the crowd was evident as they lowered their firearms. Natalie might have saved his life just now.

He made a decision. "Let's talk about it. Chuck, Ed, Marilyn, Natalie. You're welcome to come inside. Weapons will be left on the porch. Give me five minutes to turn the fence off, then I'll open the gate."

When he turned away from the subdued gathering toward his house, he almost ran into his son. Jeffrey stood with his feet planted wide and his Springfield rifle cradled expertly in his young arms.

"You were supposed to stay inside," he whispered, ushering his son up the driveway to the house.

"Dad, do you really think I would have just stayed in the house and watched those people shoot you? Seriously, you're gonna have to realize that the world has changed and I'm not a child." The delivery was the same reasonable-sounding technique Steven used in parenting.

Despite the circumstances, he smiled. He wasn't ready to relinquish control just yet though, and at the moment he needed to focus on the parley that was about to take place in his home.

Damn idiots, he thought, not for the first time. Just how many concessions would he have to make? How much of his food must he give away to keep these people from storming the gates and taking what they wanted?

He hoped Natalie had some good ideas, because at the moment, he wasn't coming up with any solutions that didn't involve an empty root cellar or dead people.

Chapter 23

Arizona

The most direct route would be north on Highway 89, then east on I40 all the way to Oklahoma City. Pablo suspected they would have to detour around Albuquerque if the mass exodus had occurred there like it had in other large cities; he had seen the automobile quagmires on the news before the power went out. He remembered the images of thousands of cars at a dead standstill on the freeways leading out of Houston, Los Angeles, and Boston. Masses of people had tried to run away, but where were they going? Was 'the country' some enchanted utopia that would magically provide safety and sustenance? Most likely they were operating on a flight directive from the amygdala, not considering what they would do nor how they would survive once there.

None of that matters now, he thought, glancing at Maddie's fluttering auburn hair. The breeze that came whipping through the Jeep's windows animated the curls, transforming them into miniature ginger-colored cyclones. The thought of hair tornados made him smile.

They had loaded up every last bottle, can, and box from their depleted supplies. In the back of the Jeep, two empty gasoline cans jostled against a dozen plastic Coke bottles filled with water from the stream. A few old blankets and Pablo's sleeping bag provided a comfortable pallet for Bruno in the back seat and would also be their community bed at night. He glanced at the rearview mirror to see the tongue of his best friend lolling out the side of his grinning mouth. Bruno's head was thrust through the open window, and all those titillating smells were igniting a firestorm of doggy brain neurons.

"Gas first, right?"

Maddie had eased back into her role of logistics manager with the natural effortlessness of a hawk circling a thermal updraft. If minds were blackboards, his would be covered in an endless, overlapping chalky scrawl of perfectly chosen words, compelling metaphors, and abstract philosophical concepts, while Maddie's would be a tidy and impeccable array of numbers, algebraic equations, derivatives, and integrals.

He smiled at this woman he loved. They were driving through Chino Valley in central Arizona, a starkly beautiful mosaic of desert flatland with stunted mesas and cerulean skies for a backdrop. The temperature was in the seventies, normal for October. The sun warmed his soul as well as the arm resting on the window casing. The aroma of hummingbird mint, surprisingly similar to that of Doublemint chewing gum, wafted across his face. All five senses were more fully alive at this moment than they had ever been in his life.

Now that they were past Prescott, this section of Highway 89 was mostly obstacle-free. They would hit I40 just west of Flagstaff and take their chances on it, passing through the eastern part of the state, then all of New Mexico, the Texas Panhandle, and finally to Oklahoma. As far as interstate highways went, surely this would be one of the least congested in the country. There was a whole lot of nothing covering the expanse of real estate between Albuquerque and Amarillo.

He would miss the desert. He'd grown up here, but the grass was literally greener in the Midwest. If they were to succeed at farming, he figured their odds improved a million percent by leaving Arizona.

Maddie could have supplied the exact number.

"There's a minivan up on the right," she said, squinting and shading her eyes with a cupped hand.

"That sounds good. I think they hold about fifteen gallons. Hopefully the tank was full when they...stopped."

Pablo's thoughts turned grim at the thought of what they might find inside. They came to a stop twenty feet behind the late model Toyota Sienna.

"Will you consider staying put?" he asked without much hope.

"Nope. Get your cute ass out there. I have your back."

She eased the hunting knife out of its thigh sheath. As he watched, Pablo was mortified to realize he had become aroused, which was inappropriate and unwelcome under the circumstances. He had a fleeting moment of self-loathing with the realization that a knife-brandishing woman turned him on. He would find a private moment later to explore that little nugget.

Think about baseball.

"You okay, Pablo? You look a little peaked."

There was an adorable smile playing around the corners of her mouth. Had she noticed?

"Yes, I'm fine. Let's just do this."

He reached in the back for the shotgun, and stepped out onto the sun-warmed blacktop. He could feel Maddie's presence behind him as he walked up to the driver's side and gazed through the filmy window. The desiccated remains of a man sat at the wheel; flesh hung like papier-mâché on the skull, and strips of hooded leather attempted to cover eyeballs that had withered and shrunk into the bony scaffolding.

The face of death. He would never get used to it even after seeing it dozens, perhaps a hundred times this past year. The passenger seat was empty. Dirt and an after-market tint job obscured the back and rear windows. He walked around to the sliding door.

"Hold your breath."

He grabbed the handle and slid open the door, the metal screeching in the runner from a year's worth of disuse.

The sight of two dead children and the pungent, vomit-inducing odor of human decomposition assaulted his senses.

"Maddie, don't come over here," he said, fighting the gag reflex that usually accompanied these events.

"Too late," she said from behind him.

"Don't look, please." His breakfast of Bush's baked beans threatened to make a return appearance.

"Go throw up, if you need to. It's okay. Then you can get the gas going." She gave his shoulders a gentle squeeze, then guided him away from the van. "I'll finish here."

"Are y-y-you sure?"

They stood on the asphalt shoulder as he gulped in fresh air. Breakfast beans and bile surged in the back of his throat.

He was going to puke.

"It's okay, Pablo. This kind of stuff doesn't bother me like it used to. I've been through worse."

The adorable Maddie from moments ago had been replaced with a grim, steely-eyed stranger. Pablo would likely never know the horrors she had been subjected to these past months, which might be best for both of them.

"I'll get the cans and the hose. Fingers crossed the guy had just filled up," he said.

He began to gather the gas-pilfering supplies. After another minute of focused swallowing, he won the vomit battle and started siphoning while Maddie investigated the Toyota's interior. Bruno sat sentinel nearby, his huge shepherd ears alert for trouble, guarding his humans while they conducted their strange activities.

He could hear her rooting around in the back as he drained the minivan's tank, which was more than half full. If it hadn't gone bad, this venture would be a home run.

Maddie hopped out of the side door. Her somber expression had changed to one that made him think of a canary-satiated cat. She held a bulging, patchwork hippie bag.

"Looks like you scored, young lady."

"I did indeed. How'd we do on gas?"

"Almost ten gallons. I'll put some in the Jeep now and see how it does. If the engine doesn't sputter, I'll assume it's still good. I would sell my grandmother's soul for a Tic-Tac right about now."

Gasoline tasted only slightly less revolting than vomit. He thought about digging out his toothbrush and the last half-used tube of Crest, but decided to gargle and brush at the next stop. He wanted to get away from the minivan and its depressing cargo.

Fifteen minutes later, they were heading north on Highway 89 again. Maddie had been in one of her quiet, introspective moods ever since finding the children. He kept silent, letting her work through what was on her mind.

Finally, a few miles farther, past a dilapidated roadside tamale stand and a Del Taco that had probably been vacant long before Chicxulub, she spoke.

"Those little girls didn't die of the pandemic."

"What? Why do you think that?"

"There were bullet holes in the back of their heads. Dad must have killed them before succumbing to the disease himself."

"Why would anyone do that? How could a father kill his children?"

"First of all, we're assuming they were his children, but I think that's a reasonable conclusion based on what I found. Secondly, I think it was because he loved them. It was the ultimate kindness, the ultimate sacrifice, and it must have taken incredible courage." She gazed at the desert landscape.

Pablo was dumbfounded. "He shot his children because he loved them? Because he was being kind?"

"Yes. Think about it. He was sick. He knew he was going to die. He's on a desolate stretch of highway with two little girls that are healthy but helpless. They were no more than four or five years old. What's going to happen to them when he's dead? Let's see. First they freak out because they just saw their dad die. Then when night comes, they have the option to sleep in the car with a corpse or sleep outside with the coyotes and wolves. Can you imagine their terror? If they make the smart choice and stay in the van, what happens when they go through all the food and water? I doubt they would have lasted a week with the provisions they had. A loving father would have thought all that through. If I'd been in that situation, I'd have done the same thing."

He didn't know what to say. The matter-of-fact way she discussed this gruesome subject shocked him. This was a more hardened version of the woman he'd left for dead in the parking lot of that Walgreens, a memory which evoked an image as unwelcome as the one where Maddie shot children in the head.

She didn't seem to expect a response, which was fortunate, since Pablo couldn't speak with the lump in his throat.

Chapter 24

Texas

"Guess Sam was right about that 'another set of eyes and hands' thing."

In addition to being the oddest-looking person Dani had ever seen, Fergus was also the most annoying. As the three unlikely companions hunkered down behind the checkout counter of a Chevron Mini Mart in North Texas, Dani was thankful that at least he'd changed into some reasonably clean clothes and a stench-free army jacket. Judging by the profound powder-fresh smell, he'd used the entire container of her baby wipes. He must have washed the hairy flames in the sink of the bike store bathroom because they were wet, droopy, and less pungent now.

A bullet zinged off the cigarette cage a few inches above their heads. The gang of Mad Max wannabes had run them into the Chevron shortly after pedaling away from the bike store. She and Sam had, again, committed the post-apocalyptic-world faux pas of bringing knives to a gun fight. She had no idea how they would get out of this one.

"Yeah, well, you don't seem to be doing much for us at the moment. Perhaps you could put that dazzling intellect to work and figure a way out of this. Or maybe you could wriggle your nose, tap your heels together, and leprechaun-magic us the hell out of here."

"Words hurt, Dani. You cut me, I bleed."

The twitching red beard belied the dramatically sorrowful expression. For some reason, this infuriated her even more. She excelled at acerbic repartee, and if she didn't piss off the targeted victim, she wasn't doing her job. She would have to try harder, just as soon as they got out of their current life-threatening predicament.

"We could make a run for it out the back," Sam offered without much enthusiasm.

"Good chance they have the back covered too. How many did you count?"

Fergus's one redeeming quality was the way he spoke to Sam. The deference in the gravelly voice was unmistakable, and anyone who respected her friend was someone she could tolerate. For a while.

"I think four at least...maybe five."

"Yes, that's what I saw too. Dani, what are your thoughts? Do you think we should try our luck through the back door?"

She tried to suspend her irritation while pondering their options. Another bullet ricocheted off the cash register.

"No, I imagine even those mouth-breathers out there would think to cover the back door. A distraction of some sort? Too bad Chevron didn't stock Molotov cocktail kits next to the Cheetos. I bet they would have been big sellers."

"A distraction!" Fergus exclaimed with a vigorous clap. "Excellent idea."

Dani hated that she felt a tiny surge of pride. What did she care if the little troll was impressed by her?

"Something tells me these dudes have more brawn than brain," he continued. "Why don't I scurry over to the other side of the store where those windows are, break out a little opening in the glass and fling some sort of incendiary device as far away from us as I can fling it. Thoughts? Suggestions?"

"I think that's a brilliant idea. Now just cross your arms, bob your head, and make an Acme dynamite stick magically appear in your hands."

He nodded, beard twitching, and opened one side of his worn army jacket, revealing two hand grenades tucked into an interior elastic band. The grenades, as well as the coat, could have been circa WWII.

"You've got to be kidding me. Where the hell did you get those? The clearance table at Bombs-R-Us? Do they even still work?"

"That's something we're about to find out. Do we agree this is the best course of action?"

Sam nodded.

"What about you, Joan Rivers?"

"Yes, we're agreed. You toss the grenade, we wait for the big KAPOW, watch these hooligans scatter, grab our bikes, and make a run for it. Does that sound about right?"

"Very good. A kiss for luck, then?"

The blue eyes sparkled in the hairy face.

Dani couldn't help smiling. "Get the fuck outta here."

"Getting the fuck outta here. If they don't have a sniper in their ranks who decides to target my lovely head, I'll meet you by the door."

In a flash of army green and fiery red, he was gone.

Sam and Dani stayed hunkered down behind the counter while bullets zinged through the broken glass at the front of the store.

"They're wasting a lot of ammo," she said, shaking her head in disgust. "Idiots. Why don't they save their resources and just starve us out? That's what I'd have done. It's not like they have any pressing social engagements or meetings with their stock broker to hurry off to."

When she glanced at her friend, she was surprised to see his face twisted up, like he might burst into tears at any moment.

"What's wrong? Are you injured? Did one of the bullets hit you?"

"If those bastards hurt my bike, there will be hell to pay the piper!"

Dani bit her lip. She would not insult him by laughing when he was so distressed. She suspected that when Sam fell in love, it was forever. If the Pivot Mach 429 survived the gunfire, she hoped the two of them would have a lifetime of happiness together.

The sound of tinkling glass came from the other side of the store. The next moment, two eardrum-assaulting explosions came in quick succession.

"One, two, three...now!"

They hopped over the counter and ran to the front, listening to the sound of voices yelling and chunks of debris hitting the pavement outside.

Fergus was right behind them when they dashed through the broken glass and to their waiting bikes. Several bullets whizzed past as they pedaled out of the parking lot and onto the access road.

In fifteen minutes, the small band of survivors covered three miles. They darted under an overpass, then came to a halt.

"That was too close for comfort," the older man wheezed.

"No shit," Dani agreed, breathing heavily. "We need to get some guns...pronto."

Sam nodded, already recovering from the exertion of their biking adventure. Dani felt mild resentment at his fitness level — he'd barely even broken a sweat, and she and Fergus heaved like two octogenarians after a sack race.

"I've never shot a gun before and I've always been kind of against them," Sam said. "But I do think we need them now. Do you know anything about guns, Dani?"

"Only what I read about them on the web before the power went down. I can't imagine they'd be that difficult to figure out though."

"What about you, Fergus?"

The blue lasers targeted Sam's face. He hesitated a few seconds before answering. Dani wondered if it was lack of oxygen or something else that caused his reticence. She thought about the ancient hand grenades.

"I know a little."

Her bullshit detector kicked into high gear. *Evasive. A guy that carries explosives probably knows a lot more than a little about firearms.*

"So what's the story on the grenades, Fergus? You want to share with the class how you got your paws on those bad boys?"

He cocked a hairy caterpillar. "How about a little quid pro quo, Clarice? What's the scoop on this Isaiah character and the arm carvings you and Sam are sporting?"

Dani scrutinized the small man, looking for a reason to deny sharing any more about herself and Sam than was necessary. She knew her friend possessed an uncanny ability to read people, much better than she. And he'd allowed this creature to join their party without hesitation. For the first time in a long time, Dani felt stirrings of self-doubt. Was she even the one running the show at this point?

She sighed. What harm could there be in telling him about their Colleyville escapades if it forced him to reveal more about himself.

"Quid pro quo, Doctor Lecter."

She took the next five minutes to paint a colorful, expletive-laden narrative of their evening with Isaiah and his not-so-merry band of creepy adolescents.

"Interesting..." A grubby hand rubbed the furry red Brillo pad of his jaw. "Clever move, Sam. It sounds like you bought your lives with those carvings." He indicated Sam's arm bandage.

"Your turn. What's your story? Don't skip over any juicy parts either." Dani couldn't deny an interest in this strange man's history.

"It all started back in 1965. It was never easy for me. I was born a poor black child..."

"Stow it, Fergus. I've seen that movie. My parents made me watch it along with a lot of other inane crap."

"Inane crap? You don't love Steve Martin? How could anyone not love Steve Martin? '*He hates these cans! Stay away from the cans!*' That's comedic genius!"

Much to her surprise, he began to laugh — deep, gravelly, resonating laughter that rumbled from the depths of his belly. Sam smiled, always happy to see others happy, even though he'd never seen *The Jerk* and didn't understand the reference.

Dani couldn't help but be amused. *The Jerk* was sophomoric humor at best, but it did have some classic moments.

"I don't need you. I don't need anything...except this ashtray..." she said, surprising herself by recalling the dialogue after all this time. The movie was already old when she watched it with her parents, but that scene had cracked her up.

"Yes! See? That's brilliant! So funny, so many great lines."

She smiled until she realized what was happening. The smile changed to an accusing scowl.

"You're stalling. Quit sandbagging and give us your stats. The Man, the Myth, the Legend: The Story of Fergus."

Blue eyes studied the underpinnings of the overpass as the newest member of their elite club gathered his thoughts.

This will turn out to be more bullshit or the most interesting life story I've ever heard, Dani thought. *Or a bit of both.*

"How about the Reader's Digest condensed version? We don't have time for the unabridged Story of Fergus."

"That'll do, Pig. That'll do," she said in a challenging tone.

"Ah, *Babe*. Another fine film. I suspect you and I have more in common than you might think, girly. Tell you what, let's get a few more miles down the highway and set up camp for the night. My memoirs demand a crackling fire, a shared flask of whiskey, and an industrial-sized box of tissues, for all the tear-jerking scenes. Does that meet with your approval?"

"Is this another stalling maneuver?"

"No, I swear it. My gut tells me it's time to get moving and to put more distance between your hooligans back there and our pretty backsides. You have my word that all your pressing Fergus questions will be answered tonight in graphic, occasionally pornographic detail. Deal?"

"Okay, but you're not getting out of it."

"My word is as good as gold. You can take it to the bank and draw two percent annually."

"More like take it to the pot on the other side of the rainbow." Dani snorted at her own joke, as they mounted their bikes and pedaled back out into the late afternoon sunshine.

"Death by a thousand paper cuts," Fergus hollered at her back. "That's your diabolical plan!"

She smiled, glad the strange man couldn't see her amusement.

***

"Look, guys!" Sam pointed at another retail strip off the I35 service road. Dani estimated they'd covered another fifteen miles, and because Sam's fancy mountain bike sported a Garmin GPS, he would happily confirm their progress if she wanted to know. For as long as they could find fresh batteries and the navigational satellites stayed in orbit, they were golden.

Dani's gaze followed his outstretched arm to a small sign at the far end of the upcoming shopping center on their right: *Bill's Guns*. Bill had either been a man of few words and zero imagination, or he'd had to pay by the letter for the signage.

The storefront glass was still intact, which was surprising. The trio rolled to a stop at the curb in front of the store.

"You'd think a gun shop would have been one of the first to get ransacked," she said, pressing her face against the pane. "It looks empty. Maybe Bill hauled ass with his merchandise before the shit hit the fan."

Sam tried the door, confirming it was locked. "Should we break in?"

"Yes, I think we need to give it a shot. We also need to consider businesses where the owners would have kept a firearm on the premises: jewelry stores, convenience stores, check cashing places. That's if Bill's doesn't pan out."

She walked back to her bike and was digging around in her backpack for something suitable for breaking glass when Fergus spoke.

"No sudden moves, people."

The strange tone in Fergus's voice evoked a feathery stirring of tiny hairs at the top of her spine. Her backside was toward the store, him, and Sam. When she turned around, would she see that machete of his next to her friend's throat? She knew she shouldn't have trusted the little bastard.

"I mean it. Slow as molasses, girly."

Dani initiated a languid pivot — a Hollywood scene where the actor turns at half-speed to face his demise.

Fergus's empty hands hovered above the colorful head. Sam stood in a similar position. On the other side of the glass was a man holding an assault rifle with the barrel aimed at her.

She lifted her arms too, empty palms facing the gun-wielding man. Her firearms knowledge was lacking, but she knew that a bullet coming from that thing would have no trouble finding its way through the window pane and into her chest.

Chapter 25

Palo Alto, California

Julia knew Steven wouldn't be happy about Logan, but she hoped the sight of seeing his long-lost sister would lessen his displeasure at gaining an unexpected mouth to feed.

If she hoped to maintain her personal integrity, her sense of honor and decency in this new world, it had to start with not abandoning a mentally-challenged young man who had sustained a recent gunshot injury and who just helped her get her vehicle started. It had been a pivotal moment for her — her gut had told her to leave him behind — but that spark of civility and kindness shared by most humans wouldn't allow her to abandon this kid. Yes, he seemed to have done all right for himself, but the shoulder wound needed to be cared for with a degree of hygiene the young man didn't understand.

Something else factored in her decision, an emotion she barely acknowledged to herself. Best not to even go there, she thought, after identifying the instinct as maternal in nature.

A lot of shifting had to be done to make room for Logan in the front passenger seat. The feline made no secret of his annoyance at being banished to his crate, wedged in the back seat between research binders and equipment. He had hissed nonstop for thirty minutes at the usurper.

"Stop it, Brains. I mean it," she hollered, as they meandered through an obstacle course of vehicles on Highway 101 south of Palo Alto.

"I don't think he likes me very much."

"Don't take it personally. He's used to being free to come and go, and his kitty survival instincts are railing against being in that cage."

"Why is his name Brains? Mr. Cheney's cat was named Mittens because his paws were white, like mittens that girls wear in the winter."

Soon after meeting the young man, she realized she must speak on his level, which was that of a nine or ten-year-old child. It didn't come naturally, having interacted with few children during her life.

"It's because when he first started coming around, I called him 'Shit for Brains' because I wasn't much of a cat lover before. Then he kind of grew on me. He kept showing up at my lab, so I brought him inside and made him a bed. At some point he became my pet, so I shortened his name to just Brains."

"I like that name. It makes me think of zombie movies."

She laughed. "Yes, I can see that it would."

"Where are we going, Julia?"

"We're going to my brother's house in Kansas. His name is Steven. I'm hoping he and my nephew Jeffrey are still doing okay there. We made a plan when the pandemic started that I would travel to his house when I got finished with my work at the university."

"Is Kansas far?"

"Yes, it's about sixteen hundred miles, and I have no idea what we'll have to deal with on the way there. We have plenty of food and water, but we're going to have to siphon gasoline after what I've brought runs out. Do you know anything about siphoning gas out of cars?"

The strange golden eyes looked up at the headliner of the Land Rover, as if the answer to Julia's question might be found there. This behavior seemed necessary when the young man struggled with complex thoughts.

"I've seen it on television, but I've never done it myself. Do you know how to do it?"

"I understand the basic principles, but I've never done it either. Guess we'll learn together." She smiled, realizing she was pleased to share this odyssey with someone, despite the intellectual disparity.

"Too bad we don't have a Harry Potter wand." Logan's sly smile implied he was joking, but she wondered if he might believe in magic wands, as any child would.

"Wouldn't that be great? We wouldn't even need to drive, we could just wizard ourselves to Kansas."

His expression became serious. "I don't think I'd want to do that. I like driving, and also I worry about what would happen to my *molecules."*

Julia had to stifle a snort. He whispered 'molecules' with the same fearful reverence used for 'infection.' It was a word he didn't understand and which seemed to hold some mystical power.

"That's a good thing since I left my Harry Potter wand at home."

He nodded, then continued to stare at her with an intensity she found disconcerting.

"I think people with magic probably don't need a wand anyway," he said, then turned his attention back to the freeway.

She felt a sense of relief when that focus shifted away from her.

"There sure is a lot of junk on this road. Maybe we should *take-an-alternate-route*," he continued, parroting every traffic reporter in California.

"I hope we don't have to."

With luck, the Land Rover's off-road capability would get them around the obstacles. She had mapped out her journey from Palo Alto utilizing secondary highways, which would take her through Yosemite, all of Nevada, and half of Utah before accessing Interstate 70. From there, she would follow it all the way through the Rocky Mountains. Snowfall could occur in October, so the timing was important.

"Do you know how to read a road map?"

"Yes, when my mom and I went places, she let me hold the Mapsco. She said I was a good navigator."

The pride in his voice was unmistakable, just as it had been when he spoke of the compliments from his friends at the gun range. Julia suspected any positive reinforcement was cherished and revisited often, like an art collector admiring a pricey acquisition. She found herself wondering again about his life. It couldn't have been easy.

"I bet you're an excellent navigator. Why don't you get the map out of the glove box and take a look at the route I've marked. Let me know what you think."

"You got it, Julia!"

She smiled at his joyful expression. Yes, she had made the right decision to bring him along. Surely they were both safer together than on their own.

Six grueling, nail-biting hours later, they arrived at the entrance to Yosemite. They had driven around countless abandoned (and not-so-abandoned) automobiles, which had blocked much of the highway system through San Jose, Modesto, and Oakdale. Julia had sent a silent message of thanks to her brother for insisting she buy a four-wheel-drive vehicle as part of their plan; she and Logan would never have made it this far otherwise. She had forced herself to gaze upon the remains of a few of the occupants in the vehicles they passed. Insulated in her lab for much of the past year, she'd been spared from seeing the worst of the ravages of Chicxulub. Seeing events play out on television while the networks still broadcasted hadn't reveal the full, gut-wrenching story.

The world she knew was gone forever.

Late afternoon was morphing into evening. Per Steven's suggestion, she would stop for the night. Nothing good would come from adding the challenge of night driving to the already adverse conditions. Besides, she knew Logan would enjoy Yosemite, and it needed to be experienced during the daytime.

He was ogling the iconic sign when they pulled off the road and stopped.

"This place will be as good as any to stop for the night. That okay with you?"

"Yes, this looks great to me!"

The crisp air was tinged with the scent of wintergreen, wafting from shrubs clustered next to the park entrance. There were fire-making supplies in one of the plastic bins from her attic — another of her brother's directives — but she doubted it would get cold enough for a campfire tonight.

As if reading her thoughts, the young man spoke.

"Can we build a fire, Julia? I think that would be fun. Sort of like camping." His boyish exuberance made it impossible to say no.

"Of course we can. Go gather an armful of sticks in different sizes and some rocks to make a ring for a pit. I'll get the food and camp stuff out of the back. I also need to let Brains out to do his business. How does that sound?"

"Perfect!" He scurried off toward the line of Ponderosa pines.

"Be careful. There may be wild animals out there."

"It's okay. I have my guns."

Guns? There was more than just the rifle?

"Just be cautious. You should probably go to the bathroom while you're at it."

Even in the dwindling light, she could see his embarrassed expression. Maybe she was taking this surrogate mother role a bit too far; he'd survived this long on his own, after all.

"Come on, Brains, time for you to stretch those orange legs." The hissing had finally stopped, but the ears remained flattened during the entire drive. He gave her a plaintive meow, then ambled out of the open crate next to the Land Rover.

This was the moment of truth. Would her furry companion come back? Cats weren't obedient like dogs, and even though they had enjoyed an equitable partnership back at Stanford, she had no idea what to expect now. She didn't have a choice though — he needed to relieve himself. The can of salmon she planned to give him later should lure him back.

She pulled out a bin containing MREs and other provisions. She bypassed the waterproof matches and magnesium fire-starter kit, opting for a long-reach disposable lighter and one of the Zippo fire starters, which was nothing more than compressed saw dust and wax. Steven called these 'little pucks of happiness,' saying they would ignite even when damp. It was going to be a lovely evening without any clouds to obstruct the stars that were just beginning to flicker in the darkening sky.

Julia breathed deeply, taking in the fresh, fragrant air and expelling much of the anxiety from the day's adventure. She had left her sanctuary and covered two hundred miles today. She was alive, safe for the moment, and on her way to family and a better life than the one she'd been living this past year. There was food and water to last several weeks, even though the trip should take less time than that. And she had company, which provided an additional layer of safety on the journey. She was feeling quite pleased with herself at the moment gunfire exploded from the forest.

Then silence.

"Logan!" she yelled, her voice piercing the solitude and echoing off the enormous trees. "Logan! Are you okay?"

What should she do? Should she go after him and perhaps expose herself to whatever danger he was facing now? She'd just met the young man and already done more for him than most people would have. How far did her personal ethics require she go?

"Damn it," she muttered. "Logan! Please answer if you can hear me!"

Still no sound came from the trees except the reverberation of her own voice.

She walked back to the SUV, opened the driver's side door, and removed the Smith and Wesson .357 Magnum revolver from the center console. There were six rounds in the cylinder and two more boxes of bullets stored below. The weapon felt heavy and baleful in her hand. After grabbing a flashlight out of the glove box, she headed for the forest.

Ten yards from the tree line, Logan answered. "I'm okay, Julia! I'm okay!"

He emerged from the shadows with an armful of wood and a wide grin on his face. Relief washed over her as they walked back to the Land Rover.

"Young man, you scared me to death. What were you shooting at?"

"There was something growling in the woods. I was trying to go to the bathroom like you told me, and I heard a crunching sound and then a growl. I thought maybe I should scare off whatever it was so I could finish doing-my-business."

"I was worried. You did the right thing though," she said, realizing her distress was causing him to squirm.

"Please don't be mad at me, Julia. I was just doing what you said, and I'm very good with my guns. I can take care of myself pretty good."

She registered the gentle admonishment.

"You're right. I shouldn't have been worried. I know you can take care of yourself. You've done a great job up until now, haven't you?"

"Yes! I've done a great job." His grin was back. "What are we having for supper?"

"Let's see," she said digging through the food bin. "You have your choice of chicken with black beans or beef stew with vegetables. Which sounds best to you?"

He pondered the question with the gravity of a child forced to select between two favorite toys. His attention shifted from the foil packages to her and a sly expression crossed his features.

"I think ladies get to pick first. I bet that was a test, wasn't it?"

"No, it wasn't a test. I just thought one might sound better to you than the other, but if you want me to choose, I'll take the chicken."

"I wanted the beef-stew-with-vegetables anyway. Ha!"

She didn't know what the game was, but decided she was too tired to play.

"Do we just tear them open?"

"Not unless you want cold food. We use the self-heating device and then we wait ten minutes. We just add a little water to the flameless heater, stick the MRE back in the box, and let it do its magic. Easy peasy."

"You put in water to make fire? That *is* magic."

"No, just basic chemistry. Did you take chemistry in school?"

He shook his head. She wondered how far he'd gotten in school and whether he'd had access to a decent special education program.

"When metal turns to rust, the oxidation process generates heat. Do you know what causes metal to rust?"

He glanced up at the darkening sky.

"Water!"

"That's right. We add water to this little packet which contains salt and metal dust and it will begin to oxidize quickly, creating heat which makes the water boil. Then when we put the food package back in the box, it's like putting a pot of soup on a hot stove. Does that make sense?"

He nodded, but the knowing smile returned. "It does make sense, especially if you mix in a little magic."

She laughed. "Maybe just a little magic." What harm was there in indulging his obsession? Besides, she wanted to get the fire going, eat their dinner, and get some sleep.

She suddenly remembered the cat.

"Brains! Here kitty-kitty-kitty!" she called, locating the salmon and pulling the lift tab. The fishy aroma was sudden and profound, perfect cat bait.

"Oh, god, I hope he isn't getting eaten by a bear, or whatever predators live around here."

"I bet he's just out hunting for mice. He'll be fine. Just like I was."

Logan busied himself placing large rocks around the pile of branches and twigs he'd gathered. "I saw this once on TV. This is the safe way to do it, right?"

"Yes, that looks good," she replied, distracted. "Here's the fire starter. Just put it in the middle, then place a few small sticks on top and light it." She handed him the disk and the lighter. "I'll get our dinners started and then I'm going to look for Brains. And, uh, also do my business. Will you keep an eye on it? We don't want to burn down Yosemite."

"Yes. I'll make sure it stays in the rock circle. No problem. Easy peasy."

For the next twenty minutes she wandered through the Ponderosa pines and enormous sequoias which became dense and oppressive the deeper she went into the woods. She was careful to keep the campfire in sight — getting lost in the wilderness looking for a cat would be unforgivably irresponsible. If Steven could see her now, he'd be wearing that disapproving frown that transformed him from cute nerd to curmudgeon.

Finally she gave up. Her food was probably cold by now and dusk was transitioning to night. Logan watched her approach. He had waited for her before eating.

"Don't wait on me. Go ahead and eat."

"Okay. You didn't find your cat?" he asked, absorbed in the task of opening his dinner packet.

"No. I'll leave the salmon sitting out here by the fire. Maybe he'll show up later. He's used to being out all night but he sure isn't prepared to deal with the wildlife that's around here." She sighed. Stupid furball.

"What if something else smells the salmon? Something bigger than Brains?"

Oh, shit. Why didn't I think of that?

"That is an excellent point. If he doesn't come back before we go to bed, we'll put it in a Ziploc bag. Good thinking."

The young man beamed with pride.

The MREs were tasty, but calorie-laden and lacking in fiber. A steady diet of them would prove challenging to her colon, but there were more pressing concerns at the moment than a backed-up lower intestine.

"I want to get an early start in the morning, okay?" she said, as a wave of exhaustion washed over her.

The fire crackled and popped. Logan had done a superb job of keeping it tended, and her middle-aged bones appreciated the warmth. Surely the stars at home had never sparkled so brightly as the ones she looked at now.

She felt herself relaxing for the first time in several days. How did the saying go? The hardest part of a journey is the first step? That was true in this case. The dread with which she'd anticipated the long road trip to

Steven's house had been exhausting. Now that it was finally happening, confidence was slowly edging out a year's worth of anxiety.

She just might make it to Kansas.

"I'll be ready whenever you say, Julia. I can't wait to drive through the mountains."

He had consumed all of his food and a bottle of water before she was halfway through hers. It seemed that he wanted to lick the inside of the container, but after a covert glance in her direction, he stuffed it back in the empty box. The protein bars eaten in the car earlier had diminished much of her hunger. Worrying about the stupid cat had affected her appetite as well.

"Do you want the rest of mine, Logan? I'm pretty full."

He gave an enthusiastic nod, then gobbled down her leftovers.

"Where are we going to sleep?" he asked

"We'll have to camp out here by the fire. There isn't room in the car unless you want to sleep sitting up. I wonder if we should take turns keeping watch. I've never been camping before, so this will be my first time sleeping under the stars."

"I've done it lots of times since everybody died."

She marveled again at how well he seemed to have managed after the apocalypse. From her research, she knew that the survivors would all have at least two characteristics in common. First, the Lixi molecule never actuated within this small group, which meant there had been no directive from their genetic code to initiate the process of necrotizing the vascular system of the host. Second, the survivors would be highly intelligent, but not all would be Einsteins. Some would be like her and Steven, generally well-adjusted, normal people who just happened to be exceptionally smart. The intellect of others would fall in the savant spectrum, like Dustin Hoffman in *Rainman* — gifted but only in a particular, specialized way.

The kicker was the last piece of the puzzle she had discovered just before leaving the lab. Approximately half of the survivor samples indicated increased levels of anxiety, neuroticism, and even psychosis. Simply put, fifty percent of the current global population would suffer from depression and panic attacks, have obsessive tendencies, struggle in stressful situations, and exhibit all the classic symptoms of neurotic behavior. This in itself wasn't alarming — one out of every five Americans had been taking anti-depressants or anti-anxiety medication before Chicxulub. The scary part was where the serotonin levels indicated psychosis. Meaning that of the fifty percent with neurosis, some of *those* would likely be bipolar or schizophrenic. She didn't know what that number was, but even erring on the low side, she estimated about one survivor in ten would have cognitive difficulties and thought disorders. They might have trouble separating reality from fantasy. In some of the worst cases, they would experience paranoid delusions and hallucinations.

Julia just hoped the imagined voices heard by the afflicted didn't tell them to kill everyone on the planet.

She studied her companion in the firelight. His facial features were quite pleasing, despite the strangeness of the golden eyes. His nose was finely shaped and his mouth was full and quick to smile when he knew he'd done well. The aroma of the blond, shoulder-length hair suggested some of the debris entwined there was fecal in nature. Perhaps she could find a delicate way to suggest he clean up a bit before they headed out in the morning. The smell in the Land Rover today would have bothered her more if she hadn't been so focused on the driving conditions getting out of Palo Alto.

"I'm going to pull out my sleeping bag, and I have a blanket under Brains' crate you can use if you don't have one," she said, stretching as she stood by the fire.

"I have my own. I've had it since I was little." He fished a grimy piece of fabric out of his backpack. It was so soiled and ragged she had no idea what it might have originally looked like, and it was woefully inadequate for a night with temperatures in the fifties.

"How about you use both of them? I think it might get a little chilly tonight." She retrieved the sumptuous fleece from the car. The soft, familiar weight of it evoked a pang of sorrow; during the winter months, it had covered the bed she shared with her husband.

"That looks fancy. Are you sure you want me to use it? I'm kind of smelly, I think. I don't want to get your blanket all dirty."

His anxious, troubled expression made her feel petty for having those exact thoughts.

"Don't be silly. You'll need something heavier than the one you have. But now that you mention it, maybe tomorrow morning before we leave, we could both do a little washing up. Plus we need to change the dressing on your shoulder."

"Okay. I don't mind a little washing up. Good night, Julia. Thank you for the blanket."

The young man was asleep a few moments after his head touched the ground.

Sleep was more elusive for her. She contemplated the ramifications of accepting his companionship. To fit the survivor profile, he must fall into the savant category, since he certainly didn't possess a high IQ. That meant that if he was as good with firearms as he and his buddies claimed, he must be quite good indeed. As for neurosis or psychosis, she hadn't seen evidence of either thus far, other than his fixation on magic.

Bringing him along had been the right thing to do under the circumstances. Now if Brains would come back in the morning, she would be feeling cautiously optimistic when they hit the road into Yosemite.

CHAPTER 26

LIBERTY, KANSAS

Six people sat at the kitchen table. Two of those were Steven and his son. The remaining four consisted of Natalie — who had saved him from getting shot by an angry mob minutes earlier — Chuck, the supermarket manager whose hostility was barely held in check, Marilyn, Liberty's former librarian who wore a carefully neutral expression, and Ed the Scarecrow, as Steven had come to think of him. Ed had coached Jeffrey's Little League team two years ago, but he couldn't remember what the man had done for a living before the apocalypse.

"I'd offer you all some coffee and Danish, but I'm fresh out," Steven said, injecting as much sarcasm as possible.

He still seethed at being forced to give away his food. He did have coffee — at least a dozen large cans of French roast beans were stashed in his cellar — but he wasn't going to share them with anyone. When the coffee was gone, it couldn't be replaced. The plants required volcanic soil, and while there were plenty of tornadoes and blizzards in Kansas, there was a marked shortage of volcanoes. Besides, coffee was a luxury, not a necessity.

Natalie had taken on the role of mediator, which suited her well. She had defused the near-explosive showdown at the gate, and so far no bullets had been fired nor punches thrown. Steven wondered how long she could keep up the streak.

She ignored his remark and said, "Let's just all agree to speak at a normal decibel level and keep the personal attacks to a minimum, and perhaps we can come to an equitable solution. Please remember, as in any negotiation, both sides must be willing to compromise."

We'll see about that.

Steven noticed Chuck scrutinizing the tubs of kale and cauliflower placed next to the stacks of mason jars.

"The fruits of our labor. That's what you're looking at. A hell of a lot of work. Right, Jeff?"

His son nodded, pleased to have been included in the grownup discussion. He had more right to sit at that table than any of the townspeople.

"Do you think I'm an idiot, Steven? Of course this isn't all you have. I bet you've got a stash in that bunker in your backyard. A man who has the foresight to install a bunker probably thought to fill it up with food. That's my guess."

Chuck knew about the bunker, which would have required willful surveillance of his property; it was only half-buried, but not visible from the street. The thought of people spying on his property infuriated him.

"I'm also guessing that a man who thought to put in a windmill anticipated there might be a power outage in the foreseeable future. Again, that smacks of the type of man who plans ahead. You see where I'm going with this, Steven? I know you're one of those doomsday prepper types, like on the TV show. The question is, how good of a prepper are you? How much food do you have? Because a lot of really hungry people want to know. Hungry people who have guns." The man's voice never rose and never wavered. His intellect was keener than Steven had originally assumed, a rush to judgment he'd made more than once in his life. Perhaps he had been one of those pedantic jerks.

Hell, maybe he still was.

The man continued. "I'm assuming that a person who has an electrified fence probably has a lot more to protect than just his own ass. What else did you squirrel away besides food? Medicine? Do you know a child in town died last week from pneumonia? A round of antibiotics would have saved her life. Antibiotics that were easy as hell to get before, and now are nowhere to be found within a twenty mile radius. We searched every pharmacy from Salina to Garden City...nothing. So that's the million dollar question: what all are you hoarding that could save the lives of children?"

Steven felt his anger drain away. Images of what these people had been through this past year wormed their way into conscious thought. His ability to compartmentalize had always frustrated his wife; he could fixate on a project or problem, and nothing could breach the mental barrier if it wasn't relevant to the task at hand. That's what he'd been doing for the past year.

And that tunnel vision might have killed a child.

Of course he had antibiotics. After his phone call with Julia, that was the first online purchase he had made. You don't need a doctor's prescription for fish antibiotics, which were exactly the same Amoxicillin and Cipro that, when prescribed for humans, cost ten times more. Pharmaceutical companies realized they could make a few extra bucks by marketing their human drugs to the fish industry without conducting expensive studies and lengthy clinical trials. He also knew that the supposed two-year shelf life was horse shit. FEMA, under the directive of the Department of Defense, had sponsored a study of the efficacy of drugs beyond their expiration dates. They found that ten-year-old antibiotics were nearly as potent as the fresh stuff. Results of that research had been difficult to find in the public domain, but Steven discovered it through his prepper network. The government wanted its citizenry to keep buying new antibiotics. It would seem that Glaxo Smith Kline and Ely Lilly made for cozy bedfellows for senators and congressmen.

Just as with his coffee bean stash, antibiotics could not be replaced. Even though he'd bought more than they would probably ever need, what would happen if he gave them away then had none when Jeffrey came down with a kidney infection, bronchitis, or pneumonia? It was a lightning rod issue in the prepping culture, and Steven had spent many hours debating this exact subject in an online preparedness forum. Just how much of your foresight and hard work should be shared with others? Who is turned away and who reaps the benefit of Steven's money, wisdom, and hard work? Why should he share with people he barely knew or didn't know at all, when it just might come down to his own son doing without later?

He stared hard into the deadly calm eyes of the supermarket manager. In those eyes he saw loss, rage, frustration, grief, and determination.

He sighed. "Okay. What do you propose, Natalie?"

"What I'm not suggesting is that you fling open your doors and allow everyone to storm in and take what they want," she said with a pointed look at the other townspeople. "What I am proposing is that perhaps a designated person — a representative from the town — could inspect your stored items and make suggestions as to what could reasonably be shared with others without depleting your supplies to a level with which you're uncomfortable."

"Let's say I agree to that. Then what? What happens when the food and medicine that I've given away is gone? Another angry mob shows up and demands the rest of it? When does it end?"

"Let's not get ahead of ourselves."

"But that's the crux of it. The reason I have all this stuff is because I did get ahead of myself. I planned and projected and worked, spent every dime I had plus every bit of credit my bank would give me, before the shit hit the fan. It was a huge gamble at the time. I leveraged my son's college education and the future financial security of my family that the world was about to change in an unprecedented and terrifying way. That gamble paid off. The reason you all are in the situation you're in is because you *didn't* do all those things. And now I'm expected to just cover everyone else's ass."

He knew he would help. Of course he would help. But damn it, he was going to bitch about it and resent it every step of the way.

"I propose two representatives from the town participate in this little inspection," Chuck countered, shifting his focus to Natalie. He wore an expression of blatant distrust as he waited for her response.

A flash of anger crossed her features, but vanished so quickly Steven wondered if he'd misread it.

"How do you feel about that, Steven? You can escort Chuck and I...you'll be with us every moment. Does that seem reasonable to you?"

"Let's address the 'what comes after' part before I consent to anything."

For the first time, Marilyn spoke. She exuded universal suspicion and general displeasure, but also a keen intelligence. His wife must have found something redeeming about this woman, aside from a mutual love of books. Or perhaps she had taken pity on a lonely spinster.

"Steven, your concern is well-founded." Her voice was cultured and pleasing, at odds with the dour features. "Like a plague of locusts, we might descend upon your home and clean you out of every last crumb. You are the toiling ant and we are the frivolous, lazy grasshoppers in this extant fable."

He nodded. She nailed it.

"But perhaps you could give us grasshoppers a second chance. Maybe we've learned our lesson? Starvation and hardship will do that to a grasshopper. Perhaps you could see this as an investment opportunity."

If nothing else, this would be interesting.

"Share with us now — not everything you have and not simply food and medicine. Share with us your knowledge along with these material items. Show us how to grow and store our own food and generate electricity through wind power, as you've done. As an engineer, I'm sure you can devise and construct systems similar to yours. Help us learn these things so we can provide for ourselves in the future, rather than be forced to further pillage your stores. And in return, you gain freedom from the burden of this moral dilemma, which so clearly vexes you, as well as the threat of future raids. But along with these benefits, I suggest we reimburse you out of the fruits of our labor next year. A tally should be kept of every jar of green beans, every can of corn, every grain of wheat, so that it can be repaid in full. Am I wrong in presuming you have a seed bank among your stored items? How better to utilize those seeds than in the ground where they can generate more? Share those seeds and your knowledge with us, Steven. Invest in us, and in the long run, you will be the wealthier for it."

It just become clear why his wife had been friends with this woman. He scrutinized the face and demeanor of the former librarian, registering all the truth and sincerity behind her words.

"I agree under one condition," Steven said with a smile. "Chuck will be one of the inspectors and Marilyn will be the other. That is non-negotiable."

The plain woman smiled for the first time that day, transforming her face into something that was still not beautiful, but appealing in its honest candor.

Steven didn't notice Natalie's angry expression because it was covered by a tight-lipped smile by the time he turned back to her. Jeffrey, however, hadn't missed a thing.

***

Three hours later, the only people still sitting at the table were father and son. Steven was drained, not just from the potentially explosive situation at the gate earlier, but also from the lengthy negotiations that came after the inspection of his root cellar and bunker. Chuck hadn't been interested in his weapons stash; firearms were not in short supply. But his eyes had gleamed at the sight of all the glass jars containing pork, chicken, and beef, the hundreds of cans of vegetables, soup, and fish, and the dozens of five-gallon buckets filled with rice, dried beans, and grains.

Steven agreed to give away half of it, which rankled more than he cared to admit to himself. He was saving lives, and he would still have plenty. It was the right thing to do.

The last hour had been surprisingly enjoyable. With input from all the roundtable members, they hammered out a plan to construct an enormous greenhouse in the center of the town square. It would allow seed planting and food production during the dormant cold months, merely weeks away now. It would be a cooperative venture — everyone would work and everyone would reap the rewards. Steven would be the agricultural director until the job could be delegated, freeing him up for engineering projects. The idea of designing and constructing windmills from scratch appealed to his inner nerd, and he would have access to all the free labor he could use. Steven would supply the know-how and the townspeople would provide the muscle.

The first order of business was to get the greenhouse built and the seeds in the ground. Scarecrow Ed's former livelihood had been new home construction specializing in energy efficiency. As he'd sketched out plans on a notepad, Steven immediately knew who their foreman would be. The man's precise freehand rendering of the post-and-rafter design appeared as if it had been done with drafting instruments; his concise explanation of how they would utilize heavy plastic sheeting and bubble wrap for insulation until windmill-powered heat could be provided was genius in its simplicity. Ed knew where to get all the necessary supplies, plus he owned a Ford F250 with a full tank of good gasoline. Later, if the cooperative proved successful, he explained how they could expand the structure and improve it, replacing the sheeting with glass and adding a heated liquid exchange system.

Ed's mannerisms and social skills seemed a little off, but Steven appreciated his cut-to-the-chase delivery, as well as the direct manner in which he addressed all the questions they had thrown at him.

Steven was excited by the prospect of what they could build together. Not just the two of them, but all the survivors in Liberty, which numbered about fifty. They would be building more than a greenhouse and a few windmills — they would be forming a new society where everyone contributed through physical labor and specialized knowledge. No slackers, unless there was a legitimate disability as in the case of Chuck's son Bradley, who suffered from bi-polar disorder. In addition to everything else this past year, Chuck had been contending with the escalating symptoms: obsessional and compulsive behavior, sudden rages, memory issues, and a recent fascination with dead bodies. The man was deeply distressed. They had run out of Lithium several weeks ago, and as with antibiotics, the pharmacies in a twenty mile radius were cleaned out of the drug. He didn't know how he would control the boy, who was the same age as Jeffrey, but who outweighed his classmate by fifty pounds.

It was just one of many problems Steven had learned of during the afternoon, and one for which he could not supply the answer. He had enough on his plate. He would help build their greenhouse, their windmills, and their community.

But he had no desire to lead it.

Chapter 27

Arizona

"Do you want to take a detour and see the Grand Canyon?" Pablo asked Maddie after her introspective silence had exceeded the limits of his patience.

He still didn't know what all she had found in the minivan, other than a dead father and two dead children, but her stoicism during the ordeal had surprised him. He might need to reassess some formerly-held constructs of the woman sitting beside him.

"No, I've seen it and I just want to get to Oklahoma. Do you want to see it?" Her demeanor seemed normal again, but she still held the bulging hippie bag on her lap, her hands resting on it in a way that seemed vaguely proprietary.

"No, I've seen it several times too. We took a few summer vacations there when I was a kid."

"What will we find in Oklahoma besides troublemaking cows and hooligan pigs?" The playful smile was back, thankfully.

"I think we will find green grass and good soil. I'd like to find a little farm somewhere that has a functional well and some fields that don't need too much tilling. Maybe we can corral some misbehaving livestock and make them hand over their milk and bacon."

She laughed. "Oh my god that sounds so good. I haven't had either in three hundred and eighty-nine days."

Pablo knew that was not a random number selected for dramatic effect. In addition to being a math wizard, Maddie also possessed the ability to summon specific dates from her past, recalling where she had been and what she had been doing. This was a talent revealed to him just before the Walgreens incident. In her old life, people found it disturbing if not downright freakish, so she'd learned to hide it. He thought it was fascinating, although somewhat unnerving. He struggled to recall yesterday's lunch.

"We'll just find one of those hoodlum pigs and make him pay for his past misdeeds by handing over his bacon. Do we want maple or apple wood smoked?"

"Smoked. I don't like the maple kind. After we get the bacon, we'll tell the cow to hand over two glasses of cold milk or we'll turn her into a chew toy for Bruno. Who are we going to shake down for some biscuits and gravy?"

"Good question. Perhaps we'll find the Pillsbury Dough Boy running a shell game in a back alley. We'll extort Flaky Layers and Crescent Rolls from the little chubster."

"I wish you hadn't mentioned biscuits," she moaned. "It's been four hundred and seventeen days since I've eaten one."

He smiled. "So what did you find back there, young lady? Are you ready to share with the class?"

The canary-eating cat was back. "I suppose I've made you wait long enough," she said. "I was letting the anticipation build."

"You're slightly evil. I love that. Now tell me. I can't stand the suspense any longer."

"I scored on several fronts." She flipped over the colorful flap and reached in, pulling out a package of M&Ms covered by plastic. "I think this is one of those Food Saver things, like they sell at Costco that sucks out the air then heat-seals the opening."

Pablo's mouth began to water. He hadn't tasted candy in more than a year, and M&Ms were a favorite, as Maddie well knew. They had spent an evening in Prescott discussing the finer points of Belgian chocolate versus Swiss.

"You are an angel sent from heaven," he said.

"You got that right. I'm Cocoarella from Hershey Heaven. But I'm also NoProcreatia, the condom angel from, uh, another part of heaven."

She pulled a second vacuum-sealed packet from her bag with a flourish. It was full of Trojan brand prophylactics.

"Minivan Dad was really into vacuum sealing, as well as not knocking up future Minivan Step Mom."

"That's...interesting. I was hoping for more candy though."

"Trust me. These condoms will be better appreciated in the long run. The last thing we want is little Pablos and Maddies running around."

"Oh."

She stared at him. "What, you want kids? In this world? After what we just saw back there?"

"Well, I'd always envisioned my life with a wife and children. I don't know why that has to change now."

Her expression of disbelief was so exaggerated it would have been comical...under different circumstances.

"I did not just hear you say, 'I don't know why that has to change now.' You can't be serious."

So, this would be the subject of their first serious argument. Might as well get it over with.

"Yes, I'm quite serious. Why should I...we... let these circumstances dictate our choices? I mean, within reason, of course. I'm pretty sure I have to give up my goal of being the United States' first Latino Poet Laureate. But why shouldn't we have children? What better way to say 'screw you' to Chicxulub than by bringing new life into the very world it sought to destroy?"

"For one thing, who knows if the baby that I just spent nine months carrying in my body will contract the disease after she's born? Did you think about that? Can you imagine how painful that would be for both of us?"

Pablo had never considered that possibility. "Whatever kept us from getting it would probably be passed on to our baby. Don't you think?"

"That's quite a gamble, don't *you* think?"

He pondered it for a long moment before answering. "I think it's a gamble we have to take. The future of humanity depends on the remaining humans' ability to procreate. I think we at least have to try."

"Said the man whose contribution to the venture is merely a sperm deposit."

"That's not fair. You know I would be by your side every step of the way, massaging your swollen feet, rubbing cocoa butter on your tummy, fetching you Rocky Road ice cream from 7-11 at three in the morning." He couldn't help smiling. The thought of taking care of a pregnant Maddie was ridiculously appealing.

He saw her anger drain away.

"What happens if there are complications?" she asked, calmer now. "What if the baby is breach and we don't have an obstetrician living on the farm next door? What if she's born with a congenital heart defect? Or Down syndrome? Or spina bifida? Or any number of birth defects that are incredibly difficult to manage under perfect conditions?"

None of those thoughts had ever crossed his mind. His fantasy was one of a plump and healthy Maddie, finishing up a normal pregnancy with the delivery of a healthy, perfect baby.

He wasn't willing to let go of the dream.

"We can 'what if' until the hoodlum cows come home. Life has always been about taking chances...even when it was safer to take those chances. There are no guarantees. The fact that we are still here is a miracle in itself, and maybe it's a sign that we're meant for something even more momentous."

"What, like a New Age Adam and Eve kind of thing? If you think I'm gonna squirt out enough babies to repopulate the world, you need to think again. Have you noticed these narrow hips? This is not a baby factory."

He laughed, relieved that they could at least have a discussion about it. There was wiggle room.

"Let's agree to return to this topic at a later date," he said. "In the meantime, I propose that we utilize Minivan Dad's other, less controversial gift."

"You and your M&M obsession. You're such a girl."

"That's not what you said this morning."

"Touché, sir! You know, M&Ms and condoms aren't the only things I found back there."

"Really? Do tell."

She set aside the candy and reached back into the bag.

"Ta da!" In her hands was a beautiful bottle with a round cork stopper. Inside was liquid sunshine.

"Oh, my..." Pablo only took his eyes off the road for a second, but it was long enough to see the label. "Añejo Patrón?"

"Yes, my good man."

"You truly are an angel."

"I am Agaverina, the tequila angel sent from Drunken Heaven, which by the way, is everyone's favorite part of heaven. Well, except for the Baptists. And they love it too, but only when no other Baptists are looking."

As the sun made a dramatic exit in a swath of orange clouds to the west, they merged onto I40, entering the southern part of the Kaibab National Forest, which skirted the Grand Canyon to the north and south. The plateau stretched for miles until it collided with a ridge of flat-topped mountains. Ponderosa pines, cedars, junipers, and massive oaks created a magnificent sanctuary for a variety of animals. Designated as a wildlife preserve by Teddy Roosevelt in the early 1900s, Pablo knew this was a habitat for deer, cougar, elk, and bald eagles. They followed the sign directing them to DeMotte Park campgrounds, hoping to find a reasonably comfortable place to spread out the sleeping gear and build a fire.

They found something better.

A well-maintained gravel road led to a large rust-colored cabin, nestled against a backdrop of woodlands. Fifty yards to the south lay a sizeable pond and beyond it, a mountain range, the name of which he didn't know.

According to the signage, the lovely Spring Valley Cabin was available for rental through the forest service at a rate of a hundred dollars per day. No pets allowed, and smoking inside was prohibited.

"Did you read that, Bruno? You'll have to sleep and smoke outside," Pablo said, stretching, while the German shepherd sniffed everything in sight.

"Don't listen to him, Bruno. You'll be indoors with us. No bears or bob cats are going to mess with my guys. You did well, my dear," Maddie said, gazing at the tidy structure. "Wonder if there's working plumbing in there?"

"Let's find out." He reached for the twelve-gauge. "What are the chances..."

"The chances are the same as they were when you wanted me to stay in the Jeep back at the minivan."

He sighed. If he'd been more observant, or perhaps less distracted by thoughts of spending the night with Maddie in this charming setting, he would have realized the cedar plank steps leading to the front door had been swept clean of pine needles and dead leaves. He jiggled the handle and found it unlocked.

The door opened with a screech of rusty hardware, too loud in the stillness of early evening. He expected a waft of musty air but instead, he breathed in the homey scent of cinnamon.

He lifted the shotgun.

"That's no way for a guest to behave." The female voice bore a faint, unidentifiable accent. He couldn't see the speaker in the darkened interior.

"You won't need that thing here. There is nothing to fear but a woman and a silly poodle with an under bite and a tendency to pee when she's excited. The poodle, I mean. Although on occasions, the same can be said about the woman."

A match was struck in a far corner, briefly illuminating a dark face framed in white-streaked braids. The flame ignited the wick of an oil lamp and a woman came into view. She could have been forty or sixty in that ageless way unique to people of dark-skinned heritage.

"I'm sorry," Pablo stammered, lowering the gun. Even after the horrors of the past year, manners overrode caution.

"No need. These are dangerous times and your vigilance is wise," the woman said, nodding at Maddie, who peered over Pablo's shoulder. "Welcome to my home. It's mine because nobody else was here. I invoked squatter's rights. My name is Amelia, but I will answer to Stands With

Fists, Pocahontas, Hey You, or anything else as long as it's spoken in friendship."

She stood, which elevated her only a few inches higher than when she'd been sitting. The tiny, ageless woman somehow conveyed the confidence and fearlessness of a much larger person. She scurried around the room lighting oil lamps and candles.

"Come in, come in. The dog is also welcome, despite what it says on the sign. Curly Sue here gets along well with all animals. She particularly likes manly, muscular canines like your boy there. She's a bit of a slut, but no worries...she's been fixed." She indicated the white poodle who watched the activity with mild interest from the comfort of a pallet.

Bruno nudged his way past the humans and trotted over to the poodle, his ears perky and his tail wagging like a furry sailor on a twenty-four hour leave.

Maddie was quick to follow.

"It's a pleasure to meet you, Amelia. I'm Maddie and this is Pablo."

She grasped the childlike hand and smiled into the dark-skinned face, receiving a friendly smile in return. Something passed between the brown eyes and the blue ones — some kind of female thing, perhaps. Pablo trusted Maddie's instincts and he could see she liked the woman. It seemed they would have a comfortable place to sleep that night. The cabin was furnished with rustic pieces that were worn but clean, and judging by the exterior, there would be several bedrooms in addition to the great room where they now stood. The thought of stretching out on an actual bed, no matter how hard or lumpy, was intensely appealing. Especially since he'd be sharing it with Maddie.

"I was just about to light a fire. You two go gather your belongings and I'll see about supper. We can get better acquainted over some warm food. Pablo, I'll need your help later gathering up more wood, if you don't mind. But we have enough for now. Let's get going, people!" she said with a clap of small hands.

Curly Sue yipped, surprised by the sudden human noise, then turned her attention back to her new boyfriend. If dogs could flutter their eyelashes, she would be doing it now. Bruno had a groupie.

An hour later, they sat in front of the stone fireplace with bowls of soup and red Solo cups containing an inch of Patrón. Amelia had been delighted by their contribution to dinner, confessing a weakness for spirits.

"Not that I'm the poster child for alcoholism in the Native American culture, but I do love the occasional snort of tequila. Or whisky. Or rum. You can keep your wine, though. I could never appreciate the subtleties. It all tastes like sour grape juice to me. Give me something that has a kick and some heat. That's what booze should be about." She took a healthy swig from the cup.

Pablo smiled. "How long have you been here, Amelia? I love what you've done with the place."

The small woman snorted. "Yes, you should have seen it when I moved in. Mice had gotten into one of the mattresses, but the others were fine. I dragged it outside and burned it, then did a thorough cleaning of the rest of the place."

Maddie nodded in understanding. "Hantavirus."

"Exactly, young lady," she winked. "After the plague killed my husband, I realized there was nothing keeping me in Peach Springs — the Hualapai Tribe — so I figured I'd see some of the world before my knees gave out. I didn't get far before I found this place and decided to stay a spell." She took a sip of tequila. "It's quite pleasant here, but I'll need to move on soon. I'm down to three cans of pears and half a case of this stuff. I hate to complain with a full belly and a warm fire, but if I never see another can of Campbell's Chicken Noodle soup in my life, I can die happy."

Maddie shot Pablo a pointed look.

Oh no. He knew what that look meant. He responded with a small but firm head shake. She countered with a curt nod, furrowed brows, and tight lips.

He had no intention of allowing a stranger to accompany them. If she were going to insist on this, they would need to know a lot more about this braided dynamo.

"I'm sorry about your husband," Pablo said. "Everyone lost someone. Most people lost everyone. Makes a person wonder what is the meaning of it all? Why did you survive and not your husband? Why me and not my parents? Why Maddie and not her entire family? They never identified the cause of the disease, or at least not that they shared with the public. Is this some kind of cleansing? A metaphorical flood wrought by God or Mother Nature? Or more likely, some white-coated bastards in a lab somewhere. We'll never know, which pisses me off. I'd like to know, wouldn't you?"

Amelia's dark eyes studied him in the firelight. When she spoke, her voice was soft and oddly tender.

"Why would it matter, Pablo? Would you do anything differently if you knew all the answers?"

"It wouldn't change my actions or my plans for the future, but it would alter how I view human life...our existence on this planet. Surely our big brains were meant for loftier purposes than building skyscrapers and launching satellites. It's what separates us from the lower species, the ability to ask such questions of ourselves. What does it all mean? Why are we here? Is there something after here? Why does it make a difference if I help this man with a flat tire, or mow the lawn of this elderly lady living alone, or steal this dog from the backyard of a neighbor because his owners leave him chained up outside all day with no food or water?" He glanced at Bruno who was oblivious to everything except Curly Sue.

Maddie smiled.

"Would you stop doing any of those things if you knew how the illness started?" Amelia asked. "I think not. You would continue being a good person because that is who you are."

"Not everyone who survived is a good person. We know that firsthand."

"Yes, that is true. And maybe someday the mystery will be solved for you, Pablo. Or maybe not. But don't you find our new reality compelling? Everything is straightforward now, reduced to its simplest form: survive, and either do so in a way that will not harm others, or in a way that might or will harm others. If there is a divine being who is judging us, would you behave differently? Or would you do the right thing because it is the right thing, even if no one is watching? Perhaps that's all that matters in the end."

"I think there's more to it than that," Maddie said. "I think we're supposed to find out what we're made of...who we are, how much we can bear. In what ways will we allow cruelty and adversity, generosity and compassion to shape us? Will we be bitter and angry, or stronger and more determined to overcome the challenges? Will we become more loving and kind, or will we build walls around our hearts so nothing can hurt us?"

"I think you've experienced a bit of all that, young lady." She reached over and squeezed Maddie's hand.

"Amelia, what did you do before? What was your life like?" Pablo asked.

The woman took a healthy sip of the tequila, then gave him a level look. "I was a midwife. And a damned good one."

Chapter 28

Texas

The man on the other side of the glass storefront — presumably Bill of 'Bill's Guns' — pointed an assault rifle at Dani's head. She held her hands up, just as Sam and Fergus were doing. Bill was a grizzled, mean-looking SOB in his sixties, with tufts of gray poking out below a baseball cap bearing the image of a coiled rattlesnake and a caption that read *DON'T TREAD ON ME*. Dani could imagine him hollering at the neighborhood kids to get off his lawn.

"What now?" she asked.

"We have two choices," Fergus said, his lips showing little movement in the bearded face. "We run like hell, probably getting killed in the process, or we try to reason with this man who seems to have taken a sudden dislike to us. Why don't you give it a shot, Miss Congeniality?"

Before she had a chance to formulate a response, Sam spoke, raising his voice to be heard through the glass.

"Sir, we mean you no harm or disrespect. We didn't know there was anybody here and we were hoping to find some guns to protect us against jerks like the ones who just tried to kill us. I think they were Democrats!"

A few painful seconds ticked by. Finally, the man shifted the business end of his weapon. It was now pointing at a kneecap rather than her forehead.

"One of them was wearing a Hillary 2016 t-shirt, and two other guys were holding hands. Makes me sick! Anyway, they were shooting at us like crazy, so we figured we needed to get some guns too. Just to level the playing stadium."

If there hadn't been a weapon pointed at her that looked like something Jason Bourne would carry, she would have burst out laughing. Where the hell did Sam come up with this? And why?

The man lowered his rifle further.

Out of the side of his mouth, Fergus whispered, "You might want to pick your jaw up off the sidewalk, girly, and thank Sam for saving your bacon...again."

"Any of you ever use a firearm before?" the man hollered through the glass.

"No, sir!" Sam yelled. "My dad wouldn't allow it even though my brothers and me all wanted to. He wouldn't even let us have a BB gun. He voted for Obama...twice!"

Dani knew for a fact that Sam's father had passed when he was quite young, and his mother had been left to raise four boys all by herself.

"What about you there?"

"I used a Colt M16A2, 5.56 caliber in the Gulf War. Does that qualify?" Fergus said, with a discreet wink in Dani's direction.

The man nodded, then turned the deadbolt on the front door.

"Get on in here," he growled, waving them in. "I'm Bill. This is my store," he continued, not bothering to see if they were behind him as he walked away. He opened a door in the back wall of the retail space and stepped through. Without hesitation, Sam followed. Dani glanced back, the question obvious on her face: *Do we trust this guy?*

Fergus shrugged. *Guess so.*

The stockroom was illuminated in the unnatural light of a battery operated lantern. As a second one was turned on, the contents of the room were fully revealed.

It might have been Charlton Heston's gun vault.

"Quite a selection you have here, Bill. I'm Fergus. It's a pleasure to make your acquaintance." He extended his hand to the older man, who grasped it in his own with an air of grudging acceptance.

"This here is Sam and that's Dani. She's got a mouth on her, so please don't hold that against Sam and me. Product of an entitled upbringing, no doubt."

The man grunted and shot her a squinting glance of disgust before dismissing her. She was about to respond, but was cut off by the pain of Fergus's boot connecting with her shin.

The message was clear. Her female opinion was not welcome here. She wanted to get her hands on some of that firepower slightly more than she wanted to utter the caustic remark hovering on the tip of her tongue.

"If you can handle an M16 then you can handle this bad boy." The man reached for a lethal-looking firearm, removing it from the peg board where it was displayed.

"Ah, the AR15," Fergus said, careful to exude equal parts enthusiasm and reverence.

"Yep. It's well-made and accurate. Not great for hunting, but it should get the job done if you're lookin' to kill some liberals," he smirked. "For Sam here, I think the Mossberg 500 Pump Action would be best. Just pump it, aim it, and pow. If those libs are within fifty yards, they're dead libs."

Fergus snorted. "Agreed, Bill. I think that's a fine choice. What about the girl there?" He indicated Dani with a disdainful gesture. Even though she understood the situational dynamics, it didn't mean she had to like it. Later, she intended to unleash the full fury of her irritation on the little man.

"You wanna give a firearm to a girl?" The contempt in the man's voice was as thick as a testosterone fog at a gun show.

Before she could spout off with a poorly-timed remark, Sam spoke. "We're worried about her being able to take care of herself, you know, if something happens to Fergus and me." The sincerity in Sam's voice was genuine. He would worry about her if she were dipped in Kevlar and had flamethrowers for hands.

"Yeah, yeah. Okay, something for the *lady*..."

She gave him a tight smile. Bill of Bill's Guns was a misogynistic dick.

"I think this little Taurus .32 caliber would be good enough for her. Don't want the kick to knock her on her ass," he said with a loud guffaw, amused by the thought of Dani on her backside. She was probably pregnant and barefoot in the fantasy as well. Her fingers twitched near the sheathed K-Bar.

"What about that Colt you got there, Bill?" Fergus asked quickly. "She's strong for a girl. I think she could handle it."

The man scowled, but reached for the revolver.

Dani smiled. Now there was a thing of beauty.

"It's an 1873 Cattleman, single action, engraved stainless steel with a mother-of-pearl grip. It also comes in a .357 and a .44 mag. Sold out of those before the shit hit the fan. This one's a .45. Pretty, ain't she? This here's my last one," he said, giving her a baleful look.

She responded with her best fuck-you grin.

"Bill, you'd be doing us a world of good. And of course, we're willing to trade."

Sudden interest gleamed in the shit-brown eyes.

"What ya got that I might want? These are worth over five grand, not that that matters anymore."

"We don't have much to offer. We've barely enough food between us to last the next two days," Fergus lied smoothly. They had enough to last a couple of weeks, thanks to Dani's careful planning. It would be painful to part with any of it though, even if they scored guns in the bargain.

"How about the Mossy, the AR15, and your Colt there, for *my* Colt." From an interior pocket deep within the army jacket, he withdrew a tiny battered weapon the size of child's hand.

The store owner's eyes came dangerously close to popping out of his head. "Is that the first model Remington derringer?"

Fergus grinned. "Yep. Rimfire, single shot, two and a half inch barrel. Cute little thing, isn't it?"

"I been trying to get my hands on one of those for years."

"I hate to part with it, but to be honest, it doesn't pack much of a punch."

The man guffawed again. Dani imagined the laughter changing to a wet gurgle as she sliced his throat.

"We got us a deal!"

"A few boxes of ammo for each, Bill? Just to be neighborly?"

"Yeah, yeah. I got plenty. I'll probably be dead long before I go through it anyway."

An hour later, they were ten miles farther north on I35 and ten miles away from Bill of Bill's Guns, which made Dani happy. The added weight of the firearms and ammunition slowed their progress, but it was a price they gladly paid. The highway had become less congested, which meant they could switch to a motorized method of transportation if they could find something suitable.

"I saw a sign for an outlet mall coming up," she yelled back at Fergus. "I bet we could find a place to stay for the night."

"Sounds good to me! My ass is killing me. I feel like the new boy in cell block 4!"

Soon after, the threesome pedaled into the parking lot of a large mall. Dani had never been to it before, mostly because she hated shopping, shopping malls, and shopping mall shoppers.

The sun hung low on the horizon. The mental and physical demands of the day made her more weary than she'd ever felt. Everything ached, but her backside was particularly agonizing. This bicycling nonsense was for the birds. She would figure out a way to tell Sam that it was time to trade in their kinetic two-wheeled transportation for four wheels powered by long-dead dinosaurs.

The sight of a Super 8 motel sign just past the bulk of the shopping center filled her with joy.

"Screw camping. Let's check in there for the night."

Fergus moaned, "Ugh, another half mile. My derriere can't handle this abuse!"

"Suck it up, sissy boy. We'll be sleeping in beds tonight."

The two-story building was painted a garish yellow but otherwise appeared promising. There were no signs of vandalism and no busted-out windows were visible from the parking lot where they now stood.

"Should we try to get the keys from the lobby?"

"Wouldn't do any good, Sam," Fergus replied. "Everything is electronic key cards these days. We'll have to break in. Which room strikes your fancy, girly? 101 or 201? Are you an upstairs or a downstairs kind of girl?" The bushy red eyebrows waggled.

"I'm a whatever takes the least amount of energy kind of girl. What will we do? Bust the window or the doorknob?"

"The window, I think." He took the butt of the new assault rifle and broke the glass pane of room 101, then did the same next door.

"Two rooms or three?" he asked. The red beard twitched.

"Three," she said. "We're just friends, if that's what you want to know."

Sam suddenly became interested in a crow flying overhead.

"None of my business. I'm just doing my job here." He busted a third window.

Dani reached for the lock through the broken glass. Moments later, she was inside. Her flashlight revealed a tidy room with a king size bed. The bed was adorned with a horrendous gold bedspread, but the pillows looked good enough to eat. She opened the door and stepped out into the cool October evening. Sam and Fergus still stood there, looking like little boys caught peeing on the neighbor's rosebush.

"What's going on here, guys?"

"Nothing," Sam said, not meeting her eyes. "We were just talking about supper and maybe starting a fire."

"Really? You look guilty. What was with all that BS earlier? The democrat thing and the story about your dad? How did you know it would soften up that sexist jerk so well? Pretty quick thinking, my friend."

He smiled, happy to change the subject. The setting sun created a golden halo around his face, and the sweet shit-eating grin was adorable. As she watched his animated face, her eyes slid to the tight-fitting t-shirt he wore, noting how it defined the contours of his chest and shoulder muscles. While he talked, her gaze fluttered down to his cargo pants. She became alarmed when she realized she'd just been wondering what her best friend looked like without his clothes.

She hoped the warmth that flooded her cheeks wasn't too visible in the dimming light.

"I knew a guy once who was just like Bill. He was a big gun lover and hated everyone who wasn't just like himself, especially Democrats and mouthy women." Sam's grin went from cute to gleeful, as he waited for Dani's reaction.

She punched him in the arm, harder than she'd intended to, perhaps retaliating for more than just the remark. The last thing she needed was to develop feelings for Sam. It would make everything more complicated.

"Dang, Dani. You hit hard."

With an evil smirk, she watched him rub the injured arm, noticing his long, tapered fingers as they wrapped around the bicep.

Oh my god, stop it!

"Okay," she said quickly, banishing further unwelcome thoughts. "What's the deal with dinner? Are we going to build a bonfire so every crazy gun store owner and Hillary-loving liberal within a five mile radius can spot us?"

Fergus snorted. "How about a discreet fire in a metal trashcan? Just enough to take the chill off our splendid cuisine."

She nodded. "And don't forget, you owe us The Story of Fergus. You gave your word."

"Fine, fine."

An hour later, they had a small blaze going in a barbecue grill at the back of the hotel property. Night had fallen, and three foil packets warmed on the rusty grate. A portable battery-operated lantern cast just enough light to see by.

They sat at a wooden picnic table next to the grill, each holding a plastic hotel cup filled with one finger of whiskey. Fergus had produced the flask from the interior of his army-green jacket. Dani had begun to wonder if it were some sort of sartorial TARDIS...roomier on the inside than it appeared on the outside.

"Is this a magic coat?" She tugged his sleeve with a sly smile. "Are you a mythical creature from the Old Country who hordes gold and grants wishes?"

"If I were, I'd be six foot two, have an enormous dong, and golden hair like Sam's that all the women would want to run their fingers through."

"Fair enough. So, let's hear it then."

The small man gave a dramatic sigh. "You're like a honey badger. You get your teeth into something and never let go."

She nodded.

"Well then, since we don't have all night and I'm dog tired, I'll make it quick. You're half right. My great grandparents emigrated from Ireland, thus the red hair and unfortunate name. 'Fergus' and my diminutive size were two things the playground bullies couldn't resist. So after high school, I joined the military to learn a trade and also how to kick ass, which I did. I can't give you any details about my service because then I would have to kill you. Top secret, black ops shit." He winked at Sam, who was happy to be the one-member audience at the Fergus and Dani show.

"I knew it was something like that! So, you're one of those badass dudes? Navy SEAL? Army Ranger?"

"Correction, *was* one of those badass dudes."

"What did you do after?"

"I did what most people with a certain specialized skill set do after they're discharged. I started a private security company."

"What about family? Wife? Tiny offspring?"

Fergus snorted. "You are relentless. It's a good thing I have thick skin and have taken a liking to you. Yes, I was married for ten years, until she decided to run off with her tennis instructor. How's that for a sad cliché?"

"Oh, I'm so sorry. That must have been painful," Sam said.

"Not as painful as giving her half of everything I'd been working for while she lunched with the girls and screwed Santiago."

"She sounds like a real bitch," Dani said.

"Yes, she was indeed, but she had perfect tits and a fanny you could bounce a dime off."

Dani laughed. "You're such a pig."

"That I am, but I'm a charming pig."

"So that's it? The Story of Fergus seems suspiciously succinct. What are you leaving out, little man?"

"Sorry to disappoint, Honey Badger. I'm afraid to say that I'm just not as fascinating as you'd like me to be. Trust me, I wish I were."

"Okay. I have just one more question: How do you get your hair to do that?"

He feigned a wounded expression.

"My hair is lovely! You are a hard woman, Dani whateveryourlastnameis. I'll have you know I cultivated this unique look. It's no accident that I have a personal style not soon forgotten. This stunning coif coupled with quiet confidence and backed by mad skills made me a rich man back in the day."

"I'm sure all that's true, but perhaps it's time to embrace a new style...one that whispers 'please don't notice me, all you would-be murderers' instead of one that screams 'I have issues and want to stand out in a crowd which would require the use of a step stool.'"

"I will make you pay for that, missy. I don't know how and I don't know when, but you can take that to the pot of gold at the end of the rainbow."

Dinner was soon over and the exhausted trio stumbled to their rooms.

Dani woke up some time later in her darkened motel room, disoriented and foggy, with the impression that a noise had roused her from sleep. Her fingers fumbled for the K-Bar which she always kept within reach. An icy wave washed over her when she realized it was gone.

A familiar, deep honeyed voice said, "Looking for your knife?"

She didn't have to see the face to know who it belonged to. She closed her eyes tight against the inevitable flashlight beam which illuminated her the next moment.

"Yes, Isaiah, and I'd like it back, please." She forced herself to remain calm while her mind raced. Did they have Sam and Fergus? Had they found the loaded Cattleman in the bedside table?

"If you're wondering about your toys, we were compelled to confiscate them. Such a bad girl doesn't deserve to have nice things."

Her eyelids were still clamped shut but she could imagine the toothy grin.

She was in a world of trouble.

"Poor Sam, he put up quite a fight."

Dani's heart leaped to her throat.

"What have you done with him, you son of a bitch?" she hissed.

Isaiah made a clicking sound of disapproval. "Such language. I find it coarse and offensive. I think I shall forbid such vulgar verbiage in my empire. I envision a polite, refined society where words are used like the scalpel of a skillful surgeon rather than the cudgel of a clumsy cretin."

Jesus. Again with the alliteration.

"If you've hurt him, I will cudgel your crazy fucking cranium until it's caved fucking in."

The deep laughter resonated in the small room.

"I can appreciate crudity when it's cleverly conveyed."

Dani imagined the obsidian eyes glowing with insanity. Hers remained closed.

Isaiah's demeanor changed to one of brusque impatience. "Your gentleman friend is not dead, but if you don't behave, I can assure you he will become that way quite soon. Put your hands above your head and stand up slowly. Any sudden movements will not only result in your untimely demise but Sam's as well. Hurry now. We have other business to attend to on this night."

She had no choice. She did as instructed, as her mind rifled through a dozen possible escape scenarios, all of which ended in the evisceration of this psychopath.

She felt her arms being jerked down in front of her while a second person zip-tied her wrists together. Someone turned off the flashlight. She opened her eyes as she was pushed through the motel door and out into a night in which starlight was obscured by scuttling clouds.

Sam stood nearby, his wrists also bound by zip ties. Three bland-faced followers held him. The only way they could have accomplished this was by catching him asleep. One of his eyes was beginning to swell shut, and blood, which appeared oily and brown in the darkness, was smeared on his face. At the sight of his injuries, a cold rage blossomed in Dani's chest. Frantic thoughts coalesced into lethally focused, strategic calculations.

Where the hell was Fergus?

That mystery wasn't allowed to intrude for long. She would handle this fine without him.

Isaiah spoke, "You disappoint me so. I thought we had an understanding. What a shame. Well, there is only one way to deal with deserters, and I feel certain you can guess what that might be. But first, you must tell me the location of your other companion. Someone was in the room next to Sam's, but he is no longer there. Tell me where he is and my soldiers will give you a quick death. If you're uncooperative, it will be protracted and painful."

Dani refused to allow the verbal theatrics to infringe on her heightened state of concentration.

"We don't know where he is." Sam had trouble formulating words with lips that were swelling as badly as his eye.

She took deep, cleansing breaths.

"Tsk, tsk. I had a feeling that might be your answer," he said, then slammed his fist into Sam's stomach. Her best friend doubled over with a groan.

She watched, blocking an emotional response and willing her rage to stay cold.

"What do you say, Dani? Do you know where this mysterious third person is?"

"You know, you're not as clever as you think you are," she said, her voice measured and calm. She kept her eyes on Sam as she spoke. He stood as straightly as his tender belly would permit, and returned her gaze with the tiniest of nods.

Isaiah took the bait. The most effective way to prevail in an encounter such as this was to make the other person angry and therefore careless. The best way to anger a narcissistic sociopath was to question his intelligence.

"What is that supposed to mean, young lady? Who are the captives here?"

"You made three fatal errors, dumbass. Seriously, I thought you were way smarter, you big douche bag."

The honeyed voice was gone. "How dare you, you little bitch!"

The fury in his voice made her smile.

She moved like a viper, raising her wrists above her head and then slamming them in a downward motion toward and against her torso. The plastic snapped. Sam's action mirrored hers a half second later.

The rest was just a matter of using the element of surprise, exhaustive martial arts training, and the fact that she could see more clearly in the dark than her assailants, whose night vision had been compromised by the flashlight.

None of them were expecting the shit storm of fists-to-throats and boots-to-groins that followed. Even injured, Sam took down all three of his captors — two young males and a middle-aged female — and had a knife pressed against Isaiah's neck by the time Dani had dealt with her two. Five people lay on the pavement in various states of agony or unconsciousness.

Sam was a damn ninja. She'd known it, but Isaiah hadn't.

There was no smile on his face now, and the eyes glowed with malevolence and madness.

"First, you underestimated your opponents. I can only assume you did so because we chose not to fight you in Colleyville."

The dark eyes narrowed. Sam shifted the blade more firmly against Isaiah's throat. A few wet drops bubbled out below it. The sight warmed her heart.

"Second, you tied our wrists in the front. Granted, we could have escaped even with our hands bound from the back, but it would have taken us longer and therefore diminished our chances of prevailing. We've practiced the zip tie snap countless times. I think you could say we have it down."

She grinned at his expression of sheer loathing.

"Third, you let your eyes lose their night vision. It was a stupid mistake and frankly...disappointing. I expected, I don't know, more of a challenge from you. Tsk, tsk."

She punched him in the stomach just as he'd done to Sam minutes before. When he bent over from the blow, she forced his head down to the pavement with her foot.

A familiar voice called out of the dark. "Have I missed all the fun?" Fergus walked toward them gripping the enormous machete-like knife.

"Where the hell have you been?"

"Couldn't sleep. Went for a little walkabout. Next thing I know, I hear the distinct thud of falling bodies. Looks like you two handled the situation without my help though. Remind me not to piss you off." He contemplated the man on the asphalt, who remained motionless with Dani's foot pinning the back of his neck.

"Your timing sucks. Secure these assholes. You'll find zip ties in their gear somewhere. Put their arms behind their backs."

"Happy to oblige."

"Now, what to do with this crazy bastard?" She shifted more weight onto the vulnerable neck. "I'm thinking *protracted* and *painful.* He's a history buff, so maybe something medieval like a good old draw and quartering. Wonder if we can get our hands on four sturdy horses?"

Fergus snorted.

"Do you happen to have a Pear of Anguish in your magical jacket, Lucky Charms?" she said to Fergus, striking a conversational tone.

Isaiah growled in frustration.

"I see you're acquainted with that devilishly delightful device."

"What's a Pear of Anguish?" Sam asked, but through his swollen lips it came out: *Waz a paw of angwiz?*

Dani smiled as she pondered the misery she would inflict on the person responsible for those injuries.

Nobody hurt Sam.

"Imagine a metal, pear-shaped object comprised of several sections with a large screw at the top. It was inserted into the vaginas of women who performed abortions and into the mouths of liars and blasphemers. Homosexuals got it in the anus. The gadget would be unscrewed, slowly spreading apart inside the orifice, causing extreme pain, mutilation, and for some, really messy future bowel movements."

Fergus guffawed. "Honey Badger, you are a gem."

"I don't think we should torture him," Sam said.

"Fine, we'll just kill him then."

"I don't think we should do that either. Can't we just leave him here?"

"What? Why?" she said, raising her voice. "So he and his Nazi youth can come after us again? So we'll always have to worry about this asshole popping up? I don't want to be looking over my shoulder every minute while we're planting corn with Dorothy and Toto."

"Killing him makes us just as bad."

Damn it. She hated when he played the personal integrity card.

"You're killing *me*."

"I'm sorry, Dani, but you know I'm right. We're better than this."

Fergus watched the exchange like it was a Hollywood thriller.

"Fine. Zip tie him. And don't be gentle."

In the process of binding Isaiah's arms behind his back, they also secured him to a concrete pillar at the corner of the building.

"You will pay for this."

His former dulcet tone was back. She suspected Isaiah was internalizing his rage just as she had done minutes earlier. She knew it was foolhardy to let him live, but executing him would do irrevocable damage to her relationship with Sam. She toyed with the idea of coming back later, but couldn't make the logistics work. They had been like an old married couple this past year; he would know what she was doing if she tried to ditch him for a few hours.

She squatted down to the eye level of her enemy. He sat on the sidewalk with his hands behind him, twenty feet of braided nylon securing him to the post.

"You are alive for one reason," she said, gunslinger's eyes staring deep into obsidian madness. "It is because my friend has a heart disproportionate to his body. You get one pass. Come after us again and I will slice you up like Han Solo gutting a Tauntaun."

Sudden laughter flowed over her, rich and genuine. Charlie Manson eyes sparkled in the dark face.

"You spoke of fatal errors. This one is yours, young lady."

She held his gaze for a dozen heartbeats, then stood, turning her back on the captive, and walked away.

Minutes later they discovered Isaiah's means of transportation: four horses were tethered to a copse of bald cypress trees near the mall entrance. She laughed at the coincidence of finding the tools needed for her drawing and quartering. For a long moment she basked in the fantasy of seeing Isaiah ripped apart...watched his bloody bits galloping away in four different directions.

It was probably fortunate that her equine knowledge amounted to a big goose egg. Horses were not what they needed anyway. It would be too easy to fall off and break an arm, leg or neck. Plus they required food and water. She'd never ridden one in her life and she wouldn't start now. Fergus seemed to know his way around the animals though. He had the saddles and tack removed within ten minutes. A slap to the rump of a gray mare sent all four off at a dead run.

Shades of violet brushed the eastern horizon. Their backpacks were heavier than before from the added weight of the supplies they'd taken from the saddlebags. What they couldn't carry, they disposed of in a dumpster behind a Gap Outlet store a block away. They left a few bottles of water back at the motel, nothing more. The water had been Sam's idea.

They pedaled to a stop at the I35 entrance ramp. Vehicles were positioned like toy cars scattered by a careless child, but not as glutted here as they had been just outside of Dallas. Dani could see a clear path between them. The next moment she made a decision without asking for input from her companions.

"The next order of business is to find a pickup truck. No arguments."

Sam and Fergus exchanged conspiratorial smiles.

Sam rolled up beside her, leaned over, and kissed her cheek with bruised, puffy lips. "Sounds great. Let's get this show on the highway!"

Chapter 29

Yosemite

"This stuff cleans your hair without water and soap?" Logan's skepticism was evident as he studied the gold can Julia had given him.

The sun's first rays crept above the Sawtooth Ridge. She sat cross-legged on her sleeping bag, warming her face in the morning light.

"Yes. Just spray it on and leave it for a few minutes. The ingredients absorb the oil and dirt on your scalp and hair. Then use the brush I gave you."

She had an extra one, thankfully. Using the same brush after him was not an option. The dry shampoo had been her idea, not her brother's. Realizing how critical water conservation would be, she'd bought several cans of it along with everything else before sequestering herself in the lab at Stanford.

Logan went about the business of grooming while she rummaged through the food bin.

"Do you want apple cinnamon or brown sugar and maple cereal?"

"You pick, Julia. Either is fine with me."

He certainly is easygoing, she thought with a smile. They had passed a pleasant evening the night before, despite her worry over Brains' continued absence. She'd slept like the dead, only waking once during the night to see him adding more wood to the campfire and stoking it with a stick designated for the task. That fire had likely discouraged predators and allowed her to get the rest she needed.

"Should I put it out now?"

After using the wet wipes on his face and the brush on his hair, she was surprised to realize there was a handsome young man under all that grime.

"Yes, that's an excellent idea. I'm going to try one more time to find Brains and then we'll just have to leave without him."

The thought of abandoning her furry companion distressed her more than she wanted to admit. Stupid cat. He'd probably gotten himself eaten by a bear or a mountain lion.

"I bet you'll find him!" he said, dumping handfuls of soil and loose rock on the embers.

She hiked over to the tree line without much hope, so when she heard the familiar meow answering her calls, a giddy laugh escaped her.

An orange blur leaped out of the forest and into her arms. The little shit was alive, and except for a few nettles and twigs stuck to his fur, he appeared unscathed.

"Damn it, Brains, don't ever do that again. No more night adventuring for you. I'm going to make a kitty leash and you're not getting out of my sight until we're in Kansas." She rubbed the soft head.

As she carried him back to their camp, Logan glanced up. A slow smile spread across his face.

"I told you he'd be fine. Are you happy now?" The earnest question struck her as odd, but perhaps her anxiety about the cat had distressed the young man.

"Yes, I'm happy. I would have felt terrible if we'd had to leave him here. It would have upset me. I didn't realize how attached I've become to this furball."

"Yes, that's what I thought. I'm glad he's okay because I don't want you to be upset."

"Thank you. That's sweet of you to say. Let's have our breakfast, put some gas in the tank, and hit the road."

"That sounds great!"

The entrance she'd chosen through Yosemite on State Route 120 was the higher elevation passage, but shorter than the 140 approach to the south. She was gambling that in October snow would not be an issue, and judging by the cloudless sky and the mild temperature, she'd made the right decision. She hoped to be through the park and at least to Tonopah, Nevada, within a few hours. They might even make it to Utah before nightfall if they didn't have any delays.

State Route 120 was a serpentine two-lane highway with breathtaking views of the western ridge of the Sierra Nevadas, Yosemite Valley, and eventually Mono Lake, which Julia had decided she'd like to see. A year ago when she and Steven had been devising their plan and plotting her course, she'd come across the online images of the eerily beautiful Tufa Towers — finger-like limestone formations which extended skyward out of the salt lake. She promised herself the small reward of seeing them, if possible.

An hour later, they stopped at Crane Flat Lookout so Logan could take in the spectacular scenery.

"I'm King of the World!" he yelled when he got to the top of the wooden structure.

His voice sounded loud in the quiet surroundings. Julia had been smiling until the shout pierced the tranquility, announcing their presence to predators...both animal and human.

"Logan, we should get going now."

"But we just got here." A petulant child's voice came from above.

She took a deep breath. "I know, but we have a lot of miles to cover today, and I don't think it's a good idea to be so loud. We don't know who or what might hear us and decide we'd make a good dinner."

The instant remorse was evident even from thirty feet below. "I'm sorry, Julia. I didn't think about that. I'm coming down now. Please don't be mad."

Twenty seconds later he stood before her wearing a contrite expression.

"I promise I won't be loud again. I hope you're not mad at me."

"Of course I'm not mad at you. Let's just remember that we're not the only ones still around, and some of the people who are left may not be very nice. You probably encountered some this past year."

He nodded.

"Plus, we're in the wilderness, and this is the natural habitat for bears and mountain lions and other large predators that could make a quick meal of tender morsels like us."

"Ha! That's funny. Tender morsels sounds like cat food."

"We'd look as appealing to a hungry bear as an open can of Tender Morsels would to Brains. Do you understand about the wild animals and the not-so-nice humans and how we need to be as quiet as possible?"

He nodded again, the contrition vanished. She wondered if he truly understood the dangers they faced.

A half hour later, as they continued their easterly route through Yosemite, Logan became silent and withdrawn. He was observing the magnificent scenery through the window of the Land Rover, but the images didn't seem to be making the journey to conscious thought.

"What are you thinking about? Is your shoulder bothering you?"

His gaze shifted from the passing landscape to her. He seemed to be analyzing her in a detached, clinical manner — a doctor scrutinizing the x-ray of an unknown patient.

She felt a pang of unease. He seemed so strange suddenly, no longer the ebullient boy of the last twenty-four hours.

"I could shoot that bear, you know," he said, ignoring her question. "I'm very good with my guns. Everybody said so."

Ah. There it was. She had insulted him by implying he couldn't defend himself.

"I know you are. I'm sorry to have suggested that you can't take care of yourself. I just worry because the world is a dangerous place now. I don't want anything bad to happen to you or me or Brains."

"The only reason Rachel was able to shoot me back at the golf place was because I had let-my-guard-down. It doesn't mean she's better than me. I've shot a lot of things, and I've never missed what I was aiming for. Never. Not once. Besides, nothing bad will happen to us if you don't let it happen. I know you can do that, Julia. You can see me. You have magic. So you can keep the bad things from happening if you really want to."

The golden eyes bored into her. She fidgeted in the driver's seat as she navigated the road, unsettled now by his tone and demeanor which seemed to convey a challenge...perhaps even a threat. Brains growled in the back seat. She thought furiously for a few heartbeats, then replied.

"Magic is not an exact art. Unexpected things can occur and there are many factors which can affect the outcome of any situation. It is best not to question what I can and cannot control."

She realized she was holding her breath.

Logan wordlessly studied her for at least the next half mile. "Okay. I won't," he said finally.

And that was it. The smile returned, the enthusiastic boy was back, and the eerie undercurrent was gone, like it had never existed.

"How much farther until we get to the lake with the fingers?"

What had just happened?

Sitting next to her in the passenger seat was the young man she'd spent the past day with. His behavior was as boyish and unaffected now as it had been all along; he was even humming a tune and patting his knee in time to whatever music he heard in his head. But for a few moments back there, he had scared the daylights out of her. Had she made a huge mistake by bringing him, or was she overreacting to this recent episode? He seemed normal now. Her allusion to possessing magical power had felt necessary at the time...had felt like her life depended on perpetuating his belief that she had it.

What the hell had she gotten herself into? Was she in danger? Should she find a way to ditch this young man, or was she blowing the event way out of proportion?

"I made something for you, Julia. When you were asleep last night. I woke up a lot because I was worried about the fire going out." He dug into the pocket of his jeans and pulled out some braided twine.

"It's a bracelet. My mom taught me how to make these. She said it was good to keep me busy with stuff. Busy hands are happy hands. That's what she told me. I made a bunch of them for her in all different colors, but I only had this one color for yours. I hope you like it."

He tied the friendship bracelet to her right wrist as she drove. She took her eyes off the road long enough to glance at it, then at the childlike happiness of the young man who had given it to her.

"It's beautiful. I love it. Thank you." She patted his knee.

He grinned. "You're welcome. I'll make you prettier ones if I can find some better string. Do you think there are any Craft Depot stores around here? That's where my mom took me to buy the colored string."

"I don't think so. It's a national park, which means the only stores would be the souvenir type, and perhaps some gas stations. We'll keep an eye out for signs, though. It would be fun to have a souvenir of our adventure in Yosemite."

"Yes! That would be great. I'll keep-an-eye-out."

They were driving on the Tioga Road section of 120 at an elevation of almost 10,000 feet. Julia had to concentrate on the winding pavement which dropped off abruptly. Skidding off this road would make for a horrific, extended plummet. The mild weather had held; she couldn't imagine navigating the road if it were icy or piled with snow. She was so absorbed now with the white-knuckled drive that the young man's odd behavior was pushed to the back of her mind. She would deal with it later.

Two hours later signs for Mono Lake began to appear on the side of the road. The terrain had leveled out now, and after a quick northerly jaunt on 395, they arrived.

"There it is! There are the fingers!"

The scenery was even eerier than it had appeared in the online images. They pulled into a parking lot adjacent to the lake. Logan jumped out the moment they came to a stop and ran to the water's edge.

Tufts of wispy clouds threaded their way across the brilliant blue sky, creating the perfect backdrop for the remarkable scene. Like remnants of gothic sand castles, the limestone formations jutted out of the water and reached toward the heavens. Their strange beauty and the solitude of the place filled her with a sudden, undefined melancholy. She didn't realize she was crying until Logan's hand slid shyly around hers.

"It'll be okay, Julia. I think this is a sad place. Do you think a princess lived in those rocks? Maybe she was waiting for her prince to come rescue her, and when he never came, she died of a broken heart. It feels sad here because her sadness was so big, it had to go somewhere when she died. That's what I think, anyway."

She wiped at her tears and looked at the young man, wondering how she could have been apprehensive of him a short while ago.

"Thank you, Logan. You may be right about the princess. I also think I'm just now realizing that almost everyone is truly gone. When I was in my lab all those months, I didn't see much. Not like you and the others who experienced it firsthand."

He nodded. "Yes. The worst part was when my mom died. After that, I kind of got used to how things were without so many people. Then I started to like it. It's really not so bad. Especially when you have a friend. I never had one before. Well, except for a girl in my eighth grade class, but all of a sudden she didn't want to be friends with me anymore and we had to move again. I'm glad I have a new friend." He squeezed her hand before releasing it, then darted back off toward the water, scattering shorebirds that had been foraging for insects in the tall grass.

She watched him run around in the sand, charging at squawking seagulls and tossing stones into the water.

A child in a man's body.

***

They made it almost to the Utah border by the time day began sliding into dusk. Julia said they should stop, but Logan wished they would keep going. He thought it would be fun traveling at night with the stars and moon overhead. He wanted to find out if the car could outrun them, but she said it would be dangerous to drive after dark. She seemed to know best about these things. She was very smart. She was a doctor, plus she had magic. How much magic he didn't know, and so far he hadn't been able to figure out if hers was stronger than his, but he suspected it was. That's why he hadn't killed her yet. He wasn't sure if a magical person could be killed with just a regular gun. Maybe it took some kind of charmed gun or a Harry Potter wand, which he didn't have.

He had started to like her too. He enjoyed how she explained things to him, and she was hardly ever bossy. She reminded him a lot of his mother, who he still missed but also didn't miss. He liked not having any rules. Except for the ones the Bad Thoughts told him about, and he didn't always have to mind them if he didn't want to. They only lived in his head, and they couldn't actually force him to do stuff. They just got really loud sometimes if he ignored them, which could be annoying.

There had been no motel in the area, so when they saw signs for Great Basin National Park campgrounds, she steered the car that direction. He was happy about that. It meant they would get to have another campfire tonight, and he'd discovered he was almost as good at making fires as he was at shooting guns.

After the fire was going, Julia did the wizard thing to their suppers. He was still amazed by how adding cold water to dust could make it hot. He figured it must be magic powder, even though she said it was *chemistry.* All the food she had was tasty, but he wished there were Twinkies. He remembered tasting them in the park that morning right before he'd seen the girl with the carrot-colored hair. Twinkies were just about the most delicious thing ever.

As he sat on a picnic table by the fire eating his dinner — it was spaghetti-with-Italian-style-meat sauce, which was not as good as the beef-stew-with-vegetables but was still pretty good — he watched Brains tiptoeing about on his long rope. Julia said he was not happy about being tied to that rope, but it was for-his-own-good. The cat had eaten canned tuna which smelled stinky to him. When he saw Logan watching him, he hissed and growled. Cats really liked to hiss. It was a funny sound, like the steam that came out of his mother's teapot.

He finished his food, then she said he should use the campground bathrooms instead of going outside like he'd been doing. He didn't see what difference it made, but she'd asked nicely, so he did. He even washed his hands without being told.

She wanted everything to be clean, so he was glad he had found those new jeans to wear before he'd seen her in the driveway that day. She might not have let him in her car if he'd still been wearing the old, dirty ones.

His shoulder was hurting badly. More so than it had been. Julia frowned at the wound when she'd changed the dressing earlier. He hoped he wasn't getting an *infection,* but she didn't say anything. She just put more gel stuff on it, then covered it with a new bandage.

He didn't sleep very well that night, despite the mild weather and the soft blanket she had given him again. He had bad dreams about a cat that wouldn't stop hissing at him, but his bullets just bounced off it. The next morning, his head felt like there was fuzz stuffed inside, and his shoulder hurt even more than the night before. Julia put her hand on his forehead, like his mother had done when he was little and had the flu. She frowned again and shook her head, then she went to the car and got out one of the storage bins.

She said, "These are antibiotics. I think your wound is infected and these will cure it. You'll need to take one of these pills three times a day until they're gone. That should do it. Okay?"

He felt groggy, like he wasn't quite awake, but he nodded his head and took the pill with a big gulp of water from the bottle she handed him.

When they loaded up the car and got on the road, he leaned back against the headrest and closed his eyes. He thought he might take a nap even though he'd already slept all night. Julia patted his knee as they drove away. He noticed the bracelet on her wrist and made a mental note to get some prettier string as-soon-as-possible.

Chapter 30

Liberty, Kansas

Steven woke from a nightmare in pitch darkness. He struggled to clear the mental fog that was the byproduct of believing just moments before that he'd been in bed — this bed — with a Medusa-like creature who had black eels for hair and fingers that ended in rough, fleshy suction cups. Earlier in the dream, he had wondered how it was able to crawl along the ceiling of his bedroom, so when she slithered into his bed and revealed her hands, the mystery was solved. Even more disturbing was that despite the eel hair (the end of each tubular shaft had a tiny, piranha-like mouth), he had been turned on by the creature's naked body and beautiful face. She'd slid down him, rubbing perfect, human female breasts down his face, chest, and belly, then peeled back the blanket when she reached his genitals.

That's when he woke up.

Even though he was alone, he was embarrassed by his erection. He sat up and swiveled, his feet finding the slippers always placed in the same spot. He fumbled for the lighter on the bedside table, then lit the candle next to it. The room was awash in dim but welcome light.

There were no eel-haired, perfect-breasted creatures lurking in the corners.

He carried the candle to the bathroom and set it on the vanity. When he raised the lid, noting the fresh water in the bowl, he pondered this little luxury: peeing in a clean toilet inside his house rather than using an outdoor latrine as many of the townspeople did to conserve water. Life had been difficult for the two of them this past year, and he hadn't spent much time thinking about how others had been coping because, frankly, it wasn't his problem. His only responsibility was the safety and health of his son.

Or so it had been until Chuck, the former grocery store manager, had rubbed his face in the details of others' hungry, uncomfortable, painful, tenuous existence after Chicxulub.

He couldn't go back in time and change what had already happened. Couldn't give a dose of his precious antibiotics to the little girl who had died from pneumonia. Couldn't save Ed's mother who had succumbed to dysentery caused by unclean water. Couldn't stop the bullet that had killed Marilyn's brother when he'd been confronted by a group of marauders at a ransacked Dillon's near Wilson Lake.

It was too late to save any of them, but he could help those who remained. As much as he hated giving away so much of his food and supplies — more than half of what he had stockpiled — he felt at peace with the decision. Profoundly so, even. It was no longer just about himself and his son; it was about rebuilding a community and planting the seeds, both literal and figurative, for the future. All the plans discussed with the board the day before — they'd settled on that verbiage for lack of anything better — had been exciting for the far-reaching and life-changing benefits. He realized he had been living in a vacuum and forcing Jeffrey to live the same way. It felt good to be involved in something bigger than just putting food on their table. They were going to reboot civilization, which was pretty damn cool, even if it only extended to the outskirts of Liberty, Kansas.

The splash of urine hitting the water was loud in the quiet of the house, but it didn't cover the sound of footsteps in the hallway.

"Jeffrey?" he called as he finished up.

He stepped back into the bedroom to see a figure languishing against the open doorway.

"Natalie, what are you doing here?"

When she dropped her coat to the floor, his next words caught in his throat at the sight of the thin nightgown. Even in the weak candlelight, he could see the outline of her breasts straining against the sheer fabric, and long shapely legs below the lace hem.

He was frozen in place, watching as she closed and locked the door, then glided toward him with the same graceful movements from earlier in the day.

Her slender arms encircled his neck. She pressed the full length of her body against him, then her soft lips found his mouth. Her tongue tasted like strawberries when it flicked against his, and he could feel her nipples through his t-shirt.

His hand slid down the curve of her back to the round bottom, drawing her pelvis against his erection. A moan escaped him as she grasped his hardness; nimble, confident fingers stroked through the boxer shorts.

The next moment they were on the floor.

He wriggled out of the boxers and lifted her gown. She wore nothing underneath. All coherent thought vanished.

"I don't think I can wait."

"You don't have to," she whispered, her hair splayed out on the braided rug below her head. She guided his penis to the warmth and wetness between her long legs. When he thrust into her, he thought he might come immediately — he hadn't felt such intense physical pleasure in more than a year — but he managed to hold off long enough to draw her climax just before his.

Minutes later, rational thought returned as his breathing slowed to normal. "How did you get in here?"

"Does it matter? Isn't this what you wanted? What we both wanted and knew was inevitable? Life is short and brutal now. Why wait a moment longer?"

She rolled over on her side to observe him. Her wide smile exuded satisfaction, but whether that was from the sex or something else, Steven could only guess.

"I need to know how you got in here."

A flash of anger distorted the pretty face. Now that he was clearheaded, he studied her with detached interest.

She sat up in a brisk, businesslike manner, adjusting the nightgown. "I unlocked one of the downstairs windows when I was here earlier. You should have done a window and door check before you went to bed. You're a smart guy, as everyone knows. It's surprising that I was able to get in so easily."

"How did you get past the fence?"

"You got what you wanted. Why are you being such an ass? I gave myself to you just now. Doesn't that mean anything? I could have had my choice of anyone...any man from the town, and I picked you. You should feel honored."

Steven laughed, a harsh, mirthless sound. "Maybe you're the one who should feel honored. How did you get past the fence?"

He stood, gazing down at her, wondering what the loveliness cloaked. Something had just clicked, slid into the place where it knew it belonged...a nagging fragment scarcely acknowledged until now, but irksome in its refusal to be banished from conscious thought.

"You told someone about my food, didn't you? That night after you and Brittany were here for dinner, you went back and told someone about what you'd seen and what you suspected I had. I think you told whoever you thought would get the word out, so you could just stand back and watch it play out."

She narrowed her eyes, but didn't respond.

"I had assumed Chuck knew about my preps because he'd seen me at the grocery store a couple of years ago with a cart full of bulk food, but when I mentioned that day, he acted like he didn't know what I was talking about. It didn't register at the time because, well, there were guns pointed at my head. So how did the townspeople — the angry mob that came to my house yesterday morning — know about my food? Chuck referred to green beans and potatoes, which was what I served you for dinner. You told him or somebody else about my food. Then it was a simple matter of getting hungry people riled up so you could swoop in and play Goodwill Ambassador."

The gray eyes narrowed further. Steven marveled how he could have considered that face so attractive just moments earlier.

"It's a shame I had to do that. If you had only invited us back, I wouldn't have had to go that far. But you didn't, and we were starving. I had to do something."

He felt a pang of remorse. Could he blame her for wanting to feed her daughter?

He sighed. "Why didn't you just tell me? Why not be direct and say what you need?"

She snorted in disgust. "Come begging? That's not my style."

He realized now that she wasn't merely slender, but terribly thin.

"Then why come back tonight? You got what you wanted. I've given everyone enough food to get them by for a while, including you and Brittany."

She stood, placing her hands against his chest. He didn't brush them away.

"Because I like you, Steven. I have from the moment I saw you, even before the plague when we were both married to other people."

That was a revelation, if it were true. He couldn't remember meeting her before, but he'd been so in love with his wife that pretty women went unnoticed in his world. The thought of Laura filled him with sadness and a sense that he had betrayed her somehow with this mindless, sexual act. He hadn't been making love with Natalie; he had been satiating carnal desire. He barely knew her. If he chose to be with another woman again, it would be for the right reasons.

With a gentle movement, he removed her hands from his chest.

"I'm sorry, Natalie, I don't want to hurt you, but I don't feel the same. I guess I'm still in love with my wife."

She seemed stunned, as if she'd been slapped instead of rebuffed. Perhaps beautiful women so rarely experience rejection that they never learn how to process it.

He stepped away, plucked the coat from the floor, and handed it to her.

"You need to go," he said simply.

The outrage and fury on her face told him he had just made an enemy for life.

***

It had been a few months since Steven had been off his own property. He felt downright giddy the next morning riding with Scarecrow Ed to the warehouse where the building materials for the new greenhouse would be found. Jeffrey sat in the back seat of the extended cab pickup.

"Your design is great," Steven said, admiring the architectural plan drafted the previous night. It was a more detailed version of the one drawn freehand at his kitchen table the day before.

Ed was a man of few words and fewer social skills, a character flaw compensated for by his knowledge of building construction and the no-nonsense manner in which he approached tasks. He didn't waste a lot of time and energy with small talk, which was a quality Steven could appreciate.

Ed didn't register the compliment, interpreting Steven's comment as self-evident. "It's rudimentary, but it's quick, and it will get the job done sooner than something more elaborate. We can upgrade it later, if that's what everyone wants to do."

Steven nodded, understanding that the man had no interest in town politics. His talents, however, would elevate his status whether he cared about it or not.

The thought nudged open a floodgate of unanswerable questions: What would their new society look like? Would they be able to feed everyone? Keep them warm and healthy over the winter? What form of government would they decide on? What kinds of laws would they create? Would they need to assign a someone to enforce those laws?

After Chicxulub, his ability to imagine worst-case scenarios and anticipate basic needs for survival under a variety of adverse conditions had served him well. Forward thinking would only distract him now, though. All he needed to focus on was getting the seeds from his seed bank into the ground and the structure in place to house them. There was nothing more important.

They'd been traveling west on I70 toward Hays, passing vast tracts of forsaken, ruined crops on either side of the interstate. A lone John Deere combine harvester interrupted the flat landscape, an alien dinosaur that had somehow escaped the asteroid annihilation of its brethren. Steven wondered if their fledgling community might someday restore those barren fields to their former splendor: golden oceans of wheat and verdant seas of corn. It was a lovely thought.

Jeffrey spoke from the back seat of the Ford F250, which hauled an empty trailer for the supplies they hoped to find. "Dad, there's a truck. I can see some guys walking around outside."

They pulled off the four-lane highway onto the service road. The warehouse was another mile ahead, but his son's youthful eyes had spotted the men and their vehicle in the parking lot.

"Shit," Steven said, drawing his Glock from its shoulder holster. Jeffrey's Springfield 30.06 rested on his lap. Ed removed a double barreled shotgun from the dashboard.

They slowed to twenty miles-per-hour as three sets of eyes studied the approaching building. He'd passed it dozens of times in his life, but it wasn't open to the public, so he'd never been inside. According to Ed, it was a treasure trove. Thoughts of all the materials they would find there — not just for the greenhouse, but also the electricity-generating windmills he planned to build from scratch — evoked a protective, greedy instinct. In the past, he'd made many pilgrimages to the Home Depot, which was situated seventy miles east of Liberty in Salina. But this warehouse was twice the size, less than half the distance, and in a rural area of the interstate devoid of the road-blocking vehicles Ed said had plagued their excursions in the opposite direction.

But should they risk their lives today?

A pickup was parked bed-first against an open bay door. The two men loading it hadn't seen them yet.

"There's a second truck," Jeffrey said.

"Maybe we should just wait them out," said Ed. "It's not like they're going to clean out the place."

Steven nodded. Of course that was the right call, even if it took several hours. They rolled to a stop on the shoulder.

There were now five men going back and forth between the bay door and their trucks. Steven began to fret, imagining an echoing, empty warehouse when they finally arrived.

"I see a woman, Dad. It looks like her hands are tied."

"Where are you looking?"

"Around the corner on the left side. Coming from the front with one of the men. He's pushing her. She's wearing a yellow sweater."

Steven saw her now. His focus had been on the back of the warehouse where the vehicles were parked. From half a mile away, he could make out a small figure with arms raised above a ponytailed head, walking in front of a man with a rifle. She stumbled and fell, struggled to stand again, then received a backhanded slap from her captor.

"Dad, we have to do something."

Ed nodded. Steven's mind raced, weighing all the risks against the possible benefit of freeing the female. There were five men, one of whom they knew to be armed. Most likely, the remaining four were as well. Would he be willing to risk the life of his son to save a stranger?

As usual, Jeffrey knew what his father was thinking.

"Dad, everything is different now. Our world is different now, but that doesn't mean it has to change who we are. We would never have let people get away with this before, and we can't now."

"Okay, let's come up with a plan then."

After a quick discussion, Ed started the engine. They crawled forward on the service road. The four men were still loading supplies, while the fifth stood guard over their prize. Her back was pressed against the building and the barrel of her captor's firearm was aimed at her head from five feet away.

"Stop here," Steven said.

They exited the pickup with minimal noise, then scrambled through the rough, weed-choked terrain which flanked the warehouse, stopping at a line of scraggly shrubs fifty yards from the building. The back of her captor was toward them, but Steven was positive the woman had spotted them. He hoped she wouldn't react.

The others emerged the next minute. A bearded giant in a KU sweatshirt hollered, "Whatdya got there, Danny?"

"Something fun for later!"

"I have him, Dad," Jeffrey whispered. He crouched behind the dead boxwoods, his scope sighting the woman's captor.

After several heartbeats and some intense mental hand-wringing, Steven said, "Take the shot, son."

The Springfield discharged, producing a recoil that was deftly managed. Rifle man crumpled to the ground. The female bolted, running full speed toward them, followed by four enraged men the next moment. As they ran, they pulled guns from inside jackets and pants pockets. One withdrew an assault rifle from a shoulder strap in mid stride.

"The guy in the plaid flannel, Jeff. Second to the right."

The 30.06 discharged. A funnel of blood burst from the back of the targeted head.

The female's legs pumped furiously, fear and adrenaline giving her a slight advantage in speed over the men who chased her. One of them fired shots as he ran; the other three were not backing off. At this distance, Steven's accuracy with the Glock was dicey and Ed's shotgun was sure to injure the girl as well.

"The guy in the KU shirt."

Jeffrey's bullet struck the big man just below his hairline. All forward motion ceased abruptly, like he'd slammed into an invisible barricade.

The remaining duo stopped, unsure now.

Please, let them stay...

The female had gained ten yards on her pursuers when one of them bellowed suddenly — an animalistic expression of outrage — and began charging after her again. His associate hesitated, then followed. There was no way to use the shotgun or the Glock without possibly harming the girl.

It would have to be a scope shot.

"Jeff, take them out."

The Springfield recoiled two more times in quick succession.

Seconds later, the woman careened through the boxwoods and collapsed on the ground next to Ed, sobs punctuating her labored breaths.

"It's okay," Ed said. "You're safe now." He patted her shoulder, awkward in his concern.

Steven studied his son. When the blue eyes watered then spilled over, he felt a weight lift from his chest. There was the remorse that had been absent in the aftermath of their dead intruders. He drew his child to him, engulfing him in a hug.

"Why wouldn't they stop, Dad? All they had to do was stop chasing her and we wouldn't have killed them."

"I don't know. Guys that abuse women aren't very smart. They usually have hang-ups about their masculinity, or they're insecure about other stuff. Maybe their egos wouldn't let them give up. It's crazy, I know."

Jeffrey nodded against his chest, then pulled away, embarrassed suddenly. Steven took the hint, shifting his attention to the woman who was still catching her breath.

From a distance, the blond ponytail had implied youth, but there were crow's feet next to the brown eyes. Ed's gaze never left the attractive face.

"Are you okay, ma'am?" Steven watched the woman struggle to regain her composure.

"Yes, I think so. I might have twisted my ankle but I'm fine."

Her voice had a melodious, silvery quality. It reminded him of the tinkling sound Laura's wind chimes made in the backyard on a summer evening.

"Thank you, gentlemen, for saving my life. I don't know how I can repay your kindness."

"No need. I'm Ed. That's Steven and his son Jeff."

"I'm Lisa." Her smile was slightly lopsided, but cute and heartfelt.

"What was going on over there, Lisa? I hope our assessment of the situation was accurate."

"I'd been to the warehouse a few times for supplies without any problems. I have a little place up the highway a half mile. I needed some fence posts. One of those guys caught me hiding behind the corrugated roofing. The rest you saw. I don't think there's any question what you all saved me from."

"You live alone?" Ed asked.

Steven winced. His new friend's inadequate social skills chose an awkward time to surface. Good grief, the woman had almost been raped. It wasn't a good time to determine if there was a Mister Lisa.

The crooked smile flashed again, thankfully.

"Yes, it's just me. I knew there was a bad element in Hays, and I guess that's who those guys were."

"Bad element?"

"Gang type stuff. You know, like a biker gang but with pickups. I mean the hardcore Hell's Angels kind, not those weekend warriors."

"Do you know how many there are?"

"I haven't been back in town for months, but a woman and her daughter passed by my place a week ago. Said things had gotten really bad there. That's why they left, except she said 'escaped.' She couldn't talk too freely in front of her girl, but she said the leader was a monster and all the women had been reduced to slave status — her words — doing all the physical labor and such, but the pretty ones were kept separate at the Best Western."

"Uh, I think I understand," Steven said with a quick glance at his son.

"If you live a half mile from here, you're too close to Hays," Ed said. "You could be in danger from those guys if they decide to expand their territory."

The ponytail bobbed. "I know. Been thinking about just that, and the incident today confirmed it."

"You should come back with us to Liberty. We can protect you there."

Arms crossed over the yellow sweater, and the brown eyes narrowed.

"I've been taking care of myself just fine for a long time, before and after the plague. It's just been me, no menfolk to make sure this helpless little female gets tucked into bed every night."

"You didn't do so well just now."

Steven groaned inwardly. The woman stood, brushing the dirt off her jeans.

"I should be going. I want to thank you again for helping me."

Ed looked crestfallen. He had no clue what he'd done wrong.

"It's obvious you're capable of taking care of yourself," Steven said. "You wouldn't be here today if that weren't the case. I think what Ed is suggesting is that relocating to a town means safety in numbers."

Ed nodded, still confused by her sudden anger.

Steven continued, "We're going to create a community there. Everyone pitching in, nobody more important than anyone else, just a cooperative system where all our individual strengths can be utilized for the collective good. Like my son here. He's not so great with a hoe, but he handles that Springfield like Doc Holliday."

She gave Jeffrey a warm smile, full of gratitude. Then glanced at Ed, who was grinning now like a man on death row who had just received a call from the governor.

"We're going to build a huge greenhouse!" Ed offered.

"You don't say," she replied. "What kind? Quonset or A-Frame?"

"Post and rafter."

"Sheeting or glass?"

"Sheeting for now, then glass next year, if everyone wants to upgrade."

"What are you going to plant?"

Steven answered, "We have a lengthy list of veggies. I have a seed bank. Do you enjoy gardening?"

She regarded him for a moment before replying. "I got my masters in Horticultural Science from A&M."

He was suddenly eager to recruit the woman, but for entirely different reasons than Ed's.

"I hope you'll consider joining our community. I bet Ed would be happy to use his truck to help you move your belongings into town."

Her gaze shifted from one man to the other as she contemplated her decision.

"I hate leaving my house. I grew up there. But I do realize it's not safe anymore." She bit her lip, then gave Ed a shy grin. "Okay, I'm in."

***

Thirty minutes later, they were inside the warehouse loading building materials on four-wheeled flatbeds and hauling them to the open bay doors where Ed's truck was now parked next to the vehicles of the dead men. Lisa's Tacoma had been on the other side but was now next to Ed's Ford. Steven had decided to requisition a Dodge Ram; it was in better shape than his Accord at home, and it had plenty of cargo space.

"You can have your pick of just about any of the houses in town," Ed told Lisa. "The one right next to mine is empty."

"How big is the yard? I'll want to have my own garden."

"About a half-acre, I'd say. It's an older neighborhood with big yards. And since I'd be right next door, I could give you a hand. Not that you can't take care of yourself, but you know, neighbors just need to help each other out."

"I'll give it a look, Ed. Thank you." She smiled.

Jeffrey glanced at his dad and rolled his eyes. Steven stifled a laugh, then said, "I think this is the last load, right Ed?"

"Yes, I think so," the foreman replied. "Once we drop off the supplies in town, I'll follow Lisa back to her house. I know you want to get started building right away, but I think it's more important to get her moved first. We don't know what's going to happen when those guys in Hays figure out their buddies aren't coming back."

"Agreed. The greenhouse can wait one more day."

As they drove past the bodies in the parking lot, Steven stole a glance at his son. Jeffrey peered at the men lying on the asphalt; heads were framed in oily halos of blood.

"That was some incredible shooting you did today. I knew you were good, but I didn't know you were that good. You okay?"

"Yeah. I wish I hadn't had to do that."

"Me too. I wish I hadn't had to ask it of you."

"It's okay, Dad. I was the one with the right tool for the job." It was one of Steven's pet phrases. "What did Lisa mean about the pretty women in Hays being kept separate?"

Oh boy. Steven formulated an age-appropriate response in his head. Just as he was about to deliver it, he thought about what he saw when he looked at Jeffrey. He wasn't seeing a child, he was seeing at a young man.

And he'd just been asked to kill five people.

"I think she meant those bastards keep the pretty ones for sex slaves."

"That's what I thought. I just wanted to make sure. I know she didn't want to say too much in front of me, but I'm not a kid. I wish people would realize that."

"They will. You did a man's job today, and everyone will know it."

Jeffrey nodded. "Good," he said, then shifted his focus to the forlorn fields as they traveled east on I70 toward home. Ten minutes passed in silence.

"Dad, we should do something about those women."

The thought hadn't even occurred to him. He had been focused on getting the supplies so they could get started on the greenhouse right away. The chilly air coming in through the half-open windows of the pickup underscored the impending threat of winter.

"Don't you think we have our hands full caring for our own people? Just a day or so ago, all we had to worry about was you and me. Now we're part of a community of fifty people who need help with water and food. It's a huge task we've set for ourselves. It doesn't seem wise putting ourselves in a dangerous situation for people we don't even know. Who's to say Lisa's information was accurate? Maybe it's not that bad there."

"I think it is. Lisa was pretty specific about what the woman said, and it sounds like they need our help. I know it won't be easy, but we can figure out a way to do it. There may be girls there my age or even younger that they're using for sex slaves too."

Steven's stomach did a queasy flip flop.

"Let's talk to the townspeople about it and see what everyone thinks. There's no way you and I can ride into Hays with guns blazing by ourselves and expect to make it out without a scratch. I'm not willing to put you in that kind of danger for people I don't even know."

Jeffrey raised an eyebrow, studying his father. "Why does it matter that we don't know them?"

Steven opened his mouth, but no words came out.

"I think if there are people being hurt, we have to do something about it, whether we know them or not." His son turned his head back to the passenger window, finished with the subject.

They drove the rest of the way in silence, but Steven wrangled with the conundrum. There were many factors in a decision such as this. Many risks that needed to be weighed against the benefits.

Jeffrey wasn't bothered by all this minutiae. The what-ifs and unknowns didn't change the core issue, nor his conclusion that they couldn't stand by and do nothing while people were brutalized.

Steven wondered if that kind of clarity would end up costing lives.

Chapter 31

Arizona

Warm sunshine filtered in through the cabin window, rousing Pablo from one of the best night's sleep he'd ever had. Maddie was awake. Golden red hair fanned out on the white pillow case and blue eyes watched him transition from slumber to full consciousness. He thought of a cat observing a mouse, deciding whether to play with it or eat it.

He groaned.

"I just woke up. Give me a minute before you list the reasons why we should bring Amelia with us."

"You're a smart guy, Pablo. I don't have to do that. You know it's not only the right thing to do for her, but for us as well. And you know why."

"The fact that she's a midwife did not escape my notice." Mental cobwebs, a residual effect of the previous evening's tequila, needed to be brushed away before he could engage in the inevitable debate.

"May I at least have a drink of water before you verbally pummel me?"

She sat up in bed and reached for the plastic cup on the bedside table.

"Here. Now, do we really need to argue about this? I think we both know how this is going to go down, so why waste all that energy? You know you'll give in because, if for no other reason, we need her to deliver the babies which are required for that family you're determined to have. Game, set, match."

"I don't even get to present my case? For starters, we don't have room in the car, and we barely have enough food for ourselves and Bruno, let alone another person and another dog."

"We'll find more food and we'll find another car."

"But I like my Jeep."

"But you like me better."

And there was the crux of it. If Maddie asked him to shave his legs and do the Macarena, he would. He hoped she would only use her powers for good.

"I do like you. Very much. But I get to win the next argument, okay?"

"We'll see." She sprang from the bed. "I'm going to go invite her!"

When he emerged from the bedroom a few minutes later, the women were nowhere in sight. He could hear low voices on the other side of the front door. When he opened it, four pairs of eyes watched him step out onto the sun-warmed wooden planks of the cabin's porch.

"Why do I get the feeling I've interrupted something?"

"Amelia has accepted our invitation. Isn't that wonderful, Pablo?" Maddie's pointed look came with a stern warning: *Be polite!*

After a second's hesitation, he replied, "Yes, wonderful. Good thing you and Curly Sue are small, Amelia."

Maddie narrowed her eyes. "The first order of business will be to find a bigger vehicle."

Pablo sighed. He would miss that Jeep. He'd had it for years, long before the pandemic. It felt like he was sacrificing a pinky finger or a big toe.

Amelia studied him with an amused expression. She'd read the subtext and didn't seem the slightest bit offended by his lack of enthusiasm.

"Where in Oklahoma do you have in mind, Pablo?" she asked, handing him a steaming mug of black coffee. It was instant, but sweet and delicious. His tequila-fuzzy tongue basked in the liquid glory.

"I'm not sure. I thought we would just stay on I40 through Arizona and New Mexico, then stop somewhere that looks like good farming country and do some reconnoitering. Ideally, we'll find a place with a well, and fields that don't require too much tilling. Along the way, we'll need to find food and water. And gasoline."

"With Amelia and Curly Sue, we have enough food and water to last three days," Maddie said. She'd done the math. "And we can probably make it to Winslow on the gas we have, but that's using the Jeep in the equation, and a new car may get better mileage."

"Or worse," he said.

"What type of vehicle are you hoping to find?"

"I haven't given it much thought, but I suppose something that has plenty of cargo space for three people and two dogs, gets good mileage...oh, and it must be a four-wheel drive, like the Jeep. Going off-road to maneuver around all the vehicles and debris would have been impossible otherwise. What are the odds we'll run across something like that along I40?"

Amelia nodded. "Come with me."

They followed the tiny woman down the steps and around the side of the cabin to the back. Parked behind the building in a grove of pine trees was a silvery blue Toyota SUV.

"It was here when I arrived. Nobody and no bodies were inside...I checked. I don't drive though. I've always preferred to walk wherever I need to go, but it would take me quite a while to stroll all the way to Oklahoma. Will this do?"

The Highlander looked brand new. Pablo opened the driver's side door to peer inside. Other than a light coat of dust, it was pristine, as if a transport helicopter had lifted it off the showroom floor and deposited here.

Would their luck hold? He slid behind the wheel, stepped on the brake, and pressed the ignition button.

The engine roared to life. The needle on the gas gauge settled at the halfway mark.

He glanced back at the two women. A statuesque red-haired enchantress and a dark-skinned braided Lilliputian wore identical smug expressions.

Pablo had to laugh. "Yes, this will do fine."

An hour later they were on the road.

"Did you find anything useful in here?" asked Pablo.

It was a sweet ride with only 157 miles on the odometer. Someone must have driven it off the lot, perhaps stolen, not long before arriving at the cabin. Still, as comfortable and practical as the new vehicle was, the sight of his beloved Jeep in the rearview mirror tugged at his heart strings. He imagined it now, abandoned and alone, like a dog left chained to a tree.

"Some supplies...bottled water, the chicken noodle soup you enjoyed for dinner last night, and the instant coffee you had with the breakfast pears. There was also a photograph album, but no people. I can only assume the worst."

"I wonder where they went to die," said Maddie.

It was an unanswerable question, but Amelia replied anyway. "Look around you," she said, indicating the panorama beyond the Toyota's windows. "When it's my time, if my knees haven't given out by then, I will find the prettiest parcel of nature I can and walk toward the sunset. Who would choose to take their last breath inside a manmade hunk of metal?"

Maddie smiled. "You're right. It's just that we've come across so many who did just that."

Amelia gave a disgusted snort. "That's no way to face death. The way I see it, there are only two ways to go: peacefully in the arms of the Earth Mother or fighting to protect those you love."

"I agree," said Maddie. These two women would likely be in accord on most issues.

"Tell us about the people in the photos," he said.

"They were a lovely mixed race couple. The woman was like me and the man was white. In their late thirties, I would say. No children, but a dachshund who appeared to have appropriated that role. They liked to travel. There were photographs of them taken all over the world."

"What did you do with it? The photo album?"

"I took it out to a pond near the cabin and found a spot that looked out over the water with the mountains in the background. A beautiful view. I left it next to an ancient bristlecone pine. It gives me pleasure to think about it still resting there. Perhaps it's close to where its owners lie. I like to think so, anyway."

He glanced at the woman in the rearview mirror; noticed a silvery tear slide down the brown cheek, but her voice remained steady.

"Maddie, you're clearly of Irish descent with that beautiful red hair and those sapphire eyes. What about you, Pablo? I gather from your name and coloring that you have Latino blood, but your eyes tell me there must be something else in the mix."

The suggestion caught him by surprise. Yes, his golden eyes were unusually light, as was his skin compared to most of the other immigrant families, but his parents had come from Guanajuato, and he'd always assumed his skin tone was the result of a rogue chromosome left over from some light-skinned ancestor. His father joked about his mother and the mailman, but they were just that — jokes. And there'd never been any other siblings with whom to compare.

"Both of my parents are...were...Mexican. I'm just your typical second generation wetback. Nothing special." He was surprised by the bitterness in his own voice. He thought he'd put those feelings behind him.

"Nothing special? I doubt that. You think like a philosopher, and you speak like a Rhodes Scholar."

Pablo felt his cheeks redden with the compliment.

"Your parents, were they also exceptional?"

He squirmed a bit under the scrutiny of those wise eyes. "Exceptional? I would say yes, but not in a way that would have been apparent to most. They came from Mexico before I was born. They worked the farms in southern California for several years before moving to Arizona. It was an arduous, difficult existence, but necessary to provide a better future for their family. It took them many years to learn the language. Even at the end, I often had to translate for them, so in the intellectual arena, I would say they were not exceptional. But I can say that I always knew I was loved and cherished. I never questioned that they would lay down their lives for me. Would that lifelong dedication to raising and loving a child make them exceptional?"

"If there had been more people like them in the world," Amelia said, "There wouldn't have been such a demand for shrinks and antidepressants. So the answer is, of course, yes."

He saw her smile in the rearview mirror. What an unusual little woman she was. The resentment he'd been feeling at being forced to include her in their journey was dissolving, like rice paper in a summer shower.

"We're coming up to Flagstaff," Maddie said, as she studied the atlas. "I think we should look for food there...on the outskirts."

Pablo felt stirrings of unease as memories of the Walgreen's incident sprung out of the dark place in which he preferred to keep it. "I don't want to make you angry, but I wish you would let me do the canvassing by myself. I can't bear to put you in danger. Again."

"I know that, but I'm not one of those women who lets her man do all the heavy lifting and bug squishing. Life these days is nothing more than one risk after another, and I won't be delegated to helpless female status. I'm sorry, but you'll just have to deal with that."

"Hey, don't forget about me," Amelia piped up from the back seat. "I'm small, but I'm wiry. And I have a mean left hook!"

They encountered more obstructive vehicles the closer they got to the city, but the Highlander handled the occasional off-roading with no problem. Pablo ignored the morbid human instinct to peer inside as they drove past. He'd already seen enough corpses to last a lifetime.

"There. A Circle K on the right. Maybe we can top off the tank too."

They pulled into the parking lot of the gas station convenience store. Two cars occupied the spaces next to the front door. A dilapidated Ford Focus was parked by the dumpster in the back. All three automobiles were covered in a fine layer of dust.

"I'm going in first, no arguing," he said.

"I'm right behind you."

"And I'm right behind you both." The little woman carried a knife the length of her forearm. She must have stored it in her battered backpack.

"Don't look so surprised, Pablo. Yes, I'm a peacenik, but I'm not a stupid peacenik."

The door was intact. When he opened it, a bell tied to a string tinkled from above the doorframe; not a high-tech security system, but an effective one. Late morning sunshine filtered in through the dirty glass half-walls, revealing near-empty shelves. Two bottles of nail polish remover and a can of WD40 were all that remained. Pablo gestured to the employees-only door at the back. The women nodded.

He held the shotgun ready and pushed open the door as Maddie clicked on her flashlight. The tinkling of another bell announced their arrival to whomever or whatever might be hiding in the stockroom. Like a divine shaft illuminating the Holy Grail, the beam exposed a dragon's treasure of processed food: boxes of Cheez-Its, plastic bags of jerky, cans of Dinty Moore beef stew, and in the center of the horde was a small, shrine-like mound of Sour Patch Kids, Whoppers, SweeTarts, and...M&Ms.

A stirring came from the farthest corner of the room. Maddie pivoted with the flashlight. In the circle of light stood a child. An elfin, smudged-faced girl with hair the color of onyx and a thin body draped in filthy rags. Enormous, sea-green eyes stared back at them with unnerving tranquility.

"We won't hurt you," Maddie said, her tone gentle.

The strange eyes blinked once. The small body made no other movement.

"What is your name?"

Not even an eye blink.

"Are you alone here?" asked Pablo, his voice louder than he'd intended.

The dark head tilted a fraction of an inch to the right. Did she not understand the question, or was she indicating the presence of someone else? Spectral fingers brushed the back of Pablo's neck.

"Can you talk? Can you tell us your name?"

No response.

Was she in shock? God only knew what she'd been through the past year.

"I'm going to walk toward you, okay? You don't need to be afraid of us. We're nice people," Maddie said.

With a calm, unswerving gaze, the child watched her approach. Pablo followed three feet behind. Amelia stayed back, an audience of one to the unfolding drama.

"My name is Maddie." She squatted down next to the little girl. "What's yours?"

Two eye blinks this time. Was that progress?

"Can you talk, sweetie?"

The dark head turned, looking at something in the far corner.

"Is there something there you want to show us?"

A quick nod.

Maddie smiled. "Let's see what you have."

The child scampered toward the back of the room, her lithe movements like those of a tiny ballerina, uncommonly graceful for one so young.

The flashlight's beam followed her. A rag-covered back was turned toward them as the child rummaged through a cardboard box. When she danced back, she carried a naked Barbie doll and the leathery remains of a human hand.

"Oh," squeaked Maddie.

"Where did you get that?" Pablo demanded, discomfited by this creature. The sea-green eyes glided toward his voice, then slid over him, either unconcerned or unseeing. They came to rest again on Maddie's face and the tiniest of grins tugged at one side of the dirty, heart-shaped face.

The cherub mouth opened and chirped one syllable:

"Pa."

"This is your daddy's hand?"

A nod of the dark head.

"And who is this?" Maddie indicated the doll.

The child hesitated, perhaps wondering if a grownup could be trusted with such proprietary information.

The crook of a grimy finger drew Maddie's ear close.

"Oh, I see. Well, that's a coincidence, isn't it?"

The dark head bobbed.

"What about you? Do you have a name too?"

Another crooked finger.

"What a pretty name! May I share it with my friends? That's Pablo with the scary gun. I promise, he only uses it on bad men and monsters. And the lady with the braided hair is Amelia."

The child's gaze settled on Pablo, as if seeing him for the first time, then traveled to their new friend, who had quietly approached. The dark head tilted again; the green eyes scrutinized the small woman for seconds longer than they'd studied him.

Finally, a slow nod.

"Pablo and Amelia, may I introduce you to Jessie? It's short for Jessica."

"It's a pleasure to meet you, Jessie," Amelia said.

"What happened to the people who drove the cars here?" Pablo asked.

She couldn't be more than seven or eight-years-old, but those eyes, unnaturally large in the thin face, were like malachite marbles and exuded no more emotion than the mineral itself. They rested again on Pablo.

He felt ashamed suddenly. What had this little girl been through the past year? What horrors had she witnessed? How had she managed to survive? What had the cost of survival been to her sanity?

The child turned and flitted to the back of the room where there was an exit door. She was through the door and outside before they had even made a move to follow.

She's a fast little shit.

When they emerged from the stockroom into the sunshine, she was thirty yards away, maneuvering through the scrub brush that surrounded the Circle K parking lot. She stopped, waiting for them to catch up.

Moments later, they stood beside three rectangular mounds of rocks. Lengths of mesquite branches were stuck into the soil at the top of each of the pilings. Tattered pieces of fabric fluttered from the childish, makeshift tombstones.

"Is one of these your daddy?"

A nod of the dark head and a gesture to the rock piling set slightly apart from the other two. In the sunlight, Pablo could see how filthy the child truly was.

"You dragged him out here all by yourself?"

Yes.

"Did he die of the plague?"

A blank stare.

"Was he sick right before he died?"

Yes.

"What about your mother? Was she sick too?"

A blank stare.

"How long have you been alone?"

A shrug of the bony shoulders.

"Who are the other two?"

Another shrug.

"Just people that came to the store?"

Yes.

"You've been living here for a long time?"

Yes.

"You've been eating all the stuff from the store?"

A slow nod. Maddie squatted down. Listened to the whispered response.

"Oh, I see. Yes, that's very smart of you." She stood, turning to her companions, her eyes glistening. "She's been careful not to eat too much of the food because she knows it has to last a long time." The words caught in her throat.

Pablo took a deep breath, then kneeled down to the child's level. He looked into the strange eyes and said, "Would you like to come with us?"

Pablo's Journal, Entry #385

I am a horrible wretch of a man. How despicable that I resent the presence of a lonely woman and a helpless child because they intrude on my world with the love of my life. There is no shame in admitting one's failings, especially when one has taken steps to rise above them. I know bringing them with us was the moral thing to do...certainly in the case of Jessie. But now I have to share my Maddie with others, and the burden of these strangers weighs on my thoughts and my heart. Maddie is attached to them both already. If something happens to either of them, it will be hard on her, and therefore hard on me. So my job is to keep everyone alive, safe, and as healthy as possible — no small task in a post-apocalyptic world.

Amelia is a gem, I must admit. An intelligent woman whose keen eyes seem to bore right into my soul. Her midwifery skills add to her value within our little troop, as I guess we are now...no longer just a couple. I suspect she has a plethora of knowledge stored in that shrewd brain that will serve us well in future challenges.

Jessie, however, distresses me somewhat, and on a level that I can't identify. She barely speaks at all, even after the long day on the road when we all became better acquainted. When she does, she prefers to whisper in Maddie's ear, as if talking too loudly might summon the monsters she fears — those same monsters which, when discussed in whispers with Maddie, provoked a visual examination of my shotgun. Jessie explained that they would skulk in the shadows of the store at night, and sometimes they would speak to her, saying terrible, scary things. Maddie asked her to reveal what they said, but she refused to elaborate. 'If I say the same words the monsters say, it will make them stronger.' And so she wouldn't do it.

At times I wonder if she might be mentally challenged, and at other times, I think there is an ancient, sagacious spirit residing behind those peculiar eyes. I'm conflicted about her, but it doesn't matter. She is with us, and time will tell whether we ultimately regret the decision to stop at the Circle K today.

At least we have plenty of M&Ms. For now...

Chapter 32

Texas

"Oh, come to momma," Dani cooed, as they pedaled up to the royal blue Ford Raptor with black pinstripes and thirty-two-inch Bridgestone all-terrain tires.

"Now that's a manly vehicle," Fergus said. "Since you should have been born a man, I can see why you love it."

She shot him the finger, set her bicycle down on the highway shoulder, and approached the pickup, K-bar in one hand and her shiny new revolver in the other. She glanced back to see Sam in ninja mode close behind. She marveled at how quickly her friend recovered from every injury he'd suffered the past year, including the beating from last night. His bruises were already in the yellow phase. She shook her head, then focused on the task at hand, peering through the filmy driver's side window. The door came open with a defiant screech.

"The peeps must have bugged out. I think this will do nicely, providing the gas hasn't gone bad and the battery isn't dead." She stepped onto the chrome running board and plopped down behind the wheel. The key was in the ignition.

Fergus laughed. "You look like a ten-year old playing in her daddy's pick-em-up truck."

It was true that she had to pull the seat up at least a foot to reach the pedal, but it was insanely kickass and if it started, she would leave a sacrifice at the altar of whatever heathen deity was in charge of combustion engines.

"Cross your fingers, gentlemen!"

She turned the key. Nothing happened.

"Damn it!"

"Hold on there, senorita. Let me try something. Pop the hood."

Dani pulled the latch as the small man removed a can of Coke from his backpack. He had to crawl up onto the front bumper to get to the battery. "Crank it again!"

The massive V8 roared to life, an angry dragon awakening from its nap.

"Woo hoo! Let's load up, boys."

Minutes later they were driving north on I35. It had been over a year since she had driven an automobile, and it felt wonderful to make such fast progress away from Isaiah.

"My ass has died and gone to heaven," Fergus said. Their bicycles and gear fit easily in the bed of the truck, so he had the entire back seat to himself.

"We'll still get to ride the bikes every now and then, right Dani?" Sam was already pining for his two-wheeled lover that had been relegated to inactive duty.

"Of course. I'm sure there will be plenty of excursions we'll need to make using them. For now, I'm just happy to be making good time. Kansas, here we come!"

This far away from the Dallas-Fort Worth metroplex, the tangle of disabled and abandoned cars had begun to dwindle. The Oklahoma border couldn't be more than another twenty miles, and Dani wanted to put as much distance between them and their adversaries as possible. She had no idea how Isaiah had found them. Back at the motel, she had glimpsed the depths of the lunatic's ego and knew that once he freed himself, he wouldn't tuck tail and run back to Colleyville.

At least he didn't know where they were going, and eventually he would give up the chase. Surely.

"Loved the Pear of Anguish thing, darling." Fergus's gravelly voice interrupted her thoughts, but had hit on the very subject of them.

"I'm not surprised. You're a freak of nature."

Fergus grinned from the back seat. She wondered how long he'd been without human companionship; he seemed to be enjoying himself immensely. She could tell he had quickly become fond of Sam, which made her accept the red-haired oddity sooner than she might have otherwise. She speculated on how much, if any, of his autobiography was true.

"Honey Badger, I'm trying to imagine you wearing overalls and chewing on a piece of straw while you plow fields. I have to say, I find the image implausible, somewhat disconcerting, and sexy as hell."

"Not nearly as disconcerting as imagining your plumber's crack while milking the cows, grandpa."

"You're a heartless woman. You remind me of the Grinch when his heart was two sizes too small."

"I love that show!" Sam said. "It's not Christmas without watching the Grinch. I think I miss TV most of all."

"Me too. And movies," said Fergus.

"It sucks not having TV. Thank goodness for books."

The words came out before she could stop them, and the crestfallen expression on Sam's face made her feel like the biggest jerk on the planet. Considering how few people there were left, she just might be.

"I'm sorry."

"It's okay. It's not your fault that I don't read well."

"What is this?" Fergus asked.

Dani shot a covert look at her friend, gauging his reaction to the question, before she answered.

"I think Sam has an undiagnosed reading disability," she said after seeing his smile. "He had a hard time in school."

"Well, young man, your other attributes certainly make up for it. I'm imagining all the cheerleaders I could have nailed if I'd been as handsome as you back in my youth."

The color rose in Sam's cheeks. She wondered if it were true for about three seconds before dismissing the idea. That wasn't Sam. He'd surely had countless female admirers since reaching puberty, but she couldn't see him taking advantage of his good looks just to bang a few chicks. He was not only a gentleman, but she suspected he would only be interested in sex when his heart was engaged.

"Cheerleaders weren't really my thing. Most of them were cute, but they could also be mean. I mostly just hung out in the gym and track field. I was good at sports."

"You know, there's no reason not to enjoy books just because printed words seem wonky," Fergus said. "Dani and I can take turns reading out loud from our novels every night before bedtime. What do you think about that, Honey Badger?"

"That may be the best idea you've had all day. I get to go first. I only had room for two in my backpack so it was a difficult decision." She found herself excited by the prospect of sharing her love of reading with Sam.

"What a co-winky-dink. I have several myself. You're lucky I didn't have more room, or I'd have brought my entire erotica collection."

"No crap books. I'm decreeing that right now. No *Fifty Shades of Grey* garbage."

"What about Gaiman, King, and Tolkien?"

"Now you're talking. This will be fun, don't you think, Sam?"

"Just promise me none of that Shakespeare stuff. I can't understand what the heck they're saying."

"Duly noted. No Shakespeare."

"And no chick books," said Fergus. "And by chick books, I mean romance novels, except for ones that contain off-the-chain sex scenes. And no sappy books about lady friendships...unless they're peppered with lesbian sex. It can even be pedestrian lesbian sex, because two chicks having boring sex is still hot."

"You really are a pig."

"But I am a lovely pig with fabulous hair."

"So what about books where two dudes are having sex? Are you a homophobe?"

For the first time, their odd friend appeared genuinely insulted.

"Certainly not. I condone all acts of love between human beings, providing it doesn't injure others. I just don't need to read about dudes getting it on...doesn't do anything for me, know what I mean?" The red eyebrows waggled. "Doesn't summon the crotch zombie or wake the one-eyed Cyclops. The pink Darth Vader never shows up. The throbbing gristle doesn't throb..."

"Enough!" Dani shouted, laughing. "You're disgusting. If I'd known you were such a little perv back at the bike store, I'd never have let you come with us."

Fergus chuckled.

"We could use more water too," Sam said, with an embarrassed grin.

"Good idea. We have plenty of MREs, but now we have room for canned goods and other supplies." Dani was feeling the effects of the heavy, salty food in her digestive tract. A nice can of carrots or green beans would taste heavenly for a change.

"And toilet paper. The good stuff too, none of that motel tree bark."

"Agreed." They had each stuffed a roll in their packs, but it was so thin it wouldn't last long. And the baby wipes were dwindling rapidly. She'd brought a supply of tampons from Colleyville, but they'd be gone after her next period.

The planning she had done before the end came was painstaking and comprehensive, and based on 'bugging in,' not taking her life on the road. This nomadic adventure was not only dangerous, but damned uncomfortable. She missed her bed back home, and her butt throbbed from all the bicycle riding. Still, for a former spoiled nerdy girl, she was doing pretty damn well.

"We also need to find a map, even though I know it's a straight shot up I35," she said. "We might need to use secondary roads, and the GPS on your bike isn't convenient."

"It would be good if we could find some gasoline cans," Sam said. "That way when we find good gas, we can store extra for the times when we can't."

"Great idea. Anything we can do to keep my poop chute on this cushy seat and off that two-wheeled torture device gets my vote."

"Uh oh, guys. Heads up," Dani said.

Two hundred yards ahead was a barricade of cars and trucks. This was no accidental twenty-car pileup. It was clear the vehicles were positioned for the purpose of blocking all through traffic.

Dani slowed the 4x4 to a crawl as they scrutinized the scene before them. There was no movement, no people, just a blockade of metal, glass, and rubber starting at the crash barrier and extending twenty yards beyond the shoulder to a barbed wire fence line.

There would be no going around it.

"Who knows how long this thing has been here," Dani said. "I don't see anybody. Maybe they're gone. Or dead."

"Or maybe they're not gone or dead, but waiting for us inside or behind the rampart of vehicles, armed with bazookas and pointy sticks," Fergus replied.

"I could flank them from the oncoming lane and do some, what's that word?" Sam said, "Reconnoitering? See what's what. They're probably mostly just watching this lane of the highway, I bet. Most of the traffic would come from the south."

"I have a bad feeling about this," Fergus said.

She nodded. "I do too. Let's think of something else. We could backtrack and use secondary roads."

Sam considered their words, then shook his head.

"The last thing we want to do is go back to Isaiah territory. We need to go forward. I'll be careful, don't worry." He was out of the pickup before anyone could argue further.

"Damn it!"

"Sam's a big boy, Honey Badger. He's smarter than you give him credit for too."

"What the hell do you mean by that?"

"You know what I mean. You may be an Einstein, but he's intelligent in a different way. Much more so than you realize. What, no droll retort this time? Ma, grab the camera!"

"Go fuck yourself, Fergus."

"If that were possible, I would have saved myself a boat load in alimony."

She was too worried to be amused. Sam was nowhere in sight. The idling of the pickup's engine seemed loud now that the conversation had stopped. She glanced at the Casio on her wrist only to see that mere seconds had passed. Finally, he materialized out of thin air next to the truck, opened the passenger door, and slid inside.

"Holy crap, son. You're like Gandalf the Grey but with better hair."

Dani felt a wave of intense relief. Without thinking, she grabbed his bruised face between her hands and kissed him squarely on his swollen lips. Embarrassment caught up the next moment, and she pulled away, feeling her cheeks redden.

Bushy red eyebrows lifted. “Clearly you were missed. What did you find out?”

“It’s a trap. There are six guys with guns hiding behind the blockade. They look like badass dudes, too.”

“Lovely.”

“Yeah, not really, but I also noticed that the highway crash barrier is in bad shape. There’s a broken section about a hundred yards ahead, like somebody rammed it with a car. There are still big chunks of concrete there, but in a 4x4, we might be able to go right over them.”

“That would put us only a football field away from the badass dudes,” Dani mused. “Risky. They’ll be shooting at us the second they realize we intend to go around their little fortress.”

“Yeah, plus they stuck a wrecked car there too, but I think I could shift it into neutral and roll it out of the way.”

She shook her head. “So while we’re being sprayed with gunfire, you’re going to leave the dubious safety of our truck, hop into another vehicle, possibly get the transmission into neutral, push it out of the way, then dash back to our truck unscathed, and we drive happily away into the sunset.”

“It’s only noon, Dani. Sunset doesn’t happen for six more hours.”

“That’s a crazy plan. Way too dangerous.”

“Hold on there, little filly,” said Fergus. “It is risky, but we have advance knowledge of our adversaries and a clear picture of what we’re facing. If we go backward, the scene gets fuzzy. Isaiah may be lurking under a rock and could leap out when we least expect it. Sam’s proposal is lacking in only one area: he didn’t factor in the help of a devilishly handsome fellow I know who has some minor skills with automobiles, as was evidenced earlier with the Coke trick. You’re welcome, by the way. I’ll go with Sam. One of us shifts and steers the barricade car while the other pushes. Perhaps you could position Big Blue here,” he patted the back seat, “In such a way as to deter some of the bullet spray while we’re exposed. I’ve grown distressingly attached to you though, Honey Badger, so please keep that exquisite head down whilst doing so.”

“I don’t like it,” she said after a full minute. “But I don’t like the alternative either. I wonder why they didn’t bother blocking off the southbound lane?”

“Don’t know.” Sam shrugged. “But other than the one car plugging the hole, that lane is pretty much smooth sail boating.”

“Perhaps they’re a bunch of radical Oklahomans who don’t care if their brethren leave, but don’t want Texans coming in and tainting the bloodline,” Fergus offered. “Or maybe they just haven’t had time to obstruct both sides.”

“Or perhaps they’re just not too bright,” Dani said.

"Don't be so quick to jump to that conclusion. It might come back to bite you in your flawless backside."

She shot him a look of disgust, then shifted into drive. They crawled toward the road block at ten miles-per-hour, an attempt to convey trepidation which she hoped would gain them the element of surprise when they made their move.

When they arrived at the damaged section of the crash barrier, Dani drove just past it, then pulled a hard left toward the breach. Big Blue was now positioned between the blockade and the place where her friends would be vulnerable while clearing the breach.

Sam and Fergus leaped out and scrambled over the chunks of concrete, hunkering down to avoid the bullets that began to fly now, as expected. Dani did the same until her nerves got the best of her. She poked her head above the steering wheel to see Fergus open the door of the blocking vehicle. A bullet exploded through the passenger side window and whooshed past the back of her head, probably taking a few brunette hairs with it.

She dived for cover, but soon anxiety forced her to peer over the dashboard again.

Sam was nudging the car from behind while Fergus steered and pushed against the open driver's side door. Excruciating seconds ticked by. Finally, it was out of the way, leaving just enough space to squeeze through.

The next moment, her ecstatic squeal changed to a shriek as she watched blood spatter against the rusted trunk. Sam staggered and fell.

"Sam!" she screamed as she opened the door and started to climb out.

"Dani, no! Get back in and get through...NOW!" Fergus hollered.

Tears of frustration made it difficult to see what she was doing. Exposed rebar clawed at blue steel as she rammed the pickup through the opening. Once she was through, she thrust the transmission into park and jumped out. Sam lay on the pavement. Fergus was lifting him by his shoulders while angry metallic hornets whizzed all around them. Dani barely noticed. Her eyes were focused on the expanding pool of blood. Too much blood.

"Grab his legs!"

Sam had been shot. He was bleeding out. All that blood. Nobody could lose that much blood and live.

They managed to get him into the back seat, but later, she couldn't recall any details. She had no idea how they'd done it without getting themselves killed in the process.

"Drive! I'll take care of these guys!" Fergus wriggled in next to a slumped over, unconscious Sam, then snatched the AR15 from the floorboard and fired at their approaching adversaries.

"Damn it, girl, snap out of it!"

His voice finally penetrated the mental fog. She tore her gaze away from the blood and slid behind the wheel. The all-terrain tires clambered over the concrete rubble scattered on the southbound lane. Bullets rained down on them, despite the lethal effects of Fergus's assault rifle.

"If we want to keep our pretty selves alive, you need to get us the hell out of here."

She gritted her teeth and punched the gas pedal, clearing the last bit of debris just as a bullet pierced the windshield. It left a jagged hole an inch to the right of her line of sight.

The tires gave an exultant screech as they found good traction and the Raptor jetted past the road block five seconds later.

An unknown amount of time passed.

"Honey Badger, easy does it now. We're well clear."

She ignored him, knowing that when she took her foot off the accelerator, they would inevitably stop. At that point, she would discover Sam's condition, and she wasn't ready to do that.

"He's breathing. Slow down, love."

The engine ticked in the sudden quiet. She had no memory of exiting the highway nor stopping on the shoulder. There was a vague notion that they'd crossed over the Red River, which meant they were in Oklahoma. Later, Fergus told her she'd driven like a NASCAR banshee for twenty minutes.

"How bad?"

"I'm not sure. Let's take a look, shall we? You need to get a grip now. You're no good to him all snotty and weepy."

Careful, steady hands lifted the bloody t-shirt from Sam's abdomen. The bruises on the handsome face appeared darker, surrounded now by an alarming pallor. Blood pooled on the seat but not as much as she feared there would be.

"The problem with the stomach," Fergus said, his tone that of a trainer speaking to a skittish mare, "Is that if any of the vital organs were hit, it usually doesn't end well."

Dani couldn't respond. The lump in her throat wouldn't allow it.

"But if it missed them, it's actually preferable to a bullet hitting other areas, like the legs or neck, where you have to worry about the femoral and carotid arteries. He would have bled out by now if that were the case."

Deft fingers wiped down Sam's stomach with a sanitary napkin pulled from his backpack. Dani was so surprised at the sight, she found her voice.

"A maxi pad? You had a maxi pad with you?"

Fergus grinned. "I never leave home without them. Well, not now anyway. Before the plague, I'd been happily ignorant of their benefits. They're the perfect field dressing, clean and absorbent. Plus they have a number of other uses I've discovered this past year. Now it gets even better."

He withdrew an even more familiar item.

"You're going to plug it with the tampon, right? I read about that before the internet went down."

"Exactly." His nose was inches from Sam's abdomen. With gentle movements, he lifted Sam's torso just enough to study his back.

"Good news. It's a perforation wound, not penetrating. I bet you know the difference."

She nodded. "Perforation is a through and through. Penetration means the bullet hasn't exited the body."

"Correct. I'm also not smelling any foul odors, which indicates the colon and intestines were probably not pierced. I'm somewhat optimistic."

She felt a fluttering of hope.

"Assuming all the important innards were missed, the potential problems now are two-fold: foreign material left in there, like fiber from his clothing, and also secondary infection later on."

"I have antibiotics. I ordered them online before the end came."

"Aren't you a clever little monkey. How did you get them? Shady doctors in Mexico?"

"No, they're for fish. But they're the exact same as the ones prescribed for people."

"Interesting," he muttered as he removed the wrapper from the tampon, careful not to touch the business end, and inserted it into the wound. The blood flow stopped instantly.

Sam's eyes fluttered open the next moment. His drowsy eyes sought Dani's face.

"Only the good die as youngsters, right Dani?"

Something between a laugh and a sob stuck in her throat. "Yes, Sam. And you're as good as they get, which is why I was so worried."

Soon color began to return to his face and his breathing was less shallow. Fergus patted her shoulder. She reached for the small man's hand and gave it a grateful squeeze.

"I think we should put some more distance between us and them," she said. "Why don't you drive for a while so I can sit with Sam?"

"Brilliant idea. Which reminds me, I'll need to change my underwear at the earliest opportunity."

An hour later they took an exit ramp and pulled around to the backside of a Love's Travel Stop. Sam was awake but Dani could see he was struggling with the pain of his injury.

"How bad does it hurt?"

"Not too much," he said between clenched teeth.

"I'll bring you some ibuprofen. And we'll get you started on antibiotics just in case."

"No, we need to save those. What happens if you need them later?"

"No arguing. You need them now and you're going to take them. It's better to stave off the infection before it begins, rather than treating it once it gets a foothold. Right, Fergus?"

"I tend to agree. However, Sam is an exceptionally healthy young man, and it might just be that his immune system is up to doing battle on its own."

She frowned.

"Don't give me that look, young lady. He has an excellent point. How many doses do you have? What if you need them later for a wound that *has* become infected? Or you get a wicked case of gonorrhea?"

Sam nodded. "Yes, let's save them, please. I will take that ibuprofen though."

She hopped out of the cab to fetch her pack from the bed of the truck.

Fergus followed. "He needs to rest, and not while being jostled around on the back seat of Big Blue."

"What do you have in mind?"

"Let's find a house somewhere in Podunk, Oklahoma, and hole up for a few days. Preferably a house with a stockpile of food and a scarcity of stinky corpses."

She nodded. "That way I can do some foraging while he's resting. Maybe everything isn't too picked over out here in the boonies."

"Let's hope. I'll see if there's a map inside this establishment. You stay put with Sam."

"Be careful, little man. Take your GI Joe gun."

"Not a good option for close quarters. I'll be fine with this." He eased the machete-like knife from its sheath, glancing up at the sky, which had turned overcast. Lumpy, green-tinged thunderheads loomed on the eastern horizon.

She did a slow twirl, scanning the perimeter of the parking lot and beyond, then said, "There are no automobiles here. There's not one car, pickup, or motorcycle in view. Don't you think that's odd?"

"Yes, very odd. Maybe I will retrieve my GI Joe gun," he said returning to the pickup.

"Everything okay?" Sam asked. Dani scurried back, handing him a bottle of water and the ibuprofen.

"Everything's fine. Just try to rest. If you won't mind me about the antibiotics, you will at least do that."

She noticed moist beads dotting his face along his hairline. He was in an enormous amount of pain and all she had was a stinking bottle of generic Advil. Prescription-strength painkillers weren't available online as the antibiotics had been, and she was kicking herself in the ass for not having faked some painful condition and wrangling a script from her GP before the end came.

"It's not so bad. Don't worry about me."

She was, of course, but she was also concerned by whatever was causing the ghostly fingertips to dance across the back of her neck.

Fergus lifted his nose like a bloodhound, scenting the sudden gust of wind.

"That's an outflow boundary," he said.

"What, you're a meteorologist too?"

"Not an expert. It was just a former interest."

He studied the thunderhead which boiled and rolled like the contents of a slow-bubbling cauldron. "See the greenish tint? That indicates hail."

"I've lived in Texas all my life. I know what green clouds mean."

"Oh, sorry, Honey Badger. I briefly forgot about your gigantic brain, which is almost as big as your ego."

She punched him in the arm.

"When thunderstorms collide with the cooler air from outflow boundaries, we get rotation. I think I'm seeing some even as we speak."

She scrutinized the eastern sky. "Yes, I see it too. Let's get moving. I bet some of these rural houses have a storm shelter. I mean, we're right in the middle of Tornado Alley. If these hillbillies don't have a basement, they deserve to get sucked up by a funnel cloud."

"You're a hard woman. You driving?"

"Yes, I'm driving. Just keep an eye on Sam."

"Will do. I'll keep an eye on your control issues as well."

She showed him her middle finger for the second time that day.

"This looks promising," she said a few minutes later as they drove down a farm-to-market road somewhere in southern Oklahoma. A large house sat on a hill a hundred yards away. Wire fencing enclosed its surrounding acreage, the type that used on horse ranches, but there were no horses now. Hopefully their human owners were also absent.

The chained gate was no match for Big Blue. They were quickly through it and barreling up the gravel driveway toward the house, sliding to a stop in front of the porch.

At close range, the house didn't appear as tidy as it had from the road. Neglect was evident here just as it had been in her Colleyville neighborhood. Next to the steps, weeds choked the flower garden, which still bloomed in October, and the white paint on the wraparound porch railings was coated with a fine layer of red soil.

"What's the plan?" Fergus asked as they stepped out of the truck and readied their weapons.

"I hate leaving Sam here alone," she said. "Why don't you stay with him and let me check out the house?"

"You're running this show, but my gut instinct is to put the shotgun in his hands and let him take care of himself until we make sure the house is safe."

"The key part of that phrase is 'you're running this show.' Look, if anything happened to him, I couldn't bear it. I almost lost him today, and I still might."

"And if anything happened to you, do you think he could bear it?"

She stopped in her tracks.

He continued, "It's a bit of a conundrum, I know. You're willing to put your own life in danger because you want to protect him, but to Sam, losing you would be much worse than whatever someone might do to him. He's conscious. He's hurting, but he's lucid. He'll be fine for the ten minutes it will take to secure this house. What do you say?"

She gave him a grudging nod.

Seconds later they stood in front of the door, peering through leaded glass at a foyer which narrowed down to a wood-floored corridor as it extended to the back of the house. She could see a living room to the left and a formal dining room to the right. She switched on her flashlight and cast the beam through the glass.

Two things struck her: a coating of dust covered the floor, and a child's doll abandoned in a corner had just totally creeped her out. It was one of those baby dolls from the forties or fifties, and which in Dani's imagination, came to life at night.

"The dust is a good sign," she whispered.

Fergus nodded and turned the doorknob. It wasn't locked. They stepped inside.

An explosive crash of thunder rattled the windows, ratcheting up her nerves another notch. She held her revolver and flashlight police-style as she surveyed the living and dining rooms. Cobwebs dangling from the light fixtures indicated a healthy spider population, but anything larger would have disturbed all the dust on the furniture and floors. They crept down the hallway, opening a closet and bathroom door along the way, finding only storage boxes and cricket husks.

By the time they reached the kitchen, Dani felt confident the house was empty...at least of people. If there were any hiding corpses, the smell of their decay had faded, leaving nothing more than musty-smelling air with bottom notes of mice urine. The upstairs still needed to be searched, but another crash of thunder followed by a lightning flash through the kitchen window cut the plan short.

"We need to get Sam out of the truck. Now," she said. "That storm is right on top of us."

They sprinted back to the front door. Within three minutes, they had him reclining on a sofa. The moment his head touched a rose-printed pillow, he lost consciousness.

"Did you notice those green clouds have turned black? I'll search for a safer place to hunker down than this living room with its glass windows."

"Hurry, Fergus."

Sam groaned while thunder boomed every few seconds now. The storm's ionized air, or perhaps the doll from the foyer, summoned the feathery ghost fingers again. She crouched next to him as the seconds ticked by...literally. A clock on the fireplace mantel contained still-functioning batteries and a noisy second hand.

"It's okay. Everything's going to be okay." She brushed sweat-darkened strands from his brow. His eyes fluttered open.

"I'm sorry to be so much trouble. That was stupid of me to get shot."

"Hush. Save your energy for getting better. Don't forget you're a goddamn ninja with supernatural healing powers."

He smiled and closed his eyes. She placed her hand on his chest; she needed to feel the lungs expand and contract. Needed to make sure he didn't slip away from her.

If Sam didn't make it through this, she didn't know what she would do. She had been discounting the newfound physical attraction and ignoring the romantic images that had been flashing through her mind these past two days. But now she embraced them. As she looked at his beautiful face, seeing all the kindness etched into every line, she knew she had fallen in love with her best friend. At the same time, she realized her arrogance had kept it from fully blossoming until now. She'd always thought she could never be in love with a man who wasn't on the same lofty cerebral level.

Funny how fate had other plans. Sam wasn't a rocket scientist, but his many wonderful qualities more than compensated for their disparate IQs. Besides, as Fergus had pointed out, he was smart...just not in the same way she was.

When the rain began a few seconds later, it was with the sudden ferocity of a monsoon. Sheets of water poured from the heavens at a near-sideways angle, buffeting the windows. Golf ball-sized hail followed the next minute. The howling wind found ingress through every crevice and loose window casing and door jamb of the house.

Fergus appeared, his red hair dripping with rainwater and an alarmed expression on his face.

"There's no safe room and no storm shelter or cellar. Our best bet is the powder room in the hallway. It's in the interior of the house and fortified by the stairway above it."

"He passed out, Fergus. From the pain."

"Let's move him quickly. The sound you hear is not that of the Amtrak Heartland Flyer."

"Is it on the ground?"

"It's rain-wrapped. Impossible to see."

The thrashing of rain and pounding of hail approached deafening levels. After they laid Sam on the floor of the small bathroom, Dani closed the door behind them, providing an instant respite from the clamor. She imagined the skeleton of the house: two-by-fours connected by tendons of sheetrock, and brick flesh draped on wooden bones.

She hoped the structure would be sturdy enough to protect them.

She clicked on the flashlight. There was no bathtub, just a toilet and sink. The beam distorted the landscape of Fergus's face, creating a caricature of the man to whom she'd recently become rather more attached than she cared to admit. The lighting didn't do him any favors; he looked as ghoulish now as the doll in the foyer.

"I assume you're not the praying type," he said.

"No, but if we survive this...if Sam lives through this, I just might convert."

"Ah. You're one of those religious Sunshine Patriots then."

"No. The logic of your metaphor is flawed. I wouldn't be fleeing a belief system when the going gets tough, but embracing one if it can be proved to my satisfaction that I have benefitted from it. See the difference?"

Under the eerie conditions, his grin was more creepy than comforting.

"So if you don't believe in God or a higher power, how do you think we got here?"

"Really? You want to debate the origins of humankind when we're about to be sucked up by a fucking F5?"

He chuckled. "I'm just trying to distract you from worrying about Sam. It almost worked."

"Maybe for a second. Thanks, Fergus. I'm worried sick about him."

Debris crashed against the house now. Dani pictured uprooted trees and unlucky cows being flung against their refuge, like detritus in the dust cup of a colossal Dyson vacuum.

"I'm fairly certain the bullet didn't hit anything critical. If we let him rest for a few days, somewhere clean, comfortable, and stationary, I have a good feeling about his prognosis. I learned a bit of first aid during my military career, so I speak with some minor authority."

She nodded, failing to keep the tears behind her eyelids where they belonged. She despised crying in front of people.

"It has a heart! I'll be damned!"

She punched him again.

"You're freakishly strong for a girl. Has anyone ever told you that? I have a bumper crop of bruises on my bicep now, thanks to you."

The noise level outside the tiny room escalated. They locked eyes as the distinct sound of an approaching train pierced the pandemonium of destruction. An ear-splitting crack came from above, the vibration causing bits of ceiling texture to rain down on them. Dani covered Sam's body with her own and waited for the end.

Chapter 33

Utah

"Do you feel better, Logan? The medicine has been in your system for almost a day. It should be working its magic by now."

The word choice was unintentional, but Julia noted the young man's sudden interest. He'd been listless and apathetic for more than twenty-four hours, a result of the infection battling white blood cells and Amoxicillin. The bullet wound in his shoulder hadn't been cleaned properly before they'd met; otherwise, she might not have been forced to use her only round of antibiotics. It was a moot point now since she had done so, and besides, Steven would have stockpiled them.

"I think so. Thank you for sharing your magic pills."

She started to explain that the medicine wasn't literally magic, then stopped herself. She remembered Logan's short-lived but distressing behavior while driving through Yosemite, and decided it couldn't hurt to perpetuate his belief that she wielded magical powers. They had been traveling east on a two-lane state highway and passing through a whole lot of nothing for several hours. Once they hit I70 near Provo, they would ride it through the remainder of Utah, over the Rocky Mountains in Colorado, detour from it briefly via the 470 bypass south of Denver (by doing so, she hoped to avoid the massive roadblock of automobiles one would expect near such a large city), back to I70 again once east of Denver, then on to Liberty. Thus far their route had been obstacle-free. When people had fled the wrath of Chicxulub, they hadn't sought sanctuary in this part of Utah, which consisted of flat, unremarkable terrain dotted with an occasional desolate-looking house in the distance and a smattering of bleak, eighties-era filling stations.

She glanced at the young man, who was starting to doze off again, then at the Rover's gas gauge, which showed less than a quarter full.

She quashed the panicky feeling this summoned and told herself they had another full five-gallon can in the back. They would stop at the next station or vehicle they found and fill up the others.

As it turned out, the next opportunity came a few minutes later in the form of Bobby's Fill-and-Go Shell Station. Road signs informed her they were almost to Delta, population 3,436, whose claim to fame was being near an attraction called U-Digg Fossils where one could find a rich supply of trilobites if one were willing to drive off the main highway for twenty-eight miles and excavate the quarry oneself.

"Logan, wake up. There's a gas station up ahead. We need to fill up if we can."

"Okay. What do I need to do?"

She steered the Rover down the exit ramp and stopped next to the parking lot.

"Get your gun ready for starters. We need to make sure there's nobody around. See that car parked behind the building? Somebody was here at some point. They may have left on foot, or may still be inside, although probably dead. Best to be safe than sorry."

"You got it, Julia. I'm very good with my guns."

"I know you are. Just keep an eye out."

She drove onto the weed-choked concrete slab, surveying the structure for any evidence of recent activity, then continued around to the back.

On her brother's recommendation, she had purchased a hand pump, a Super Siphon, and a twenty-foot hose for the purpose of acquiring gasoline from underground tanks. But also per his advice, she would try to get it from automobiles first, thus the purchase of a second, shorter hose. The critical part was making sure it hadn't oxidized, and of course Steven had an easy way to test it before loading up the SUV with what could be injector-clogging sludge. Dribble a bit onto the ground and ignite it. If it burned, it was probably good. If it didn't, it wasn't.

She explained all this to Logan, who was more interested in securing the perimeter with his rifle than in her tiresome speech on acquiring fossil fuel in a post-apocalyptic world.

"I don't see any movement in the windows, but they're pretty dirty. Should I go inside? There might be Twinkies."

She laughed. "There might be, but we have plenty of food already so let's not take a chance."

She peered through the glass of the Accord's driver's window. No bodies, living or dead. She tested the handle, found it unlocked, and opened the door. A minute later she located a release lever, pulled it, then inserted the hose into the tank. Next came the part she was dreading because some of it would escape into her mouth.

It did, and was as disgusting as she imagined it would be.

"Ha! You should see your face! Does it taste bad?"

She spit for a half-minute while holding her thumb over the open end of the hose.

"Yes, it's horrible. I need you to take one of the lighters and try to set fire to the gas that spilled on the ground."

"You got it!"

He acted like he felt better and seemed to bask in the glory of being assigned such an important task. Maybe he had been paying attention after all.

Much to Julia's relief, the small puddle burst into flame. Hopefully there was enough gasoline in the Accord to justify the revolting taste in her mouth.

"Can I please go check the store? There might be other stuff in there we could use. I did this all the time when I was by myself."

He was right, of course. Why in the world was she being so overprotective with this young man who had survived quite well on his own for the past year?

"Sure. Go ahead." She stopped herself from adding a litany of warnings. Even though he was childlike, he wasn't a child.

He darted off and stayed gone the entire time she loaded two of her five-gallon tanks. Ten gallons was worth the taste in her mouth. Now that she knew just how bad it was, she would dread it even more the next time.

When he strolled back to the Rover, he wore a satisfied expression and the pockets of his jeans were bulging.

"Find any Twinkies?"

"No, but I found some other good stuff." He seemed reluctant to share more and Julia decided not to push it. He was an odd one for sure, but the same had been said about her over the years.

"We got ten gallons, which is good. But we're going to need more soon." She spat one last time before climbing behind the wheel. Logan slid into the passenger seat, watching her facial contortions with interest.

"If you want me to suck the gas next time, I will."

"It's really awful. I can't ask you to do that."

"I don't think it will bother me as much as it bothers you. I don't mind, really."

She glanced at the young man, gauging his sincerity, while relief flooded over her. She relished the thought of never having that taste in her mouth again.

"That would be wonderful. Maybe we could take turns?"

"Whatever you say, Julia. But I know I won't mind. If you don't want to take a turn, that's okay."

"Let's see if you still feel that way after you've done it the first time."

He grinned and nodded.

Moments later they were back on the highway driving with the windows down because of the fumes.

"I think you must have found something good back there, even though you didn't find Twinkies."

A grubby hand crept into one of the jeans pockets and withdrew a Snickers bar, then a second one. It had been a long time since she'd eaten candy, and she had a particular weakness for Snickers bars.

"Oh, nice score!"

"Would you like one? There were just two. I found them in the back of the store."

What was the shelf life of milk chocolate, caramel, peanuts, and the mysterious substance known as nougat? She didn't know and didn't care. It tasted stale and delicious.

"Anything else?"

"I was hoping to find some string to make you a prettier bracelet, but they didn't have any."

"That's okay. The one you made for me looks very nice."

He frowned and didn't respond. She could see him struggling with something, a concept that was difficult to articulate.

She waited.

"I need to find purple string and just a little bit of green. Those are your colors."

"I love those colors. How did you know?"

"Because those are the colors that I see around you most of the time. Especially purple, but sometimes green too."

Interesting, she thought. As a scientist, she was disinclined to believe in such things as auras, but as an open-minded person, she knew there were many mysteries still in the world because science had yet to discover ways to explain them. An aura was said to be a person's electromagnetic energy, which some individuals claimed they could see. Bio electromagnetics was an actual field of study, so perhaps those people were seeing something. It was a fascinating notion. She'd always been interested in fringe subjects — psychic phenomena, ghosts, extraterrestrials — but had never revealed those interests to her peers at Stanford. There was her reputation to consider, and brilliant scientists could be surprisingly childish. It wasn't completely implausible that a savant, as she suspected Logan to be, might also possess other abilities beyond the norm.

"Do you see colors around everyone?"

He pondered the question, studying the ceiling of the SUV which was his habit when wrestling with a complex thought.

"Not all the time. Not everyone's are as bright as yours, and it's hard to see them unless I really think about it. A lot of the people I saw back home after everyone else died just had black and gray around them. My mom was a yellow. The bracelets I made for her always had yellow in them so they would match her."

"Ah, I see now about the bracelets. Can you see your own colors? Like when you stand in front of a mirror?"

"No. I don't think it works that way. I thought I saw something once when I looked in the mirror. Something sort of around the edges, but it was fuzzy and it made me feel bad, so I stopped looking."

"Well, if it made you feel bad then that was the right decision. I hope you don't always feel that way when you look at yourself. You're a handsome young man, you know."

They were making good time on the state highway and soon they would intersect with I70, which filled her with cautious excitement. It would be the road that carried her to safety, providing everything had gone according to plan on Steven's end. At this rate and barring any unforeseen issues, they would arrive in Liberty in several days.

"Thank you, Julia. My mom said that too, but I figured she did just because, you know, moms say that kind of stuff. Girls don't really like me. I think they think I'm weird."

She could imagine the cruelty he must have endured as a good-looking but mentally challenged boy. Girls would have been drawn to him because of his appearance, then once they discovered his intellectual limitations, they would have lashed out from embarrassment. It must have been difficult for him. Teenage females could be such bitches.

"I don't think you're weird," she half-lied. "I think you're sweet and funny and talented. Those are all qualities to be proud of."

"Thank you. I think you are too. Plus you're really smart, and you have magic."

She sighed.

***

Another car was up ahead and Julia said they would check it for gas. She was always worried about getting more. Logan thought that was funny because he'd done okay without gas and a car for the past year. Still, he was enjoying the drive. They were making-good-time, and even though the cat still hissed a lot, he thought Julia liked him. It felt good because not many people did. Just his mother and Mr. Cheney next door, who taught him stuff, like popping-the-clutch that time, and also how to tie knots and how smart it was to always carry duct tape. Duct tape was good for everything, which is why when he found a pink-colored mini roll of it back at the Shell station, he'd stuck it in his pocket. He didn't tell Julia about it because the Bad Thoughts said he shouldn't, plus it was fun to have secrets.

Julia was nice, but she didn't need to know everything. He also hadn't told her about the little man who had been hiding in the back where the Snickers bars were. He had a gun that he tried to point at Logan, but his hands were shaky and he was slow. It was disappointing that there were no Twinkies, but that's not why he'd killed the little man. He'd killed him because he wanted to know how it felt to choke the life out of someone with his own hands, which he thought would feel different than shooting them from a distance. The Bad Thoughts agreed it was a good idea, so he did it. He was strong even though his shoulder still hurt, and the little man was old, so it hadn't been hard to hold him down and squeeze his wrinkled throat until his eyes bulged and his tongue stuck out. Logan had laughed at that. It made him think of that Simpsons cartoon where Homer always choked Bart. Bart never died, but the little man sure did. It also reminded him of the time he'd done the same thing to a classmate's hamster in the eighth grade. The eye-bulging part was so funny.

Logan decided he liked the way it made him feel. He was very good with his guns and enjoyed seeing blood fly out of animals and people when he shot them, but the feeling of having his strong hands around the skinny throat of the little man, and slowly...ever so slowly...squeezing the breath out of him, was the neatest thing he'd ever done. He hoped he would get the chance to do it again soon. The little man must have had some magic because he'd been able to see Logan, but it hadn't been strong enough to save him.

When they stopped behind a car that was parked on the side of the road, he wondered again how strong Julia's magic was. She said she would let him suck the gas this time and he thought that might be fun, although not as fun as the little man. He liked making her smile, just as he'd liked making his mom smile. But he also knew he had to be careful. He knew he shouldn't tell her that he enjoyed killing things...he never told his mom, either. He also hid his drawing pad from his mom, except for those first few pictures. He told her he was bored with drawing, but that wasn't true at all.

He had been careful not to let her know about the cats and dogs that went missing in the neighborhoods where they lived because it would upset her. For that same reason, and because Mr. Cheney had said he should, he had hidden his well-used drawing pad under a lot of junk in a bottom drawer. His mom never looked in that drawer.

He figured he should keep it hidden from Julia too, even though he was pretty proud of those drawings. Mr. Cheney loved them. He'd said that he and Logan 'had similar urges,' which Logan thought meant they both enjoyed killing things. He missed Mr. Cheney too, but he felt that part of Mr. Cheney was still with him.

Chapter 34

Liberty, Kansas

While a gathering of townspeople helped unload the building materials in the square, Steven decided to broach the subject of the enslaved women in Hays. Reactions were varied and heated.

Natalie had refused to make eye contact with him since the incident in his bedroom the night before. He sensed a slow-boil anger lurking beneath the cool demeanor. It was understandable; he had sex with her then promptly kicked her out of his house. Even though he'd been justified, he felt guilty. She and her daughter had been hungry. Yes, she manipulated the mob to get to his supplies and almost gotten him killed in the process, but who could blame her? Wouldn't he commit far worse acts to feed his son?

"I don't mean to sound heartless," Natalie said in that reasonable, crowd-calming way, "But we can barely provide for our own people. If we take on more mouths to feed, everyone will have to go with less, or even without, depending on how long our current provisions last." Her glance in Steven's direction didn't reach his face. "We don't even know if those women are truly prisoners. Perhaps they're just enterprising females utilizing the barter system. Goods for services, you know. Some might find that's an easier life than grubbing in a garden or conducting dangerous forays to acquire food."

Chuck's snort was derisive and bitter. "Seriously, Natalie? Leave it to you to put a positive spin on a bunch of assholes raping women."

The crowd had burgeoned at this point to include most of Liberty's tiny population. She shot him a poisonous look.

"Even if that's true, and I'm not saying it is, the issue is the danger," she continued. "It's likely our own people will get hurt or killed in the process of rescuing these strangers. Why would we take that chance?"

Her words were met with a smattering of applause.

Steven kept his mouth shut. She had a point. He had voiced a similar notion to Jeffrey that morning.

"You are one cold bitch, Natalie," Chuck replied. "What if Brittany were one of those women? How would you feel then?"

"But she's not. They're strangers. Why risk life and limb for people we don't even know?" Her tone was calm and judicious even in the face of his insult, scoring additional points from the onlookers.

A musical voice came from the back. One Steven recognized immediately.

"They're not prostituting themselves, if that's what you mean."

The crooked smile was gone from the face of Liberty's newest resident, replaced by a grimness which was at odds with the gentle nature he had sensed earlier.

"And who are you?"

"I'm Lisa. I just moved here." People stepped aside as she walked toward Natalie.

"I see. You're a stranger with an opinion about whether we should put ourselves in jeopardy for other strangers."

"I didn't say that. I said they weren't prostituting themselves."

"And how do you know that?"

"Because a week ago I spoke to a woman who had just left there. She mentioned armed guards and chains. That doesn't sound like any barter system I've ever heard of."

Steven interjected. "Everybody, Lisa has just moved to town. She is a horticultural scientist, so she'll be of enormous help getting our community garden off the ground."

A few 'welcomes' came from the townspeople but the general focus was not to be shifted so easily from the topic of the Hays women.

"Even if what you're saying is true..." Natalie began.

"It is. I'm no liar." The brown eyes flashed but the lovely voice remained steady. Ed, who had edged his way through the packed bodies to stand next to her, didn't say a word. His body language conveyed a protective instinct; Steven was relieved that he didn't try to insert himself into the discussion. If he had, it just might have been the end of his would-be romance with his new neighbor before it had even gotten off the ground.

"Be that as it may, it doesn't change anything. We simply cannot afford injury or death of our own to save others. In case you haven't realized it, the world is no longer the cakewalk it used to be. Civilization is hanging by a thread. We have a chance to do something here in our own town that could mean the very continuance of humanity. If there's any risk to our citizens, it should be in endeavors which benefit us. We are not the world's saviors."

There was more than a smattering of applause this time. Steven had to admit, Natalie was damn good at oratory. And he also had to admit, grudgingly, that he tended to agree with her. At least about this.

"You're right," Lisa said. "Everyone can't be saved. But it seems to me that a few women in a nearby town who are being kept captive for the purpose of rape would qualify as worth saving."

"We certainly have a conundrum, don't we?"

Steven searched for the speaker. Liberty's former librarian maneuvered through the onlookers without grace or finesse but with the quiet dignity he had recently come to appreciate. Three very different women stood in the center of the crowd now, all assuming diverse postures and expressions.

Marilyn continued, "There is no wrong or right answer. The dilemma is not complicated, but the effects of our decision have far-reaching implications. Like a stone tossed into a pond, the ripples or repercussions of our behavior now will affect our future later. We are in the infancy of this venture...the formation of a cooperative community in which everyone will have a voice...where we all contribute and reap the rewards equally. These are bold plans we've made. If only we had a producing vineyard, it might be a paradise. Alas, our soil isn't suited for grapes, but perhaps if we play our cards right, there will someday be bathtub gin and hard apple cider."

A wave of laughter passed through the gathering, diminishing the tension. Good. Clear heads meant better judgment. Steven watched the woman talk, her elegant prose had captivated everyone, himself included.

The smile came then, transforming the plain features into something that almost rivaled the beauty of the women next to her. "What path shall we take? Down which road will our fledgling community travel? The one where we make smart, detached, clinical decisions based on threat assessment and risk-reward ratios? Or the one where we do the right thing because we know in our hearts it is wrong to let people suffer in bondage if there is something we can do about it? Both sides of the argument are compelling, but even more important is understanding that the decision we make now, on this slippery slope, will establish the fundamental nature of our future society. Once we set sail, it will be difficult to change course."

"Wise words, Marilyn," Natalie said loudly, shifting the attention back to herself. "I for one would like to live in a world where sense and reason prevail. I say we put it to a vote."

Lisa turned her back and walked away in disgust. Ed scurried to follow.

"Maybe people would like to think about it, Natalie," Steven said from the tailgate of the Ram pickup where he'd been sitting. "I know I would."

This time her gray eyes bored directly into his; he almost reeled backward from what he saw there.

"Fine. Let's meet back at this time tomorrow, people."

The crowd dispersed, leaving just the construction volunteers: six young people who were capable of hard physical labor.

Steven sighed as he watched their new foreman struggling to keep up with an agitated, bobbing blond ponytail a block away.

"Do I get a vote, Dad?"

"You sure as hell do. You're working as hard as everyone else. Harder than most. You've earned it."

He regretted his words the next moment when he considered their talk earlier about helping those in need. His mind skipped forward to what a rescue operation would look like, and beyond to the recruitment of his sharp shooting son for the mission. A part of him wished he could take Jeffrey back to their house with the electric fence and the well-stocked cellar, tend only to their needs, and leave this quagmire behind. But even though he could be content to live as a hermit, it would be no life for his son.

"Get the word out," Steven said to those who remained. "Tomorrow morning we're going to vote on more than a rescue mission. We're going to make a lot of other decisions too. Every one of us, not just a board of four or five people." He smiled to himself at the thought of Natalie's face when she discovered he had circumvented her assumed authority. If there was to be a feud between the two of them, better to have it out in the open.

He had a lot of work to do on the greenhouse today, then he would pull an all-nighter getting his notes together for tomorrow's town meeting. If he couldn't live with his head in the sand, he would at least play a major role in designing and building the sandbox.

The next day dawned clear and mild but soon turned overcast. The wind picked up as the townspeople gathered in the square again. Noses lifted to the sudden breeze, detecting the rain that was close behind. Longtime residents of the Midwest knew what that could mean even in October, so the meeting was relocated to the interior of the courthouse, where a variety of hastily lit candles created a warm, inviting atmosphere in one of the courtrooms.

Fifty pungent bodies squeezed onto the wooden benches. Steven decided he would browse his *Encyclopedia of Country Living* — no self-respecting prepper would be without a copy — for a homemade antiperspirant recipe as soon as there was time.

Natalie glided to the front, positioning herself between the tables at which opposing legal counsels would have pleaded their cases, and where all eyes would be focused on her. But this wasn't a trial. There were no lawyers or judges, and Steven was determined that everyone would feel equal.

He raised his voice, "I think we should move the benches around so they form a circle. Like the Knights of the Round Table." He hoped his smile was self-deprecating, not just awkward and goofy, as it felt to him. Public speaking had never been his forte, but if he were going to be instrumental in the creation of this new community, he would do it in a way that made sense to him. He'd stayed up all night, making lists and scribbling half-formed ideas, but also spent time considering the personalities of the people he knew and how best to interact with them.

Natalie would be his biggest problem. He sensed she had an agenda, but he could only speculate on the details. Even though he was late to the party — people had been surviving without him for the last year — his largess of food and medicine had bought him a bit of deference. He intended to exploit it for the greater good.

"I'd like to emphasize that just because a few of us came up with the concept of the cooperative greenhouse and some other ideas, it doesn't mean that anyone's opinion carries more weight than anyone else's." He glanced at Natalie, who arched a delicate eyebrow. "Having said that, some people are better suited for certain tasks than others. We'll need to vote on positions such as construction foreman," he nodded in Ed's direction, "Head gardener," a nod at Lisa who sat next to Ed with a foot of bench space in between, "And so on. The way I see it, getting seeds in the ground is our number one priority, which means it's crucial to get the greenhouse built quickly. Our water situation is tolerable for now but will need to be improved. I have some thoughts on windmill-generated electricity, which will help with the water supply to our crops in the short term and can be expanded upon later. But in the meantime we'll have to truck in water from the lake." He stopped for a moment to catch his breath and take measure of the crowd.

So far, so good. He was relieved to see that the general mood seemed upbeat and friendly.

"I know there have been some waterborne illnesses in the past, so I'm happy to assist anyone who would like to build a gravity-fed water filtration system for their personal use."

A number of hands went up.

"Winter is right around the corner, and we'll need to make sure everyone stays warm. We need a group of volunteers to locate, chop, and deliver wood to all those who can't get it for themselves."

His gaze found Marilyn, who had been assigned the task of taking notes from the meeting. She jotted down names on a notepad as several men and two women volunteered for the fuel crew, as it would be called.

"What about people that don't have fireplaces?" The question came from an older man Steven didn't recognize.

"There are plenty of houses in town that do and which are no longer...occupied. I suggest moving."

"I'm no squatter. I've lived in my house for thirty years. Lost my wife to the plague in that house. Raised two sons and a daughter in that house. You're suggesting that I abandon it now and move into some stranger's house just because they're dead and they have a fireplace?"

"How did you manage in your house last winter?"

Atmos Energy had kept the natural gas running until too many employees stopped coming to work. Heating oil systems weren't common in Kansas, so once the power had gone out and the gas stopped flowing in December, people must have gotten very cold.

"I insulated the hell out of it and wore a lot of sweaters," the man replied, unsmiling.

Steven sighed. "I understand the inclination to cling to the past, but this is about survival, and if you want to stay warm, I encourage you to find a house with a fireplace. It's a free country though, so do what you want."

He appreciated the irony of those last words and the easy manner in which they had fallen unthinkingly out of his mouth. But this was not the appropriate time to get bogged down in a discussion of whether there was still a United States of America and if it were, in fact, free. Other matters were far more pressing.

"Let's move along, shall we? We've touched on the most important issues: food, water, and warmth," he counted three of his fingers. "Next comes illness and other medical concerns. I understand there's a nurse practitioner here?" He had learned of the woman at the impromptu meeting at his house two days earlier but had yet to meet her. She had helped with some injuries and sickness the past year. Several people had described her as 'peculiar.'

All heads swiveled toward the courtroom door where a woman stood. Steven hadn't noticed her until that moment.

"That would be me." The high-pitched, spindly voice was at odds with the stout figure, itself an anomaly in a room filled with half-starved people. She said nothing else but merely waited for him to continue.

"You're Cate?"

A curt nod of the mousy-brown head.

"As a nurse practitioner, you are the most qualified person to head our medical group. Is that something you'd be interested in?"

Steven realized why the others thought the woman strange. Beefy arms were crossed over a generous bosom and the ruddy face wore an expression of amusement. What she found so funny was a mystery.

"I'm guessing it doesn't pay much," she said.

"You're right about that."

The amused smirk intensified. "Sure. I'll head up your group, as long as I get to do it my way. I don't want to be bothered with hangnails and nosebleeds either. And if my methods seem unorthodox, I don't want to be second guessed. If you all agree to that, I'll take the job."

With that, she turned and walked out of the room. Steven followed her progress, catching a glimpse of the storm clouds through the corridor windows beyond.

***

"I think it went well," Steven said to his son as they sat down to a late dinner in their kitchen. As ominous as the approaching storm had appeared earlier, it had been all blustery bravado and produced only a few raindrops. He would bet his last can of coffee that the weather system had spawned tornadoes somewhere though. Perhaps Arkansas or Oklahoma.

During the town hall meeting, which would occur weekly from now on, they voted on a number of issues and formed several other crews. Eventually, the greenhouse would be expanded upon not only physically, but in the broader sense of broaching into the town's outlying fallow fields next spring. They touched on ideas for planting wheat, oats, and a few other grains, a berry patch for currants, blackberries, and strawberries, and an orchard grove with pecan, hazelnut, plum, and cherry trees — all indigenous crops.

"Don't you think it went well?" He pressed his son. "Everyone seemed excited to be pulling together and planning the community."

"I guess," Jeffrey replied. Hostility over the rescue vote was still evident on a face which was just beginning to lose some of its youthful roundness to an angular jawline.

It had been close. Twenty-three for, twenty-six against.

Steven sighed. He had voted in favor of the mission but couldn't deny the relief he felt when it went the other way.

"Pretty exciting that you're on the security crew. Only the best marksmen got picked for it."

His son's face brightened. "Yeah, that's cool. I like Chuck, and the other people seem okay."

Chuck, the former grocery store manager, had done a six-year stint in Afghanistan as an MP, so the closest thing to a police officer left in Liberty was awarded the position of head of security. His crew consisted of two burly young men in their twenties and a girl of eighteen who could hit the bulls-eye of a target fifty yards away with a rifle, handgun, or compound bow — a claim which several people had corroborated. With the help of Ed and Lisa, who confirmed they had witnessed his sharpshooting skills the day before, Jeffrey had been the last person accepted in. It had taken every bit of self-control Steven possessed not to interfere when his son volunteered. Its members would be responsible for keeping the town safe from marauders, as well as handling the delicate issue of enforcing any laws they legislated, none of which had been decided upon that day.

Steven was relieved about that. He hated the inevitable politicking that would begin when bellies were full and minds less preoccupied with keeping them that way. After the assemblage, they had made tremendous progress on the greenhouse build-out. At the rate they were going, it would be ready for seeding in a week. His seeds were in good hands with Lisa. She knew her stuff, and abdicating his role as head gardener to her would allow him to focus on projects for which he was better suited.

His first order of business was getting limited electricity running for the greenhouse. Then he intended to develop a grid system utilizing both wind and solar power; he envisioned it as a mini version of the grid at Kansas Electric. The lofty goal of having everyone's lights back on within a year was presented at the end of the meeting and met with thunderous applause.

He reined in thoughts of wind turbines and solar panels, focusing again on the young man across the table.

"I agree," Steven said. "I like Chuck a lot and the others seem nice. That girl sounds like a real Annie Oakley." He laughed at the blank expression. "Way before your time. Hell, way before my time too."

"Dad, I can't stop thinking about those women."

"Jeff, there's nothing we can do about it. The vote went the other way."

"You and I could do something."

Steven groaned. "Son, we can't. I'm not going to risk my only child on such a dangerous operation. Can't you understand that?"

"Maybe it wouldn't be that dangerous. We don't have all the facts. You always say, 'We don't have enough information to make a decision.' Right?"

Steven had no response ready. Jeffrey pounced. "So let's get more information."

"And how do you propose we do that?"

"We'll ask Lisa. Just the two of us and her. Let's see if there's anything else that lady who left Hays told her. Then we'll go from there."

Steven cocked an eyebrow at the smooth manner in which his son had just manipulated him.

"Fine. We'll talk to her."

Jeffrey's rare smile was still more little boy than young man, and it melted Steven's heart every time.

CHAPTER 35

ARIZONA

Pablo was grumpy. He'd been deprived of sleeping with his love the night before. They crashed at a Days Inn on the eastern outskirts of Winslow, and Maddie insisted that Jessie — the strange little girl with the sea-green eyes — sleep with her. She promised it was a temporary situation, and as soon as the little girl felt safe, Maddie would return to his bed. How long that would take, he could only guess. He knew he was being a jerk about it, but he'd just gotten her back. Their relationship had barely progressed from friends to lovers, and already he was being denied physical intimacy.

The other reason for his surliness was bad gasoline. The last three attempts at obtaining more had been a bust, resulting in nothing more than a foul aftertaste. A year after the pandemic, it was turning. He was no chemist nor interested in the process that converted good gas to bad. All he knew was that much of what they were siphoning out of abandoned cars had oxidized, and that meant more gas-sucking down the road.

Maddie watched him with amusement from the passenger seat.

"I'll suck the gas next time."

He shook his head. "No, that's my job."

She laughed. "Really? And that's based on what? The fact that you have a p-e-n-i-s?"

Great. Now we're spelling out the naughty words...

"I'm surprised you remember," he replied before he could stop himself.

"And there it is, folks! The true source of Pablo's poutiness. Somebody didn't get l-a-i-d last night. Poor Pablo."

"I'm sorry. I know I'm being a d-i-c-k. I just missed you."

"It won't be long. I think Jessie is feeling better already. Aren't you, Jessie?"

The child nodded. They had gotten her cleaned up and changed into some clothes scavenged from a corpse-free vehicle. The dress was too large, but clean and intact. Now that the grime was gone and her hair freshly washed and braided (just like Amelia's, per Jessie's request), she looked more like a child and less like a female Gollum. Still, those enormous eyes unsettled him...made him think of a placid tropical ocean and the toothy creatures gliding beneath its surface.

"We should be crossing into New Mexico soon," Maddie said, studying the map in her lap.

Pablo gazed out his window at the relentlessly uninviting desert landscape. "That's good. I'm ready to see Arizona in the rearview mirror."

"That sounds like the title of a country western song. Let's write it!"

He laughed. "Right now?"

"No better time than the present," Amelia piped from the back. "Come on Mr. Poet Laureate. Writing a song is child's play for someone like you."

He grinned, caught up in the infectious excitement. Even the little girl smiled.

It took several hours to compose the lyrics, then another two to put a melody to their creation. By the time they pulled into the parking lot of a Motel 6, the three grownups were singing "Arizona in the Rearview Mirror", even working out some three-part harmony in places, with Pablo taking the tenor, Maddie the alto, and Amelia's sweet soprano stealing the show.

They piled out of the Highlander, which they parked in front of room 106. With a hand to his brow, Pablo scanned their surroundings. To the west, a colossal mesa pulled the sun toward itself like a greedy lover, and to the east, burgeoning cities of clouds scuttled in the direction they would be traveling in the morning.

Pablo reconnoitered the vicinity, shotgun in hand and Bruno trudging along behind. There were no automobiles and no people. Not surprising since Gallup, New Mexico, was in the middle of nowhere.

"I think this'll be okay," he said, when he joined the group again.

Something whizzed past his left temple.

He lunged for Maddie and pulled her to the asphalt. Amelia reacted even faster. She wedged herself beneath the under carriage, covering Jessie's body with her own.

Another bullet ricocheted off the side mirror. He couldn't tell from what direction it had come.

"See that second story window on the far right? Room 218, I think," Maddie said.

A third bullet pierced the passenger door where she had been sitting moments earlier. He followed her gaze to the tip of a rifle poking through the window.

He couldn't see the number on the door, but he had no doubt it was 218. She had a calculator for a brain, so tracking the trajectory and configuring the room number without seeing the silver-plated numerals was not remarkable...for her.

"Shit," he said. "Get under the car. Please."

Surprisingly, she did so. He scrambled in after her. Bruno darted behind one of the front tires. Curly Sue whimpered from inside the Highlander where Amelia had yet to release her.

"That's eight so far. How many bullets does an average rifle hold?" Maddie asked in a calm voice. She might have been pondering the caloric content of a Big Mac.

"Five or so, I think. Of course that might not be his only gun or he might be using a high capacity clip."

"He's no more than thirty yards away and he can't hit a non-moving target with a rifle. He must not be a good shot."

"He doesn't have to be. If he has enough ammo, he can just play the odds."

"Or maybe he's not trying to hit us," she said. "You're not going to like this, and it will take too long to explain because it's all very mathy. But I'm going to do something and I need you to not freak out."

Bullets nine and ten hit the asphalt a few feet from the Toyota. From this angle, they looked like miniature bombs exploding. Before he could argue, she squirmed back out. Eleven and twelve struck the pavement two feet in front of her.

With raised arms, she walked toward room 218. Pablo's heart was in his throat as he crawled out after her.

"Stay back. I mean it. You will not get any n-o-o-k-i-e tonight if you don't," she hissed.

He stopped. Maddie continued toward the source of the gunfire. The barrel still extended through the window, but was no longer firing now.

She called out, "We're no threat to you! We're just looking for a place to sleep for the night!"

No response, neither verbal nor ballistic.

"We have a child! We're two women and a child!"

A voice came from the window of room 218, gruff yet frail-sounding. "I see a man too!"

"Yes, but he's a poet!"

Pablo was too anxious to be offended. Ten seconds passed that felt like ten minutes. Finally, the door of room 218 opened and a white head poked out.

Maddie stopped just below the balcony where an old man emerged, holding a hunting rifle pointed directly at her.

A nauseating flashback of the Walgreen's nightmare caused Pablo to break out in a cold sweat.

"How do I know you're harmless? I've met a lot of nasty people this past year."

"Do we look like nasty people?" She allowed the old man a long examination of her open face and guileless beauty.

At that moment, Pablo knew she would be safe.

"I'm Maddie. That's Pablo. Amelia is there under the car with Jessie. Is it okay for them to come out?"

"Yeah, yeah. I've never shot a woman or child, and I don't plan on starting today. You there, poet fellow. You watch yourself. No sudden moves and put that shotgun on the ground."

Pablo nodded, feeling the sting now of the emasculating nuance.

"May I ask your name?" Maddie said.

"I'm Alfred. I don't have much food or water, so don't think you're invited to dinner. You can stay here for the night but you're gone in the morning. We clear?"

"Yes, sir."

Pablo could only see her backside from his vantage, but he saw the effect of her smile on the face of the old man.

If Maddie carried a gun, she could have etched another notch in it.

"Why the hell Oklahoma? There's nobody there but goat ropers and shit kickers."

During dinner, provided by Alfred despite the earlier caveat, the old man showed himself to be cynical and somewhat racist, but also intelligent and kind-hearted. He shared room 218 with a tabby kitten he'd found near death the previous week and had been nursing back to health ever since. Nevertheless, his offhand comments regarding Pablo's and Amelia's ethnicity made it difficult to be in his presence.

"We're just looking for fertile farmland and a safe place to live. The farther away from people the better," Pablo replied.

Alfred's faded blue eyes regarded him. "You ever do much farming, young man?"

"A little. My family kept an extensive vegetable garden. In Arizona, no less. I figure the rich soil and regular rain in Oklahoma will provide conditions light years beyond what we had back home."

The old man gave a grudging nod. "You come across any troublemakers so far?"

Pablo darted a look at Maddie. She nodded.

"There were some bad people in Prescott. So bad that they ran me out of town and into the desert for the last six months. They had Maddie for a while, but she got away."

"Ya don't say?" The old man's eyes were drawn again to her face. He reached out and gave her knee a grandfatherly pat. The light eyes became watery and he brushed at them with the back of a liver-spotted hand.

"What about you, Alfred? Have any problems with troublemakers?" Amelia asked from one of the double beds in his hotel room. Curly Sue and Bruno were curled up on the bed next to her. Jessie and the kitten had fallen asleep an hour ago on the other bed. The naked Barbie doll was held in a tiny death grip.

"Oh, yeah. That's why I'm here, smack dab in the middle of nowhere. That's also why I shot at you folks. Sorry about that, by the way."

"No problem," Maddie said quickly before Pablo could get in a snide remark. "You didn't know we weren't unsavory types."

"Still don't know about that poet fellow," he said with an ornery grin at Pablo.

Pablo sighed and shook his head in mock exasperation. "We poets get such a bad rap. So, how did you get here? We didn't see any cars in the parking lot."

"Unloaded all my supplies then drove my pickup into the ditch a mile up the road. Didn't want anyone to know I was here."

"What happens when you run out of food?" Maddie asked.

The old man smiled, displaying teeth so pristine they must have been dentures. "That will be the end of Alfred then."

"What do you mean? You're just going to let yourself starve to death?" The distress in Maddie's tone made Pablo cringe on the inside. He began tackling the logistics of squeezing an elderly man and a small feline into the overloaded SUV.

In his gruff, quavering voice, the old man surprised everyone with a poem recitation. It was one Pablo knew well.

"I said unto myself, if I were dead,What would befall these children? What would beTheir fate, who now are looking up to meFor help and furtherance? Their lives, I said,Would be a volume wherein I have readBut the first chapters, and no longer seeTo read the rest of their dear history,So full of beauty and so full of dread.Be comforted; the world is very old,And generations pass, as they have passed,A troop of shadows moving with the sun;Thousands of times has the old tale been told;The world belongs to those who come the last,They will find hope and strength as we have done."

"Longfellow. Very nice, Alfred." Pablo gazed at the old man with new respect.

"More relevant now than ever." He paused. "I'm not long for this world, Maddie. I've lived on this planet for eighty-seven years. I've kissed a lot of girls," he winked at Amelia, "done a lot of bad things and then a lot of good things. I think I'm square with my maker, but if I'm not, well, at least living in the desert has gotten me used to the heat. *'The world belongs to those who come the last.'* I just hope it's folks like you and your poet fellow who rise to the top. Not the punks and riff raff I've seen so much of this past year."

"Me too, Alfred," Pablo replied. "Me too."

***

"What do you think will become of him?" Maddie asked, scrutinizing the map the next day. They were entering the outskirts of Albuquerque, and it would soon be time to locate an alternate route through the city. People had resorted to using both sides of I40 in an effort to flee. Pablo hated this part, never knowing if there would be bodies inside or not. So far, about fifty percent of the time there were. Maddie could have provided the exact number.

"He'll die," he said, steering the Toyota onto the shoulder to bypass a snarl of cars.

"It seems wrong to die alone."

"It's the way he wanted to go," Amelia said. Jessie gazed at the older woman with a thoughtful expression as she stroked the kitten in her lap. Of course they'd allowed the child to accept Alfred's gift; the alternative would have been a death sentence for the feline.

A shy, peach-smooth hand reached across the back seat and grasped Amelia's, encircling the brown fingers, slightly crooked from early onset arthritis. When the child released her grip minutes later, Amelia studied her own hand with surprise.

"It just makes me sad," Maddie continued.

"I know what will turn that frown upside down," Pablo said with an evil grin.

"What? Chocolate? Tequila?"

"Nope. Gas sucking. I was recently informed that this task does not require a p-e-n-i-s, so you're in luck. All you need is good lungs, great lips, and a weak gag reflex. What do you say?"

She punched him in the arm. "Fine. I'll do it. And I'll do it without all the girly complaining too."

As it turned out, she couldn't make good on her vow.

"Holy s-h-i-t! This is horrible!" she said ten minutes later next to a late model Suburban. On the eastern horizon the low skyline lay nestled against a backdrop of mountains.

"Told you." The visual of her sputtering and gagging would have been funnier if he wasn't concerned about how her kisses would taste that night.

"I gotta give you this one, Poet Fellow. You're right. Let's hope it's the gas is good this time."

They dribbled some of it onto the pavement. Per Alfred's instructions, they touched the edge of the puddle with a lighter, transforming it into a miniature inferno.

"If nothing else constructive came from our encounter with Alfred, this little trick will have been worth it. Houston, we have good gasoline."

Pablo was still kicking himself that he hadn't thought of this litmus test before. Although the smell test was also fairly reliable. Good gas smelled like gas and bad smelled sweet. The Suburban's enormous tank allowed them to top off the Highlander, plus fill their two dented cans. Maddie was elated knowing they could make it to Oklahoma on what they now had. Of course she could calculate it down to the yard, even switching to the metric system if asked. So far he hadn't, but sometimes it was fun to throw her a mathematical curve ball just to watch the adorable process.

"We should take the Atrisco Vista exit."

"I see a sign up ahead."

Jessie had fallen asleep in the back seat with the kitten on her lap, the dogs were doing god-knows-what in the third row, which had been folded down to accommodate them, and Amelia was wedged in between the supplies that wouldn't fit in the back. They were crammed into the SUV like a box of human crayons.

"I think I see..." Maddie began, just as something smashed through the windshield and silenced whatever she was going to say.

After that, everything became hazy and dreamlike. Maddie slumped against the passenger side door, a rag doll dropped by a careless child. On some level he knew he was screaming, but the feeling was detached from himself, like it came from another Pablo in an alternate dimension. He could hear Amelia yelling now.

Drive Pablo drive!

It barely registered because it was directed at that other Pablo, the one who physically sat behind the wheel and was capable of movement and action. Not this Pablo who couldn't take his eyes off the rag doll next to him.

Then, like a soul crashing back into its body after a near death event, he returned to himself and followed the directive to *drive Pablo drive!*

He couldn't look at the rag doll. All he could do was *drive and get them the hell out of here!*

Fifteen chaotic minutes later, they came to a stop on a residential street somewhere in Albuquerque, where there were no longer rough-looking men and women approaching them and brandishing an array of weapons and firearms. He still couldn't bear to look at the rag doll, because if he did, he might see its lifelessness. So instead, he opened the driver's side door and fell to the sidewalk of what was once a lovely ranch-style home with pale yellow siding and a cacti garden next to the front porch.

He vomited by the mailbox.

He lifted his head a minute later when all he could do was dry retch, to see Amelia tending to Maddie. He wondered if her midwife skills extended to neurosurgery because the bullet hole in Maddie's left temple would require it.

"She's alive, Pablo." There was an odd edge...a shading...to Amelia's voice he hadn't heard before, but his brain wasn't functioning well enough to analyze what it meant.

He opened his mouth to speak, but all that came out was a sob.

"Pablo, get a grip. You're not doing her any good now. Let's get her inside. Now, young man!"

The sharp words penetrated the fog, and gently-oh-so-gently, he carried Maddie inside.

Per Amelia's instructions, he laid her down on a tidy bed in one of the bedrooms. He was aware that the house smelled musty and stale, but his olfactory senses didn't register the pungent, sour aroma of human decomposition. Was that because there were no bodies or because they were so far gone their odor was no longer off-putting? He found that it helped to wonder about such things at the moment, because otherwise all he could think about was losing his love. Again.

"Pablo, listen to me. Go back to the car and get my pack and some water. Quickly now." Amelia's voice still carried that perplexing quality which he couldn't be troubled to identify at the moment. He did as he was told without a verbal response. He didn't want to hear the agony in his own voice.

When he returned with the items, the strange little girl and the tiny braided woman sat on either side of Maddie. She looked less like a rag doll now and more like an angel who hasn't had a proper bath in a while. The thought made him smile. What was the name of that old black and white movie? *Angels with Dirty Faces?* Something like that.

"Now, leave us, please." The tone was still strange, but he was more disturbed by the command itself.

"I'm not leaving her. I will never leave her. Never again."

He watched the slow rise and fall of Maddie's chest. It gave him minor comfort. He tried not to look at how starkly her freckles stood out against the pallor of her face. Back to the chest. It was still rising and falling.

That had to be a good thing, right? Her beautiful hair...that luxurious, tangled mess of red and gold, was so perfectly, exquisitely disheveled, lying against the powder blue pillow case. Who could die with hair that gorgeous? He smiled again. *The Hair Gods wouldn't allow it*, was something Maddie would say. *I am Folliculitia, the Angel of Fabulous Hair! I must stay on earth to provide an example for all those females who also desire fabulous hair! I cannot be summoned to heaven on a whim...my job here is too important!*

"Pablo, it's not a suggestion. If you want to give her a fighting chance, you will leave now and shut the door."

That snapped him out of his reverie. The expression he saw in the old-soul eyes was congruent with the curious voice.

He didn't know why he did so, but he turned around and walked out of the bedroom, closing the door behind him.

Chapter 36

Oklahoma

Something had crashed down on Dani's back, pinning her body to Sam's. She couldn't see his face in the dark bathroom. The flashlight had fallen from her grasp at some point in the last few seconds, but she felt him breathing. She could barely hear Fergus's shout above the savage howl of the wind and the incessant pounding of debris.

"Dani, are you okay?"

"Yes!" she screamed, her voice almost lost in the storm's cacophony. What was holding her down? Sheet rock? Cabinetry? It was heavy as hell, but she managed to wedge herself like a human gasket between Sam and whatever had fallen on them.

"I think it's passing! Just stay put!"

Seconds later, the pounding tapered off and the shrieking wind subsided. The residual quiet so soon after the deafening noise of the storm was eerie but welcome. She could feel Sam's steady breathing and enjoyed how it felt to just lie there, her body covering his, and their hearts beating close together. She had no idea how long it lasted. Five minutes? An hour? But the moment was shattered by the sudden lifting of weight from her back and blinding sunlight in her eyes.

"What the hell?"

"That's right, Honey Badger. That glowing bright orb in the sky is, in fact, the sun. Why, you might ask, can one see it through the ceiling of a house? To which I would reply in that charming yet direct way I have, because a fucking F5, as you referred to it earlier, ripped the entire second story off our sanctuary. Kind of annoying since we'll have to relocate now, but at least we're alive, yes? I assume by the dreamy look on your face and the salacious manner in which you're groping Sam that he's still with us?"

He continued the running dialogue while excavating them from a sea of splintered lumber, chunks of porcelain, mangled shingles and, oh my god, was that a dead Holstein in the destroyed living room?

"Unlucky cow!" she said, with a manic chuckle.

"Indeed," Fergus replied. "I intend to capitalize on its bad fortune in the form of steaks for dinner. Help me with Sam, love. Careful, now."

In the sporadic way tornadic destruction results in one suburban house being demolished and the one next door escaping unscathed, Big Blue was parked where they'd left it and in good condition despite hail damage that looked like metallic cellulite.

If anyone in the truck had glanced back at the mountain of rubble as they drove down the winding gravel driveway, they would have seen a figure: a ragged, frantic human rummaging through the debris. He? She? It was grasping at objects with filthy, claw-like fingers, then flinging them aside in anger. Just as the pickup turned left onto the road, it came upon the object it sought — the sentinel doll from the foyer. It pressed the toy against its bony torso next to a sheath containing a blood-stained knife.

They found an intact house a mile down the road, although it took some stunt driving around uprooted trees to get there. While Sam rested in bed, Dani and Fergus sat outside in companionable, exhausted silence next to a charcoal grill. She had left the butchering of the unlucky Holstein to him. They found some Kingsford briquettes in a shed, and the aroma coming from the Weber mini Death Star was heavenly.

"Two things would make this better: a cold Sam Adams in my hand and a bodacious blond on my lap," he said.

She smiled but was too tired to think of a clever response. The glowing bright orb from earlier, now a not-so-bright half orb, was on the brink of committing planetary suicide in the western horizon.

Going, going, gone.

She breathed a deep, soul-cleansing sigh. Sam was doing remarkably well despite the pain, and had swallowed the first dose of antibiotics without too much arguing. He was situated in a bedroom, as comfortable as possible after cleaning his wound and changing the dressing. Before she left the bedroom, he pulled her face gently down to his and kissed her with more love and tenderness than she had ever before experienced, then promptly passed out on a king-size field of pink tea roses.

"I think he's going to make it," Fergus said, guessing the subject of her thoughts. He flipped the sizzling steaks, testing their doneness with a barbecue fork.

"He has to."

She could feel the keen blue eyes studying her, but no additional comment on Sam or her love life was forthcoming.

Instead, he said, "I'm having a difficult time picturing you in overalls, plowing fields, and milking cows. You have this sexy Milla Jovovich Resident Evil vibe going at the moment...you know, badass brunette with a brain to match her brawn? No, wait. No, I'm seeing you more as an Angelina Jolie aka Laura Croft type. Yes, that's it. Would you mind braiding your hair and donning some hot pants? I could die a happy man."

If she were sitting closer, she would have added to his bruise collection. He had, however, hit upon something that had been bothering her for a while. Could she be content in such a bucolic setting? Before Isaiah came along and pissed in their sandbox, her nighttime forays in Texas had been exhilarating. She would never confess this to Sam, but sometimes she left him at home with the objective of increasing the danger element and thus the excitement.

She *was* a badass, thanks to her intellect and Sam's training. The challenges of the past year had taken the soft bookworm and transformed it into a force to be reckoned with. Despite the loss of her parents — those gentle souls who had shared their home and their love, but not their DNA — she couldn't deny that she was happier in this perilous, post-apocalyptic world than she had ever been in her safe, indulgent restaurant-on-every-corner life.

The thought triggered a recent memory.

"Why do you think there were no cars back at that Love's station?" she asked. "I mean, there were fast food joints, some houses, and other buildings, but not one vehicle parked at any of them. There have been abandoned cars everywhere we've gone."

"Yes, it was odd," Fergus replied, flipping the steaks again. "Perhaps everyone tucked their automobiles neatly in their garages before kicking the oxygen habit."

"That seems unlikely based on past experience. Think about it. We haven't seen any vehicles since we left that gas station. Not one. I don't know what to make of it."

"I don't know either and, frankly, I don't care at the moment. I'm taking these off now. Medium rare, yes?"

She nodded absently.

Between mouthfuls of the most delicious steak she'd ever eaten, she said, "When people are sick and dying, they're not worried about parking their cars in the garage. They leave them wherever they happen to be, or they die inside them if they're trying to get somewhere else to die. I mean, I'm not pulling this out of my ass. That's what we've seen for the past year."

Fergus sighed. "Yes, I'm sure that's true and the reference to your sublime ass is duly noted and appreciated. I'm wondering why you're wondering, is all. I suppose it's the nature of the honey badger to wrangle with enigmatic mysteries such as this until they get to the bottom of them."

He belched loudly and set his empty plate on the picnic table where they'd been eating. The night sky was an indigo canvas awash with a giant's fistful of silver glitter.

"Let's do process of elimination," he continued, resigned now to the fact that bedtime would be delayed until Dani had solved the riddle. "Number one: you say it's unreasonable to assume all the cars are parked in garages while their owners are busy being dead inside the house. I concede that point. Possibility number two: space aliens swooped in and confiscated every wheeled vehicle in Podunk, Oklahoma, because there is a shortage of steel, aluminum, plastic, leather, and glass on their planet."

She gave him a slow, annoyed blink.

"What? I'm conducting a process of elimination. Don't get testy. I think we can rule out space alien vehicular abduction. Okay, number three: The local survivors rounded up the vehicles after everyone else was dead."

"Bingo. That's what I'm thinking. So let's ask ourselves why? Why round up all the automobiles? To scavenge parts or gasoline?"

Fergus didn't respond, enjoying the show as she worked through the puzzle herself.

"Let's assume it was for the gas. Wouldn't it be easier to get it if they're all close by?"

"That sounds logical."

"Right, so someone, or a group of someones, transported them to a central location for the sake of convenience. That's plausible, right?"

He nodded, but she could tell he was holding something back and she could guess what it was.

"But there's a more compelling explanation, and I hope I'm wrong. They didn't round up those vehicles for gas or spare parts, but to create a barricade on I35 that makes that last one we busted through look like a poor kid's Matchbox Car collection."

The expression on his face told her he had come to the same conclusion.

"Damn it," she said.

"Yes, I think that's most likely."

"I guess we need to check the GPS on Sam's bike," she said. "We'll have to use secondary roads, assuming those aren't barricaded as well."

"And what if they are? Perhaps we should just take a right and head to Arkansas."

"No. We'll figure it out. If these Oklahoma fuckers think they can keep me caged in their shitty state, they have another think coming."

"Goodness, such foul language from such a delicate flower. What did Oklahomans ever do to you?"

She shrugged. "Nothing. But we're heading to Kansas, and if they try to stop me, it won't go well for them."

"I see." Fergus's Mona Lisa smile was ignored as she mentally tackled the logistics of getting them through the next two hundred miles.

***

"You're looking remarkably chipper for a man with a bullet-shaped wormhole in his abdomen," Fergus said to Sam the next morning as he watched Dani clean his wound. Sam's smile turned to a wince when her ministrations became too vigorous.

"Easy there, Honey Badger. He's a tough one, but even our Sam has limits."

"It's okay. You're not hurting me."

Fergus laughed that deep, rumbling sound that made her think of giant boulders rolling downhill...so incongruous with the small man himself.

"I have a feeling if she pressed hot coals to the bottoms of your feet, you'd say the same thing. Good grief, witnessing this tender blossoming of love between the two of you may be more than I can stomach."

"Nobody has a gun to your head." Dani's retort was intended to be harsh, but her joy at Sam's rapid recovery undermined it. She also realized at that moment that she would be sad if their new friend parted ways with them.

"How long do I have to stay in bed?"

His color was good, the bruises he'd received courtesy of Isaiah were almost gone, and the best news: the bullet injury was showing no signs of infection. She could swear it was already healing, but surely that was just wishful thinking.

"You were shot in the belly yesterday. How long do you think you should stay in bed? Two hours? Three?"

"I think I'm fine to go right now. I feel pretty good and the pain isn't nearly as bad. I slept really well last night." His smile was dazzling as he reached for Dani's face and pulled it toward his own.

"Oh, geez. I think I may hurl," Fergus groaned.

After a kiss which left her head a spinning, she said, "Bed rest for one day minimum. No arguments. Right, Lucky Charms?"

"As I said before, I'm no doctor although I'd have gotten laid a hell of a lot more if I had been, but my dubious credentials tell me a couple of days at least. No matter how perky he may be feeling nor how freakish his ability to heal quickly, his body needs to conserve its energy to recover. A week of bed rest would be better, but I know how antsy you are to kick some Oklahoma ass on your way out of the state."

When he locked eyes with her, she knew he had ferreted out her secret adrenaline addiction.

"A compromise then," she said. "I think two days is reasonable. That will give me time to do some scouting and maybe pick up supplies. I'm getting sick of these MREs. I feel like I have a bowling ball in my colon."

"Please, Dani. Don't go out alone. Wait until I'm better, or take Fergus with you."

"Yes, take Fergus with you," the small man parroted. "Unless you think having a capable gun-wielding stud covering your delightful backside is a bad idea."

"Fine. He can come with me."

"Good. I know you like to do this stuff on your own, but with me not being a hundred percent now, this isn't the time to go thrill-looking."

Her mouth formed a surprised 'O'.

Fergus's guffaw was so ear-splittingly loud, she wondered if he might hemorrhage something. **She hoped he would.**

CHAPTER 37

WESTERN COLORADO

"That's Grand Junction coming up," Julia said, navigating around a cluster of abandoned cars on I70. "And those mountains in the distance are the Rockies. Pretty cool, huh?"

She was excited to be in the last state she would need to get through before arriving in Kansas. Granted, it required getting over and through one of the highest mountain ranges in North America to do so, but it was only October. She hoped her luck would hold and an early blizzard wouldn't make the passes too treacherous. This decision had been a point of contention with Steven. He felt that she should detour south to New Mexico to avoid possible snow, but that would require more time on the road. And more gas siphoning.

"Those were the mountains you were telling me about?" Logan leaned toward the windshield as if an extra foot would take him closer to the massive peaks in the distance.

"Impressive, aren't they? I wish we could have taken US Route 40 through Rocky Mountain National Park. That road goes up really high...right over the top at an elevation of 14,000 feet. But we're going to stay on I70 and go through a section that's not quite as high but still scenic and hopefully not full of snow. Have you ever skied?" she asked before thinking. She knew more of his life story now: single mom raising a special needs child without benefit of a decent-paying job. Of course ski trips hadn't been an extravagance they could afford.

"No, but I've seen people do it on TV. It looked fun but also cold. I don't like being cold. I remember it snowed once when I was little, but it melted as soon as it got to the ground."

"You're right, it is fun but cold. We'll be going through Breckenridge which is a — well *was* — a resort town. I went there with my family a couple of times when I was growing up. The best part was being in the cabin at night with a fire going in the fireplace and drinking hot chocolate. We played *Scrabble* and *Monopoly* with our parents. Those are some wonderful memories."

Melancholy struck, a violent blindside of sadness and loss. Her world had vanished. She wished she had known then what she knew now so she could have cherished every happy moment, every tiny bit of joy from that life that was gone forever.

"Why do those good memories make you sad?" Logan shifted his attention from the view to her face.

She hated being emotional and weepy, especially in front of someone. But it was happening frequently now after leaving the vacuum of her lab and being forced to confront the reality of the altered world firsthand.

"Because it's all gone. Everything is gone. No more ski trips, no more hot chocolate by the fire, no more lazy Sunday mornings reading the paper in bed, no more Domino's pizza delivery when I don't feel like cooking, no more internet when I need to Google something, no more double-shot lattes from Starbucks, no more anniversary dinners at fancy restaurants, no more blockbuster movies, no more pedicures, no more birthday cakes. No more of anything the way it used to be." She ran out of steam and took a deep quivering breath.

Logan watched her with that now-familiar dispassionate expression. "You're blue. Well, kind of blue-green and there's still some purple around the edges. It's very pretty."

She laughed, feeling the sorrow loosen its grip. Laughter would be a valuable commodity here in the new world.

"I think it's so interesting that you see people's colors. Maybe when we get to Kansas we can learn more about that talent of yours. Would you mind being the subject of a scientific study?"

"Would you stick me with needles? I don't like needles."

"No, no needles. I'm not sure how it'll be done, but we'll figure it out. I'm going to need something to occupy myself with other than gardening and chopping wood."

Which was one of the reasons she was bringing so much of her equipment with her. If she knew her brother, there was power going at his house. And if she had electricity, she could continue her current research and even venture into other areas. She had almost exhausted the genetic angle of Chicxulub, and what she'd found was fascinating. She knew the 'what' but she didn't know the 'how' nor the 'why', and probably never would. The Lixi DNA molecule had suddenly become active in most humans causing their sudden, unpleasant demise. She didn't know why it hadn't flipped on in everyone, but she did know the survivors would possess either marked intelligence, savant type abilities, or both. Some of them would also suffer from mood and personality disorders. Perhaps if there were at least a handful of people still living in Liberty, she could expand her research beyond that of the electron microscope wedged into the back of the Land Rover. She could examine and interview actual human subjects. The thought of continuing scientific study of any kind, made her happy. Whether it involved auras or deadly rogue DNA molecules.

"I think we should stop in Breckenridge for the night," she said. "It's about a three-hour drive from here, which will put us there around sundown. How does that sound?"

"Can we stay in the cabin where you played *Monopoly*? Maybe there are other games too. I don't think I'd like *Scrabble* though."

"It's doubtful I could find it again. It's been a long time since I was there."

She saw the look of disappointment on his face and something else she couldn't identify. Petulance? She hadn't raised any teenagers but surely that same expression could be found on the face of any fourteen-year-old boy denied a four-wheeler or dirt bike.

"We'll look, okay? Maybe if we can't locate the same cabin, we'll find an even better one."

With any luck, it won't contain dead bodies or violent schizophrenics.

***

"This will be fun!" Logan whooped, clambering out of the Land Rover.

The log house was narrow with a steep roofline and long sides to accommodate the two levels. A wooden railing girded the porch as well as the second story balcony. Julia was certain it wasn't the same cabin in which she had vacationed as a child because this one was newly constructed — probably no more than five years ago and likely with a price tag over a million dollars. Nestled on some lovely wooded acreage and with views of the Tenmile range, the location alone would have driven up the value to seven figures.

On the way, they passed through downtown Breckenridge without any issues and no people sightings. That was good. She hoped they were as isolated as they felt. She couldn't imagine that any survivors would have stayed in this area, which would be cut off from resources and the rest of the world when the snow began falling. Breckenridge town proper, charming and picturesque before Chicxulub, felt despondent and defeated when they drove through. No families would meander down its sidewalks looking for dinner after a long day of activities. No couples would window shop while holding hands and stealing kisses. No iPhones would capture the shimmering gilded leaves of the aspen trees which punctuated the street, an arboreal ellipsis, from one end of town to the other. They were just now achieving their most vibrant shade, thousands of golden treasure coins strung on white-barked limbs.

I'm doing it again, she thought to herself as she opened the hatch and extricated Brains. She hadn't given him a potty break for hours and the sheer loathing on the feline face made her laugh out loud.

"I think it will be fun, too," she smiled at Logan's exuberance. "Do you have your gun ready?"

"Yes. I'll be careful. I've done this a lot."

He was on the mend. The bullet wound in his shoulder was healing nicely and the antibiotics were doing their magic. Literally, according to Logan.

"Okay. It doesn't look like anyone has been here in a long time, but take it slow. Please," she added, mindful of the bossy tone. It was difficult not to slip into a maternal role with him.

The sun hung low in the western sky, and she thought how delicious a nice soft bed would feel. They had made excellent time today. Ideally, they would be through the horrific gridlock she expected to encounter near Denver and to the Kansas border by this time the next day.

A cold breeze lifted strands of hair from her face, then rushed through the tops of the surrounding pine trees. From the needled branches it compelled a paean that was both beautiful and despondent. As music so often does, it transported her back to those childhood vacations and happy memories. The next moment, she identified something less pleasant carried by the wind.

The smell of snow. What she had assumed was part of a mountain range on the horizon, she now realized was a cloud bank. While unloading what they would need for their brief stay, she toyed with the idea of driving on to outrun the approaching storm. Steven's warnings about traveling at night won out, though.

The interior of the house was as impressive as the view. Flickering candles and an electric lantern made it feel inviting. Logan ran in and out of rooms, up and down the stairs like a kid on Christmas morning. Brains avoided the manic activity while inspecting his lodgings for the night.

"Can I sleep in the room with the bunk beds, Julia? I always wanted bunk beds but mom said since there was just me, it would be *wasteful*."

"Of course you can have that room. I'll take the one with the king size bed and the down comforter." Oh my, that bed was going to feel heavenly. But first, they would light a fire in the stone fireplace, eat their dinner, and play one of the board games found in the upstairs game room. Water still ran to the cabin, but it was frigid, so she planned to heat a pot of it in the fire and have an actual sponge bath later, a vast improvement from Wet Wipes.

It was the strangest feeling, but with Logan darting happily about and Brains stretching his legs, sniffing everything and not hissing for once, there was a sense of family. Crazy, yes, but there nonetheless. She pondered the fireplace and the neat stack of dry wood on the hearth.

Too bad they didn't have hot chocolate and S'mores.

"Julia, look what I found!" Logan hollered from the kitchen. He ran into the living room holding a box of Swiss Miss. "It says all we have to do is add boiling water. We can have hot chocolate like you did on your family trips."

The young man's excitement was contagious. "How about a mug before dinner?" she said with a smile.

"Yes! Before and after too. I can start the fire. I'm very good with fires. Remember?"

***

Julia wasn't sure what a banshee was supposed to sound like, but surely it was similar to what she was hearing outside while she luxuriated in the decadent comfort of the Tempur-Pedic bed. She hadn't been this comfortable in more than a year, and despite the wintry mayhem on the other side of the walls, she was enjoying the soft slice of heaven on this side.

That line of thinking didn't last more than a few seconds before her tired brain kicked into survival mode. The snowfall wasn't thick, nor was it accumulating...yet. But the fierce wind rattled the window panes in their casings and flung an occasional branch on the roof, making her jump every time.

A candle flickered by her bed, lighting the path to the bathroom. She had told Logan to do the same thing, and of course to not leave the flame near anything that could catch fire. His expression said 'duh' when he turned away. Managing him was a balancing act. Earlier, she had expected him to select Battleship or checkers for their evening entertainment, but chose Clue. After learning the rules, he wasn't interested in playing any other game. He was mesmerized by the characters and the different ways they might meet their demise...or cause the demise of their associates. Coincidentally, it had been her favorite board game as a child.

What if we wake up to two feet of snow in the morning? What if the road is blocked through the pass? We're down to a quarter tank of gas...need to find some first thing in the morning. Maybe we should backtrack to town? I think there were a few cars scattered about. Should have done that before we went on through.

A loud crash from overhead yanked her from an uneasy sleep. She had no idea if she'd been out for minutes or hours. It must have been a sizeable branch from one of the Ponderosa pines, but in her fuzzy mental state, she imagined a helicopter landing on the house and paramilitary men in heavy combat boots spilling out and tromping around up there. She slid her feet into the slippers placed next to the bed and shuffled to the window.

There were no soldiers rappelling from the roof and no snowflakes falling from the sky. The wind still howled, but a full moon had risen, adding its luminosity to the starlight. Moonlight and starlight meant no clouds, and no clouds meant no two feet of snow. She breathed a sigh of relief.

Another, quieter sound came from the interior of the house. Its source was downstairs, not Logan's room in the other direction.

She glanced around the room looking for Brains. He had been nestled in a mountain of goose down at the foot of her bed the last time she saw him. Now he was gone.

It's probably just him skulking around downstairs. Damn that little shit and his nocturnal nature.

The sound came again, louder and more defined this time: human footsteps on a hardwood floor. It could be Logan wandering around, but when she heard his snores down the hall, a surge of adrenaline propelled her from the bed.

She grabbed her revolver from the bedside table, tiptoed to the door, and peered through. Her bedroom was situated at the top of the stairway; from her vantage she could see the living room and the still-glowing embers in the fireplace.

She was halfway down the carpeted steps when she heard another noise. She pressed her back against the wall that separated the living room from the kitchen, holding the gun in a two-fisted grip. She continued to the bottom, then moved toward the corner.

"Don't be a stranger. Come on in. I was about to make myself some hot chocolate, if you two haven't guzzled it all." The voice was male and carried the unmistakable timbre of agedness. She heard a match being struck and saw a flicker of candlelight.

She rounded the corner. Standing in the kitchen was an old man with skin the color of antique mahogany and a grin punctuated with several gold teeth. His hair made Julia think of a giant Q-tip. He wore a Denver Nuggets sweatshirt and was pouring water into a coffee mug from the pot they'd used earlier for the same task. The box of Swiss Miss sat on the dining table.

Her mouth was open but she couldn't manage to formulate a sentence.

"Shocking, I know, waking up in the middle of the night to discover a gentleman of color in your house. Under normal conditions, finding a strange man in your kitchen would be mighty scary, but look at me. I'm so old I buy the swimsuit edition of *Sports Illustrated* for the articles. Doubt I could do anyone much bodily harm." He extended a hand as dark and gnarled as an ancient oak.

"I'm Abe. Although recently some people have taken to calling me Thoozy, which is short for Methuselah...get it? On account of my advanced age. But you can call me whatever you'd like so long as you put that hunk of metal down. Don't have need of that among friends."

Julia found her voice. "What are you doing here? How did you get in? I thought we'd secured the house."

"I may be old, but the day I can't get into a house I've set my mind on getting into is the day I'll just shuck it all." The gold-toothed smile was engaging, but Julia noticed he hadn't answered her question.

"What do you want, Mister, uh..."

"Why don't you just call me Thoozy? Everybody else does, and I admit I've grown to like it."

"What are you doing here? Surely there are any number of empty houses you could have chosen instead of this one."

Twinkling candlelight reflected in the warm, caramel brown eyes and when his laughter gurgled out from behind the golden smile, it was as rich and sweet as maple syrup.

Holy crap. I've been burgled by a skinny, black Santa Claus.

"I wanted *this* house, young lady. I knew there was hot chocolate here, and well, it's a weakness of mine. Anything chocolate and any kind of chocolate. Milk chocolate, dark chocolate, mint chocolate, but don't give me any of that white chocolate because we all know there ain't nothin' chocolate 'bout that nonsense."

She smiled before she could stop herself.

"And besides, unless your name is on the deed to this piece of high-dollar real estate, you're just as much of an intruder as me."

He had her there.

"So your Swiss Miss obsession overrode all common sense, compelling you to venture out on a cold night during a storm and break into a house that was occupied by two armed individuals? Does this sound reasonable to you?"

The chuckle was delightful, but she resisted the urge to be charmed.

"Don't forget about your attack cat," he gestured to Brains who was curled up against the man's well-worn Reeboks.

Good grief. The cat hated Logan and barely tolerated her. His embracing of this stranger felt...significant.

She placed the revolver on the tabletop and sat down across from him. "Okay, Thoozy. I'm Julia. What's your story?"

***

"Logan, wake up. It's morning and we have a guest." He must have slept like the dead not to have heard them talking for the past two hours.

"What?" He sat up in the top bunk bed, dirty blond hair sticking out at odd angles like an '80s rocker.

"There's someone you need to meet. He's in the kitchen and his name is Thoozy. He'll be coming with us to Kansas."

He scrambled out from under a heap of blankets and clambered down the railing. "I don't understand. Where did he come from?"

"Long story. Come downstairs and you can meet him. Then we'll have breakfast and get on the road. We're going to backtrack into town to find some gasoline. Are you sure you don't mind sucking the gas again?"

"No, I don't mind," he replied, distracted and foggy. "He's coming with us? Does he have magic?"

"I think he might. But I'm pretty sure it's good magic. None of that wicked dark stuff."

He followed her down the carpeted stairs to the kitchen.

Early morning sunlight filled the room, backlighting the old man who sat at the table, obscuring his face. "I found some instant coffee, Julia. Something tells me a hot cup of joe would be something you'd appreciate."

"Oh, god, yes. Logan, this is Thoozy also known as Abe, but I think most people don't call him that any more. Thoozy, may I introduce you to Logan?"

She watched the young man's reaction, seeing displeasure in his body language; his frown had turned downright hostile. Well, he would just have to accept this new addition to their diverse little family. She had no intention of leaving an old man on a mountain by himself with winter approaching.

"It's a pleasure to meet you." Thoozy extended the gnarled oak again, but Logan ignored it.

"You can see me?"

She was glad she had already explained Logan's obsession with magic and her decision to perpetuate that belief system.

"I can indeed. I appreciate that you're allowing me to come on your journey with you. I promise not to get in the way or eat too much."

Was it Julia's imagination or did the gold-toothed smile seem less genuine now?

"I'm very good with my guns."

"Of that, I have no doubt."

"What can you do?"

"I can play the saxophone, I can whittle sailboats from scraps of tree bark, I can recite the Pledge of Allegiance backwards, I can tie fifty-seven different knots, and I can make a mean martini."

Julia grinned.

Logan studied the old man, then asked, "Would you show me how to do the knots?"

The caramel eyes never wavered from the boyish face. "Young man, knot-tying is something I will never share with you. But if you're interested in carving sailboats, I'm your guy."

Chapter 38

Kansas

"The woman was scared, that's for sure," Lisa said from the comfort of an overstuffed chair.

Steven and his son sat on a sofa across from her, in a house that smelled strongly of cinnamon and vaguely of decomposition.

"Can you remember exactly what the lady said?" Jeffrey pressed Liberty's newest citizen. Steven noted the intense expression on his son's face.

"She said they were keeping women, the pretty ones, in the Best Western. She said the rest of the women did all the grunt work, hauling water and such, while the men ordered them around. She said the town had grown from just the few survivors who had lived there before the plague. She said a lot of rough types had moved in recently and she didn't know where they were coming from. They were bad news, though, and it seemed to this woman that they were creating some kind of 'misogynist mecca' — her words. That's why she and her daughter left during the night. Their house was on the far outskirts of town and they had somehow kept off the radar, but she knew it couldn't last. She knew she was taking a huge chance leaving because they had a good stockpile of food, but it wasn't worth the risk of staying. So, they packed up as much as they could carry and left on foot."

"Why on foot?" Steven asked. "They could have brought more of their provisions if they'd used a car. There's still good gas to be found."

"She said they have I70 blocked," Lisa replied, anger in her voice now. "On both sides of the town. If you try to leave, they'll stop you. If you try to go through town, they'll detain you. If you have anything valuable, they'll take it from you, and if you have any skills or are attractive enough, they'll make you stay."

That's when he thought of his sister.
"Oh, shit."
"What, Dad?"
"Your Aunt Julia will be driving right through there on her way to us."

***

As with any task Steven had ever tackled, he approached the dangerous rescue operation with obsessive attention to detail. He broke it down into three components. First: he would elicit help from those citizens of Liberty who had voted in favor of rescuing the captive women. He understood the precedent that going against the popular vote might set within their fledgling community, but he would deal with the backlash once Julia was safely through Hays. Second: he would conduct a scouting mission to determine what they were dealing with so as to formulate the safest and most effective plan possible. Third would be the rescue operation itself, which had evolved in his mind beyond merely saving some women. He planned to annihilate the bastards who had decided to create their oppressive, testosterone-fueled despotic empire only thirty miles from his town.

Steven felt a sense of relief. This was what he should have been loudly and vigorously advocating for all along. Jeffrey knew it. Lisa knew it. He had known it too, but fear and worry kept him from acting. So now he could focus on what needed to be done rather than whether it should be done at all.

He assigned his son the job of notifying the other twenty-one residents who had supported the rescue that there was to be an informal meeting at his house at sundown. Jeffrey had taken off on his bike down the gravel driveway like a post-apocalyptic Paul Revere.

By the time people began to arrive, he had a smorgasbord ready for them. It was the least he could do for the people whose lives he'd be putting at risk. As he beckoned them into his home, he managed to remember most of their names. Of course Marilyn was among their number, as was Lisa, Ed, Chuck and the other members of Chuck's Security Crew, which consisted of two young men and the sharp-shooting girl.

They were already attacking the canned chicken and sweet corn when he began to pull his front door closed. He stopped when he noticed a final person walking toward his house. He didn't recognize the face in the twilight and still couldn't identify him even when the man stepped onto the porch with his hand extended.

"Hello. You must be Steven," he said with a smile that didn't quite reach the almond-shaped eyes. "I've heard a lot about you in my short time here. My name is Tung. Tung Wong. Clearly my parents hated me, but since they spoke no English when they arrived in this country from China, I know I should forgive them. And I have...mostly. Anyway, I'm here to sign up for your cause."

Despite his exotic features, the accent was pure Midwest. Steven liked him at once.

"It's a pleasure to meet you. What's your story? Condensed version, please. We'll be starting the meeting soon."

"Brevity is my middle name. Okay, former Supervisor of Mining Operations at Hutchinson Salt. Advanced degrees in chemistry, geology, and mathematics...yes, the math is a Chinese cliché. Moved here from San Francisco after grad school. Never married because it seems I'm kind of a dick to live with. What else do you need?"

He barely heard anything after 'mining operations.' "Are you saying you're an expert with explosives?"

"Yep. I'm great at blowing things up."

"Come on in, Tung. We have a lot to talk about."

More than twenty people crammed their pungent bodies into Steven's living room and all were in various stages of inhaling his food. He didn't begrudge it.

"Tung, grab a plate and find a spot. Everyone, this is Tung. He's from Hutchinson and is great at blowing things up. I figure he'll come in handy. First, I need to be up front about what prompted all this. My sister will be arriving from California soon, and she'll be driving right through Hays to get here. I'm aware this endeavor was voted down the other day, and I realize by acting in direct violation of that decision, I'm instigating trouble and setting a bad example. But I also think it's the right thing to do.

"I'm paraphrasing Marilyn when I say we're creating a societal archetype here and now. We're shaping our future and we're choosing the path of decency and compassion. It's not about being the world's police or trying to save everyone. That's not realistic, and I think we're all smart enough to know that. And this isn't just a rescue mission either. After hearing what is happening in Hays, there's no question that the situation there is a ticking time bomb and we need to eradicate it before it gets worse. Before that gang becomes stronger and bigger."

"Steven, what exactly are you proposing?" Marilyn asked, her plain face set in an expression of careful neutrality.

He took a deep breath. "First we need to confirm Lisa's information and see for ourselves that things are as grim as we believe them to be. If they are, once we release the captives, I propose we blow those apes to kingdom come."

***

Steven noticed Tung held back from the rest of the departing crowd. It was close to midnight. The moon glowed in the night sky like a white-hot sickle.

"You ever consider running for mayor?" Tung's smile seemed genuine as he stood next to Steven and watched the last of the stragglers disperse in one direction or the other.

"After this little infraction, I don't think that will be an option," he replied, feeling exhaustion kick in. He'd managed to convince every person at the meeting to join him in the dangerous undertaking.

"Well, if the job opens up, I'm just saying you might think about it. You have a way with people, you know. Getting them to do what you want." The words, delivered without rancor, still carried a sting.

"I'm not a manipulator. I didn't sugarcoat anything, and I outlined all the risks."

"Agreed. I don't mean to sound adversarial, just stating a fact. Not everyone has that talent."

"Talent? I don't know about that, but I'm happy to have their backing. My son and I can't get this thing done on our own."

Tung rubbed the stubble on his chin and gazed at the electric moon.

There was something else the man wanted to say, and he was too valuable to risk offending with an abrupt dismissal. If he were right, and Steven did have a way with people, it was a newsflash to him. He'd always considered himself awkward in social situations, and public speaking was something to get through, not a task he relished.

"I realize these men in Hays are despicable. I get that. But is it your place...our place...to kill them because we've decided that's what's best for everyone else? What if people from a town thirty miles on the other side of Liberty decide that we're the bad guys? Is it appropriate for them to eradicate us based on their perception? Morality is subjective. If we do this thing, we're murderers. We believe we're justified in the act of murder, but we're still murderers. Are you okay with that?"

Steven followed the man's gaze toward the night sky. A lone whippoorwill serenaded anyone who might still be awake. *Whip or WILL. Whip or WILL. Whip or WILL.*

He pondered the question for almost a minute before answering. "Yeah, I'm okay with that."

Tung nodded, then extended his hand for the second time that evening. "Okey dokey, then. See you tomorrow." His smile was friendly, but the Sphinx eyes gave away nothing.

Chapter 39

New Mexico

Pablo's Journal, Entry #389

What now? Just wait here all day for that door to open so I will be told what I already know? Without proper medical attention, it's not possible that Maddie could survive brain trauma. She needs skilled surgeons and state-of-the-art equipment and medicine and machines that beep and monitors that display a heartbeat and nurses that scurry about with confident expressions and magnetic imaging coffins that can pinpoint the location of the bullet and show the swelling that's happening in her skull. As much as I admire Amelia, I have no delusions that her midwife skills can rise to the challenge.

I should be in there, holding her hand, breathing every breath with her, savoring every microscopic movement of her face or her fingers or her eyelashes. Why did I allow myself to be thrown out? Why did that strange little girl remain?

What the hell am I doing scribbling in this journal instead of charging into that room? Something about her voice. Something about the expression on her face. What was it? I never got the sense that Amelia wasn't what she presented herself to be, yet it was almost as if a mask — benevolent and genial, but nevertheless a mask — slipped away and revealed someone who was still Amelia, but also something else. Or perhaps something more.

Two dogs and one tabby kitten sprawled on the rug at Pablo's feet. He lifted his pen from the notebook and gazed at their indifferent slumber.

"Bruno, you will miss her. Not as much as me, but you will miss her."

The German shepherd's ears twitched but the eyes didn't open. Whatever his human was babbling about could wait until after his nap.

Pablo leaned back against the cushions of a well-worn sofa. There was a hole in his chest...an abyss so vast it couldn't possibly fit within the confines of his physical body...black and bottomless...full of despair and expanding by the minute.

He couldn't go on. Not without Maddie. For the first time in his life, he entertained thoughts of suicide. They weren't full-blown nor well-articulated thoughts. But they were spawning, stirring to life in the fertile soil that separates consciousness and sub-consciousness. Insidious, poisonous fungi of possibilities.

His eyes flew open. The sound of the bedroom door behind him set his heart racing. *Don't look. When you see the face of the woman with the old soul eyes, you will know that your Maddie is gone.*

"Pablo." Amelia's voice. It was back to normal. The odd quality from before was gone.

"Pablo." Softer now. Kind, compassionate. The voice of a doctor delivering news of cancer. "Do you plan on sitting there all day or would you like to come say hello to your sweetheart?"

He leaped to his feet when he heard the smile in the voice, before the words' significance even registered.

The next moment he stood beside Maddie's bed. Her eyes were closed. A white bandage encircled her head and hair stuck out at spiky angles; none of the clumps were more than an inch long. Her chest was still rising and falling. He felt a kittenish squeeze of his fingers.

Then the exquisite smile.

"Hello there, Poet Fellow."

"Hello there, Angel Girl."

"Not very angelic at the moment, I'm afraid. I hope you like pixies." A weak hand touched the reddish gold stubble. Her eyes were still closed but the smile remained.

"You're more beautiful than ever. All that hair detracted from your perfect face." He intended a white lie, but realized it was true. "How do you feel?"

"Like a mob of tiny construction workers are jackhammering my skull. Meh. I've felt worse." The eyelash canopy fluttered open. "You look like crap. What happened to you?"

"I almost lost the love of my life."

"Well, you didn't. At least not today. I think I'll sleep now. Love you, Pablo."

"Love you, Maddie."

He lingered long after she had fallen asleep, watching the rise and fall, rise and fall, of the powder blue sheet. A few minutes or perhaps an hour later, he felt a hand on his shoulder.

"Let her rest," Amelia whispered.

He sighed, kissed the pale, freckled cheek, and closed the door behind him.

Jessie was curled up on the floor with the sleeping animals, but she watched him enter the room. Amelia sat on the sofa.

"How did you do it? I'm no expert, but I know that people don't survive a head shot without proper medical attention."

"It seems they do."

"Will she live?"

"Yes. I'm certain of it."

"How is that possible? What did you do in there? Is the bullet still in her head?"

"No. It went through, which is probably what saved her. The exit hole allowed a release from some of the pressure. Also, I suspect it was small. A .22 caliber, perhaps."

"How will she be...later?"

"You mean did she suffer any brain damage? Impossible to say now. Her speech is fine. There might be some loss of motor skills. We'll know more soon."

Sea-green eyes and brown eyes watched him with benign interest.

A thought, forged during the wretched chaos earlier, surfaced like a bubble in a tar pit. "Why did you allow Jessie to stay in the room?"

Amelia held his gaze for a long minute. She would make an excellent poker player, he thought. Despite the stoic expression, he could tell something important was going on between those gray-streaked braids. When she spoke, some instinct told him that whatever she'd been pondering — words weighed, some chosen, some discarded — it hadn't gone in his favor. He wasn't going to get the full truth.

"I thought she should begin to learn some of what I know. What better way than a hands-on first-aid lesson?"

It was a plausible explanation, and probably even true. But there was more. He began to ask another question, when a youthful, straight-fingered hand cut him off.

"She's alive, dear. Be happy. Sometimes it's best for us not to know all the answers. Not to solve all the mysteries. Then there will always be a bit of magic in the world. I think that's rather wonderful, don't you?"

As their gazes remained locked, something passed between them, a heightened awareness, or perhaps some sort of collective consciousness. He knew he shouldn't press her. Maddie was alive and according to Amelia would remain so.

He took a deep breath and conceded the staring contest.

"When can she be moved? We're not safe here. The people who did this could be close. We must get out of Albuquerque as soon as possible."

"Let's see how she is by morning. I think we could leave then if her vital signs stay strong through the night."

Pablo shook his head. "That's crazy, you know."

An indulgent smile. "I know it sounds that way."

He mirrored her smile. "I'll move the car. We shouldn't advertise our location. We'll take shifts standing watch through the night. I don't need a lot of sleep, but I'll need some."

She nodded. "Bring that tequila when you come back. I think we could both use some."

***

"Good grief, Pablo. Quit being a grandma. You're making me crazy," Maddie said from the back seat of the Highlander the next morning. Amelia had changed the dressing before they left and declared her satisfaction at what she saw.

They'd been on the road for an hour, driving slower and more carefully than he'd ever driven in his life. Every bump, every pothole, summoned a wave of anxiety when he considered what the jarring might do. He glanced in the rearview mirror. Her eyes were closed but her color was good. Actually, she looked amazing, despite the bandage.

He'd heard of bizarre accidents involving head trauma and their subsequent miraculous recoveries: the construction worker who didn't realize he'd shot a four-inch nail into his skull until six days later, or the man who walked into a London emergency room with a knife sticking out of his head. Both men had not only survived, they'd suffered no lasting ill effects from their injuries.

Maddie was alive. Rather querulous, but alive. It was a miracle, and he would just leave it at that. Now it was time to focus on getting them to Oklahoma.

Jessie and her kitten seemed content to take Maddie's place in the front seat. He could feel those unsettling eyes on him from time to time. Would he ever get used to this creature? She still didn't speak much. Only an occasional hand-cupped whisper to Maddie or Amelia. Was she averse to him specifically, or men in general?

Two quiet hours later they were through the snarled, dead traffic of Albuquerque and approaching the town of Santa Rosa, which proclaimed a population of 2,802. The two women were asleep in the back. Pablo was pondering whether to wake them and try for more gas on their way through, when a lilting, elfin voice floated from the passenger seat.

I can see the end of the story
I know where my future must be
It's not about money or glory
It's a place to live honest and free
You don't have to bring your possessions
All that you need will be there

Forget all your former transgressions
Abandon your sometime despair
Arizona in the rearview mirror
Every passing mile takes me nearer
I swear I can already hear her
That sweet angel's whispers of love

He kept his eyes on the road, afraid that reacting with too much enthusiasm might scare the child back into silence. He could feel her eyes on him again and he hazarded a glance. A tiny grin played about the corners of her mouth. There was also a sense of expectancy.

"Jessie, that was beautiful. You knew all the words, too. Good job. Can you sing the rest of it?"

A quick bob of the dark head.

If I said I was certain she's waiting
You'd know I was lying for sure
But I feel all my sorrows abating
I can sense that our love will endure
So I packed up this rusty old Chevy
I gave my two weeks to the Man
My heart no longer feels heavy
The best of life finally began
Arizona in the rearview mirror
Every passing mile takes me nearer
I swear I can already hear her
That sweet angel's whispers of love

He marveled at her perfect pitch and that she had remembered every word without hesitation. This must have been her first time singing their improvised song out loud, yet she knew it better than he did. He winced at the cheesiness of it. Maddie told him to stop being an insufferable Poindexter and go with the flow. Songs didn't have to be sublime poetry set to music. They just needed to be heartfelt and catchy. Hearing it now, he realized the truth of her words. The ethereal voice imbued it with a poignancy the adults failed to achieve in their rendition.

Too bad the world had ended. It just might have been a hit on the country music charts.

When she finished her solo performance, they had just reached the outskirts of Santa Rosa, home of the famous *Blue Hole*, according to the highway signage for the past ten miles. He knew more than he ever wanted to know about the artesian well measuring eighty feet in depth, boasted crystal clear waters, and proclaimed itself, ironically, to be the SCUBA diving capital of the Desert Southwest. At a constant temperature of sixty-one degrees, they wouldn't be doing any diving today.

He felt a tug on his shirt sleeve as another *Blue Hole* billboard loomed fifty yards ahead.

"What is it, Jessie?"

She pointed at the sign. Pablo knew instantly what she wanted, and decided to use the opportunity to draw the child out.

"What? What are you pointing at? That telephone pole?"

A frustrated head shake while a stern finger jabbed in the direction of the billboard.

"Is there a coyote? Oh, I think I see it. Out there, off to the right."

An exasperated breath blew wisps of dark hair up from the brow.

"It's not a coyote? What then? What is it you want to tell me?"

When she spoke, her non-whispering speaking voice was as melodious as the singing version. "I wish we could go there. It looks very pretty." Her head tilted to one side, and for once, the green eyes beseeched rather than contemplated.

There would be no denying that face anything, certainly nothing as simple as a quick visit to the *Blue Hole*.

"We'll make a side trip. It's only a few miles off the highway. But we can't stay for long. Just a few minutes and then we have to go. Deal?"

She nodded.

"You have to say it."

"Deal."

"Let's shake on it then."

When he grasped her small hand in his, it felt warm. Hot, actually.

"Do you feel okay? Your hand is hot. Let me feel your forehead." He pressed the back of his hand to her head. It felt normal.

"I feel fine. I don't feel sick at all. Are we still going to the *Blue Hole*?"

"We shook on it, didn't we?"

He had only seen the shy half-grin since finding the child back at the Circle K, so when she regaled him with a full-blown smile, he was unprepared for the transformation.

The small body and face hadn't caught up with the adult incisors, which was a bit disconcerting. But with the expression of sheer joy (*the Blue Hole!*), Pablo got a glimpse of the future young woman. Soon she would grow into those enormous eyes and largish teeth and cast off all remnants of Female Gollum forever.

She was going to be breathtaking.

With the sudden realization, concerns of a fatherly nature began to formulate. How would he keep all the randy young boys away from this beautiful girl when she reached puberty? An image flashed through his mind: he stood at the front door of a farmhouse, shotgun in hand, watching a line of boy-filled cars snake up their driveway.

He sighed. "Let's go to the *Blue Hole*!"

Her squeal woke up the occupants of the back seat.

Good thing there aren't many boys left in the world.

Chapter 40

Oklahoma

"Once again you underestimated him," Fergus said from the passenger seat of the dented pickup.

They had left Sam in bed, sleepy and sore, yet recovering quickly. He truly must have some kind of self-healing super power, Dani thought. The circumference of the gunshot wound in his abdomen already looked smaller, which was crazy, and the Cephalexin should be thwarting any lurking infection. Sam would be fine to leave whenever they were ready.

And that would happen after they reconnoitered I35 north of Podunk, Oklahoma. The town's actual name was Davis, and it lay in the rural boonies south of Oklahoma City. If a colossal roadblock had been constructed near there, as they suspected, they would need a plan to circumvent it.

"Yes, clearly I underestimated him. Now shut the hell up. I'm thinking." She studied the Rand McNally map from the Love's Travel Stop. They sat behind the building in the exact spot they'd been the previous day when the sky had been lumpy, sick-ward green, and spoiling for a fight with an outflow boundary.

"I like you, Honey Badger. Why that is, I have no idea. You're actually quite unpleasant most of the time."

She reached out a distracted hand and patted his knee. The anchored GPS on Sam's bike still worked, but wasn't convenient. Besides, she liked the feel of the crisp folded paper which was bisected, trisected, and quadrisected by a thousand colorful veins of information.

She pointed at a dot. "Norman. I'd bet my grandmother's dentures that's where these bumpkin shitheads have it set up. Just south of Oklahoma City."

Dusk had slipped away and night was upon them. Fergus held the flashlight so they could see the map.

He nodded. "Could be. Do you think they're keeping people in or people out?"

"Both, probably. The big city is close enough so they could pick its carcass on a regular basis, but Norman is far enough into the country for farming. If they were smart, they'd have two roadblocks creating a safe zone in between. That's what I'd do. I also think it's likely they have smaller barricades on all the secondary roads. Again, that's what I'd do. I don't want to waste a lot of time and gas that we don't have traveling all over BFE to find out, so we're going to concentrate on I35 tonight."

"She has spoken."

Dani felt the familiar tingling of anticipation, like an injection of some delicious narcotic. Sam was right. She was a 'thrill looker.' There was no denying it, to herself or anyone else. And now she no longer had to hide her dirty little secret. It felt both shameful and liberating...like a drunk bringing a six-pack to an AA meeting.

Fergus watched her as she shifted the ravaged Ford Raptor into drive. It would be difficult to see with the headlights off, but stealth demanded it. They would travel for fifty miles or so, then park on the service road and hike the rest of the way to mile marker 113, just south of Norman. From there, they would traverse into whatever terrain lay to the west of I35. Farmland, most likely. She intended to survey the route they would take with Sam when they would flank the hypothetical blockade from that side. It would be a long night and potentially a dangerous excursion — they may encounter sentries or other would-be assailants. The thought elicited a predatory smile.

"What if you're wrong? What if it's set up north of Norman? What if doesn't even exist?"

She'd been anticipating every potential complication and pitfall and the manner in which she would react to each of them.

"I'm not wrong," she said. "If there's no roadblock, we're golden. But I'm not wrong."

An hour later, she had proof. After leaving the pickup parked on a narrow road that ran perpendicular to the highway, they hiked through fallow fields until they reached an inky, sluggish stream.

"It's Walnut Creek, which feeds into the Canadian River to the east," she whispered, gazing at the brackish water. "It's the perfect natural barrier to deter people from doing exactly what we want to do. Of course, most people are stupid and would approach on the highway, then fall right into their trap. See that firelight about a hundred yards out? Past that clump of trees? That would be the blockade."

Fergus reached into his jacket, withdrew a pair of binoculars, located a switch on one side and flipped it.

"You're kidding me. You have night vision binoculars in your magic coat? I swear to god, you're a damn leprechaun. Don't deny it."

He smiled in the dark and lifted the smallish device to his face. Dani thought of a Navy SEAL attending the opera.

"I'm surprised you didn't think to purchase some when you were buying your fish antibiotics."

"Touché. What do you see?"

"I see a prodigious heap of car-shaped steel piled up on both the northbound and southbound lanes of the highway. Just as you predicted. Good job, Honey Badger. I also see five armed men milling about in front of and beside said pile."

"Yes, yes. That's what I figured."

"You have a plan for this?"

"Of course. But you won't like it."

He groaned. "Does it involve my ass connecting with the seat of that two-wheeled torture machine?"

"Yes. You should be happy about that. I would prefer to just pull up in Big Blue and go postal on those redneck sons of bitches, but I can't put Sam at risk like that. So we ditch the truck, load up as much as we can in our packs and carry the bikes across the creek. I can see sticks and rocks in the water. It can't be more than a couple of feet deep, which is what I estimated it would be. That's why we're on the west side and not the east side where it's deeper. Tributaries typically swell just before they flow into a river."

"What a coincidence. I also swell right before I flow into something."

She snorted. "Okay, Pervus Maximus. Let's head back. I bet Sam is worried sick."

***

"I don't like the idea of getting so close to that roadblock," Sam said from a sofa in the living room. He refused to stay in bed any longer. The day had dawned much too early for Dani after only a few hours of sleep the night before. "Why can't we just try some other roads?"

She stifled a yawn. "Because we don't have much gasoline and all the cars we might have pilfered from are being used for roadblocks. Look at the bright side. You'll get to ride your bike again. At least until we get clear of Norman."

"Maybe we could get more gas from underground tanks."

"Don't you think the local yokels have already drained them? If they're organized enough to accomplish the barricade, they're probably smart enough to have scavenged what was left in these parts."

Sam frowned and nodded.

"We'll be wading through a bacteria-ridden creek, so we'll need to waterproof your dressing."

"Will duct tape and a Glad Trash Bag do the trick?" Fergus waved the items from the kitchen doorway.

"Yes. Perfect. Once we're through the creek," she tapped at the map on the coffee table, "We'll have to get past the barricade. That means riding through some fields for a few miles until we hit a residential area to the west of I35. If I'm right about the safe zone, there will be another roadblock here," she pointed, "Just south of I40 which runs east and west. Once we're past it, we can decide whether to stay on I35 through Oklahoma City or keep to secondary roads.

"We'll rest today and head out just after dark. How does all that sound?"

Sam nodded. Fergus appeared noncommittal.

"Why take the bicycles? We can just filch some new ones."

She glanced at Sam, knowing before she looked that she would find wide-eyed panic. She leaned over and kissed his cheek. "The bikes come with us," she said.

"Oh god. There it is again. A nauseating testimony to young love. It might get us killed, you know. Those things are heavy, cumbersome, and will slow us down."

"They will. But they're still coming with us."

"Do you think there are alligators in this creek? Piranhas? Great Whites?" Fergus's whisper seemed loud to Dani's ears, despite the noise from the crickets, cicadas, and gurgling water. The crescent moon provided adequate light for their endeavor — barely. There would be no free hands for flashlights. If the Oklahomans were smart, they would have posted sentries not only on the highway but at this location as well. Maybe they weren't concerned about a few stragglers getting past their barricade. Or maybe they were waiting for them on the other side of the creek. The thought made her edgy and exhilarated.

"Stow it, Fergus," she hissed. "Let's get this over with."

The burden of their packs was shared by both back and leg muscles, but the bicycles must be carried with arm strength alone. She watched Sam step into the stream. He hoisted his beloved Pivot Mach 429 over his head and held it well above the water with ease, more effortlessly than a man with a bullet hole in his belly should be capable of.

"There's a low spot here," Fergus said a few feet in front of them.

The water was chilly and moved faster than anticipated. Even at thigh level, the inky flow could wash their feet out from under them.

She gritted her teeth against the onset of muscle fatigue. They were at the halfway point, and the waterlogged clay pulled at her boots with the slimy suction-cupped hands of a backwoods creek monster. Her passage was made more arduous by the .45 Cattleman pistol, attached to her waist in an improvised duct tape holster. It had been a last minute decision, prompted by the thought of their vulnerability during the crossing. It might have been overkill though, and she was regretting it now. *Just twenty more feet. Don't be such a pussy. You can do this.*

Fergus sloshed out of the water and onto the far bank.

"Made it!" he whispered, just as two men stepped out of the surrounding brush. One of them struck a blow to the back of his head. He collapsed to the rocky ground like a puppet with severed strings.

"Come on out, both of you. Slowly." The nasal drawl sounded lazy, almost bored.

Sam shot her a backwards glance. They exchanged a tiny nod and she began to fight the mud again, watching every movement of his body.

The two men stood close to the water's edge now, holding rifles which gleamed black in the moonlight. Ill-fitting military fatigues hung on thin frames, and the hands holding the firearms seemed tentative, awkward...teenage boys unhooking their first bra.

Dani noted these details with her peripheral vision. Her focus was on Sam's back. When his shoulder muscles tensed, she was ready.

He heaved his bike at the man on the left. It didn't knock him down, but it surprised and distracted both men long enough for her to release her grip on the bike and level her pistol. Two shots rang out. The man on the right fell to the ground with a yelp. The man on the left was still struggling with his rifle when Sam darted from the water and took him down with a chisel fist to the throat.

The movement might have killed him, but Dani knew better. At least the redneck would be unconscious for a while. She floundered the rest of the way out of the stream. Sam was already checking for a pulse in her victim.

"Is he dead?" she asked.

"No. You just winged him. Shoulder and bicep. He'll be okay. Good job!" The wounded man groaned in disagreement.

"I was aiming for center mass. Guess I need more practice."

She ignored Sam's distressed look and knelt beside Fergus. She turned his head one way, then the next, exploring the skull with careful fingers through the matted red hair, then breathed a sigh of relief. When she slapped his bearded face, his eyes fluttered open.

"Is that an angel of mercy I see? Or a raven-haired hellhound bent on inflicting misery and pain? What happened, Honey Badger? Everything's a bit fuzzy after I got out of the water."

She smiled, removed a small flashlight from her pack, switched it on and aimed it into the blue eyes.

"Is there no satiating your sadistic pleasure?"

"Your pupils are even, but we'll check them again in a few minutes. I think you'll live."

"I'm wondering if that's necessarily a good thing," he grumbled as he sat up and rubbed the back of his head.

"Your bike is in the water, Dani," Sam said. He might have been speaking of a cherished pet.

"I know, and it's going to stay there. They're all going to stay right where they are, and we're getting the hell out of here. I love you Sam, but this is crazy. We'll get more soon."

He had been inspecting the damage to his bicycle, when his head jerked up, and the bike fell to the ground with a satisfying thud. In three steps, he stood facing her. He cupped her face between his hands and gazed into her eyes.

"I love you too. So much. More than anything in the world," he said, then he kissed her.

A year's worth of suppressed emotion traveled through his fingertips, through his lips, his languid tongue, and into her. She dropped the flashlight and wove her fingers into his hair, that beautiful, golden hair. She pressed the length of her body against his, felt his hardness, then grasped his hips and pulled them against hers.

There was nothing but Sam. The cicadas, the crickets, the gurgling water, the dangerous situation, vanished. Just Sam. His mouth, his tongue, his body, his love so intense it was almost a tangible entity.

"Oh for god's sake, can we please get the hell out of here? You kids can bump uglies later. My head is killing me."

She pulled away with a laugh. "Yes. Let's get the hell out of here," she said. The normal predatory smile was replaced by one as goofy and love-struck as the one Sam wore.

Chapter 41

Colorado

"Can we have a potty break, Julia?" Logan asked, squirming in the front passenger seat. For the past hour, they had been maneuvering around a metal and rubber quagmire on the outskirts of Denver.

"Can't you hold it? This is a mess, and I don't think it would be safe to stop here."

"I promise I'll be fast. Really fast."

Thoozy, the skinny black Santa Claus, spoke up. "Best to let him go. It's not good for a man to keep his sluice gate closed when the water has risen to the top."

She sighed, slowing the Land Rover to a stop. "Okay. Be fast, please."

"Should I take my gun?"

She scanned the area. So far, they had found ways of getting around and over the debris, but the obstructions were getting worse with every mile. It was time to get off I70 and onto secondary roads.

She shook her head, thinking of people fleeing in cars to escape a pandemic.

"I can't take my gun?" The petulant teenager was back.

"No, I didn't mean that. Yes, you may take it. Just hurry, okay?"

She contemplated the ocean of vehicles left in situ, many still occupied. Mother Nature had begun the job of housekeeping. Scouring winds and corrosive precipitation, both frozen and liquid, had wrought considerable damage in only a year. With the help of thermal energy from the sun, plus a hefty dose of time, this ugly landscape would one day become beautiful again. Perhaps in a thousand years, or ten thousand. It might even take a million. But the earth would abide, as she always had, whether or not there were people scratching and clawing along her surface.

The voice from the back seat interrupted her musings.

"That one is a handful," the old man said.

"He can't help how he is." She could hear the defensive tone in her voice. "But yes, he is a handful. It's been a challenge figuring out the best way to deal with him. I've never raised children, so I'm flying by the seat of my pants here."

"He's not like most children, so I doubt that would have helped much anyway. Besides, he's no longer a child. He's a grown man."

Julia felt a prickling of irritation. Black Santa better not piss her off or she just might leave him by the curb. "Yes, I know that. But he's developmentally and intellectually challenged, so he can't be treated like an average adult."

"Why is that?"

She was getting exasperated. "Because he's not average. He needs special handling."

"He looks fine to me."

"Thoozy, come on. You know I'm referring to his mental capacity. At best, he's low IQ, possibly coupled with Asperger Syndrome."

"And at worst?"

She glanced at the rearview mirror. The old man smiled when he noticed her eyes upon him. The golden-toothed grin seemed curious, not contentious. She hesitated. Should she share with this stranger what her research had revealed?

"Worst or worst-worst?" she asked.

A rich chuckle. "Both?"

"Worst is, he's a low IQ, high functioning autistic with bipolar disorder. Worst-worst, he's a low IQ, high-functioning autistic with bipolar disorder and schizophrenia."

"Oh, my. Are you also a psychiatrist as well as a molecular geneticist?"

"No. Psychiatry and psychiatric disorders were interests of mine. Before."

"I see. Is there anything else I should know about my traveling companions?" The smile in the mirror remained warm. He didn't seem to be goading her, and he did have a right to know, after all.

She took a deep breath and said, "There is a worst-worst-worst option."

"That sounds ominous."

"If his childhood development had been...influenced in a harmful way, or if he experienced unhealthy urges that weren't dealt with professionally and in a timely manner, it could be bad."

"I think I follow. What you're saying is that we might be sharing our adventure with a sociopath."

She hated hearing the word spoken aloud. She nodded.

"And this sociopath also has certain skills with firearms?"

"So he says. I've not seen him in action though. There's something else you probably should know."

"Goodness, there's more? Okay, lay it on me, Doc."

"You're familiar with savant syndrome?"

"I believe so. That's someone who has an extraordinary talent or ability in a specific area. Did I get it right?"

"Yes. That's it, basically. There are different types of savants...splinter skill, talented, acquired, etc. Oftentimes, they're mentally disabled, but in some cases they're not. Those people are considered prodigies. The splinter skilled and talented savants are by far the most common types. Splinter skilled savants show a remarkable ability to memorize things: historical facts, license plate numbers, phone books. There was a German boy who memorized *The Rise and Fall of the Roman Empire* verbatim and could recite it forward *and* backward.

"Then there are the talented and acquired savants. They are either born with a savant ability or acquire it as a result of brain trauma. I believe Logan falls into one of these two categories. These individuals exhibit vastly superior skills in a specific area. That area may be music or mathematics, or a mechanical talent that requires exceptional eye-hand coordination."

She paused in her explanation, hesitant to continue.

"So there is a worst-to-the-fourth-power option as well, Doc? In addition to everything else, am I hearing that our companion might be a sociopathic weapons expert?"

It sounded more sinister coming from a stranger's mouth than it had in her head.

She nodded.

"Julia, why have you hitched your wagon to such a potentially dangerous young man?"

She had asked herself that same question more times then she could count. She still didn't have the answer.

***

Logan knew he had to be quick. He'd been thinking of ways to get rid of the old man ever since he refused to show him how to tie all those knots. Also he just plain didn't like him. Something made him want to squeeze the old man by his skinny black neck and watch his eyeballs bulge like the little guy back at the Shell station. But what he really hated was how Julia talked to him. It was different from how she talked to Logan. She used lots of big words and the old man seemed to understand them. It might even be some kind of code, but he wasn't sure if it had anything to do with magic. He had seen evidence of Julia's magic, but so far not one of the tricks the Thoozy person claimed to know. Sometimes those black eyes would just stare at him when Julia wasn't looking. It felt like they were looking deep down inside him. The old man didn't smile when he did this. Not like he always smiled at Julia. Maybe when he stared like that, he was seeing what Logan was thinking. Could that be how his magic worked? What if he could see Logan's memories and knew what he'd done to all those animals and people?

Hopefully when the Thoozy person had been looking at his thoughts, he didn't spot Logan's plan for getting rid of him. It was a plan that would happen in the next few minutes.

His trick of saying he needed to do-his-business was pretty smart. He didn't need to go at all and was now hiding behind a truck a little ways-away from their car. He was on the same side as the Thoozy person. He would have preferred to use his rifle for this shot, but he thought Julia might tell him not to take any gun at all, or worse, she might raise her eyebrow at him. She always did that when he said stuff that he probably shouldn't have said out loud. The Bad Thoughts told him to shut-the-hell-up and to only talk about safe stuff.

He rested his forearms on the bed of the truck, holding his Ruger 9mm in a relaxed two-handed grip. Even though he shot better with the Sig Sauer tactical rifle, he loved his Ruger the best. It was a beautiful killing machine, and it felt at home in his hands. One eye squeezed shut while the other sighted the white cotton ball head in the back seat of the Rover. He breathed out half of his breath, just like always, and began to squeeze the trigger.

"Logan! Are you done? What's taking you so long?" Julia's voice came from the car. With a smile, he continued the gentle squeeze.

The cotton ball head vanished.

What the heck? It was like he just disappeared-into-thin-air. The old man must have vanishing magic.

"Logan!"

"Coming, Julia!" he hollered, baffled by what had just happened. "I had to go number two!"

Frustrated, he replaced the pistol in its holster and jogged back to the Rover. When he hopped in, the old man still sat in the back seat, just as before.

Yes, he definitely had vanishing magic. No doubt about it. Logan would need to be very careful of the Thoozy person.

The old man said, "Would either of you like a protein bar? I had a few stashed in my pack on the floor." He waved the cellophane packages.

Logan ignored him. He didn't want anything from the Thoozy person. They were probably poisoned anyway.

Chapter 42

Kansas

After driving twenty-five miles on I70, they pulled off the highway, parked, and then headed into the surrounding farmland on foot. According to Lisa, the interstate would be heavily monitored east and west of Hays. Steven's plan was for two small scouting parties to approach from the north and south. Each group would contain three people, a Motorola walkie talkie, a pair of high-powered binoculars, and a variety of firearms in case they got into trouble.

The Indian summer sun bore down on Steven, Jeffrey, and Tung as they crouched in a desiccated cornfield. Steven thought the noise of the cicadas, which ebbed and flowed, sounded like castanets played by a thousand tiny Spanish dancers. He squinted through the lenses, frowning at what he saw.

"What is it, Dad?"

"I can see the Best Western. There are two men standing out front with rifles."

"Lisa was right, then."

"That only corroborates part of our suspicions, Jeff."

"Do we actually have to see them hurt people to know they're doing it?"

He looked at his son. "What we're contemplating is serious business. We need proof that those men are as bad as we think they are before we act. While I have no doubt Lisa is telling the truth, we don't know anything about the woman who gave her the information."

Jeffrey processed the words then nodded. "Okay, you're right."

Tung watched the exchange without comment.

Steven lifted the binoculars. "Someone is coming out. It's a female. Young...maybe early twenties. There's a man behind her. She's standing with her hands behind her back. The two men that were outside are talking to the man with the girl. They all have guns. Now the one that came out with the girl is pushing her from behind. They're walking down the street. I think I see handcuffs, which explains why her hands are still behind her back. Uh oh. She stopped and is shaking her head. Damn it, the bastard just hit her. They're walking again. She just stumbled. She's on her knees now. The man is pointing his gun in her face. Oh shit. They have some kind of pillory or stocks set up on a wooden platform in the middle of the street. Looks like something from the 1800s. He's making her put her head and arms across it so he can close it on top of her. Oh no."

"What's happening, Dad?"

"There's a crowd around the stocks now. Mostly men, but a couple of women too. They're cheering while the man is...violating...the girl."

Steven handed the binoculars to Tung, wrestling with the urge to vomit.

Tung peered through the lenses, then spoke in that Midwestern drawl so at odds with his exotic features.

"Yes. It's as bad as you suspected." His mouth was turned down and the almond eyes glistened.

Jeffrey frowned, then said, "Do you have the proof you need?"

***

"I don't want to wait even one more day!" Chuck bellowed in Steven's living room later that evening. The face of the former grocery store manager, now Liberty's head of security, was flushed with outrage.

"We're going to do this the right way," Steven replied.

After what he had witnessed, and after hearing similar reports from the other scouts, he wanted to ride into Hays like the Union army at Gettysburg. But that wasn't rational thinking. People were going to die, and if he orchestrated the assault well enough, the casualties on their side would be few, or dare he hope, zero.

"You saw what they did to that girl! How can we just sit here and let that happen?"

"We're not going to rush into this. We're going to do it the smart way."

"Of course, because we all know how smart you are!"

It was the second time Chuck had made that remark to him in the same disparaging tone.

"That's right. I am smart, and I'm not going to apologize for it. We should all be thankful for whatever gifts or talents we possess, because we're going to need them in the days and months to come. More than ever before."

He waited to see if the man would respond. When he didn't, Steven continued.

"Let's consider our resources," he said to the subdued gathering. "We have firearms and several people who are proficient with them. We have plenty of vehicles but need to find more gas. We have a munitions expert," he indicated Tung, "But we'll need to find materials for the devices he intends to build, as well as steady-handed volunteers."

Nervous laughter.

"We have Cate, who has offered her medical expertise for any injuries our people might sustain, and also with the victims once we've rescued them." He gestured to the woman who occupied his favorite chair.

Her arms were crossed over a shelf-like bosom, as they had been at the town hall meeting. She wore the same amused expression. He had been surprised when she showed up at his door for the strategy session; she didn't seem like the volunteering type. Even though she was off-putting, he was grateful for her assistance.

"Most importantly, we have brave, caring people who are willing to put their lives on the line to help others. We are the good guys here. We will prevail."

Applause filled the room. When it diminished, Steven nodded to Ed, the skinny man with the exquisite draftsman's skills. There was a drawing pad on his lap and a sharpened pencil in his hand. Someone had laid out a Kansas road map on the coffee table.

"Okay, let's get down to business."

Chapter 43

New Mexico, Texas Panhandle, Oklahoma

The Blue Hole had yielded more than just a few minutes of entertainment for Jessie. Pablo was again relegated to gas-sucker, since Maddie wasn't up to doing much of anything other than resting in the back and occasionally snorting at his lame jokes. He hit the jackpot at the third derelict car which had been left in the parking lot of the local attraction. In a morbid moment, he wondered if perhaps those former occupants of the three empty automobiles were at the bottom of *The Blue Hole*. He kept that thought to himself while Jessie frolicked about the edge of the turquoise water.

Soon after leaving, he scored twelve gallons of gasoline from a late model Cadillac. It had fueled their way past the state line of New Mexico and through the flat, unremarkable terrain of the Texas Panhandle. As they approached Oklahoma City from the east, the gauge was edging into the red zone. The deserted interstate was becoming less so with every mile, populated now with a smattering of vehicles.

"Why Norman? What about any of these other rural burgs we've driven past?" Amelia asked.

"I want to be south of Oklahoma City, which is north of Prescott's latitude. We decided we didn't want to live any farther north than where we came from, so we'll start heading south as soon as we can get more gas. If not Norman, maybe Chickasha. Maddie likes to say that word."

He glanced at his shorn and bandaged angel in the rearview mirror. Her eyes were closed but she smiled at the funny name.

"How's the headache?" he asked.

Her eyes remained shut. He was about to repeat the question when she finally spoke.

"It ebbs and flows, like the sound of cicadas on an Indian Summer day...castanets played by a thousand tiny Spanish dancers." Her voice had taken on a drowsy cadence.

Pablo felt a jolt of alarm. "Amelia, is she okay?"

The older woman frowned then touched the back of her hand to Maddie's forehead.

"She's not feverish. Maddie dear, how are you doing? Does the headache feel like distant thunder or a raging storm?"

He was too distracted to register the poetic analogy.

The drowsy cadence again. "It's not an F5. Big Blue looks like metallic cellulite." She giggled.

Pablo parked the Highlander in the middle of I40 and turned to face the back seat. Jessie stroked the kitten in her lap and regarded the surrounding landscape.

"What does that mean? Is she hallucinating?" he demanded.

"Pablo, hush. Maddie, what do you see?"

"My head feels fuzzy. Julia said the pills will make it better though. I wish I could tie fifty-seven knots."

"Amelia, do something!"

The brown eyes narrowed at him, somehow managing to exude affection and disdain at the same time. She lifted an eyebrow, then focused her attention on Maddie again.

"Why do you want to tie knots, dear? Can you tell us what is going on inside your head? Is there a movie projector in there? What do you see?"

Maddie gave a weak snort. "I like you, Honey Badger. Why that is, I have no idea. The little man's eyes bulged. His colors were orange and red. His magic must not have been very strong. It wasn't hard at all, and it was fun too."

Jessie turned in her seat now to gaze at Maddie.

Pablo didn't notice the fear in those huge sea-green eyes, but Amelia did.

"You're a damn leprechaun. Don't deny it. If these Oklahoma fuckers think they can keep me pinned in their shitty state, they have another think coming."

"You said you wanted to live in Oklahoma!"

"I don't think these are her thoughts, Pablo. Try to stay calm. I don't think she's in any danger. Let her ride this out. Jarring her out of a hallucinogenic or trance state could be harmful."

His stomach churned, but he kept quiet.

"I've never raised children. Flying by the seat of my pants here. Some kind of pillory or stocks set up in the street. Oh no!"

Maddie's eyes flew open but he knew she wasn't seeing the interior of the car.

She moaned, an unwilling captive to some nightmarish vision. Bruno whimpered in the back, igniting a burst of firecracker yips from Curly Sue. Just when Pablo thought he couldn't bear the clamor a second longer, it stopped.

Maddie took a deep, quivering breath and said, "We are the good guys here. Let's get down to business."

The moment the last word was out, her eyes squeezed shut and her head lolled against the window, the same ragdoll posture from when she'd been shot.

Amelia placed a fingertip at her throat, then pressed an ear against her chest. She smiled.

"She's fine, Pablo. I promise. At least physically."

"What do you mean, at least physically? What is going on? What the hell was all that gibberish?"

Jessie's enormous eyes followed every movement of the older woman's face when she spoke again.

"I think our Maddie came away from that injury with more than a headache and a bad haircut."

***

"You're saying she has psychic powers now?" Pablo didn't bother hiding his skepticism. "Do you know how crazy that sounds?"

Maddie remained in a deep sleep, nestled in the bed of a downstairs room at the Cambria Inn in Yukon, Oklahoma. The small suburb just west of Oklahoma City would mark the end of their journey eastward and the beginning of the final southern leg.

"Psychic powers? That's a cheesy term for a wordsmith such as yourself." Amelia's chastisement carried a delicate sting.

They sat in motel chairs on the sidewalk outside Maddie's room. Jessie played with the animals in the parking lot, uninterested in the conversation of the grownups. The kerosene lantern cast a warm glow, keeping the night shadows corralled at its perimeter.

"But some form of telepathy, certainly," she continued. "I can't say what newfound abilities she has, but she seemed to be receiving the thoughts of others. I think at one point she was witnessing a horrific event. Is she a clairvoyant? Lucid projector? Remote viewer? There are many terms for these people, and please wipe that patronizing smirk off your face, young man."

This time the sting wasn't so delicate.

"How do you know she wasn't just dreaming?"

The brown eyes bored into him. The gentle Amelia mask went askew for a moment, then soon returned.

"Do you think she was merely dreaming?"

He shrugged. "She's had a head injury. Who knows what damage that bullet did? I think jumping to the conclusion that she's suddenly Edgar Cayce is a bit premature."

She sighed. "You have a point. Further speculation now would serve no purpose. We'll simply wait for her to wake up and ask her."

"Please don't be angry. I've just never bought into all that stuff." He watched the little girl chase Bruno in the dark parking lot.

She followed his gaze, then said with an enigmatic smile, "There are more things in heaven and earth, Horatio, than are dreamt of in your philosophy."

"Shakespeare. Very nice," he said.

"Very nice, indeed." The voice came from the darkness beyond the lantern's reach.

Pablo grabbed the shotgun from the ground beside his chair. Jessie scooped up the kitten and ran to Amelia and Curly Sue. Bruno growled.

"Who's out there?" he demanded, underscoring the question with a click of the shotgun's safety.

"Just friends. No need for the gun, Wyatt Earp."

The voice belonged to a small figure stepping into the meager circle of light. He had never seen such an odd looking person in his life.

"You seem like decent folks, which is why my hands are devoid of weaponry. See?" The small man wagged empty palms. There was a smile buried within a muzzle of red wool.

Pablo chambered a round.

"Okay, amigo, we'll cut you some slack because you're clearly the protective type, but I'll need you to stop pointing that flintlock at my tiny friend."

The voice was female, a fact confirmed the next moment when a tall, slender young woman with dark hair wearing a black t-shirt and camouflage pants, glided into the dim light. She would be stunning if it weren't for her vaguely savage demeanor. The revolver aimed at his chest didn't help either.

"Right," he said. "I'll lower mine when you lower yours."

The next moment, the shotgun was plucked from his hands and held by a smiling man who might have just stepped off the cover of GQ Magazine.

"Who the hell are you people?"

"Survivors," the golden-haired man replied. "Just like you."

Now that they were fully in the lantern's light, Pablo saw tired, dirty people. The girl lowered her revolver but still managed to appear menacing, like a coiled viper.

"Don't worry about that one," the small man said with a smile. "She's housetrained. Mostly."

The man winced from the bicep punch the girl delivered with lightning speed, then said, "I'm Fergus. The Greek god over there is Sam. You can trust him. He's aces. The scary female is Dani. You'd be wise not to test her patience, especially when she's on her period."

Another bicep blow elicited a pained yelp.

The bloodthirsty smile on the girl's face was rather unsettling, but he felt himself relaxing. He glanced at Amelia, who wore an amused expression. Jessie's gaze slid from one new face to the next, her mouth agape.

His gut instinct told him he needn't fear these people, but Pablo still hesitated.

The GQ guy, Sam, offered the shotgun back with the business end pointed downward. His other hand was extended in greeting. "You've been carrying the weight of the earth on your back. It makes sense you'd be cautious." Kindness was evident in the voice.

Pablo returned the handshake. The handsome man's grip felt warm in his, despite the coolness of the October evening.

"Yes." He paused, then said, "I'm Pablo. This is Amelia and the little girl is Jessie. Maddie is inside. She's my girlfriend," he added with another glance at Sam's face. "She's been injured. Long story, but we think she'll recover."

"What a co-winky-dink," the red-haired man said. "Sam here has had a recent injury too. He's healing remarkably fast though. I hope your Maddie does too. It's a pleasure to meet you, Pablo. And Amelia, what a delicious creature you are." He reached for the small hand and lifted it to his lips.

Was Amelia blushing? It was difficult to tell in the low light, but there was no mistaking her flirtatious grin. This little guy was a real character.

Maddie called from inside. He snatched up the lantern and dashed to her bed just as her eyes fluttered open.

"What's going on? Where are we?" She frowned at the newcomers in the doorway. "Who are they?"

The small man, Fergus, introduced himself and his companions.

"How do you feel? How's the headache?" Pablo asked, stroking her cheek. Her skin felt cool to the touch. No fever.

She didn't acknowledge his caress or his questions; her attention remained fixed on the strangers. Suddenly her sleepy eyes opened wide as she stared at the young woman in the doorway. "Honey Badger!"

"Oh my," the small man said, his attention shifting from Maddie back to Amelia. "What do we have here?"

Amelia returned his gaze wearing the same enigmatic smile from before.

"Who is Honey Badger? Do you remember what happened in the car earlier?" Pablo felt left out of the loop, like everyone else knew the punchline to a not-very-funny joke.

In a bemused voice, the woman said, "I'm Honey Badger."

"What does that mean? Is that some kind of code?" He was getting more frustrated by the second.

Maddie patted Pablo's hand. "It's okay, Pablo. We're not staying in Oklahoma. We're going to Kansas with these people. We're needed there. And soon."

***

Two small figures came together under cover of night. One of them reached out a hand to touch the hair of the other.

"You've more gray now, my darling. It becomes you."

"I've been out longer this time than ever before. My bones ache." A coy smile in the darkness.

"My bone also aches...for you."

Silvery laughter.

"You're still the same lascivious creature after all these years."

"Of course. Why mess with perfection?" A smile in the deep voice.

"Not much longer now."

"Yes. A respite will be welcome."

"For me too. I think I will sleep for a year. Will you be joining me?"

A pause.

"I may travel east before I come in. I have a hankering to see the Atlantic Ocean again."

"Oh." Disappointment in the voice.

"But after that..."

"Very well. Just don't wake me when you slip under the covers."

A low, rumbling chuckle.

"My darling, I intend to wake you in a most exquisite way."

The two shadow figures merged briefly into one before separating and gliding in separate directions.

Chapter 44

Kansas State Line

"See that sign, Logan? We're about to cross the Kansas state line! We're very close now! Look at the map and see if you can figure out how many miles to Liberty."

"Okay! I can do that!"

Julia's enthusiasm was contagious. Everyone in the car seemed a bit giddy. Even Brains had shed his chronic pissed-off demeanor and was sitting upright in his cage.

"I think we'll have just enough gasoline without having to siphon more."

"I'll suck the gas if we have to get more. I don't mind."

She smiled at him. Ever since accepting the old man into their group, Logan had been well-behaved. And Thoozy had proven himself the perfect travel companion: good natured, charming, funny, and someone with whom she could have an intelligent, adult conversation.

"Have you ever been to Kansas, Thoozy?"

"Yes ma'am. A remarkably flat place, quite windy, hot as Hades in the summer, and I seem to remember a lot of curvy, blue-eyed goddesses."

Julia laughed. "Yes, I remember those things as well. It's been many years since I've been there. Steven and his family traveled to California for visits, rarely the other way around."

"Your brother sounds like a fascinating gent. I'm looking forward to meeting him."

"What's wrong, Logan?" she asked, noticing the sudden downturned mouth.

"I'm worried about the people in Kansas. I'm afraid they might not like me, like lots of other people didn't like me before they all died. It's been nice with just you and me." He shot a pointed look into the back seat.

She considered her words carefully before responding. "You have many good qualities. You're helpful and funny and enthusiastic, just to name a few. Perhaps if you make more of an effort to show people these nice traits, and talk less about your guns and such, they'll like you better. But even so, there will always be some who just don't like you. I'm sure there were people who didn't like me before," she laughed. "Not everyone will like us. That's life. But I like you, and no matter what happens there, you will always have a friend."

The shy smile told her she had chosen her words well.

She glanced at the rearview mirror, wondering if Thoozy would contribute, but the old man seemed lost in his own thoughts as he watched the passing terrain and the darkening sky.

Unbidden, she heard his voice in her head: *Julia, why have you hitched your wagon to such a potentially dangerous young man?* She shrugged the voice away.

"This will be our last night on the road. I think we should have a celebration. What do you think about that, Logan?"

"You mean a party? Will there be clowns and balloons? I hope there won't be clowns."

"Of course there won't be clowns. No balloons either, but how about extra desserts from our rations?"

"That sounds great! Can I make a fire? I'm very good at making fires now."

She sighed. "Yes, you may. Maybe we'll have a few games of Clue. Since you insisted we bring it with us, we might as well play it. Thoozy, I have something for you too."

"What would that be, Doc?"

"Something tells me you're a scotch drinker, and I just happen to have some twenty-five-year-old Macallan saved for a special occasion. I think this qualifies."

"Oh my, yes. That would be delightful."

Just as the sun began sinking below the horizon, they found a roadside motel. It might have been built during the Carter administration, but there were no cars in the parking lot, nor other signs of life. It would do fine for their last night.

The chill in the air justified the small fire Julia let Logan build on the cracked pavement, but she knew she would have allowed it even on a ninety-degree evening. The poor boy must have led such a lonely life, ostracized by his peers, perhaps neglected by a harried working mom, no real fatherly influence in his life except the neighbor he'd spoken of a few times. She vowed to make up for those years. Fate had thrown them together for whatever reason, and with some patience, kindness, and some trips to the library where she planned to learn more about his condition, she hoped to provide a suitable environment for developing positive, useful skills.

"The first thing I plan on doing when we arrive is to take a long bubble bath."

"Where will we live?" Logan's anxiety was still evident.

"We'll probably stay with Steven for a few days until we can find other, uh, accommodations."

She watched the old man over the fire. His white head contrasted with the backdrop of the night sky and reflections of flames danced in his ebony eyes. He wore only a ghost of a smile tonight, not the usual broad grin. He held her gaze, sphinx-like, until she finally looked away.

She knew what he was thinking. How could she bring this young man into the home of her brother and nephew? It was one thing to take on that risk herself, but quite another to expose others. Well, she and Steven would figure it out. She would explain her research findings in detail, and give him a full description of the occasional troubling behavior during their journey from Palo Alto. Then she would let her brother decide what to do. His house, his rules.

The decision brought a measure of relief.

Logan set up the Clue board with the obvious happiness of a child. In a grand gesture, he turned to Thoozy and asked, "Would you like to be Professor Plum or Mister Green? I'm Colonel Mustard, so you can't be him. I'm always Colonel Mustard."

"Of course you are. I'll be Professor Plum. I've always aspired to higher education. 'Professor' makes me sound like I must know a lot of important stuff," he said with a wink for Julia.

She returned the wink with a grin.

Logan watched the exchange with narrowed eyes.

Chapter 45

Liberty, Kansas

"We can't allow it, Steven. She would be risking more than just her life, you know."

Marilyn wore the pinched, worried expression that he had begun to appreciate. It meant the keen intelligence was hard at work, approaching problems from all angles at once, unlike his method, which was laser-focused and sported blinders.

"I'm open to suggestions, but I don't see any other way to do this. We have to have a mole in place. Someone who can corral all the victims in one location. Otherwise, we risk injuring them along with the bad guys."

Tung's IEDs sat on Steven's driveway, four of them in all. Each of the five-gallon buckets from The Home Depot contained a cotton sack steeped in diesel fuel and then filled with ammonium nitrate. Two-foot lengths of gasoline-soaked rope snaked out of drilled holes in the lids, converting the innocuous orange buckets into some nasty business. Explosives didn't get any simpler than this, and that was fine with Steven. Even if they'd been able to locate dynamite or black powder, Tung said the handling of those types of incendiary items was unsafe for novices. He refused to build them. Besides, in a farming community such as theirs, ammonium nitrate had been easy to find at the local feed and grain store.

Everyone but Marilyn and Tung had left. The final meeting before the rescue mission had lasted three hours and resulted in a plan that was almost as simple as the bucket bombs. It would begin by allowing one of their own to be taken captive.

Marilyn pursed her lips even tighter, then said, "Perhaps I could do it?"

Steven gazed at the plain face in the fading light as he struggled with a diplomatic response. He glanced at Tung, whose expression was as stoic as always except for a slight twitching around the corners of his mouth.

Marilyn laughed. "Oh, Steven. If you could see your face. Yes, I know I'm no beauty queen, but perhaps those men aren't picky. I could put on some lipstick and wear a push up bra. I actually have an acceptable décolletage for a woman in her forties."

That was one of the qualities he appreciated in the former librarian: her candor. He understood now why his wife, who had many friends, had allowed this woman into her inner circle.

"No offense, but we need a sure thing. And Lorilee has a good head on her shoulders for an eighteen-year-old."

He was referring to the sharpshooting female in Chuck's security team who had volunteered for the job of mole. It was inherently risky and his stomach knotted up when he thought about the danger this young girl would face, but the decision had been made. Lisa was furious at being turned down for it. Not because of vanity, but because they were sending this teenager directly into the wolves' den. Steven had flat-out refused to risk Lisa's horticultural skills. An entire hour had been devoted to this decision and a few people, Lisa included, left angry.

It was important to think beyond the rescue operation, to their future and the food that would be needed to survive.

Marilyn sighed. "Very well. We'll let this dead horse rest in peace."

"Good. I suppose we should all get to bed. Tomorrow is a big day."

Just then, two sets of headlights appeared at the end of the residential street.

"What now?" Steven was exhausted and wanted nothing more than to eat the dinner Jeffrey was preparing inside, then fall into bed. He placed his hand on the Glock in its holster.

Three pairs of eyes watched the unfamiliar vehicles inch down the street, then stop at the end of the driveway. The passenger window in the first vehicle, a Toyota Highlander, slid down with a mechanical hum. A bandaged head with short-cropped hair poked through the opening.

"We're here to help!"

***

"You're asking a lot of me. I've never believed in psychic nonsense."

Steven would get little sleep that night. The group of strangers sitting in his living room were an eclectic mix. The assertive female, Dani, reminded him of someone but he couldn't place who. The young Hispanic man hovered near the pretty, 'psychic' girl with the bandaged head, while covertly studying everyone else. The red-haired fellow was an oddity for sure. The Native American woman had barely said ten words and kept the little girl close by — another curiosity with those huge unblinking eyes. The kitten she clutched seemed content to stay in her arms. He wondered if the child were mute since she hadn't spoken during the hour they had been there. The good-looking guy was obviously in love with the self-assured young woman, but her body language didn't reveal if they were a couple. The poodle and German shepherd were well-behaved and already bonding with Molly.

"Let's skip on down," Dani said. "We'll assume we're all on the same page regarding the ESP stuff. Tell me the plan. You said it's going down tomorrow?"

Wordlessly, Steven sought input from Tung who stood across the room, then from Marilyn next to him on the sofa. Marilyn's shrug said: W*hy not?* Tung remained impassive.

He took a deep breath, then relayed the plans for the rescue operation that would occur the next day. Dani leaned forward in a chair, elbows on her knees. Her intensity was almost palpable, an invisible aura of ferocity.

"I'll be the mole," she said when he was finished.

"We already have a volunteer." Even as he spoke the words, he knew this girl would be a vastly superior choice.

"Right. An eighteen-year-old who's handy with a gun. Please. Sam, let's show them what we can do. Push the chairs back."

All eyes watched as the two sparred in an unknown form of hand-to-hand combat, moving with lethal grace but not quite landing blows. It was a thing of beauty. The lithe bodies glided and gyrated with feline fluidity, anticipating the action of the other in perfect synchronicity. The demonstration lasted five minutes but Steven was convinced thirty seconds in. She was right. She had the physical allure they needed to ensure she would be taken into the enemy's camp, plus the chops to handle the danger.

The two came to a balletic stop and turned to face him. He laughed and broke into grudging applause. When the girl smiled, he realized in a flash who she resembled.

"So I have the job?"

"You have the job."

"Smart decision. Now, here's how we're going to do it."

Steven raised an eyebrow but kept his mouth shut until he heard her plan. Afterward, he knew he'd been wise to do so.

Two hours later, Jeff, who was sharing his dad's bed so the others could use his room, whispered to his father, "She looks like Aunt Julia. Don't you think?"

"Yes, she does. She looks exactly like your Aunt Julia when she was young. It's crazy, isn't it?"

"Yes, a little, I guess," Jeffrey said, drowsy voiced. Soon he felt his son breathing the regular pattern of sleep.

Steven remained wakeful. He knew it wasn't as crazy as it should have been. He contemplated the odds of this happening, but soon gave up trying to figure them out. Maddie's alleged psychic ability was tough enough to swallow, so to speculate whether Dani might be the baby Julia gave up for adoption was an immense stretch. Even more incredible — if it were true — was the timing of her arrival: his sister would be here any day.

Believing in that kind of serendipity would require a Grand Canyon leap of faith.

Pablo's Journal, Entry #392

Strangeness abounds. We are not in Oklahoma, but rather nestled in a Kansas farmhouse which boasts running water, flushing toilets, and an electrified fence.

I may have died and gone to heaven.

Between Curly Sue and Molly the yellow lab, Bruno has acquired his own doggy harem. I don't think he's ever been so happy.

I can't explain Maddie's newfound psychic ability other than to surmise that the bullet, like a ballistic switch, flipped it on. Perhaps she always had it. Hell, maybe we all have it, a latent talent which most are unable or unwilling to access. There's no denying she heard the thoughts of others and saw through their eyes...that was confirmed this evening. She has only experienced the one episode, and I hope it was the last.

The heinous act she witnessed, seemingly through the eyes of Steven, our host, has changed her on a fundamental level. She's still my Maddie in most ways, but I have the sense that now a part of her belongs to everyone, and I will have to share her even more than I did with the addition of Amelia and Jessie. This vexes me.

Yes, I know that makes me a selfish prick. So be it. And if I die tomorrow in this showdown, at least she is sleeping next to me tonight...my battered and beautiful enchanting mystic angel.

Next to Pablo, Maddie slept. And dreamed.

A troop of shadows moving with the sun. Alfred smiled and patted her knee. Shift. Now the old man with the pristine dentures lay in his motel bed. The chest didn't move. Didn't rise and fall. She stood next to him.

Sadness. Nobody should die alone. The ancient eyelids fluttered open, but she wasn't afraid.

Maddie, do you know? Do you feel the life inside you?

Surprise.

Fragile like a dandelion in the wind. Be cautious for yourself and the baby, my dear. There are many to fear, and one most of all.

Surprise and now unease.

Malicious malevolent malignant, this one. He would rule the world or see it burn. Soon you will see him clearly and you will recognize him for the destroyer he is. Take care.

She nodded in the dream as well as in the bed. The grandfather hand squeezed hers, then the pale eyes closed.

Don't go.

I must, child. The world belongs to those who come the last.

Maddie moaned in her sleep. Pablo set his notebook on the bedside table, blew out the candle, and wrapped a protective arm around her waist. He was asleep in seconds.

Chapter 46

Western Kansas

Logan wasn't sleeping. He'd been working on the plan in his mind all day. He would wait for Julia and the Thoozy person to go to bed, then after he waited long enough for them to fall asleep, he would press a pillow against the old man's face and keep it there until there was no breathing or moving. He had thought carefully about all the necessary steps. It wasn't that he didn't want to do it — he actually found the idea exciting — but because it was important that the death looked...what was the word?

Natural, the Bad Thoughts said.

Yes, that's it. His death must look natural, which meant no squeezing the skinny black throat until the eyes bulged. Holding the pillow over the wrinkled face was the best way. It would appear that he passed away in his sleep. Since he was very old, Julia wouldn't question it and he would be rid of the pesky man for good.

It was time. They had gone to bed more than an hour earlier in three separate rooms at the motel. The doors were locked, but they had found the keys in the office. What Julia didn't know was that Logan had spotted a duplicate set under the counter. She had been so happy the motel used the old-key-system instead of an electronic-key-system, that she hadn't noticed them.

It would make his plan even easier.

He slipped out of his room. He was sure that he couldn't be seen by anything or anyone that didn't have magic, even though the stars and the moon lit up the parking lot. The bonfire was just a pile of wet ash and black wood now. Julia was impressed that he'd thought of pouring water on it before they went to bed.

He was quiet-as-a-mouse as he entered the motel office and snatched the key labeled with the number 103. That was the Thoozy person's room. For a few seconds he considered the one marked 102. He lifted it from the hook and brushed his thumb across the numbers.

Her magic is weakest when she's sleeping, the Bad Thoughts said.

Logan stared at the key. Finally, he put it back on the hook under the counter.

As he tiptoed past his room and then Julia's, he pretended he was one of those burglars in the cartoons. He imagined himself as a black shadow with a mask where just the white part of his eyes showed through, his back hunched and his feet tiptoeing in careful, high steps.

The thought made him giggle.

Quiet! the Bad Thoughts said.

He pressed his hand against his mouth and nose. No more giggling.

The key slid into the doorknob without any noise. His tennis shoes made no sound on the carpet. A moment later he stood next to the old man's bed. A bit of starlight came through the curtains, reflecting off the black skin and the closed eyelids.

He reached for the pillow on the other bed. When he turned back, he could see white eyeballs in the dark.

"You certain you want to do this?" The voice was low and not even sleepy sounding. Had he been playing possum?

Logan grinned. Nodded. Then sprang.

Chapter 47

Liberty, Kansas

"What happens if they don't take her?" Jeffrey whispered to his father. They both peered through binoculars from a withered hayfield a hundred yards from the roadblock east of Hays.

The red-haired man, Fergus, answered before Steven could. "If the Honey Badger wants to be taken, she will be," he said with an affectionate smile. He was using a pair of field glasses pulled from an inner pocket of the oversized Army jacket he wore.

Steven lowered his binoculars and studied the small man, who studied him right back. "You seem confident of her abilities."

"That's because I am. I've seen her in action. I don't know what's more impressive: the big brain, the physical prowess, or the perfect backside."

Steven frowned, considered a response, and then lifted the binoculars again. "It seems you're right. They're handcuffing her now. Looks like they're using tie wraps."

Fergus smiled.

***

"What kind of medieval shit-hole operation you running here, semen breath?" Dani said to her captor as she scanned her surroundings.

The stocks Steven had described were positioned in the section of I40 that would be considered Main Street during its short migration through the small town. Rough men lounged against storefronts or sat on benches, eyeballing the new merchandise as she pretended to stumble along the sidewalk. All carried weapons of some kind: rifles, a few handguns, and knives. Lots of knives.

The two women she saw were scrawny and grimy, and engaged in physical labor. One pushed a wheelbarrow full of canned goods and the other lugged two buckets of water on an archaic wooden shoulder yoke, a scene right out of the Old West. The woman weighed less than a hundred pounds and struggled with the cumbersome weight.

You lazy assholes. Payback is a bitch with sharp teeth and razor claws. And she's right around the corner.

Dani smiled.

"Shut up. And what the hell you smiling about, bitch?" the farm boy next to her asked. He couldn't have been more than eighteen or nineteen, but he stood well over six feet — a meat sack filled with equal portions of muscle and baby fat. He smelled of stale sweat and fresh shit.

"I'm smiling because I know how little your dick is. Guys like you with tiny hands and blubbery bellies always have little dicks."

When he backhanded her, she didn't have to pretend to fall.

"Get up. I'll show you how big my dick is later."

She spat blood onto the concrete, then stood. She faced the man-boy, stared unblinkingly into his close-set eyes and said, "I bet you like sticking your Vienna sausage into your farmer boyfriend's butt."

The meaty hand raised to strike again, but a voice halted it in midair.

"Enough, Jacob. She's just trying to rile you up."

The voice belonged to a man who was likely her captor's father. He wore the flannel shirt and Levi's typical of these Midwesterners; had the same washed-out blond hair and ruddy face as his son, but there wasn't an ounce of fat on this one. With his Aryan features and wintry smile, a swastika on his chest would have looked more natural than the plaid. When Dani gazed into the glacier-blue eyes, what she saw there made her bravado slip.

"You'll get your revenge soon enough," the man spoke to his son but held Dani's gaze. "In the meantime, we don't want to damage the wares."

The final words, meant to demean, had the opposite effect. She returned the chilly smile but kept her mouth closed. She had a job to do.

Jacob shoved her through the entrance of the Best Western. Immediately, her nostrils were assaulted by the pungent tang of urine and feces mingling with the unmistakable musk of sex. She felt the bile rise in her throat. Several more creeps sprawled on the chairs in the hotel lobby. She ignored their catcalls and sophomoric innuendos.

"Up the stairs, bitch."

The man-boy was still pissed, which was what she wanted — but she needed to keep it at a slow simmer. It wasn't time to let him boil over. Yet.

As she was hustled along the upstairs corridor, she stole quick peeks into the rooms she passed. The doors had been removed so the shackled women could be easily viewed, like trussed up poultry at a Thai market.

He pulled her to a rough stop at one that wasn't occupied. "This is yours. Your very own home with a bathroom and everything, except there ain't no running water so you'll have to shit and piss in that bucket." He indicated a plastic wastebasket with a Best Western logo on the side.

It was already half full.

He chuckled when she retched. "Yeah, maid service ain't too reliable. You'll get used to the smell. All the others have."

"Go to hell," she managed.

"That all you got?" he laughed. "Ain't so cocky now, are you?"

He shoved her down onto the soiled bedspread, looped a length of chain around her waist, then secured it with a padlock. The other end was attached to a metal eyebolt in the wall. He noticed her glance.

"Don't get any ideas. It's screwed into the stud."

She kept her face expressionless and stared straight ahead.

"Yeah, nice and quiet now, ain't ya? That's what always happens. Stupid bitches."

She blinked, clenched her jaw, and said nothing.

He grunted, bored now that he wasn't getting a reaction. "Dumb Dolores will be here in a few minutes. She's the maid. She'll give you the lowdown on how things work. Be good and you'll eat. Be bad and you won't. Plain and simple."

He grabbed her face in one of his pudgy hands, pressed his mouth against hers, and stuck his fat tongue between her lips. At the moment she thought she might vomit, he pulled away.

"I'll see you later, hot stuff," he said with a painful squeeze of her breast.

Finally he was gone. She spat on the stained carpet.

The situation was worse than expected, but her plan should still work. They hadn't found the handcuff key in the heel of her boot, but she wouldn't need it. When the time was right, she would have no problem with the zip tie that bound her hands in the front. It wasn't even the heavy-duty type...idiots. They discovered a switchblade during the pat-down at the roadblock, as she'd planned. It was a decoy. The Leatherman multi-tool folding knife was concealed inside her, along with a Bic lighter. And they were becoming more uncomfortable by the second. Should she extract them now, or wait for the servant girl? She decided she couldn't bear another second of the discomfort, despite the Vaseline-coated cotton gauze the items had been wrapped with. The package felt like the Sword of Damocles inside her vagina.

She laid back on the bed and wriggled her pants down to her knees, alert for footsteps in the corridor. She tugged on the string that had been tied to the bundle. The relief was instant, but her nether regions ached like the worst case of PMS cramps in the history of PMS cramps. She wondered if she'd done some permanent damage to her uterus.

Oh well. Didn't want rug rats anyway.

She unwrapped the gauze and slid the Leatherman and the Bic into her boot. The next moment, a girl appeared in the doorway.

Dani couldn't stop the reflexive gasp. There was nothing symmetrical about the features — not the eyes, the mouth, nor the taxicab door ears. One of the emaciated arms ended in fleshy crablike pinchers. The other hand held an empty bucket with its thumb and pinky, the only fingers present.

The next moment, the girl stood next to her.

She moves like a ghost, Dani thought, then was nearly overcome by the stench coming off the poor creature.

"What's your name?" The voice was the opposite of what she might have expected to emerge from the hygiene-challenged mouth. Lilting, melodious.

"I'm Dani. You must be Dolores."

"Dumb Dolores. That's my name."

Dani frowned. "I bet that wasn't your idea."

"It's because I'm not smart." A shrug of the uneven shoulders.

She thought for a moment before answering. "Well, I'm just going to call you Dolores. I don't like ugly words like 'dumb.'"

The girl shrugged again.

"You're the one who explains things here?"

"Yep. It's bad. You won't like it. It's just the way it is, though. The men will come and stick their thing in you. Sometimes they want to put it in your mouth. Don't bite when they do that or they'll kill you. Doesn't matter how pretty you are, they'll still kill you. If you're good, I'll bring you a plate of food in the morning and at night. If you're not good, I don't bring any food."

"Do you determine whether I'm good or not good?"

The girl snorted. "No, silly. Jacob tells me. He's my boss. His daddy runs the town."

"Yeah, I figured it might be something like that."

"Every day or two I'll empty your bucket." She nodded toward the wastebasket. "I'll bring you one roll of toilet paper every Sunday. It has to last a week, okay?"

Dani smirked.

The girl paused, studying her face. "You don't want to mess around with these guys. They will hurt you or kill you. I mean it."

"If they're such bad guys, why do you work for them?"

Another shrug. "What else would I do? Least I have my own room. Never had my own room before. Pa made me sleep in the woodshed."

Something shifted inside her. She imagined the horror this girl's life must have been before. Hell, Chicxulub was probably a blessing for her. Fewer people around to gawk at her appearance. The thought prompted an idea, a minor change to her plan. In exchange for her help, Dani could offer a life that didn't include emptying shit buckets in a sex slave bordello.

She reached out and took the pincher hand in her own. The uneven eyes flew wide, but the girl didn't pull away.

"What if I could offer you a better life than this? A life with your own room, where people would be kind to you, and where you would have clean clothes to wear. Would you like that?"

Another snort. "Nobody's ever touched my hand before. I don't know what you mean about people being kind to me. Jacob gave me this job, and I get enough to eat most of the time."

Dani sighed. "You could have a better job and more to eat. People would be nice to you. They wouldn't call you dumb. They would just call you Dolores, like I do."

She gave the hand a squeeze. The help of this girl would increase their chance of success. If she didn't get it, her mission would be a hell of a lot harder and more people could get hurt.

The girl squinted, then tilted her head. Scrutinized Dani's face for another minute. Glanced at the doorway. Looked at the window where the drapes had been drawn against the sunlight. Studied Dani's face again.

"At this new place, what would my job be?"

Dani smiled.

***

Thirty minutes later, Dolores returned to Dani's room. By then, Dani had used the Leatherman on the padlock with success, but kept the chain draped around her waist for appearance. If a man, any man, came to her room, it would be the biggest mistake he'd ever made.

"I told them," the girl said.

"All of them?"

"Yes. There are only seven other girls like me that don't do the sex."

"Seven is a lot of women though. And they're spread out all over town, right? Do you think anyone noticed what you were doing?"

"No, I'm very fast and nobody saw me. That's because I can be invisible." The girl grinned.

Dani decided the first order of business, if she survived the day, would be to get her a toothbrush.

"I'm joking. I know that's not possible, but I feel that way a lot. People don't see me most of the time. And if they do, they usually say ugly things. It's better to be invisible."

Dani felt a tiny crack in her Grinch heart. Fergus would be so proud.

"And you told all the sex girls to stay away from their windows, right?"

Dolores rolled her eyes and huffed out a breath.

"Sorry. You understand why we have to be so careful, right?"

"Yes, because there's going to be an explosion of epic proportion and everyone who has a dick will be blown to fucking smithereens."

Dani laughed at her own words parroted back verbatim. She liked this girl.

"That's right. Now I think it's time to go find your boss. Do you remember what you're supposed to say?"

"Yes. *'Mister Jacob, you gotta come quick. The new girl is fiddling with her lock. I think she's trying to escape!'* How's that?"

Dani raised her eyebrows. "Perfect. You got every word right. And your acting ability is stellar."

"I remember everything. Pa hated it. Said it wasn't natural for a person to be able to do that."

"You have a photographic memory?"

A quick nod. "Yes, the correct term is eidetic. I read about it in a book once. Pa wouldn't let me go to school. Said I would be an embarrassment to the family because of how I look. So they just gave me books instead. Ma taught me to read before she died. I was three."

"You learned to read when you were three?"

"Yes. I love books. They're my most favorite thing in the world. When we get to your town, I want to work in the library."

She grabbed the girl's deformed hands in her own bound ones. "You're not dumb at all. You know that right?"

"Yes, of course I know that. I learned a long time ago it's better to let everyone think that. I can be more invisible if they think I'm not bright. When you look like I do, it's best not to be noticed."

Dani gazed into the uneven eyes and said, "Those days are over."

***

"What the hell do you think you're doing, bitch?" Jacob's bulk consumed most of the open doorway. Dani feigned surprise then leapt off the bed toward the window. He caught her around the waist and threw her back on the bed.

Deep, even breaths.

She grinned up at the man-boy with the fat belly. "What's that smell? Oh, I know. It's the stink of your boyfriend's ass on your tiny dick."

When he struck her this time, she almost passed out from the pain.

Deep breaths.

"Shut the hell up. You don't know shit!"

Had she stumbled upon some truth? If so, she would exploit the hell out of it. "Oh, come on. You know this is just an act. You don't even like girls, do you? You'd much rather be rolling around in the hayloft with your boyfriend." She gazed up at the chubby face inches from her own, seeing nothing but malevolence. Just a little further now...

"I doubt you can even get it up for a girl. I think the only thing that makes your dick hard is the sight of another dick."

He grabbed her by the arm and flung her into the hallway. She hit the wall hard, but controlled.

"I'll show you how much I like girls. In front of everyone!"

Dani hid her smile. As he pushed her down the corridor, she glanced back. Dolores stood at the opposite end. She lifted the hand that contained a pinky and a thumb. The thumb pointed up.

When Dani stepped outside, it took a second for her eyes to adjust to the bright sunlight.

Not enough people. It was speech time.

"Hey, everyone! Come on out! Jacob here is going to show us his wiener! Just like candy at Halloween...it's *Fun Size* and loved by adolescent boys!"

He shoved her hard from behind. Her arms were still bound in front by the zip ties, so she let her shoulder take the force of the fall. From ground level, she could see the Home Depot buckets under the wooden platform. They hadn't been moved from where she and Sam placed them the night before.

Above, the prisoner stocks exuded a silent message: obey or suffer the consequences. She wondered how many people had felt its baleful embrace since Chicxulub.

Deep breaths.

She stood. People spilled out of buildings, rubberneckers at a grisly traffic accident. The show was about to start and nobody wanted to miss it. Dani didn't want them to miss it either.

"Jacob thinks he's going to teach me a lesson, but I don't think he can rise to the challenge. Anybody want to place a bet? I'm giving ten to one odds!"

"Shut your damn mouth!"

Another backhand sent her flying to the pavement. That was a bad one. She could barely spot Sam in the gathering crowd through the stars in her vision. He started toward her, but she shook her head. He stopped.

This was the weakest part of her plan. He would have to watch her take a beating without coming to her rescue.

When she could see clearly again, she gave him a covert wink while ignoring his pained expression.

Deep breaths.

More people now. Lots of people. Who could resist the spectacle of a brutal rape? It was topnotch entertainment. Too bad there weren't any lions and Christians handy.

Fifty more feet to the wooden structure. She looked around. Men everywhere, eager-faced and smiling.

Closer.

"Come on up folks and witness Jacob's shame. Where's your daddy, Jacob? Shouldn't he be watching too?"

"I'm right here, young lady." The voice came from too far away. She needed that one in the front row.

"There he is! You're the one who runs this place, right? You're Mr. Big Shot? The Big Kahuna?"

"That's right. And Jacob is my son. He's the one who's going to pull off your pants and show you who's in charge until you're screaming for mercy."

The pale blue eyes and wintry smile reduced the surrounding crowd to soft focus. Here was the prize. Here was the king cobra slithering among the coiled rattlesnake horde.

Closer now.

"Is that so? He's a chip off the old block then, huh, pops?"

The burgeoning mob filled the street. She spotted asymmetrical features and taxicab door ears. Why was Dolores next to Jacob's father?

Icicles blossomed in her stomach.

The girl flashed her appalling smile. Tugged on the man's sleeve and whispered something in the lowered ear.

Oh no. Oh no. Oh no.

She found Sam's face. Tried to convey a wordless warning. Shifted back to the pale eyes. The frigid smile was an ear-to-ear grinning glacier.

Damn it. She'd been so cocksure of herself. So convinced she'd schmoozed the girl with her promise of a better life. The freak's brilliant performance had tricked her instead, with a little help from some overconfidence on her part.

Where was Sam? She'd lost him among all the bodies. She placed one foot onto the lowest of the warped pine steps, then slowly climbed the remaining three to the top. Her mind raced.

"You won't be needing these anymore. Boys, remove those orange buckets. Carefully."

She watched as several men came forward, then crawled under the planks and removed the fertilizer bombs. Everything was going to hell more quickly than her mind could process.

"Now, what were you saying, young lady?"

Glacier Man stood next to the platform now. She glared at him from three feet above while his son squeezed her bicep in a meaty vice grip.

"I was saying that cockroaches like you need to be eradicated. You, and others like you, are what was wrong with society before. You won't be allowed to get away with it any longer. People like me will whip out our industrial-sized cans of Raid and exterminate you. Bing, bang, boom." She made a dismissive brushing gesture with her zip-tied hands. "No harm, no foul, and no legal system."

"Is that so? You fancy yourself a vigilant? A bringer of justice? A righter of wrongs? You're pathetic. In truth you're just a weak female with delusions of grandeur. It's a man's world, sweet pea. Always has been, always will be. Besides, you're about to die, so your ridiculous little speech was not only absurd, it was ill-timed.

"Jacob, proceed."

Dani locked eyes with the man responsible for the atrocities that had been daily occurrences in this place. She didn't know his name but she knew him...his type. Not long ago, she'd seen a similar expression worn by a man who was the physical opposite of this one, but who exuded the same lack of compassion, the same need to dominate, and the same desolate wasteland where a conscience should be.

While she had been stalling for time with improvised rhetoric, the bigger part of her brain was formulating a new strategy. One without the explosives below her feet, which would have killed most of these jerk-offs in one fell swoop.

The man-boy began tugging at her pants. She continued to contemplate the father while working out the logistics of her new game plan. As she did so, the throat beneath the face with the pale eyes opened up, a bloody jack-o-lantern smile under the chin.

Sam!

"Run, Dani!"

Most of the crowd didn't realize yet what had happened. She had five seconds to bust out of the zip tie, then fish the Leatherman out of her boot.

She did both in three.

The next moment, the son went the way of the father, receiving three quick jabs to the groin as a bonus.

That's for all those girls.

Piggy eyes flew wide in surprise and a pudgy hand clutched at the injured genitals; he seemed oblivious to the eruption of blood at his collar. First the knees, then his remaining bulk collapsed onto the wooden boards.

She leaped off the platform just as the mob began to press in.

She moved faster than everyone, a balletic assassin dancing through bodies, slicing and stabbing and punching and kicking...eluding fists that swung, fingers that snatched, and blades that swished at the place she'd occupied a half-second earlier.

She emerged from the throng just as a barrage of gunfire began.

Sam grabbed her by the arm, a beautiful smile on his face. "Run like the wind!"

As she took off, she thought: *He got one right!*

Behind them, the street exploded in a cacophony of gunshots and screams. After fifty yards, she glanced back to witness a massacre, and stopped in her tracks.

"What's happening?"

There were people on the roofs of the buildings that lined Main Street, firing down into the crowd. She spotted at least a dozen shooters up there, maybe more. The noise was deafening. Primal, pain-filled shrieks mingled with the rapid and sustained firecracker explosions of automatic weapons. Some of the victims scrambled for cover, but most were dying on the quaint cobblestone street of downtown Hays.

Sam pulled her behind a concrete pillar next to an empty ice cream parlor.

"It's plan B," he said with a grin.

"What plan B? Whose idea?"

"Steven and Fergus came up with it. Just in case yours didn't work."

She couldn't decide whether to be elated or pissed off. "Why didn't anyone tell me about it?"

He took her bruised face gently between his hands and said, "Because you're a bully, Dani." He kissed her. "It's okay, though. I love you just the way you are. Anyway, they knew you would argue. It put more people at risk, but there were plenty of volunteers."

She started to object but realized that only proved his point. "I suppose it's a good thing they did. What do we do now?"

"We stay out of the way until most of the guys are dead, then we'll do a sweep through the town and take care of the rest. That's what Steven said. You and I are supposed to wait here until someone brings us our guns."

Several minutes later, the cacophony tapered off, reduced now to single sniper shots rather than the battery of automatic rounds. Return fire came from the street, which meant some of the enemy still lived.

Standing by, doing nothing, and missing all the action was almost more than she could take.

Sam watched her, frowning.

"Dani, please don't. Somebody will be here any minute."

"I can't stand it!"

"You're not ten foot tall and bullet proof."

He got another one right!

She was so surprised, it stopped her from darting back into the fray. "Sam, are you okay?"

"I'll be a lot more okay if you don't do something reckless."

She laughed. "All right, all right. What about the girls? Did plan B cover the part where somebody gets them out of that shit hole?"

"They figured the girls weren't going anywhere, so they should be okay long enough to secure the town."

"What about the eastern and western barricades? There are at least a dozen more of those bastards between the two of them."

"That part of the original plan is still in effect. We should be hearing the explosions any minute now."

"How did all the shooters get in place, Sam? We had to dodge a lot of security placing those bombs last night. How did they all just waltz into town during broad daylight?"

"They waited for you to draw them away. Any of the enemy that stayed at their posts were to be taken out by our snipers. Steven has a couple of kids who are sharpshooters."

"So what the hell is the delay at the barricades?"

The gunfire had diminished now to just an occasional pop-pop sound every few seconds, the last obstinate kernels of microwave popcorn.

"I don't know." He glanced at his watch. "We should have heard them by now."

Just then, a thunderous explosion from the east of town jarred ear eardrums. She could feel the vibration in her bones.

"Woo hoo! That Tung knows his stuff!"

Sam didn't share her enthusiasm. He was gazing back at all the bodies in the street.

"Sam, they were horrible, vile, loathsome creatures. Every one of them. And the one you killed was the worst of the worst. He ran this despicable town. You did a good thing."

He nodded but didn't speak.

Thankfully, feeling remorse about killing bad guys wasn't something she had to wrangle with. She looked up to see a small, red-haired figure zigzagging toward them.

"Over here!" she hollered from behind the concrete pillar. Fergus held Dani's revolver and Sam's shotgun as he ran.

"Honey Badger, you are a sight for sore eyes," he said with a grin. The next moment, the smile changed to a grimace of surprise. A hole, surrounded by a blossoming red stain, appeared on the front of his shirt.

***

On the western outskirts of Hays, Pablo was close to panic. The vehicle containing one of the four Home Depot buckets wouldn't start. He'd tied the steering wheel into place, leaving the tires pointing forward. A brick and a bungee cord on the passenger seat were ready to secure the gas pedal to the floorboard. But, stupidly, he'd turned off the engine while preparing the car for its suicide mission.

"Come on!" he yelled. The Nissan Sentra sputtered but wouldn't turn over. It was an older model with a hundred thousand miles on the odometer, but had been functioning fine on the drive from Liberty.

If he was a better shot or had possessed Bruce Lee skills like Dani and Sam, he wouldn't be in this predicament. He'd been delegated the task of lighting the fertilizer bomb and setting the car in motion toward the western roadblock. Maddie had been the one to work out the logistics of how far away the car should be when the fuse was lit, and at what speed it should be going to make contact with the barricade at the precise moment the device detonated. Pablo knew her calculations were perfect. And since everyone else had volunteered or been recruited for other jobs, he'd been obligated to do this one. If he hadn't offered, he would have looked like a schmuck.

Not an option.

His assignment required a cool head but no special skills other than to be able to inconspicuously roll out of the car once it got moving. But if it didn't start, what the hell was he supposed to do?

Through the windshield, he could see men with rifles standing around the roadblock a hundred yards ahead. So far they were just watching him, but they were alert.

No explosion from the east yet, but it could happen at any moment. And if he didn't get this piece-of-shit Nissan started, he would have failed, losing Maddie's respect as well as the townspeople's...also not an option since she had decided they would be staying.

"Damn it." He slammed a fist against the steering wheel.

Something caught his eye in the rearview mirror. A white SUV was approaching at a crawl. Were these more bad guys or harmless travelers? He gave the key another twist in the ignition. The engine refused to cooperate.

He glanced again at the mirror, opened the car door, and stepped out slowly. He walked toward the SUV, a Land Rover, with empty hands in the air. A man with dirty blond hair and a crazy grin emerged from the passenger side holding a rifle pointed at Pablo's head.

"Don't shoot! I need to talk to you!"

He heard the mechanical hum of the driver's window. A woman with gray strands in her dark ponytail stuck her head out. "What's going on here?"

He peered back at the barricade. The guards hadn't left their post, but all the firearms were in position now. He needed to act fast.

He approached the woman, talking as he walked. His thirty-second explanation brought a broad smile to her face.

"If I know my brother, he has this planned down to the minute. You're right, we better get moving. Logan, cover this man while he moves the bucket from his car to ours. I'll get Brains."

"Your brother?"

The woman's smile faded when she stepped out and saw half a dozen men pointing rifles at them.

"No time for explanations. Logan, if those men start shooting at us, shoot back."

"Can I shoot now, Julia? I think they're about to start anyway."

"No. Wait for them. Thoozy, do you think you can stand on your own? We've got a situation here."

Pablo had no idea who else was in there, and he didn't care. He dashed back to the Nissan and slung the Home Depot bucket out of the backseat just as the bullets began to whiz past him.

"Now, Logan!" the woman yelled as she helped an elderly black man out of the backseat.

On the other side, her companion placed his rifle on the window casing, using the open door for cover. One shot. Two shots. A third. Measured, smooth.

"I got three of them, Julia!"

The remaining men were scrambling now but still returned fire. Pablo ignored the zipping bullets while he transferred the bomb to the Land Rover, then went back for the brick, rope, and bungee cord. The woman had removed a wire cage containing a hissing cat.

Just then, an explosion thundered from the far end of town. They paused to watch a molten yellow fireball appear in the east followed by a bulbous smoke cloud.

"We have to do this now!"

"Wait," the woman replied, dismay in her voice. "I need to remove my equipment. And my research."

"We don't have time. Please," Pablo begged.

The woman frowned, then nodded. "Logan, let the man do his job."

The blond, still wearing the crazed grin, continued to take methodical shots even as he moved away from the safety of the car door. The old black man sat on the highway shoulder next to the caged cat. The woman looked like she might cry.

Pablo slid behind the wheel, steered the Rover around the Nissan, got the speed up to seventeen miles-per-hour, secured the brick, lit the gas-soaked fuse, and rolled out of the car. He landed on the gravel-strewn asphalt of I70 with a painful thud, then watched the SUV continue toward the barricade. The few guards who remained renewed their gunfire for the excruciating seven seconds the car bomb took to reach its destination.

Finally, it exploded.

***

"Fergus, talk to me." Dani managed to keep her voice low and even.

Inside the ice cream parlor, the sound of sporadic gunshots was muted. Fergus remained unconscious. He had passed out after they placed him on the checkered linoleum. His breathing was ragged, and despite the pressure she applied with the palms of her hands, his chest wound continued to bleed heavily.

Sam searched the pockets of the blood-stained army jacket, looking for anything useful. "Nothing but a lot of weird stuff. I'll look in his pack."

She nodded, remembering the items he produced when Sam had been shot. She stared at the wooly face of the odd little man. Thought about his calming presence, his sage advice, his pervy sense of humor...and how insidiously he had wormed his way into her heart.

Please don't die.

The blue eyes fluttered open.

"Is that an angel floating above me? Or am I in that other place, and my punishment for the debauched life I've led is to be saddled with an enchanting demon who will torment me throughout eternity?"

His speech was labored, but surely it was a good sign he could speak at all.

"How are you feeling? Do you think we can move you? What should I do?"

Sam handed her a sanitary napkin from the backpack. She pressed it against the wound with as much force as she dared.

"I'm going for help," Sam said. "That nurse lady should be here by now. I'll go find her."

"No," Fergus said, then coughed. Blood dribbled from the corner of his mouth. "Find Amelia. She'll know what to do."

"Amelia?" Dani asked, puzzled. "The Native American woman? Is she a doctor? I thought Cate was the doctor here."

"Just do it, Sam. Be careful. My life isn't worth yours."

He nodded and was gone.

"What's going on? What am I missing?"

"Questions, questions. Always with the questions. I wonder if all honey badgers are so curious."

"Stow it. If you weren't mortally wounded, I'd be grilling you like a T-bone."

A weak chuckle. "You are a peach. I'll miss you."

"Don't talk like that. You're not going anywhere."

The familiar, lecherous grin. "You love me. I realize that now. The first time you saw this hot little package, your honey badger brain said, *'I must have that fine specimen of a man!'* Don't deny it."

"You're delusional, Lucky Charms. Now stop talking. You need to conserve energy."

An explosion, this time from the west, rattled the store front windows.

"Sounds like the mission is going as planned." The gravelly voice was barely a whisper.

She glanced at the grime-streaked glass panes just as several figures darted past. Good guys or bad guys? There was no way of knowing. Her revolver lay next to Fergus on the ground, just in case.

"You hate to be missing all the action, don't you?"

"I told you to quit talking, crazy man."

The maxi pad was now a soggy, red sponge.

"It's mystifying, this existence we humans call life. We scuttle about on the surface of a tiny blue marble in the middle of an unremarkable solar system, which is merely a dust mote in an otherwise average galaxy, a galaxy which is one of a hundred billion in the universe."

"This isn't the time to get all philosophical."

A faint snort. "I think dying is the perfect time to get philosophical."

"You're such a drama queen." The words stuck in her throat.

The beard twitched and the crow's feet next to the bright blue eyes — azure slits now — deepened. "Anyway, it makes a person feel small, doesn't it? Then, when you add the concept of time to the mix, it gets truly puzzling. A typical lifespan is, let's say, eighty years...hardly a blip when you consider the billions of years the universe has existed. Why so little time for such a magnificent species? It doesn't seem right, does it?"

"You're not dying. I won't allow it."

He smiled. "I believe you mean that. You're quite exceptional, Honey Badger, but despite your remarkable talents, I'm fairly certain you can't control lofty matters such as this. If I die, I die. Just like every other human being who has drawn a breath, but no longer does so. I would have preferred to see the Atlantic Ocean again, but it seems that wasn't meant to be. And besides, I have lived a life fuller and richer than most. I'm a lucky man. A Lucky Charms man!"

"Fergus, shut the hell up. I mean it."

The eyelids fluttered and closed.

"Fergus! Stay with me!"

A bell above the door of the ice cream parlor tinkled.

She swiveled and stood, pistol in hand.

"Young lady, put that weapon down and move out of my way."

The tiny woman nudged her aside, none too gently. The little girl with the strange green eyes watched Dani with mild interest.

"He's still breathing," Dani said. "He was just talking right before you came in. Are you a doctor?"

Amelia took Dani's place on the floor and removed the blood-soaked pad, ignoring the question.

"Oh, what have you done, my darling?" the small woman murmured, studying the wound.

Dani knew she wasn't addressing her. Why the familiarity with Fergus, whom she had just met the day before?

"You two, out." Amelia's gesture was meant for her and Sam, who lingered in the doorway. The strange child sat cross-legged on the floor now, watching the behavior of the grownups with those unsettling eyes.

Dani began to object, but Fergus's weak whisper cut her off. "Do what she says, Honey Badger." His eyes remained closed.

"We don't know these people. You want me to trust this woman with your life?"

She had to lean in to hear his response.

"I want you to trust *me*, Dani. Please, just go."

Her eyes locked with those of the small woman. She saw intelligence and determination in their depths. And something else...sorrow?

"Fine. You better take care of him. You have me to answer to."

The next moment, she and Sam stood outside. The gunfire had stopped completely and an eerie silence filled the town. There were bodies everywhere; some were still moving. The pungent aroma of gunpowder and scorched rubber tainted the air, like the noxious atmosphere of an over-industrialized alien planet. There were also top notes of something that was vaguely pleasant — at least until she realized it reminded her of backyard cookouts.

It was the smell of burning flesh.

Good. Those assholes had it coming.

With Sam at her back, she picked her way through the carnage, confirming that everyone who appeared to be dead actually was. Those who weren't became so, courtesy of the Leatherman's largest blade. Several others from Steven's group were doing the same grisly work. Sam vomited twice before the job was complete.

She wiped his face with her shirtsleeve.

"What now, Dani?"

"Let's go to the Best Western. There's nothing else to do here. And there's nothing else to do for Fergus."

Infuriating tears streamed down her face. Sam knew better than to offer her comfort. He followed her in silence as they walked.

It seemed everyone had gathered in the hotel lobby while she tended to Fergus. Pandemonium reigned.

"Quiet down, people!" Steven tried to manage the raucous gathering.

Three men sat in chairs in the center of the room. Their wrists were handcuffed and they were gagged with strips of filthy bed linens. Twenty women, all thin, bruised, and dazed, huddled in a corner. The woman known as Cate tended to them with the help of two volunteers.

"Why wait? Let's shoot them!" someone in the agitated crowd hollered.

Steven yelled, "Everyone, please! Let's calm down. The worst is over. Let's take a deep breath and get our emotions under control. Cold-blooded murder is different from what we just did. Remember, we're setting precedents here."

Dani could see that Steven carried a lot of weight with the townspeople. She found a section of wall to lean against and watched.

Sam gravitated toward the victimized women, anxious to help. She smiled as she followed him with her eyes. She would never possess that instant likeability that he did. She was abrasive, and she knew it. But it gave her joy to see others react to him with shy smiles and double-takes at his handsome face.

A female voice cut through the clamor. "These men were hiding under the beds of the women they were brutalizing. Just because they aren't shooting at us, doesn't mean we're not justified in killing them now. The girls have told us they were routinely raped and beaten by the very men sitting in these chairs. Do you think due process is necessary? I think we've set a few precedents at this point already. Namely, going against the vote to not intervene here in in the first place."

That got everyone's attention. All eyes turned now to Marilyn and Steven. Dani thought she caught a shadow of a wink from the skinny woman, who could have been Meryl Streep's malnourished, less attractive sister. Something was going on between these two, but what it was, she had no clue.

"That's true. But this isn't about them. Yes, they're horrible men and deserve the very worst punishment we can give them. The issue is with us, and our behavior as a society. Do we want to resort to vigilante justice or maintain at least some form of a civilized judicial system?"

Steven was a charismatic speaker, but she got the impression the dialogue between the two had been rehearsed. She watched Marilyn's face and realized that the woman didn't want to kill the men in cold blood. She was merely presenting that side of the argument in a manner he could address more effectively than that of a lynch mob. Pretty clever, actually, but it stunk of manipulation. She would tuck that bit of information away for the future if they decided to stay. She already knew Sam's thoughts on the subject: he would prefer to be around people. She would need to know a lot more before making the decision.

"What are you suggesting? A jury trial?"

"Yes, a scaled down version of that, where the accused have the opportunity to present their own case and the jury can cast a secret ballot for guilty or innocent. Quick, fair, and decisive."

Marilyn nodded, appearing to consider the weight of his words, acting her part. The majority of the gathering nodded too.

"Chuck, let's get these men back to the jail in Liberty. Cate," he raised his voice to be heard by the heavyset woman tending to the victims. "Are you ready for transport to the hospital?"

"Ten minutes," was the curt reply.

The crowd started to break up now that the show was over. Dani escaped the oppressive smell of the Best Western for the marginally improved air outside. She had seen plenty of horrors in the past year, but the gruesome scene in the town square of Hays, Kansas, was the worst to date. Amidst a sea of bodies and blood, the prisoner stocks towered, an ominous symbol of a civilization which had reverted to barbarism and brutality.

Well, at least life wasn't boring.

Someone was behind her, sharing the dreadful panorama in shared silence. When she turned, she saw Steven had been watching her with a small smile.

"What?"

"You did a great job. You put your life on the line for strangers, and I want you to know how much we appreciate it. You and Sam have a place in our town if you want it."

She shrugged. "Thanks. I'll let Sam make that decision, but we've been doing fine on our own."

"I'm sure that's true. You both seem quite capable. I won't push you, just know the offer stands. Where's Fergus, by the way?"

Dani felt her stomach knot up. "He's been shot. Amelia, is with him. It didn't look good to me."

Steven squeezed her shoulder. "I'm sorry. He seemed like a good guy."

"Seems."

He nodded, then shifted his attention westward, down Main Street. She followed his gaze. Four figures were making their way toward them. When she looked back at Steven, he was wearing a broad smile.

He vaulted off the sidewalk and jogged toward the small group. She watched as he scooped up a tall female in a sweeping, twirling hug. Their laughter echoed over the blood-stained cobblestones. It felt inappropriate, discordant, considering their surroundings.

She frowned as they ambled in her direction. She knew Pablo, but the other three were strangers.

"Dani, there's someone I'd like you to meet. This is my sister, Julia. Jules, this young lady is a local heroine and soon-to-be...hopefully...Liberty's resident Wonder Woman."

The older woman was attractive but haggard. She could see a strong resemblance to Steven in the facial features and the same intelligence gleamed in her eyes. The woman extended a hand.

Dani took it firmly in her own. Something passed between them as their hands touched...a sensation that felt almost electrical. She studied the woman with more interest now as introductions were made. The old black man looked like he was on his last leg, and the blond guy totally creeped her out. In one hand he held a wire cage which contained a pissed-off orange cat. A scoped sniper rifle was in the other.

"Your colors are green and purple, like Julia," the blond man, Logan, said to her.

Steven's sister gave her a wink that said, *"Please just play along."*

"If you say so," Dani replied, unsmiling. There was something profoundly wrong with this guy. His grin evoked images of Rorschach inkblots and strait jackets.

"Steven, can we get Thoozy inside? You said you had a medical person?"

"Yes. Her name is Cate. Lots to tell you, Jules, but first things first. Hold your breath!"

He ushered them into the lobby of the Best Western.

Dani turned and headed east toward the ice cream parlor.

The bell above the door tinkled again. The little girl and the small woman sat on either side of a body whose face had been covered by a bloodstained army jacket.

"I'm sorry," the woman said. Her dark eyes were full of sorrow. The little girl just stared.

Dani stumbled back out of the ice cream parlor into Sam's arms. After more than a year of banishment, the grief and heartache demanded to be acknowledged. Sobs racked her body. Not just for Fergus, but for her parents too, those wonderful people who didn't share her DNA but who had given her an enviable life and unconditional love. She had never allowed herself the time and emotional energy to properly mourn them in the aftermath of Chicxulub. Now, the sadness of losing Fergus mingled with that grief, surprising her in its depth and intensity.

Her legs collapsed and she was suddenly sitting on the concrete. The despair expanded in her chest, fanged and molten now. It was as defined, as tangible, as the tears that streamed down her face and the fingernails that clawed against the dirty palms which sought to imprison them.

She felt Sam's arms engulf her. Silently he rocked her, comforted her. Thank goodness he didn't offer any platitudes. Instinctively he knew not to, it seemed. And he would have massacred the typical clichés people always say in situations like these anyway.

At least she had Sam.

"He's on a better planet now, right, Sam?"

"Yes, that's right."

She could hear the smile in his voice.

"Time heals all gunshot wounds?"

"Well, not all of them. I think Fergus is an example of when it didn't."

Dani barked a sound...a hybrid laugh-wail-sob.

"I'm just so sad." Salty tears and slimy snot crept into her mouth. She pulled up the hem of her t-shirt to wipe her face. "Gross."

"Yeah, you're no beauty contestant right now. But you're gonna be fine. I promise."

"How do you know that?"

"Because this is true love. You think this happens every day?"

"Nice reference," she said, with a shaky smile. "I loved *The Princess Bride.*"

"What's that?"

CHAPTER 48

"You know there's going to be hell to pay, Steven," Marilyn said from the sofa in Steven's living room. "Not only did we act in direct violation of what the town decided in the vote, but now we have more mouths to feed."

She sipped her coffee, which must have been nirvana in a cup judging by the way she was savoring it. Despite her words, she seemed pleased at what they had accomplished that day. It made him feel good to see her sitting there, enjoying the French roast he hadn't shared with anyone else. It also made him feel good to have earned her approval and admiration.

"And you know who's going to be the biggest problem..."

"Natalie," they both said in unison, laughing.

There it was again — that transformative smile.

They kept their voices low so as not to disturb his guests upstairs. Julia and her fellow travelers took precedence over the people who had slept there the night before. He didn't feel too badly about that; it wasn't like there weren't plenty of other beds in Liberty.

He was exhausted but happy, which was strange considering the day's events. He had killed people today, but when he searched his feelings, he found no remorse or guilt. He sipped his coffee and gazed at Marilyn, not as the former friend of his wife, but as an intelligent, compassionate, interesting woman.

He knew that Laura, wherever she was, would approve.

***

"I'm worried about Thoozy," Julia said to the orange cat curled up at the foot of the bed in Steven's guest room. "He might have had a mild stroke or some other kind of heart event. First thing tomorrow I'm going to visit him."

The old man had been taken to Liberty's hospital, along with the Hays women. She supposed he was in good hands, but she still fretted about him. Something happened the night before in the motel; he had barely been able to wake up the next morning and they practically carried him to the Land Rover. She realized she had become fond of the old guy. She enjoyed his cheerful disposition and quick mind. She wished Logan felt the same way, but he was jealous of anyone who took her attention away from him, including Steven and Jeffrey.

He would have to accept that he had to share her now. She could hear Logan's snores from her nephew's room down the hall.

She smiled. They'd made it. She was with what remained of her family, and they would start rebuilding society together. Even though she had sacrificed her equipment and notes, she would still be able to conduct research, and she was excited at the prospect of having so many survivors gathered in one location. Knowing what she knew about them from the past year's work, it would be a fascinating study.

She took a deep breath and let it out slowly, feeling safer and happier than she had in a long time.

***

Logan was worried, but he was also tired. He thought he'd pressed the pillow against the Thoozy person's face hard enough and long enough to make him dead. His chest was no longer rising and falling. Thought he *was* dead when he slipped out of the old man's motel room and back into his own last night. The next morning when the old man was still alive, he began to worry. Would he tattle to Julia? So far he hadn't. Logan thought that was a good sign. Although the Thoozy person wasn't saying much of anything now. Maybe when he got better, he would tell Julia about the pillow. Or maybe he wouldn't remember. Or maybe he thought Logan being in his room was just a dream.

There was just no way of knowing. At least until the Thoozy person started speaking better. If he ever did.

Logan frowned when he thought of the nephew down the hall and the brother-Steven. He hated the way they all looked at each other and also the way they all looked kind of alike. Like he and his mother did. There was that other girl too that looked like them. He *really* hated the Dani person. Something about her and Julia having the same colors bothered him a lot.

The Bad Thoughts began talking in his head then. He was very sleepy, but he listened for a while. When he fell asleep, he was smiling.

***

"I'm so proud of you, Pablo," Maddie whispered, lying next to him in the dark. The house they found to stay in smelled stuffy, but there were no bodies. After an inspection and light cleaning earlier, they moved in. Amelia and Jessie shared a room on the other side of the small ranch house, but there was a third bedroom for Jessie whenever she was ready to sleep alone. In the meantime, Pablo knew Amelia didn't mind the company; she seemed quite attached to the strange little girl.

"Aw, shucks, ma'am. Tweren't nothin'. Just doin' my job."

Their laughter was tinged with a dose of manic relief. It had been an extraordinary few days, and they had managed to not only survive, but perhaps find their future home. Not in Oklahoma, but here in Liberty, Kansas. Maddie wanted to stay for now, and he would deny her nothing. Her wound was healing nicely, according to the local nurse, although he put more credence in Amelia's assessment. There was something off-putting about the heavyset woman with the perpetual smirk. Thankfully, there had been no other psychic events since that day in the car. Maddie's beautiful smile had turned a bit mysterious lately, but he would discover why only when she was ready.

He watched her fall asleep in the moonlight with the smile on her lips, then saw it fade away as dreams took over. Breathy moans escaped her, and every few seconds her body twitched...like Bruno's when he dreamed of chasing rabbits. He lay motionless beside her until she became still and her breathing slowed, indicating a dreamless, restorative sleep.

Soon after, he followed, a protective arm draped across her waist.

Chapter 49

Epilogue

A crescent moon cast its meager light on a neglected wheat field somewhere in what would be considered the Midwest by the few remaining people. If anyone cared to calculate the exact longitude and latitude, they would discover the location lay in the precise center of the land mass formerly known as the United States, which resided in the continent of what had been called North America for a few fleeting centuries.

Many hundreds of feet beneath the wheat field, the golden light of a late afternoon autumn day filled an open, cavernous space. The inhabitants there preferred subdued illumination to glaring noonday brightness. The light, and other technology there, was powered by a process similar to what the surface dwellers would have called *cold fusion*, but which the occupants referred to as something else entirely.

The chamber where some gathered now, after months or years of conducting research on the exterior of the planet, was home.

All was as it had been there for a span of time that numbered many tens of thousands of annual earth cycles. The gathering of humans was perhaps more animated than usual, due to the residual excitement of come recent above-ground excursions. Soon though, it would be time for those newly returned individuals to enjoy the deep sleep, while others who had just awakened would take their place on the surface. Although some might forgo the deep sleep and return again after just a short rest – if they so desired – to mentor, to watch, to study, and on the rare occasion, to recruit.

"No newcomers this time?" a man with enigmatic eyes and an easy smile said to the others. He spoke in a language heard soon after Pangaea had broken apart into many continents.

"Not yet. There is one who must gain some growth and knowledge before she joins us." The woman was small, as they all were, as all their brethren had been when they lived above.

Humankind had recently grown taller.

"The child is the reason this rascal is still with us." She indicated a man next to her with hair like flames and bright blue eyes.

The man kissed her on the mouth while the others looked on with affection.

"A healer, then?" said the man with the mysterious, almond-shaped eyes.

"Oh, yes. Quite special, that one. She just needs to marinate a bit longer." The woman smiled. Her translation of *marinate* into their language was a humorous word choice in the context.

Everyone nodded and smiled with her.

"So you'll be going back up?"

The woman began unbraiding her hair. She seemed saddened by the question and shook her head.

"No, this time was arduous. Perhaps even the worst. Look at all the gray in my hair! It'll take a century in bed to catch up on sleep, I think." She winked at the man next to her. As with *marinate*, the meaning of the translated word *bed* was similar to that of the surface dwellers in some ways, yet also profoundly different. Their beds were more analogous to something found in a hyperbaric chamber than to the furniture slept on by those above.

"What about the girl then?"

"She's in good hands for now."

The others all nodded in understanding.

"Your decision is made?" she asked, turning to the man beside her.

"Yes, my dear. Your time above was longer than mine. There is business I must attend to, women to fondle, and an ocean to gaze upon. I'll be back soon enough, though. Try not to miss me," he said, then grabbed the woman and pressed the full length of her body against his.

She giggled with delight, then kissed him long and thoroughly.

Most dispersed soon after, while some began dressing themselves in the type of apparel worn by the recent pandemic's survivors.

By the time they were appropriately outfitted and had traveled to the surface, the crescent moon sat much lower in the night sky. The eastern horizon was beginning to blush with shades of lilac and pink. The small group took a moment to gaze upon the laboring sunrise, then after affectionate hugs and smiles, they walked away in separate directions.

***

Harold's body shivered from the chill of the marble floor. The only warm place in the building was in front of the British Academy's baroque fireplace, and he only slept there a few hours each night. He barely noticed the cold, though. His mind was on matters far more important than creature comforts.

He pondered the chiseled verbiage in front of him. All seven Urak tablets were spread out on a library table located in an archive room of the British Institute for the Study of Iraq, housed in the British Academy building in the St. James district of London. Also on the table lay piles of books, most open to specific pages, along with Harold's own papers: his research from the prior year, conducted without benefit of the internet nor the BISI's superior reference materials, and utilizing photographs rather than the tablets themselves.

Until now.

The anthropologist's mouth was agape in a manner decidedly undignified for such an accomplished and respected scientist. If any of his peers could have seen him, they would know he had discovered something monumental. Dr. Harold Clarke was as stoic as he was brilliant. He had been almost as famous for his reserve and use of understatement as he was for his intellect. Everything in the world of anthropology interested him, but nothing so much as written language...the older the better.

Before Chicxulub killed off most of humankind, he was considered the world's leading expert on ancient logophonetic languages. How fortuitous that he had been one of the two men to uncover the artefacts at the dig site in As-Samawah. His American colleague had also grasped the implication of the double helix chiseled onto the fourth of the seven tablets before him. As Harold had been, his colleague was careful to keep his theories grounded in science and not conjecture. Sadly, neither his associate, nor the handful of experts who would have comprehended the significance of this recent achievement, were present to witness the final deciphering of previously unknown cuneiform signs.

With this final breakthrough, he now understood their message, secrets grudgingly given up, like those wrestled from the locked diary of a madman. The analogy was appropriate since the artefacts before him were a journal, of sorts, authored by a tribal shaman. Harold's tired eyes scanned the tablets again, then focused on his scribbled notes:

"The One came to me appearing as he had before

Wearing the face of People but not of my People

And said Brother your toil and hardships may end if you wish it to be so

It is your choice as one of the Exceptional to decide your fate

Remain with your common brethren here on the surface of the Mother or follow me below where you shall know Life Everlasting and the Knowledge of the Cosmos

For it shall come to pass as it has for millennia before that the Mother shall cleanse herself of the current People and start anew

We from below will make it so

A New People will inherit the Above Ground

As before We shall begin anew and with the (symbol for the double helix here) *we shall improve upon our species*

They and their children will inherit the Mother

They will serve Her and serve their Brethren

Know this Brother

The Bright Star in the night sky will return thrice then once more

Twenty Mother cycles will pass and a Great Pestilence will come to the People

The Mother shall be cleansed of all but the Exceptional

So it shall come to pass as I have said

Know this

We are You and You are We

Not Divine

We are Shepherds of the Mother and Keepers of the People"

These were the words the One spoke to me upon discovering my talents

As shaman for our village I fear I may not leave my brothers though they are not exceptional as I am

The Bright Star fills me with dread

Harold shook his head at the words his own hand had written, disbelieving yet confident of his translation, despite the modern English language fillers. Astronomy was not his forte, but the British Academy contained reference materials on all core science subjects. It had been easy to count back twenty years to a significant astronomical event that would produce a 'bright star in the sky.' The Hale-Bopp comet, of course. The comet appeared every 2,392 years, so the tablets' author must have lived almost twelve thousand years ago.

More importantly, if he was correctly interpreting the Urak tablets — and he felt with every fiber of his being that he was — they told of a superior humanoid race (*We are You and You are We, Not Divine, We are Shepherds of the Mother and Keepers of the People*) that lived underground, and utilizing genetic engineering, had orchestrated the demise of humanity, manipulating human DNA to self-destruct at a predetermined time twelve thousand years in the future.

As monstrously inconceivable as all that was, Howard found the paramount question to be not *what? Or how?*

But *why?*

***

"I don't understand why we can't just stay here," the boy said in the petulant tone of a tired teenager, which he was.

The dark man's gaze swiveled toward the youth. A magnificent grin spread across his face, revealing teeth that gleamed like perfect strands of pearls against skin of midnight marble. The smile was still in place when the man swung his fist, knocking the boy to the ground. Blood jettisoned from a nose that was certainly broken.

"Because, you belligerent, bellicose boy, there is a reckoning I must tend to. A settlement of accounts, so to speak. I suspect she's in Kansas by now, if I understood her 'Dorothy and Toto' reference. And I'm sure I did. Stupid girl. Truly, she's not nearly as intelligent as she thinks."

His army of recruits numbered close to a hundred now. No longer were the ranks filled mostly with youngsters who had been drawn to his charismatic leadership and were susceptible to promises of respect and power in their new civilization. Hardened men and women encountered along their way north had joined as well. People with a taste for violence and the subconscious need to be told what to do.

Pliable, pliant putty, they are.

The man's smile remained as he gazed at the eastern horizon, where the watercolors of sunrise were edging out the cobalt and gray. He estimated how many days their journey would take them, which was precisely how long he must wait for his reckoning.

To be continued...

Continue the journey with book two in the Troop of Shadows Chronicles, *Beauty and Dread*

EXCERPT FROM BEAUTY AND DREAD

BOOK TWO IN THE TROOP OF SHADOWS CHRONICLES

British Institute for the Study of Iraq

"Pity there's no one left to share this with," Harold muttered to himself.

Dr. Harold Clarke's final decoding of the seven mysterious Urak tablets had been gratifying and exhilarating; the pinnacle of his career, actually. It was the culmination of more than a year's tireless research, done first in his barricaded Twickenham flat, and then continued at the BISI housed in the British Academy Building in London. It had been a harrowing adventure making the pilgrimage from his home to London, but he had done it. It was vital to view the tablets themselves, not just pixilated photographs. Even more importantly, he needed to touch the cuneiform symbols chiseled into the stone, allowing the author's message to seep into his fingertips, travel along his body's nervous system, then find the appropriate neurons in his brain to explain what the fingertips had discovered.

Dr. Harold Clarke, brilliant anthropologist and world-renowned expert in ancient logophonetic languages, had a secret. Yes, he was a genius; his IQ was in the high 150 range. But he also possessed a hidden talent that had helped propel him to the lofty professional position he enjoyed before the end of the world happened. He had never told anyone about it. Not his family, nor his few friends, and certainly not his colleagues. His talent was something mainstream science would have ridiculed and dismissed. But because Harold was smart, he had used his gift to make himself a better scientist during his career, and again recently to decipher the ancient stone tablets before him. After weeks of studying them, touching them, coaxing from them their long-dead secrets, there had been a breakthrough, and it went beyond just the translation. He had connected, telepathically, with their author who should have died more than twelve thousand years ago.

LIBERTY, KANSAS

"What the hell do you mean, she's gone?" Maddie's pale face was flushed with frustration. Her red gold hair stuck out at odd angles, a follicular casualty of her recent head injury. After the necessary butchering, Pablo had said all that luxurious hair actually detracted from her beauty, and he meant it. But now, he had to bite his tongue to keep from laughing. She looked like a reject from a casting call of Peter Pan's Lost Boys.

"Jessie said she wasn't in her bed this morning, and she wasn't in the front or backyard. I'll keep looking though. Please, lie back down. In case you forgot, your beautiful noggin is still recovering. Getting upset can't be good for you."

A bright spot of blood blossomed on the white gauze bandage which encircled her shorn head, underscoring his concern.

Once he got her tucked back into bed, he would search for Amelia. But right now there was nothing more important than taking care of Maddie, making sure she didn't cause further harm to herself or the graphing calculator that was her brain.

Jessie stood in the doorway. He felt her presence there before he saw her. Those unusual sea-green eyes studied him, but he no longer found the child disconcerting. Somehow, Amelia had pulled Maddie through the devastation of a bullet wound in her skull, an injury that happened outside of Albuquerque the previous week. Jessie had been a witness to the doctoring, but Pablo had been banished from the room and would probably never know how Amelia had done it. Even more astonishing than Maddie's survival was the apparent lack of residual brain damage. So far the only side effect of the head trauma had been her newfound 'psychic' ability which had brought them to Liberty, caravanning with the other group of oddities which included the scary female warrior, the handsome guy, and the red-haired man, who died during the Hays mission.

That was a shame. He had liked the cheeky little fellow.

Pablo ushered the little girl out of the bedroom and closed the door behind them.

"You've searched all around the yard and up and down the street, Jessie? She can't have gone far."

The child nodded, but then remembered her agreement with Pablo. She must vocalize rather than gesticulate.

"Yes, Pablo." The singsong voice perfectly suited her. The elfin otherworldliness had diminished somewhat now that she was clean and communicative.

"Do you want to stay here while I go search? She's probably just exploring...chatting to the locals and whatnot. I don't think we have anything to worry about," he added when he noticed the distress on the child's face. They had all bonded with Amelia. Her easygoing nature, inherent wisdom, and tranquil demeanor had made her the perfect travel companion, and now, an invaluable friend.

"Yes, I'll stay with Maddie. Please go now."

"Okay, okay." He smiled at the child. "You're worrying for nothing though. I know she'll turn up any minute now."

For the rest of the morning and a good portion of the afternoon, he canvassed the surrounding area, returning every hour to check on the girls at their new home – a small ranch-style dwelling near the center of town where the community greenhouse was being built. Then later that day when he arrived at the meeting taking place in the former courthouse, he asked everyone he met if they had seen Amelia. No one had.

"Come on, people. Let's take it down a notch." Steven, Liberty's unofficial leader, raised his voice to be heard above the din.

Pablo hadn't yet decided how he felt about the man. He seemed insufferable at times, but little fault could be found with his decisions thus far. Sometimes exceptionally smart people were oblivious to their own pedantic natures; he had learned that lesson from his parents who had encouraged his creativity and supported his lofty literary goals but were quick to bring him down a peg when he complained about his less than articulate peers. So many people in his culture never embraced English, even though they lived in the United States. This baffled Pablo, who was a wordsmith in both English and Spanish. His parents had been proud of their son's exceptionalism but would often point out that nobody liked a *puto arrogante...a*rrogant asshole.

"Where the hell do you get off acting in direct violation of the vote, Steven?" The speaker's angry voice came from the row behind, but Pablo kept his eyes on Steven at the center of the room. "Is that how it's going to be from now on? Everyone has to abide by the rules except you? Is this what you bought with the food you shared?"

"The rescue operation was an exception, I promise. The circumstances demanded action and since we suffered no casualties, I think we should just let it go for now. There are more pressing matters to discuss. May we proceed?"

"Do we have a choice? You seem to be running the show now."

"We always have choices, but why waste valuable time and energy debating the semantics of government and majority rule when we won't make it through the winter with our current food supply levels?"

The man didn't respond.

Game, set, match.

"You're wrong about the casualties."

The voice came from a bench in the back row of concentric circles. The speaker was the intimidating young woman, Dani, and judging by the look on her face, she was either about to cry or kill someone. Maybe both. Pablo was glad he wasn't the one who had upset her.

"Of course. I misspoke. Your friend Fergus was a tragic loss, but also not yet a member of our town."

"No, but he volunteered for your dangerous, unsanctioned mission, and now he's gone. So there were casualties."

Steven tilted his head a degree, studying the girl. "You volunteered too."

"I had to. No one else on this planet could have done what I did, and clearly it was a job that needed to be done. As for all you assholes who voted against saving those women, fuck every last one of you. Sam, do you want to live in a town where half the people wanted to let those girls suffer?" She spoke to the Greek god sitting next to her.

Pablo watched Steven's face. Was he trying not to smile?

"Give us a chance. Let us prove to you that we're good folks. Scared folks, but good folks. You and Sam would be huge assets to our town, and we have a lot to offer in return," Steven said.

The girl opened her mouth to reply, but Sam reached for her arm and gently pulled her back onto the bench beside him. If any other person had tried that maneuver, he would have broken fingers now.

"We'll talk later, Dani. Candidly and with no sugarcoating, I promise. Now, Marilyn, what's first up on the agenda for today's discussion?"

Before focusing his attention on the spinsterish librarian, Pablo saw Steven wink at his sister, who sat with her strange companion in one of the front rows.

Now there's a human oddity, he thought, observing the wild blond hair and vacant smile of the person sitting next to Julia. Inspiration for a new poem came to mind as he covertly watched the young man.

Goodness is a notion in which all may not partake Kindness is a choice not everyone must make. Be true to the nature at one's core Love the dark things others abhor

Whatever dark things that nutcase might love, Pablo hoped never to find out.

"You're like a mother hen. Please don't fret so. I'm sure I'll be fine in a few days. These ladies are taking excellent care of me."

Julia stood at the bedside of her friend. The town had set up a makeshift medical clinic in the former Liberty Regional Hospital. There was no power, but plenty of sunlight streamed through the windows, and a kerosene lamp sat on a table next to a water cup and a plate with Thoozy's half-eaten lunch. He still didn't have his appetite nor his strength back after the morning she had found him barely conscious in his motel room.

"You must eat, old man. Come on, finish that tuna fish."

The dark-skinned face assumed the universal expression of disgust; the normally smiling mouth turned down in an exaggerated grimace. "It's just so fishy! If God intended for people to consume creatures that breathe water and swim in their own toilet, he'd have made them taste better."

"You big whiner. When I come back in the morning, I'll bring some land-based food. Steven has some canned pork and beans. How does that sound?"

"Sounds like I'll be able to entertain the nurses with my butt trumpet tomorrow night."

The warm grin was back to normal, but the haggardness around his eyes and the tight-lipped way he glanced at Logan hovering by the door bothered Julia. Something was deeply amiss with her friend, but it seemed there was nothing she could do to draw him out.

"Okay, Thoozy, we'll be back tomorrow bearing flatulence-creating, non-fishy-tasting gifts." She smiled at one of the women from the medical crew who had just breezed through the doorway. She remembered her name was Natalie, but that was all she had gotten from Steven about her other than some visibly discomfited foot shuffling. Her big-sister radar told her the two must have some history, but there had been no time yet for an extended conversation with her brother. She hoped to have one later once Logan and her nephew Jeffrey were in bed.

"One more thing, Doc," he said to her in a low, conspiratorial voice with another glance at the blond young man who was absorbed in studying the woman who'd just entered. Julia recognized that face: he was analyzing her 'colors.'

"Have you had a chance to talk to your brother about that thing we discussed in the car the other day?" The cotton ball head twitched in Logan's direction.

She read the subtext: *Have you told your brother about Logan? Explained his behavioral and psychological issues which could range from harmless Asperger's and manic depression to more dangerous disorders such as schizophrenia or psychopathy? And by the way, have you mentioned to your brother, in whose home you and your ward are guests, that your former traveling companion also exhibits savant-level abilities with firearms?*

She felt a flash of annoyance. This was her problem, not Thoozy's.

"Not yet, but I will, I promise. We had the town hall meeting this afternoon, and Steven has been busy preparing for it. See you tomorrow, Thoozy."

"When we can have a moment alone...just the two of us..." another head twitch in Logan's direction, "I need to talk to you about something. It's important."

She nodded, kissed the old man on the top of his Q-tip head, and hustled Logan through the door. A minute later they were outside of the hospital and walking toward their bicycles. A fierce wind gusted straight out of the north; the weak setting sun was no match for it. It would be a chilly ride back to Steven's house which was five miles from Liberty's town square.

"The nurse's colors weren't as pretty as yours."

"I saw you looking at her," Julia said, as they mounted their bikes. "It's good that you can do that, Logan. I believe it's quite a gift you have, but I wonder if it's something we should keep to ourselves. Some people might find it a bit off-putting." She noticed the sudden frown, his response when he didn't understand a word. "Unpleasant, I mean. It might feel to people that you can see inside their heads, which is not a comfortable feeling. Most of us like our privacy, and we all have secrets, don't we?"

"Oh, yes. I think that's true. There's nothing bad about having secrets. My mom said so. She said I should not tell people about all the things I keep in my head. She said *oversharing wasn't good.*"

"I think your mother was a smart lady. What colors did you see, by the way? Around Natalie the nurse?"

"It was kind of weird. They kept changing. For a while they were yellow and orange, then they would get brownish. For a minute they were almost black, then they went back to yellow and orange again. Not pretty colors, like yours. Your colors are my favorite."

Julia laughed between the puffing and pedaling. She thought ahead to the talk with her brother and wondered if revealing all the details regarding Logan was necessary. Much of it was conjecture on her part...nothing more than amateur psychiatry. Having an interest in a subject and reading up on it doesn't make one an expert.

###

"Good grief, Julia. Am I hearing this right? You're saying that man upstairs, the one sleeping in my son's bedroom, could be a sociopath? How could you bring him into my home?"

"Steven, please calm down. You're overreacting." She splashed another ounce of amber liquid into his glass. "I'm just trying to describe the kinds of people that survived Chicxulub. Roughly fifty percent of all the survivors will have emotional issues of some kind, but only a small percentage of those may present with more troublesome symptoms."

"Troublesome? Shit. I consider sociopathic tendencies a hell of a lot worse than troublesome."

"Those would be rare cases. Please just hear me out. I've seen no evidence of psychopathy in Logan, and I've been with him for a week. If he were dangerous, I'd know it because I'd be dead now."

Steven frowned.

"And he's really just a boy in a man's body. I doubt his emotional and intellectual maturity is even at the same level as Jeffrey's."

"Not a good comparison. Jeffrey is a fifty-year-old in a fourteen-year-old's body."

"Well, you know what I'm saying. He is childlike in many ways. Who knows if I'd have made it here without him? Remember how he helped with those men at the Hays roadblock?"

"Yes, I heard the story of his shooting prowess. Not sure if that makes a constructive argument for your case though. Great, he's effective at killing people."

Julia's eyes narrowed. "You probably have a number of marginally dangerous people in Liberty even now. It's just the new reality of our world."

"They're not living down the hall from my son."

"Fine. If you want us to leave, we'll leave. It's not like there aren't plenty of houses to live in."

He knew that expression. He had pissed off his big sister and now she would slip into 'ice queen mode,' a term coined during their teen years. Nobody could do chilly reserve better than Julia.

"That's not what I want and you know it. You're much safer here than anywhere else. I just don't understand why you're so defensive of this young man whom you've only known a week. Please tell me there's not a Mrs. Robinson thing going on here."

He regretted the words the moment they tumbled out.

"Don't leave, I'm sorry!" he said to her backside as she stormed toward the stairs. "Come back and let's discuss this. I promise I will listen with my ears open and my mouth shut." It was their father's favorite directive; he had been a man with his hands full raising two gifted children who challenged him at every turn with logical and loud rebuttals.

She paused at the bottom step.

"I have chocolate." He waved a Dove Bar. He had saved a box for his sister whose love of dark chocolate was legendary in their family. "And there's more where this came from."

She turned, intending to scorch her little brother with her best go-to-hell look. Instead, she laughed. The goofy grin had the desired effect, melting her anger. She snatched the candy from his hand and plopped back down on the sofa.

"God, you look like dad now with that silver in your hair." She took a huge bite of chocolate. "I can't explain it. I admit, I've wondered the same thing. Maybe I got sucked in a little. When I first met him, he had just been injured, and he was so filthy I knew the wound would get infected. Then the more time we spent together, the more his childish innocence worked on me. It was almost refreshing in a way, I suppose, after hobnobbing with all the self-important blowhards at Stanford. Plus don't forget, I was alone for almost a year. I didn't realize how much I missed human companionship until I got used to Logan sitting next to me in the car. And," her voice lowered, eyes falling upon everything in the room but Steven's face, "I suspect there's some residual maternal instinct. You know, from before."

Steven nodded in understanding; pieces of a Julia jigsaw puzzle were snapping into place. He saw the pain on his sister's tired face. Was this a good time to mention her resemblance to the young woman who had been largely responsible for the success of the rescue mission? Probably not. Not yet.

"The baby you gave up for adoption back in undergrad school," he said.

"Yes."

"Of course that makes sense. Still," now it was Steven's turn to lower his voice, "I can't help that he gives me the creeps."

"I know. You're not the first person to have reservations about him." She thought of Thoozy back at the hospital. "But he's had a difficult life. He was a special-needs kids raised by a single mom. He got bullied and made fun of and has been shunned his entire life. I promised that Liberty would be a new start for him. Everything is different now, and there are so few people left. Most of them will also be special...in one way or another."

What Julia had just explained about the survivors made sense when he considered his personal experience from the past year. He had encountered a lot of smart people recently, as well as people with extraordinary talents. The mental capacity of some of those with remarkable abilities did seem lower than average, although not always, as evidenced by his son. Then there was Ed, who was brilliant at building and design but whose social skills were lacking, which could be attributed to Asperger's. He thought of Marilyn and Natalie, two very different women with exceptional intelligence, and Natalie's daughter Brittany, a musical prodigy who didn't seem especially bright. The intellectual disparity didn't stop Jeffrey from ogling the girl every chance he got though; she was beautiful. If surviving and keeping his son safe hadn't forced him to have tunnel vision, he would have realized sooner that something strange was going on. Now it all began to make sense.

Julia interrupted his thoughts. "There are no longer institutions and hospitals to stick these people in, or medication to alleviate their symptoms. No advanced placement classes or magnet schools for the gifted ones. We'll just have to figure out ways to manage them all."

Steven had an unpleasant thought.

"What about the men in Hays? What would have compelled them all to behave so despicably? How did so many of those bastards end up in the same small town?"

"I'm not sure. It could have been a combination of events. Suggestibility isn't an inherent trait, but if they had low self-esteem or borderline personality disorder, they could have been receptive to the influence of a strong leader. There's so much I don't know, and don't forget this is by no means my area of expertise. I think we could learn a lot by conducting a scientific study of the townspeople."

Steven nodded. "Yes, I'm sure you're right. I'm just not sure everyone will want to be put under your microscope."

"Well, there's no problem there. It got blown up along with all my data and other equipment."

"I meant figuratively, of course. Anyway, the bigger question is, how will people react when they discover the nature of some of the individuals they may be rubbing elbows with?"

"That's impossible to answer."

For the first time since Julia's revelation, Steven pondered the wisdom of sharing this newfound information with the rest of the townspeople. How would the social dynamic change if everyone were always wondering who was gifted, psychotic – or perhaps both? And more importantly, how would that altered dynamic affect their cooperative plans for survival?

###

Logan had very good hearing. His mother always said he could hear a pin drop on the other side of the house. He crouched at the top of the darkened stairwell and listened to Julia's conversation with her brother. He wasn't surprised to discover that Steven liked him about as much as he liked Steven, which wasn't very much at all. He didn't understand a lot of the words they used, like *psychopathy* and *sociopath*, but it didn't matter because Julia had stood up for him against her own brother. That meant a lot. Other than his mother and Mr. Cheney, their neighbor who had taught him about duct tape and knives and how to trap stray animals, he'd never had a friend. Julia was his friend. She had just shown him that. And even though the Bad Thoughts said he should...*KILL HER!*

KILL THEM ALL!...he wouldn't do it. Not yet, and never Julia. When the time came, though, he knew exactly who he would start with: that mean girl who always gave him the stink eye and who looked so much like Julia.

You can continue reading *Beauty and Dread* here.

Dear Reader

Dear Reader,

I hope you enjoyed this book. I'd love it if you posted a review about it on Amazon or Goodreads. Reading a well-written book in the company of snoring doggies is my favorite pastime; receiving feedback and reviews from readers about my own books is my second favorite pastime. I look forward to hearing what you think! Who was your favorite character (I have a couple), and which scenes did you like best? Did you want to punch the gun store owner in his face? Who is the better pet, Brains or Bruno?

On a side note, if you've spotted a typo, please email me at nicki@nickihuntsmansmith.com. I hate those insidious little buggers as much as the next reader. If you're a native Kansan and noticed that my fictional Liberty, Kansas is nowhere near the real Liberty, please know that I changed the name from Russell (the town that actually resides there) to Liberty. I just liked it better. I hope you won't find my creative license too annoying. You can follow me on Facebook https://facebook.com/AuthorNickiHuntsmanSmith/. I look forward to hearing from you!

Nicki Huntsman Smith

Your Opinion?

What Did You Think of Troop of Shadows?

First of all, thank you for purchasing Troop of Shadows. I know you could have picked any number of books to read, but you picked this book and for that I am extremely grateful.

I hope you were surprised at a few points, shocked at a few points and entertained overall. If so, it would be really nice if you could share this book with your friends and family by posting to Facebook and Twitter.

I'd like to also make a small request of a review on Amazon or Goodreads, or both! Reviews are the number one thing people consider prior to buying a book.

You can follow me on Facebook at https://www.facebook.com/AuthorNickiHuntsmanSmith/

I look forward to hearing from you!

Nicki Huntsman Smith

Books by Nicki Huntsman Smith

All my books are enrolled in the Amazon Kindle Unlimited program. So if you are a Kindle Unlimited subscriber, like me, you can read all of my books for free.

The Sublime Seven

Troop of Shadows – Book 1

Beauty and Dread – Book 2 (Troop of Shadows Chronicles)

Moving with the Sun – Book 3 (Troop of Shadows Chronicles)

What Befalls the Children – Book 4 (Troop of Shadows Series)

Those Who Come the Last -Book 5 (Troop of Shadows Series)

Dead Leaves, Dark Corners (includes The Lighthouse – a novella)

Secrets Under the Mesa

Perceptions (a Short Story)

Stay in Touch

Those fortunate people on my mailing list are always the first to know about my newest book. They get fist notice of publication dates as well as updates on things like audiobooks, and large text format availability, and all other things book/writing related.

There's no spam and you can unsubscribe at any time.

https://nickihuntsmansmith.com/webs

Made in the USA
Columbia, SC
05 March 2023

13386459R00187